SOON TO BE A MAJOR MOTION PICTURE

Praise for Ruth Ware's instant *New York Times*, *USA Today*, and *Los Angeles Times* bestseller *In a Dark, Dark Wood*

An NPR Best Book of the Year • An *Entertainment Weekly* Top Ten Summer Read • A *BuzzFeed* "31 Perfect Books to Get Excited About This Summer" Pick • A *Publishers Weekly* "Top Ten Mysteries and Thrillers" Pick • A *Bookreporter* Summer Reading Pick • A *New York Post* "Best Novels to Read This Summer" Pick • A *Shelf Awareness* "Book Expo America 2015 Buzz Book" Pick

"Prepare to be scared . . . Really scared! When I read this page-turning book about a bachelorette party gone wrong, I almost bit all my fingernails off!"

—Reese Witherspoon

"Who pulls a gun at a bachelorette party? The answers are unveiled with Gillian Flynn–style trickery."

—*O, The Oprah Magazine*

"Reese Witherspoon's making it into a movie, so read the book now. Before bed at your own risk."

—*theSkimm*

"Just try to guess how sinister this plot can get (hint: VERY)."

—*Marie Claire*

"[It] packs a noirish punch that would make the Queen of Crime herself proud."

—*Bustle*

"Ware hews [close] to the new genre of twisty-mystery women's books."

—*Vulture*

"Ruth Ware has written an exciting and amazing book that never stops circling the reader and clapping its cold hands over her eyes."

—Peter Straub, *New York Times* bestselling author

"The pulse-quickening plot will keep you up until the small hours."

—*Good Housekeeping*, UK

"Read it on a dark and stormy night—with all the lights on."

—*Kirkus Reviews*

"An enchantingly unsettling thriller with mysterious characters and a classically spooky setting."

—*Shelf Awareness*

"[It] will appeal to fans of Gillian Flynn's *Gone Girl* and Paula Hawkins's *The Girl on the Train.*"

—*Publishers Weekly*

"You'll find it almost impossible to put this twisting, electrifying debut down . . . [The] foggy atmosphere and chilling revelations will leave you breathless."

—*Entertainment Weekly*

"A sinister mood lurks in [*In a Dark, Dark Wood*]."

—*ELLE*, UK

"Ware writes with verve and energy, building up the suspense and keeping the pages flying."

—*Library Journal*

"Ware's debut novel sets the stage for her to become a household name . . . Engaging, suspenseful and mysterious."

—*RT Book Reviews*

"Haunting."

—*styleboston*

"WARNING: This book is hot. Do not pick it up late at night or if you are in a dark, dark wood . . . Ruth Ware has a gift. This British author's first foray into fiction is a hit . . . it delivers a punch and keeps you guessing—an ideal August psychodrama that reminds us why mysteries remain such fun—except at night."

—*New York Journal of Books*

"I raced through this, totally unable to put it down . . . Dark, smart, and compulsive."

—Nicci Cloke, author of *Lay Me Down*

"So gripping. So glad my hen days are behind me. It's going to be huge."

—Tamar Cohen, author of *Dying for Christmas* and *The Broken*

"Likely to be the next *Gone Girl*."

—*Surrounded by Books*

"If the premise might be the sort that Agatha Christie would have toyed with had she been a twenty-first-century graduate, Ware's analysis of the power games some women revel in—and the toxicity in the undertow of some female friendships—is more reminiscent of Sophie Hannah, Christobel Kent, or even Gillian Flynn and Harriet Lane."

—*Independent*

"The best thing about *In A Dark, Dark Wood* is the eerie atmosphere it creates for this ill-fated weekend, never overwrought, just ominous enough, the glass house where the guests are trapped 'dark and silent, blending into the trees, almost invisible.'"

—USAToday.com

in a dark, dark wood

ruth ware

SCOUT PRESS
New York London Toronto Sydney New Delhi

SCOUT PRESS
An Imprint of Simon & Schuster, Inc.
1230 Avenue of the Americas
New York, NY 10020

First Scout Press trade paperback edition April 2016

For information about special discounts for bulk purchases, please contact Simon & Schuster Special Sales at 1-866-506-1949 or business@simonandschuster.com.

The Simon & Schuster Speakers Bureau can bring authors to your live event. For more information or to book an event contact the Simon & Schuster Speakers Bureau at 1-866-248-3049 or visit our website at www.simonspeakers.com.

Interior design by Jaime Putorti

Manufactured in China

10 9 8 7 6 5 4 3 2 1

The Library of Congress has cataloged the hardcover edition as follows:

Ware, Ruth.
In a dark, dark wood / by Ruth Ware.—First Scout Press hardcover edition.
pages cm
Summary: "What should be a cozy and fun-filled weekend deep in the English countryside takes a sinister turn in Ruth Ware's suspenseful, compulsive, and darkly twisted psychological thriller."—Provided by publisher.
ISBN 978-1-5011-1231-7 (hardback)—ISBN 978-1-5011-1233-1 (paperback)—ISBN 978-1-5011-1232-4 (ebook) 1. Women novelists, English—Fiction. 2. Female friendship—Fiction. 3. Murder—Investigation—Fiction. I. Title.
PR6123.A745I53 2015
823'.92—dc23

2015005077

ISBN 978-1-5011-1233-1
ISBN 978-1-5011-1231-7 (hardcover)
ISBN 978-1-5011-1232-4 (ebook)

For Kate; for the other three-fifths. With love.

In a dark, dark wood there was a dark, dark house;
And in the dark, dark house there was a dark, dark room;
And in the dark, dark room there was a dark, dark cupboard;
And in the dark, dark cupboard there was . . . a skeleton!

—traditional Halloween tale

I am running.

I am running through moonlit woods, with branches ripping at my clothes and my feet catching in the snow-bowed bracken.

Brambles slash at my hands. My breath tears in my throat. It hurts. Everything hurts.

But this is what I do. I run. I can do this.

Always when I run there's a mantra inside my head. The time I want to get, or the frustrations I'm pounding away against the tarmac.

But this time one word, one thought pounds inside me.

James. James. James.

I must get there. I must get to the road before—

And then there it is, a black snake of tarmac in the moonlight, and I can hear the roar of an engine coming, and the white lines shine, so bright they hurt my eyes, the black tree trunks like slashes against the light.

Am I too late?

I force myself down the last thirty yards, tripping over fallen logs, my heart like a drum in my breast.

James.

And I'm too late—the car is too close; I can't stop it.

I fling myself onto the tarmac, my arms outstretched.

"Stop!"

chapter 1

It hurts. Everything hurts. The light in my eyes, the pain in my head. There's a stench of blood in my nostrils, and my hands are sticky with it.

"Leonora?"

The voice comes dim through a fog of pain. I try to shake my head; my lips won't form the word.

"Leonora, you're safe—you're at the hospital. We're taking you to have a scan."

It's a woman, speaking clearly and loudly. Her voice hurts.

"Is there anyone we should be calling?"

I try again to shake my head.

"Don't move your head," she says. "You've had a head injury."

"Nora," I whisper.

"You want us to call Nora? Who's Nora?"

"Me . . . my name."

"All right, Nora. Just try to relax. This won't hurt."

But it does. Everything hurts.

What has happened?

What have I done?

chapter 2

I knew, as soon as I woke up, that it was a day for a park run, for the longest route I do, nearly nine miles in all. The autumn sunlight streamed through the rattan blind, gilding the bedsheets, and I could smell the rain that had fallen in the night, and see the leaves on the plane tree in the street below, just turning to golden-brown at the tips. I closed my eyes and stretched, listening to the tick and groan of the heating, and the muted roar of the traffic, feeling every muscle, reveling in the day to come.

I always start my morning the same way. Maybe it's something about living alone—you're able to get set in your ways, there's no outside disruptions, no flatmates to hoover up the last of the milk, no cat coughing up a hairball on the rug. You know that what you left in the cupboard the night before will be in the cupboard when you wake up. You're in control.

Or maybe it's something about working from home. Outside of a nine-to-five job, it's very easy for the days to get shapeless, meld together. You can find you're still in your dressing gown at five p.m., and the only person you've seen all day is the milkman. There are days when I don't hear a single human voice, apart from the radio, and you know what? I quite like that. It's a good existence for a writer, in many ways—alone with the voices in your head, the characters you've created. In the silence they become very real. But it's not necessarily the healthiest way to live. So having a routine is important. It gives you something to hang on to, something to differentiate the weekdays from the weekends.

My day starts like this.

At six thirty exactly the heating goes on, and the roar as the boiler starts always wakes me up. I look at my phone—just to check the world hasn't ended in the night—and then lie there, listening to the pop and creak of the radiator.

At seven a.m. I turn on my radio—already tuned to Radio 4's *Today Programme*—and I reach out and flick the switch of the coffee machine, preloaded with coffee and water the night before—Carte Noire filter grind, with the filter paper folded just so. There are some advantages to the size of my flat. One of them is the fact that I can reach both the fridge and the coffee machine without getting out of bed.

The coffee is usually through by the time they've finished the headlines, and then I lever myself out of my warm duvet and drink it, with just a splash of milk, and a piece of toast with Bonne Maman raspberry jam (no butter—it's not a diet thing, I just don't like the two together).

What happens after that depends on the weather. If it's raining, or if I don't feel like going for a run, then I shower, check my e-mails, and start the day's work.

Today was a beautiful day, though, and I was itching to get out, get wet leaves beneath my trainers, and feel the wind in my face. I'd shower after my run.

I pulled on a T-shirt, some leggings and socks, and shoved my feet into my trainers, where I'd left them near the door. Then I jogged down the three flights of stairs to the street, and out, into the world.

- - -

When I got back, I was hot and sweating and loose-limbed with tiredness, and I stood for a long time under the shower, thinking about my to-do list for the day. I needed to do another online shop—I was nearly out of food. I had to go through the copy edits on my book—I'd promised them back to the editor this week, and I hadn't even started them yet. And I should go through the e-mails that had come through from my website contact form, which I hadn't done for ages because I kept putting it off. Most of it would be spam, of course—whatever kind of verification you put on it, it doesn't seem to deter the bots. But sometimes it's useful stuff, requests for blurbs or review copies. And sometimes . . . sometimes it's e-mails from readers. Generally, if people write to you, it's because they liked the book, although I have had a few messages telling me what a terrible person I am. But even when they're nice, it's still odd and uncomfortable—someone telling you their reaction to your private thoughts, like reading someone's opinion on your diary. I'm not sure I'll ever get used to that feeling, however long I write. Maybe that's partly why I have to gear myself up for it.

When I was dressed, I fired up my laptop and clicked slowly through the e-mails, deleting as I went. Viagra. A promise to make me "satisfy my woman." Russian cuties.

And then . . .

To: Melanie Cho; kate.derby.02@DPW.gsi.gov.uk; T Deauxma; Kimayo, Liz; info@LNShaw.co.uk; Maria Tatibouet; Iris P Westaway; Kate Owens; smurphy@shoutlinemedia.com; Nina da Souza; French, Chris
From: Florence Clay
Subject: CLARE'S HEN!!!

Clare? I didn't know any Clares except . . .

My heart began beating faster. But it couldn't be her. I hadn't seen her for ten years.

For a minute my finger hovered irrationally over the Delete button. Then I clicked, and opened up the message.

> HI ALL!!!
>
> For those of you who don't know me, my name is Flo, and I'm Clare's best friend from university. I'm also—drum roll—her maid of honor!! So in time honored fashion I will be organizing her HEN DO!!!
>
> I've had a word with Clare and—as you can probably guess—she doesn't want any rubber penises or pink feather boas. So we're going to have something rather more sophisticated—a weekend away near her old college stomping ground in Northumberland—although I think there may be a few naughty games snuck in under the radar!!
>
> The weekend Clare has chosen is 14-16th November. I know this is VERY short notice, but we didn't have a lot of choice between work commitments and Christmas and so on. Please RSVP promptly.
>
> Love and kisses—and hoping to meet old friends and new very soon!!!!
>
> Flo xxx

I sat, frowning uneasily at the screen, chewing the side of my nail, trying to figure it out.

Then I looked again at the "to" list. There was one name on there that I recognized: Nina da Souza.

Well, that settled it. It must be Clare Cavendish. There was no one else it could be. And I knew—or thought I remembered—that she'd gone to university at Durham, or maybe Newcastle? Which fitted with the Northumberland setting.

But why? Why had Clare Cavendish asked me to her hen night?

Could it be a mistake? Had this Flo just plundered Clare's address book and fired off an e-mail to anyone she could find?

But just twelve people . . . that meant my inclusion could hardly be a mistake. Right?

I sat, staring at the screen as if the pixels could provide answers to the questions shifting queasily in my gut. I half wished I'd just deleted it without even reading.

Suddenly, I couldn't sit still any longer. I got up and paced to the door, and then back to my desk, where I stood, staring uneasily at the laptop screen.

Clare Cavendish. Why me? Why now?

I could hardly ask this Flo person.

There was only one person who might know.

I sat. Then quickly, before I could change my mind, I tapped out an e-mail.

To: Nina da Souza

From: Nora Shaw

Subject: Hen???

Dearest N, Hope you're well. Must admit I was a bit surprised to see us both on the list to Clare's hen night. Are you going? xx

And then I waited for a reply.

For the next few days, I tried to put it out of my mind. I busied myself with work—trying to bury myself in the knotty minutiae of the copy editor's queries—but Florence's e-mail was a constant distracting presence in the back of my mind, like an ulcer at the tip of your tongue that twinges when you least expect it, the ragged nail that you can't stop picking. The e-mail got pushed farther and farther down the in-box, but I could feel it there, its Unreplied flag like a silent reproach, the unanswered questions it posed a constant niggle against the background of my daily routine.

Answer, I begged Nina in my head, as I was running in the park, or cooking my supper, or just staring into space. I thought about calling her. But I didn't know what I wanted her to say.

And then, a few days later, I was sitting having breakfast and scrolling idly through Twitter on my phone when the "new e-mail" icon flashed.

It was from Nina.

I took a gulp of coffee and a deep breath, and clicked to open it.

From: Nina da Souza

To: Nora Shaw

Subject: Re: Hen???

Dude! Long time no chat. Just got yr e-mail—I was on lates at the hospital. Christ, in all honesty it's the last thing I want to do. I got the wedding invitation a while back but I was hoping I'd escaped the hen. R you going? Shall we make a pact? I'll go if you go?

Nx

I drank my coffee while I looked at the screen, my finger hovering over Reply but not quite clicking. I'd hoped Nina would answer at least some of the questions that had been buzzing and building in my head over the last few days. When was the wedding? Why invite me to the hen, but not the wedding? Who was she marrying?

Hey, do you know . . . I started, and then deleted it. No. I couldn't ask outright. It would be tantamount to admitting I hadn't the first clue what was going on. I've always been too proud to admit to ignorance. I hate being at a disadvantage.

I tried to push the question to the bottom of my mind while I dressed and had a shower. But when I opened up my computer, there were two more unread e-mails in my in-box.

The first was a regretful "no, thanks" from one of Clare's friends, citing a family birthday.

The second was another e-mail from Flo. This time she'd attached a read receipt.

To: info@LNShaw.co.uk

From: Florence Clay

Subject: Re: CLARE'S HEN!!!

Dear Lee,

Sorry to chase, but just wondering if you got my e-mail the other day! I know it has been a while since you saw Clare, but she was so hoping you might be able to come. She often talks about you, and I know feels bad that you lost touch after school. I don't know what happened, but she'd really love for you to be there—won't you say yes?! It would really make her weekend complete.

Flo xxx

The e-mail should have made me feel flattered—that Clare was so keen for me to be there, that Flo had gone to such trouble to track me down. But it didn't. Instead, I felt a surge of resentment at being nagged, and a sense of invaded privacy at the read receipt. It felt like being checked up on, spied upon.

I shut down the e-mail and opened up the document I was working on, but even as I got down to it, determinedly pushing all thoughts of the hen from my mind, Flo's last sentence hung in the air like an echo, niggling at me. *I don't know what happened.* It sounded like a plaintive child. No, I thought bitterly. You don't. So don't go prying into my past.

I had sworn never to go back.

Nina was different—Nina lived in London now, and she and I ran into each other occasionally around Hackney. She was as much part of my London life as my Reading one now.

But Clare—Clare was resolutely part of the past—and I wanted her to stay there.

And yet a small part of me—a small nagging part that pricked at my conscience—didn't.

Clare had been my friend. My best friend, for a long time. And yet I'd run, without looking back, without even leaving a number. What kind of friend did that make me?

I got up restlessly and, for want of anything better to do, made another cup of coffee. I stood over the percolator while it hissed and gurgled, worrying at the side of my nail with my teeth and thinking about the ten years since I'd last seen her. When at last the machine had finished, I poured myself a cup and carried it back to my desk, but I didn't start work again. Instead, I opened up Google and tapped in "Clare Cavendish Facebook."

There were a lot of Clare Cavendishes, it turned out, and the coffee had gone cold before I found one that I thought might be her. The profile picture was a snap of a couple in *Doctor Who* fancy dress. It was hard to tell beneath the straggling red wig, but there was something about the way the girl was throwing her head back and laughing that made me stop, as I scrolled down the endless list. The man was dressed as Matt Smith, with floppy hair, horn-rimmed glasses, and a bow tie. I clicked on the picture to enlarge it and stared at the two of them for a long time, trying to make out her features beneath the trailing red hair, and the more I looked, the more I thought it *was* Clare. The man I definitely didn't recognize, I was sure of that.

I clicked on the "about" tab. Under "mutual friends" it said "Nina da Souza." Definitely Clare. And under the "relationship" header, it said "in a relationship with William Pilgrim." The name made me do a slight double take. It seemed familiar in some indefinable way. Someone from school? But the only William in our year had been Will Miles. *Pilgrim.* I couldn't remember anyone called Pilgrim. I clicked on the profile picture, but it was an anonymous shot of a half-full pint glass.

I pressed the Back button and returned to Clare's profile picture, and as I looked at it, trying to work out what to do, Flo's e-mail echoed inside my head: *She often talks about you . . . she'd really love for you to be there.*

I felt something squeeze at my heart. A kind of guilt, maybe.

I had left without looking back—shell-shocked, reeling—and for a long time I'd concentrated on putting one foot in front of the other, keeping going, keeping the past firmly behind me.

Self-preservation: that was all I could manage. I hadn't allowed myself to think of everything I'd left behind.

But now Clare's eyes met mine, peering out flirtatiously from beneath the red wig, and I thought I saw something pleading in her eyes, something reproachful.

I found myself remembering. Remembering the way she could make you feel like a million dollars, just by picking you out of a crowded room. Remembering her low, gurgling laugh, the notes she'd pass in class, her wicked sense of humor.

I remembered sleeping over on her bedroom floor, at maybe six years old, my first time away from home, lying there listening to the soft purr of her nighttime breath. I'd had a nightmare and wet the bed, and Clare—Clare had hugged me and given me her own bear to cuddle while she crept into the airing cupboard to get new sheets, and hid the others in the laundry basket.

I heard her mother's voice on the landing, low and groggy, asking what was going on, and Clare's swift reply: "I knocked over my milk, Mummy, it made Lee's bed all wet."

For a second I was back there, twenty years ago, a small frightened girl. I could *smell* the scent of her bedroom—the fustiness of our night breath, the sweetness of the bath pearls in a glass jar on her windowsill, the fresh laundry smell of the clean sheets.

"Don't tell anyone," I whispered as we tucked the new sheets in, and I hid my wet pajama bottoms in my case. She shook her head.

"Of course not."

And she never did.

I was still sitting there when my computer gave a faint *ping,* and another e-mail popped up. It was from Nina.

What's the plan then? Flo is chasing. Yes to the pact?

Nx

I got up and paced to the door, feeling my fingers prickle with the stupidity of what I was about to do. Then I paced back, and before I could change my mind, I typed out, Ok. Deal. xx

Nina's reply came back an hour later.

Wow! Don't take this the wrong way but gotta say, I'm surprised. In a good way I mean. Deal it is. Don't even think about letting me down. Remember, I'm a doctor. I know at least 3 ways to kill you without leaving a trace.

Nx

I took a deep breath, pulled up the original e-mail from Flo, and began to type.

Dear Florence (Flo?)

I would love to come. Please thank Clare for thinking of me. I look forward to meeting up with you all in Northumberland and catching up with Clare.

Warm wishes,

Nora (but Clare will know me as Lee).

PS best to use this e-mail address for any updates. The other one is not checked as regularly.

After that the e-mails came thick and fast. There was a flurry of regretful Reply All "nos"—all citing the short notice.

Away that weekend . . .

So sorry, I've got to work . . .

Family memorial service . . . (Nina: It'll be a funeral for the next person who abuses the Reply All button.)

I'm afraid I'll be snorkeling in Cornwall! (Nina's reply came back to me on that one within two minutes: Snorkeling? In November? She couldn't think up a better excuse? Man, if I'd known the bar was that low I'd have said I was stuck down a mine in Chile or something.)

More work. More pre-engagements. And in between, a few acceptances.

At last the list was set.

Clare

Flo

Melanie

Tom (bit of a surprise that one—Nina's reply back to me: ???)

Nina

Me

Just six people. It didn't seem many for someone as popular as Clare. At least, as popular as she'd been at school. But it *was* short notice.

Was that why she'd invited me? To make up numbers, on what she knew would be a barrel-scraping do? But no, that wasn't Clare, or not the Clare I once knew. The Clare I knew would have invited *exactly* who she wanted and spun it as soooo exclusive that only a handful of people were allowed to come.

I pushed the memories aside, burying them under a blanket of routine. But they kept surfacing—halfway through a run, in the middle of the night—whenever I was least expecting it.

Why, Clare? Why now?

chapter 3

November came round frighteningly quickly. I did my best to push the whole thing to the back of my mind and concentrate on work, but it became harder and harder as the weekend approached. I ran longer routes, trying to make myself as tired as possible when I went to bed, but as soon as my head hit the pillow, the whispers started. *Ten years. After everything that happened.* Was this a huge mistake?

If it hadn't been for Nina, I would have backed out, but somehow come the fourteenth there I was: bag in hand, stepping off the train at Newcastle into a cold sour morning, with Nina beside me, smoking a roll-up and grumbling for England as I bought coffee from the kiosk on the station platform. This was her third hen of this year alone (drag on cigarette). She'd spent the best part of five hundred quid on the last one (drag) and this one would be more like a grand, once you took into account the wedding itself (exhale). Honestly, she'd rather write them a check for a ton and save herself the annual leave. And please, as she ground the butt out under her narrow heel, remind her again why she couldn't bring Jess?

"Because it's a hen night," I said. I scooped up the coffee and followed Nina towards the car park sign. "Because the whole point is to leave partners at home. Otherwise, why not bring the fucking groom and have done with it?"

I never swear much, except with Nina. She brings it out of me somehow. It's like this sweary inner me is in there, waiting to be let out.

"Do you still not drive?" Nina asked as we swung our cases into the back of the hired Ford. I shrugged.

"It's one of the many basic skills of life I've never mastered. Sorry."

"Don't apologize to me." She folded her long legs into the driver's seat, slammed the door, and stuck the keys in the ignition. "I hate being driven—driving is like karaoke—your own is epic, other people's is just embarrassing or alarming."

"Well . . . it's just, you know. Living in London, a car seems like a luxury rather than a necessity. Don't you think?"

"I use Zipcar to visit Mum and Dad."

I looked out of the window as Nina let in the clutch. We did a brief bunny hop across the station car park before she sorted it out. "Australia's a bit of a trek in a Volvo."

"Oh God, I forgot your mum emigrated. With, what's his name? Your stepdad?"

"Philip," I said. Why do I always feel like a sulky teenager when I say his name? It's a perfectly normal name.

Nina shot me a sharp look, and then jerked her head at the sat nav.

"Stick that on, would you, and put in the postcode Flo gave us. It's our only hope of getting out of Newcastle town center alive."

Westerhope, Throckley, Stanegate, Haltwhistle, Wark . . . the signs flashed past like a sort of poetry, the road unfurling like an iron-gray ribbon flung across the sheep-cropped moors and low hills. The sky overhead was clouded and huge, but the small stone buildings that we passed at intervals sat huddled into the dips in the landscape, as if they were afraid of being seen. I didn't have to navigate, and reading in a car makes me feel sick and strange, so I shut my eyes, shutting out Nina and the sound of the radio, alone in my own head with the questions that were nagging there.

Why me, Clare? Why now?

Was it just that she was getting married and wanted to rekindle an old friendship? But if so, why hadn't she invited me to the wedding? She'd invited Nina, clearly, so it couldn't be a family-only ceremony or anything like that.

She shook her head in my imagination, admonishing me to be patient, to wait. Clare always did like secrets. Her favorite pastime was finding out something about you and then hinting at it. Not spreading it around—just veiled references in conversation, references that only you and she understood. References that *let you know.*

We stopped in Hexham for lunch, and a cigarette break for Nina, and then pushed on towards the Kielder Forest, out into country lanes, where the sky overhead became huge. But as the roads grew narrower the trees seemed to come closer, edging across the close-cropped peaty turf, until they stood sentinel at the roadside itself, held back only by a thin drystone wall.

As we entered the forest itself, the sat nav coverage dropped off and then died.

"Hang on." I scrabbled in my handbag. "I've got those printouts that Flo e-mailed."

"Well, aren't you the Girl Scout of the year," Nina said, but she was relieved, I could hear it in her voice. "What's wrong with an iPhone anyway?"

"This is what's wrong with them." I held up my mobile, which was endlessly buffering and failing to load Google Maps. "They disappear unpredictably." I looked at the printouts. *The Glass House,* the search header read. *Stanebridge Road.* "Okay, there's a right coming up. A bend and then a right, it must be anytime—" The turning whizzed past, and I said, mildly, I thought, "That was it. We missed it."

"Fine bloody navigator you are!"

"What?"

"You're supposed to tell me about the turning *before* we get to it, you know." She imitated the robotic voice of the sat nav, "Make a left in . . . one hundred fifty . . . feet. Make a left in . . . ninety . . . feet. Turn around when safe to do so; you have missed your turning."

"Well, turn around when safe to do so, lady. You have missed your turning."

"Screw safe." Nina stamped on the brakes and did a fast, bad-tempered three-point turn just at another bend in the forest road. I shut my eyes.

"What was that you were saying about karaoke?"

"Oh, it's a dead end—no one was coming."

"Apart from the other half-dozen people invited to this hen do."

I opened my eyes cautiously to find we were around and picking up speed in the opposite direction.

"Okay, it's here. It looks like a footpath on the map, but Flo's definitely marked it."

"It *is* a footpath!"

She swung the wheel, we bumped through the opening, and the little car began jolting and bumping up a rutted, muddy track.

"I believe the technical term is 'unpaved road,'" I said, rather breathlessly, as Nina skirted a huge mud-filled trench that looked more like a watering hole for hippos, and wound around yet another bend. "Is this their drive? There must be half a mile of track here."

We were on the last printout, the one so big it was practically an aerial photograph, and I couldn't see any other houses marked.

"If it's their drive," Nina said jerkily as the car bounced over another rut, "they should bloody well maintain it. If I break the chassis on this hire car, I'm suing someone. I don't care who, but I'm buggered if I'm paying for it."

But as we rounded the last bend, we were suddenly there. Nina drove the car through a narrow gate, parked, and killed the engine; we both got out, staring up at the house in front of us.

I don't know what I'd expected, but not this. Some thatched cottage, perhaps, with beams and low ceilings. What actually stood in the forest clearing was an extraordinary collection of glass and steel, looking as if it had been thrown down carelessly by a child tired of playing with some very minimalist bricks. It looked so incredibly out of place that both Nina and I just stood, openmouthed.

As the door opened I saw a flash of bright blond hair, and I had a moment of complete panic. This was a mistake. I should never have come, but it was too late to turn back.

Standing in the doorway was Clare.

Only—she was . . . different.

It *was* ten years, I tried to remind myself. People change, they put on weight. The people we are at sixteen are not the people we are at twenty-six—I should know that, more than anyone.

But Clare—it was like something had broken, some light inside her had gone out.

Then she spoke and the illusion was broken. Her voice was the only thing that bore no resemblance to Clare whatsoever. It was quite deep, where Clare's was high and girlish, and it was very, very posh.

"Hi!!!" she said, and somehow her tone gave the word three exclamation marks, and I knew, before she spoke again, who it was. "I'm Flo!"

You know when you see the brother or sister of someone famous, and it's like looking at them, but in one of those fairground mirrors?

Only one that distorts so subtly it's hard to put your finger on what's different, only that it *is* different. Some essence has been lost, a false note in the song.

That was the girl at the front door.

"Oh my God!" she said. "It's so great to see you! You must be—"

She looked from me, to Nina, and picked the easy option. Nina is six feet one and Brazilian. Well, her dad's from Brazil. She was born in Reading, and her mum's from Dalston. She has the profile of a hawk and the hair of Eva Longoria.

"Nina, right?"

"Yup." Nina stuck out a hand. "And you're Flo, I take it?"

"Yah!"

Nina shot me a look that *dared* me to laugh. I never thought people really said *yah,* or if they did, they got it punched out of them at school and sniggered out of them at university. Maybe Flo was made of tougher stuff.

Flo shook Nina's hand enthusiastically and then turned to me with a beaming smile.

"In that case you're . . . Lee, right?"

"Nora," I said reflexively.

"Nora?" She frowned, puzzled.

"My name's Leonora," I said. "At school I was Lee, but now I prefer Nora. I did mention it in the e-mail."

I'd always hated being Lee. It was a boy's name, a name that lent itself to teasing and rhyme. *Lee Lee needs a wee. Lee Lee smells of pee.* And then with my surname, *Shaw: We saw Lee Shaw on the seashore.*

Lee was dead and gone now. At least I hoped so.

"Oh, right! I've got a cousin called Leonora! We call her Leo."

I tried to hide the flinch.

Not Leo. *Never* Leo. Only one person ever called me that.

The silence stretched, until Flo broke it with a slightly brittle laugh.

"Ha! Right. Okay. Well, this is going to be so much fun! Clare's not here yet—but as maid of honor, I felt I should do my duty and get here first!"

"What hideous tortures have you got lined up for us then?" Nina asked as she yanked her case across the threshold. "Feather boas? Chocolate penises? I warn you, I'm allergic to them—I have an anaphylactic reaction. Don't make me get my EpiPen out."

Flo laughed nervously. She looked at me, and then back at Nina, trying to gauge whether Nina was joking. Nina's delivery is hard to read if you don't know her. Nina stared back seriously, and I could tell she was wondering whether to dangle the bait a bit closer.

"Lovely um . . . house," I said, to try to head her off, although in truth *lovely* wasn't the word I was thinking of. In spite of the trees to either side, the place looked painfully exposed, baring its great glass facade to the eyes of the whole valley.

"Isn't it!" Flo beamed, looking relieved to be back on safe ground. "It's actually my aunt's summer house, but she doesn't come here much in the winter—too isolated. Sitting room's through here . . ." She led us through an echoing hallway the full height of the house, and into a long low room with the entire opposite wall made of glass, facing the forest. There was something strangely naked about it—it felt like we were in a stage set, playing our parts to an audience of eyes out there in the wood. I shivered and turned my back to the bare glass, looked around the room. In spite of the long squashy sofas, the place felt oddly bare—and after a second I realized why. It wasn't just the lack of clutter and the minimalist décor—three pots on the mantelpiece, a single Mark Rothko painting on the wall—but the fact that there wasn't a single book in the whole place. It didn't even feel like a holiday cottage—every place I've ever stayed in has had a shelf of curling Dan Browns and Agatha Christies. It felt more like a show home.

"Landline is in here." Flo pointed to a vintage dial-and-cord phone that looked strangely lost in this modernist environment. "Mobile reception is very glitchy, so feel free to use it."

But I wasn't looking at the phone. Above the stark modern fireplace was something even more out of place—a polished shotgun, perched on wooden pegs drilled into the wall. It looked as if it had been transplanted from a country pub. Was it real?

I tried to tear my eyes away as I realized Flo was still talking.

". . . and upstairs are the bedrooms," she finished. "Want a hand with those cases?"

"No, I'm fine," I said, at the same time Nina said, "Well, if you're offering . . ."

Flo looked taken aback, but gamely took Nina's huge wheeled case and began to lug it up the flight of frosted glass stairs.

"As I was saying," she panted as we rounded the newel post, "there're four bedrooms. I thought we'd have Clare and me in one, you guys in another, Tom will have to have his own, obvs."

"Obvs," said Nina, straight-faced.

I was too busy processing the news that I'd be sharing a room. I'd assumed I'd have my own space to retreat to.

"And that just leaves Mels," Flo was saying, "Melanie, you know—as the odd one out. She's got a six-month-old, so I thought out of us girls, she probably deserved a room of her own the most!"

"What? She's not bringing it, is she?" Nina looked genuinely alarmed. Flo gave a honking laugh and then put her hand up to her mouth, smothering the noise self-consciously.

"No! Just, you know, she'll probably need a good night's sleep more than the rest of us."

"Oh, okay." Nina peered into one of the bedrooms. "Which one is ours then?"

"The two back ones are the biggest. You and Lee can have the one on the right if you like, it's got twin beds. The other one's got a four-poster double, but I don't mind squishing up with Clare."

She stopped, breathing hard, on the landing and gestured to a blond wood door on the right-hand side.

"There you go."

Inside there were two neat white beds and a low dressing table, all as anonymous as a hotel room, and—facing the beds—the creepily obligatory wall of glass, looking north over the pine forest. Here it was harder to understand. The ground sloped up at the back of the house, and so there was no spectacular view as there was from the front. Instead, the effect was more claustrophobic than anything—a wall of dark green, already deepening into shadow with the setting sun.

There were heavy cream curtains gathered in each corner, and I had to fight the urge to rip them across the enormous expanse of glass.

Behind me Flo let Nina's case fall with a thud to the floor. I turned, and she smiled, a huge beam that made her suddenly look almost as pretty as Clare.

"Any questions?"

"Yes," Nina said. "Mind if I smoke in here?"

Flo's face fell.

"I'm afraid my aunt doesn't like smoking indoors. But you've got a balcony." She wrestled with a folding door in the glass wall for a moment and then flung it open. "You can smoke out here if you like."

"Super," Nina said. "Thanks."

Flo struggled with the door again, and then swung it shut. She straightened, her face pink with exertion, dusting her hands on her jeans.

"Right! Well, I'll let you get unpacked. See you downstairs, yah?"

"Yah!" Nina said enthusiastically, and I tried to cover it by saying "Thanks!" unnecessarily loudly, in a way that only managed to make me sound weirdly aggressive.

"Um, yeah! Okay!" Flo said, uncertainly, and then she backed out of the doorway and was gone.

"Nina . . ." I said warningly, as she made her way over to gaze out across the forest.

"What?" she said over her shoulder, absentmindedly. And then, "So Tom's definitely of the male persuasion then, judging by Flo's determination to quarantine his raging Y chromosomes from our delicate lady parts."

I couldn't help but snort. That's the thing about Nina. You forgive her stuff that other people would never get away with.

"I think he's probably gay—don't you? I mean, why would he be on a hen night otherwise?"

"Um, contrary to what you seem to believe, batting for the other team doesn't actually change your gender. I think. No, wait . . ." She peered down her top. "No, we're all good. Double D's all present and correct."

"That's not what I meant, and you know it." I banged my own case down on the bed, and then remembered my wash bag, and unzipped it more gingerly. My trainers were on top, and I set them down neatly by the door, a reassuring little "emergency exit" sign. "Hen nights are partly about an appreciation of the male form. That's what women have in common with gay men."

"Christ, *now* you tell me. Perfect excuse lined up and you never trotted it out until now. Could you 'reply all' to my next hen night invitation saying, *Sorry, Nina can't come as she doesn't appreciate the male form*?"

"Oh, for God's sake. I said *partly* an appreciation."

"It's all right." She turned back to the window, peering out into the forest, the tree trunks dark streaks in the green gloaming. There was a tragic crack in her voice. "I'm used to being excluded from heteronormative society."

"Fuck off," I said grumpily, and when she turned around she was laughing.

"Why are we here, anyway?" she asked, throwing herself backwards onto one of the twin beds and kicking off her shoes. "I don't know about you, but I haven't seen Clare in about three years."

I said nothing. I didn't know what to say.

Why had I come? Why had Clare invited me?

"Nina," I started. There was a lump in my throat, and I felt my heart quicken. "Nina, who—"

But before I could finish there, the sound of pounding filled the room, echoing up through the open hallway.

There was someone at the door.

Suddenly, I wasn't at all sure I was ready to get the answers to my questions.

chapter 4

Nina and I both looked at each other. My heart was thudding like a stray echo of the door knocker, but I tried to keep my face calm.

Ten years. Had she changed? Had *I* changed?

I swallowed.

There was the sound of Flo's feet, echoing in the high atrium of the hallway, then metal shrieking on metal as she opened the heavy door, followed by the murmur of voices as whoever it was came into the house.

I listened carefully. It didn't sound like Clare. In fact, beneath Flo's laugh I could hear something that sounded distinctly . . . male?

Nina rolled over and raised herself up on one elbow.

"Well, well, well . . . sounds like the fully Y-chromosomed Tom has arrived."

"Nina," I said warningly.

"What? What are you looking at me like that for? Shall we go downstairs and meet the cock in the henhouse?"

"Nina! Don't."

"Don't what?" She swung her feet to the floor and stood up.

"Don't embarrass us. *Him*."

"If we're hens, naturally that makes him a cock. I'm using the term in its purely zoological sense."

"Nina!"

But she was gone, loping down the glass stairs in her stockinged feet, and I heard her voice floating up the stairwell.

"Hello, don't think we've met . . ."

Don't think we've met. Well, it definitely *wasn't* Clare then. I took a deep breath and followed her down into the hallway.

I saw the little group from above first. By the front door was a girl with smooth, shiny black hair tied in a knot at the base of her skull—presumably Melanie. She was smiling and nodding at something Flo was saying, but she had a mobile in her hand and was poking distractedly at the buttons even while Flo talked.

On the opposite side was a bloke, Burberry case in hand. He had smooth chestnut hair and was immaculately dressed in a white shirt that must have been professionally laundered—no normal person could produce creased sleeves like that—and a pair of gray wool trousers that screamed Paul Smith. He looked up as he heard my feet on the stairs and smiled.

"Hi, I'm Tom."

"Hi, I'm Nora." I forced myself down the last few steps, and then held out my hand. There was something incredibly familiar about his face, and I tried to figure out what it was while we shook, but I couldn't place it. Instead, I turned to the dark-haired girl. "And you must be . . . Melanie?"

"Um, hi, yeah." She looked up and gave a flustered smile. "Sorry, I just—I left my six-month-old at home with my partner. First time I've done it. I really wanted to call home and check in. Isn't there any reception here?"

"Not really," Flo said apologetically. Her face was flushed—with nerves or excitement, I wasn't sure which. "Sorry. You can sometimes get a bit from the top end of the garden or the balconies, depending on what network you're on. But there's a landline in the living room. Let me show you."

She led the way through to the living room, and I turned back to Tom. I still had an odd feeling I'd seen him somewhere before—but that was impossible, surely.

"So, how do you know Clare?" I asked awkwardly.

"Oh, you know. Theater connections. Everyone knows everyone! It was actually through my husband originally—he's a director." Nina gave me a theatrical wink behind Tom's back. I frowned furiously and then rearranged my face as I saw Tom looking puzzled.

"Sorry, go on," Nina said seriously.

"Anyway, I met Clare at a fund-raiser for the Royal Theatre Company. Bruce was directing something there, we just got to talking shop."

"You're an actor?" Nina asked.

"No, playwright."

It's always strange meeting another writer. A little feeling of camaraderie. A masonic bond. I wonder if plumbers feel like this when meeting other plumbers, or if accountants give each other secret nods. Maybe it's because we meet comparatively rarely—writers tend to spend the bulk of their working life alone.

"Nora's a writer," Nina said. She eyed us both as if unleashing two bantamweights into the ring to scrap it out.

"Oh really?" Tom looked at me as if seeing me for the first time. "What do you write?"

Ugh. The question I hate. I've never got comfortable talking about my writing—never got over that feeling of people riffling through my private thoughts.

"Um . . . fiction," I said vaguely. Crime fiction was the truth, but if you say that, people want to suggest plots and motives for murder.

"Really? What name do you write under?"

Nice way of saying, Have I heard of you? Most people phrase it less gracefully.

"L.N. Shaw," I said. "The *N* doesn't stand for anything—I don't have a middle name. I just put that in because L. Shaw sounded odd, whereas L.N. is more pronounceable, if you know what I mean. So you write plays?"

"Yes. I'm always rather jealous of novelists—the way you get to control everything. You don't have to deal with actors massacring your best lines." He flashed a smile, showing unnaturally perfect white teeth. I wondered if he'd had porcelain veneers fitted.

"But it must be nice working with other people." I ventured. "Sharing the responsibility, I mean. A play's a big thing, right?"

"Yes, I suppose so. You have to share the glory, but at least when the shit hits the fan, it's a collective splattering, I guess."

I was about to say something else when there was a *ching* from the living room as Melanie put down the phone. Tom turned to look towards the sound, and something about the angle of his head, or his expression, made me suddenly realize where I'd seen him before.

That picture. Clare's profile picture from Facebook. It was *him*. So the person in her photo wasn't her new partner at all.

I was still processing this when Melanie came out smiling.

"Phew, got through to Bill. All absolutely fine on the home front. Sorry I was a bit distracted—I've never been away for the night before, and it's a bit of a leap of faith. Not that Bill won't manage, I'm sure he will, but—oh anyway, I should stop rabbiting on. You're Nora, is that right?"

"Go through into the living room!" Flo called from the kitchen. "I'm making tea."

Obediently, we trooped through, and I watched Tom and Melanie as they took in the huge room, with its long glass wall.

"That view of the forest is quite something, isn't it?" Tom said at last.

"Yes." I stared out into the woods. It was growing dark, and somehow the shadows made it feel as if all the trees had taken a collective step towards the house, edging in to shut out the sky. "It makes you feel a bit exposed somehow, doesn't it? I think it's the lack of curtains."

"Bit like having your skirt tucked into your knickers at the back!" Melanie said unexpectedly, and then laughed.

"I like it," Tom said. "It feels like a stage."

"And we're the audience?" Melanie asked. "This production seems a bit boring. The actors are rather wooden!" She pointed out to the trees, in case we hadn't got the pun. "Geddit? Trees, wood . . ."

"We got it," Nina said sourly. "But I don't think that's what Tim meant, was it?"

"Tom," Tom said. There was a slight edge to his voice. "But no, I was thinking of it the other way around. We're the actors." He turned to face the glass wall. "The audience . . . the audience is out there."

For some reason his words made me shiver. Perhaps it was the tree trunks, like silent watchers in the growing dark. Or perhaps it was the lingering chill that Tom and Melanie had brought with them from the outside. Either way, leaving London, I'd thought the weather had felt like autumn. Suddenly, so much farther north, it felt like winter had come overnight. It wasn't just the close-growing pines shutting out the light with their dense needles, nor the cold crisp air with its promise of frost to come. The night was drawing in, and the house felt more and more like a glass cage, blasting its light blindly out into the dusk, like a lantern in the dark. I imagined a thousand moths circling and shivering, drawn inexorably to its glow, only to perish against the cold inhospitable glass.

"I'm cold," I said, to change the subject.

"Me, too." Nina rubbed her arms. "Think we can get that stove thing working? Is it gas?"

Melanie knelt in front of it.

"It's wood." She struggled with a handle, and then a door in the front popped open. "I've got one a bit similar at home. Flo!" she shouted through to the kitchen. "Is it okay if we light the stove?"

"Yep!" Flo yelled back. "There're fire lighters on the mantelpiece. Inside a pot. I'll be through in a tick if you can't work it out."

Tom moved across to the mantelpiece and started peering into the pots, but then he stopped, his eyes arrested by the same sight that had stopped me in my tracks earlier.

"Ker-rist." It was the shotgun, perched on its wooden pegs, just above eye level. "Haven't they heard of Chekhov around here?"

"Chekhov?" said a voice from the hall. It was Flo, edging through the door with a tray on her hip. "The Russian guy? Don't worry, it's loaded with blanks. My aunt keeps it for scaring off rabbits. They eat the bulbs and dig up the garden. She shoots at them out of the French windows."

"It's a bit . . . Texan, isn't it?" Tom said. He hurried forward to help Flo with the tray. "You know, not that I don't enjoy the redneck vibe, but having it right there, in your face . . . it's a bit disconcerting for those of us who tend to keep morbid thoughts further at bay."

"I know what you mean," Flo said. "She probably should have a gun cabinet or something. But it was my grandfather's, so it's sort of a family heirloom. And the veg patch is right outside these doors—well, in the summer anyway—so it's just more practical having it to hand."

Melanie got the fire going, Flo began to pour out tea and dish out biscuits, and the conversation moved on . . . to hire car charges, the cost of housing . . . whether to put the milk in first. I was silent, thinking.

"Tea?"

For a minute I didn't move, didn't answer. Then Flo tapped me on the shoulder, making me jump.

"Tea, Lee?"

"Nora," I said. I tried to force a smile. "I'm—I'm sorry. Do you have coffee? I should have said, I'm not that keen on tea."

Flo's face fell.

"I'm so sorry, I should have . . . no. We don't. It's probably too late to get anything now—the nearest village is forty minutes away, and the shop'll be shut. I'm so sorry, I was thinking about Clare when I was doing the food shop, and she does love her tea. I never thought—"

"It's fine." I cut her off with a smile. "Honestly." I took the cup she held out and took a sip. It was scalding, and it tasted utterly, revoltingly like tea—hot milk and gravy browning.

"She should be here soon." Flo looked at her watch. "Shall I run through proceedings so we all know what's happening?"

We all nodded, and Flo got out a list. I felt, rather than heard, Nina's gusting sigh.

"So Clare should be here at six, then I thought we'd have a little drinky—I've got some champers in the fridge, and I picked up the bits for mojitos and margaritas and stuff. I thought we wouldn't bother with a proper sit-down supper"—Nina's face fell, visibly—"I've just got some pizzas and dips and stuff, and we can stick it all out on the coffee table in here and dig in. And I thought while we did that we could play a few getting-to-know-you games. You all know Clare, obvs, but I don't think many of us know each other . . . is that right? In fact, we should probably do a quick round-the-table introduction before Clare gets here, maybe?"

We all looked at one another, sizing one another up, wondering who was going to have the chutzpah to begin. For the first time I tried to fit Tom, Melanie, and Flo in with the Clare I knew, and it wasn't entirely easy.

Tom was obvious—with his expensive clothes and theater background it wasn't hard to see what they had in common. Clare had always loved good-looking people, women as well as men, and she took an uncomplicated generous pride in the attractiveness of friends. There was nothing snide about her admiration—she was beautiful enough herself to be unthreatened by beauty in others, and she loved helping people make the best of themselves, even the less-promising candidates like me. I remembered being dragged around to shop after shop before a big night out, with Clare holding up dresses against my skinny bust-less frame and pursing her lips in appraisal until she found the one that was perfect for me. She had an eye for what flattered. She was the one who had told me I should get my hair cropped. I had never listened to her back then. Now, ten years later, I wore it short, and I knew she'd been right.

Melanie and Flo were more mysterious. Something Melanie had said during the early e-mails had made me think she worked as a lawyer, or possibly an accountant, and she did have the faint air of someone who would be more comfortable in a suit. Her handbag and shoes were expensive, but the jeans she was wearing were what Clare, ten years ago, would have called "mum jeans"—generic blue, unflatteringly cut to bunch at the top.

Flo's jeans, on the other hand, were pure designer, but there was something oddly uncomfortable about the way she wore them. The entire outfit looked like it had been picked wholesale off a display in All Saints with no regard for whether it fitted or flattered her frame, and as I watched she pulled awkwardly at the top, trying to tug it down over the soft chubby bulge where the waist of her jeans cut into her flesh. It looked like the kind of outfit Clare might have picked out for herself, but only someone cruel would have suggested it to Flo.

Flo and Melanie together made a strange contrast with Tom. It was hard to imagine the Clare I'd known with either of them. Was it just that they had been friends at university and had stayed in touch? I knew those kinds of friendships—the ones that you make in Freshers' week and realize as time goes on that you've nothing in common besides staying in the same halls, but somehow you keep sending birthday cards and Facebook likes. But then, it was ten years since I had known Clare. Maybe the Melanie-and-Flo Clare was the real one, now?

As I looked around the circle, I realized that the others were doing the same thing; sizing up the guests they didn't know, trying to fit the strangers in with their mental image of Clare. I caught Tom's eye as he stared at me with a frank curiosity that bordered almost on hostility, and dropped my own gaze to the floor. No one wanted to go first. The silence stretched until it threatened to become awkward.

"I'll begin," Melanie said. She pushed her hair back off her face and fiddled with something at her neckline. I saw that it was a tiny silver cross on a chain, the kind you get at christenings. "I'm Melanie Cho, well Melanie Blaine-Cho now, I guess, but it's a bit of a mouthful and I've kept my own name for work. I shared a house at university with Flo and Clare, but I took two years out before uni, so I'm a bit older than the rest of you guys . . . at least I don't know about you, Tom? I'm twenty-eight."

"Twenty-seven," Tom said.

"So I'm the group granny. I've just had a baby, well, six months ago. And I'm breast-feeding, so please excuse me if you see me running out of the room with giant wet patches on my boobs."

"Are you pumping and dumping?" Flo asked sympathetically, and over her shoulder I saw Nina go cross-eyed and mime strangling herself. I looked away, refusing to be drawn in.

"Yes, I thought about trying to bag it, but I thought, well, I'll probably be drinking and taking it back down will be a right pain. Um . . . what else? I live in Sheffield. I'm a lawyer, but I'm on maternity leave, my husband's looking after Ben today. Ben's our baby. He's—oh well, you don't want to hear me bore on. He's just lovely."

She smiled, her rather worried face lighting up and two deep dimples forming in her cheeks, and I felt a pang at my heart. Not broodiness—I didn't want to be pregnant in any way, shape, or form. But a pang for that complete, uncomplicated happiness.

"Go on, show us a piccie," Tom said. Melanie dimpled again and pulled out her phone.

"Well, go on then, if you insist. Look, this was when he was born . . ."

I saw a picture of her, lying back on a hospital bed, her face bleached to clay-color and her hair in black rat tails around her shoulders, beaming tiredly down at a white bundle in her arms.

I had to look away.

"And this is him smiling—it wasn't his first smile, I didn't catch that, but Bill was away in Dubai, so I made sure I snapped the next one and texted him. And this is him now—you can't see his face very well, he's got his bowl on his head, bless."

The baby was unrecognizable from the angry blue-black stare of the first picture—a chubby fat-faced little thing, crowing with laughter. His face was half obscured by an orange plastic dish, and some kind of green goop was running down his round cheeks.

"Bless!" Flo said. "He looks just like Bill, doesn't he?"

"Oh my God." Tom looked half amused, half horrified. "Welcome to parenthood. Please abandon your dry-clean-only clothes at the door."

Melanie tucked her phone away, the smile still on her lips.

"It is a bit like that. But it's amazing how quickly you get used to it. It seems completely normal to me now to check my hair for gobs of porridge before I leave the house. Let's not talk about him anyway, I'm already homesick enough, and I don't want to make it worse. What about you, Nina?" She turned to where Nina was sitting beside the stove, hugging her knees. "I remember we met once at Durham, didn't we? Or did I imagine that?"

"No, you're right, I did come up once. I think I was on my way to see a mate at Newcastle. I don't remember meeting Flo, but I definitely remember running into you in the bar—was that right?" Melanie nodded. "For those of you who don't know, I'm Nina, I was at school with Clare and Nora. I'm a doctor. Well, I'm training to be a surgeon actually. In fact, I just spent three months overseas with Médecins sans Frontières, where I learned a whole lot more than I ever wanted to about gunshot wounds . . . in spite of what the *Mail*'d have you believe, we don't see a whole load of those in Hackney."

She rubbed at her face, and for the first time since we'd left London I saw her veneer crack a little. I knew Colombia had affected her, but I'd seen her only twice since she came back, and both times she hadn't talked about it, except to make some jokes about the food. For a moment I got a glimmer of what it might be like to patch people together for a living . . . and sometimes fail.

"Anyway." She forced a smile. "Tim, Timmy-boy, Timbo: shoot."

"Yes . . ." Tom said, with a slightly wry look. "Well, I suppose the first thing that you should know about me is that my name is *Tom*. Tom Deauxma. I'm a playwright, as previously advertised. I'm not huge, but I've done a lot of fringe stuff and won a few awards. I'm married to the theater director Bruce Westerly—maybe you've heard of him?" There was a pause. Nina was shaking her head. Tom's eye traveled around the circle looking for recognition until it rested hopefully on me. Reluctantly, I gave a little shake. I felt bad—but lying wasn't going to help. He gave a small sigh. "Oh well, I guess if you're outside the theater, maybe you don't notice the director as much. That's how I know Clare—via her work for the Royal Theatre Company. Bruce does quite a bit with them—and he directed *Coriolanus,* of course."

"Of course," Flo said, nodding earnestly. After my previous failure I felt I could at least pretend knowledge of this, so I nodded along with Flo—maybe slightly too enthusiastically: I felt my hair band slip. Nina yawned and got up to leave the room without a word.

"We live in Camden . . . what else? We have a dog called Spartacus, Sparky for short. He's a labradoodle. Two years old. He's completely adorable but not the ideal dog for a couple of workaholics who travel a lot. Luckily, we have a brilliant dog walker. I'm a vegetarian . . . what else? Oh dear, that's a terrible indictment, isn't it? Two minutes and I've run out of interesting things to say about myself. Oh—and I have a tattoo of a heart on my shoulder blade. That's it. How about you, Nora?"

For some unfathomable reason, I felt myself flush scarlet, and my fingers lost their grip on the teacup, slopping tea onto my knee. I busied myself wiping it up with the corner of my scarf and then looked up to find Nina had slipped back inside. She was holding her tobacco pouch and rolling up with one hand, watching me steadily with her wide dark eyes as she did.

I forced myself to speak.

"Not much to tell. I, um . . . I met Clare at school, like Nina. We—"

We haven't spoken for ten years.

I don't know why I'm here.

I don't know why I'm here.

I swallowed, painfully.

"We . . . lost touch a bit, I guess." My face felt flushed and hot—the stove was really starting to throw out heat. I went to tuck my hair behind my ears, but I'd forgotten it had been cut, and my fingers only skimmed the short strands, my skin warm and damp beneath. "Um, I'm a writer. I went to UCL and I started work at a magazine after university, but I was pretty crap at it—probably my own fault, I spent all my time scribbling my novel instead of doing research and making contacts. Anyway, I sold my first book when I was twenty-two, and I've been a full-time writer ever since."

"And you support yourself entirely on your books?" Tom raised an eyebrow. "Respect."

"Well, not *entirely*. I mean, I do the odd bit of online teaching here and there . . . editorial reports and stuff. And I was lucky—" Lucky? I wanted to bite my tongue. "Well, maybe not lucky, that's not the right word, but my granddad died when I was in my teens, and I got some money, enough for a tiny studio flat in Hackney. It's absolutely minuscule, only room for me and my laptop, but I don't have any rent to pay."

"I think it's really nice that you've all kept in touch," Tom said. "You and Clare and Nina, I mean. I don't think I've kept in contact with any of my friends from school. I've got nothing in common with most of them. It wasn't the happiest time for me." He looked at me steadily, and I felt myself flush. I went to tuck my hair again, and then dropped my hand. Was it my imagination, or was there something slightly malicious in his gaze? Did he know something?

I struggled for a moment, wanting to answer, but not sure what I could say that wasn't an outright lie. As I floundered, the silence growing more uncomfortable by the second, the wrongness of this whole situation struck me all over again. What the hell was I doing here? Ten years. *Ten years.*

"I think everyone has a shit time at school," Nina said at last, breaking the pause. "I certainly did."

I looked at her gratefully, and she gave me a little wink.

"What's the secret, then?" Tom asked. "To long-lived friendships? How have you managed to keep it up all these years?"

I looked at him again, sharply this time. Why the hell couldn't he just let it drop? But there was nothing I could say—not without looking like a crazy person.

"I don't know," I said at last, trying to keep my voice pleasant, but I could feel the strain in my smile. I could only pray that my expression wasn't as obviously fake as it felt. "Luck, I guess."

"Significant others?" Melanie asked.

"No. Just me. Not even a labradoodle." It was meant to raise a laugh, and they duly did, but it was a thin, lackluster chorus with a pitying note. "Flo?" I said quickly, trying to get the spotlight off myself.

Flo beamed.

"Well, I met Clare at university. We were both studying Art History, and we got allocated to the same accommodation block. I walked into the Common Room and there she was, sitting in front of *EastEnders,* chewing her hair—you know that funny way she's got of twisting a lock around her finger and nibbling on it? So sweet."

I tried to remember. Had Clare ever done this? It sounded disgusting. A faint memory came—Clare sitting in the café next to the school, twisting her plait around her finger. Maybe she had.

"She was wearing that blue dress—I think she's still got it, can't believe she fits into it! I've put on at least a stone since uni! Anyway, I went up and said hi, and she said, *Oh, I like your scarf,* and we've been BFFs ever since. I just— She's just great, you know? She's been such an inspiration, so supportive. There's not many people who—" She gulped, and broke off, struggling, and to my horror I saw she was welling up. "Well, anyway, never mind all that. She's my rock, and I'd do *anything* for her. Anything. I just want her to have the *best* hen night ever, you know? I want it to be perfect. It means *everything* to me. It's like—it's like it's the last thing I can do for her—you know?"

There were tears in her eyes, and she spoke with an intensity so fierce it was almost frightening. Looking around the circle, I saw that I wasn't the only one taken aback—Tom looked frankly startled, and Nina's eyebrows had disappeared beneath her fringe. Only Melanie looked totally unconcerned, as if this was a normal level of emotion to feel for your best friend.

"She's getting married, not going to prison," Nina said dryly, but either Flo didn't hear or she ignored the remark. Instead, she coughed and swiped at her eyes.

"Sorry. Oh God, I'm such a sentimental moo! Look at me."

"And, er, what do you do now?" Tom asked politely. As he said it, I realized Flo had told us entirely about Clare—almost nothing about herself.

"Oh." Flo looked down at the floor. "Well, you know. A bit of this. Bit of that. I . . . I took some time out after uni. I wasn't in a good place. Clare was amazing. When I was . . . Well, never mind that. The thing is she's just—just the best friend a girl could have, honestly. God. Look at me!" She blew her nose and stood up. "Who's for more tea?"

We all shook our heads, and she took the tray and went through to the kitchen. Melanie took out her phone and checked the signal again.

"Well, that was weird," Nina said flatly.

"What?" Melanie looked up.

"Flo and the quote unquote perfect hen," Nina spelled out. "Don't you think she's a little . . . intense?"

"Oh," Melanie said. She glanced out of the door towards the kitchen and then lowered her voice. "Look, I don't know if I should be saying this, but there's no sense in beating around the bush. Flo had a bit of a breakdown in her third year. I'm not sure what happened, but she dropped out before her finals—she never graduated as far as I know. So that's why she's a bit, you know, *sensitive,* about that period. She doesn't really like discussing it."

"Um, okay," Nina said. But I knew what she was thinking. What had been alarming about Flo wasn't her reserve about what happened after uni—that was the least odd part of the whole thing. It was everything else that had been unnerving.

chapter 5

I want to sleep, but they shine lights in my eyes. They test and scan and print me, and take away my clothes, stiff with blood. What's happened? What have I *done*?

I'm wheeled down long corridors, their lights dimmed for night, past wards of sleeping patients. Some of them wake as I pass, and I can see my state reflected in their shocked expressions, in the way they turn their faces away, as if from something pitiable or horrifying.

The doctors ask me questions I can't answer, tell me things I can't remember.

Then at last I am hooked up to a monitor and left, drugged and bleary and alone.

But not quite alone.

I turn painfully onto my side, and that's when I see: there's a policewoman sitting patiently on a stool.

I'm being guarded. But I don't know why.

I lie there, staring through the wire-hatched glass window at the back of the police officer's head. I want so badly to go out there and ask questions, but I don't dare. Partly because I'm not sure if my woolly legs will carry me to the door. But partly because I'm not sure if I can bear the answers.

I lie, for what feels like a long time, listening to the hum of the equipment, and the click of the morphine syringe driver. The pain in my head and legs dulls, and becomes distant. And then at last I sleep.

I dream of blood—spreading and pooling and soaking me. I am kneeling in the blood—trying to stop it—but I can't. It soaks my pajamas. It spreads across the bleached wood floor . . .

And that's when I wake up.

For a second I just lie there, with my heart pounding in my chest and my eyes adjusting to the dim nighttime lights of the room. I have a raging thirst and a pain in my bladder.

There's a plastic cup on the locker, just by my head, and with a huge effort I reach out and hook one trembling finger around the rim, pulling it towards myself.

It tastes flat and plasticky, but my God, drinking never felt so good. I drain it dry and then let my head flop back on the pillow with a jar that sets stars dancing in the dim light.

For the first time I realize there are leads coming out from under the sheets, connecting me to some kind of monitor, its flickering screen sending dim green shadows across the room. One of the leads is attached to one finger of my left hand, and when I lift it up to examine it, I see to my surprise that my hand is scratched and bloodied, and my already bitten nails are broken.

I remember . . . I remember a car . . . I remember stumbling across broken glass . . . one of my shoes had come off . . .

Beneath the sheets I rub my feet together, feeling the pain in one, and the swollen bulge of a dressing on the other. And across my shins . . . I can feel the stretch and pull of some kind of surgical tape across one leg.

It's only when my hand strays to my shoulder, my right shoulder, that I wince and look down.

There's a vast spreading bruise coming out from beneath the hospital gown, running down my arm. When I shrug my shoulder out of the neckline, I can see a mass of purple spreading out from a dark swollen center, just above my armpit. What could make such an odd, one-sided bruise? I feel like the memory is hovering just beyond my fingertips—but it remains stubbornly out of reach.

Have I had an accident? A car accident? Was I . . . was I attacked?

Painfully, I slide my hand beneath the sheets and run my palm across my belly, my breasts, my side. My arms are slashed with cuts, but my body seems okay. I put my hand to my thighs, feel between my legs. There's some kind of thick nappy thing, but no pain. No cuts. No bruises on the inside of my thighs. Whatever happened, it wasn't that.

I lie back and shut my eyes, tired, tired of trying to remember, tired of being afraid, and the syringe driver clicks and whirs, and suddenly nothing seems as important anymore.

It is just as I'm drifting off to sleep that an image comes to me: a shotgun hanging on a wall.

And suddenly I know.

The bruise is a recoil bruise. At some point in the recent past, I have fired a gun.

chapter 6

"Flo." I stuck my head around the kitchen door. Flo was loading the dishwasher with cups. "Oh, you shouldn't be doing that all by yourself. Can I help?"

"No! Don't be silly. It's done." She slammed the dishwasher shut. "What is it? Anything I can help with? I'm so sorry about the coffee."

"What? Oh—honestly, it's fine. Listen, I was just wondering, what time did you say Clare was due to get here?"

"About six I think." She looked up at the kitchen clock. "So we've got an hour and a half to kill."

"Okay, well, I was just wondering—have I got time to go for a quick run?"

"A run?" She looked startled. "Well, I guess—but it's getting dark."

"I'll be quick. It's just . . ." I shifted awkwardly. I couldn't explain it to her. I have trouble explaining it to myself, but I had to get out, get away.

I run almost every day at home. I have about four different routes, variations going through Victoria Park in fine weather or street runs when it's wet or dark. I give myself a couple of days off a week—they say you should, to let your muscles repair, but sooner or later the need builds up and then I have to run. If I don't, I get . . . I don't know what you'd call it. Cabin fever, maybe. A kind of claustrophobia. I hadn't run yesterday—I'd been too busy packing and tying up loose ends. And now I felt a powerful itch to get out of this boxlike house.

It's not about the physical exercise—or at least, it's not only that. I've tried running in a gym, on a treadmill, and it's not the same. It's about getting out, not having walls around myself, being able to get *away*.

"I guess you've got time," Flo said, glancing out the window at the deepening twilight, "but you'd better be quick. When it gets dark here, it gets really *really* dark."

"I'll be quick. Is there a route I should go for?"

"Hmm . . . I think your best bet would be to take the forest path down—hang on, come through to the living room." She led me through to the main room and pointed out the huge window wall to a shadowy gap in the forest. "See, that's a footpath. It leads down through the wood to the main road. It'll be firmer and less muddy than the drive—much easier to run. You just follow it down until you hit tarmac, but then I'd turn right along the main road and come back up the drive—it'll be too dark by then to run back through the forest; the path isn't fenced and you could end up going in totally the wrong direction. Come on . . ." I followed her as she returned to the kitchen and rummaged in a drawer, then pulled out something that looked like a set of badly folded suspenders. "Take this—it's a headlamp."

I thanked her, and hurried up to my room to pull on my running gear and trainers. Nina was lying on her bed, looking up at the ceiling and listening to something on her iPhone.

"That Flo's quite the fruit loop, isn't she?" she said conversationally as I came in, pulling out her earbuds.

"Is that a technical medical term, Dr. da Souza?"

"Yes. From the Latin, *Fruitus lupus*, fruit of the moon, associated with the pagan belief that insanity was connected to bathing in the light of the full moon."

I began laughing as I pulled off my jeans and yanked on my thermal running leggings and top.

"*Lupus* is Latin for wolf. You're thinking of *luna*. Where are my trainers? I left them by the door."

"I chucked them under the bed. Anyway, werewolves turn crazy at the full moon. Same diff. Speaking of crazy, are you going out?"

"Yes." I bent to look under the bed. There were my trainers, miles underneath. Thanks, Nina. I knelt and began fishing with my arm, my voice muffled by the bedclothes as I asked, "Why?"

"Let me see." She began ticking off the reasons on her fingers. "It's dark, you don't know the neighborhood, there's free wine and food downstairs—oh, and did I mention it's *pitch-fucking-black* outside?"

"It's not pitch-black." I looked out of the window as I tied my trainer laces. It was pretty dark, but it wasn't pitch-black. The sun had set, but the sky was clear and still illuminated with a diffuse pearly gray light in the west, and a round white moon was rising from the trees in the east. "And it's going to be a full moon, so it won't be *that* dark even after the sun sets properly."

"Oh really, Miss Leonora 'I've lived in London for the past eight years and never strayed more than fifty yards from a streetlamp in all that time' Shaw?"

"Really." I double knotted the trainers and stood up straight. "Don't give me grief, Nina, I've got to get out or I really will go crazy, moon or no moon."

"Huh. You're finding it that bad?"

"No." But I was. I couldn't explain why. I couldn't tell Nina how it had made me feel, having the strangers downstairs picking over my past with Clare, like someone picking at the edges of a half-healed wound. I'd made a mistake in coming—I knew that now. But I was stuck here, carless, until Nina chose to go. "No, I'm fine. I just want to get out. Now. See you in an hour."

I set off down the stairs, with her mocking laugh following me as I slammed out the door.

"You can run . . . but you can't escape!"

Out in the forest I took a breath of the clean, crisp air and began to warm up. I stretched my limbs against the garage, looking out into the forest. The sense of menace, nearing claustrophobia, that I'd had inside had gone. Was it the glass—the feeling that anyone could be out there, looking in, and we'd never know it? Or was it the strange anonymity of the rooms that made me think of zoo cages, of social experiments, of hospital waiting rooms?

Out here, I realized, the sense of being watched had quite gone.

I began to run.

It was easy. This was easy. No questions, no one prodding and poking, just the sharp, sweet air and the soft thud of my feet on the carpet of pine needles. It had rained a fair bit, but the water could not sit on this soft, loose-draining soil the way it could on the compacted rutted drive, and there were few puddles, or even boggy bits, just miles of clean springy pathway, the drifted needles of a thousand trees beneath the soles of my shoes.

There are no other runners in my family—or not that I know of—but my grandmother was a walker. She said that when she was a girl and in a rage with a friend, she used to write her friend's name on the soles of her feet in chalk, and walk until the name was gone. She said by the time the chalk had worn away, her resentment would have faded, too.

I don't do that. But I hold a mantra in my head, and I run until I can't hear it anymore above the pounding of my heart and the pounding of my feet.

Tonight—although I wasn't angry at her or, at least, not anymore—I could hear my heart beating out her name: *Clare, Clare, Clare, Clare.*

Down, down through the woods, I ran, through the gathering dark and the soft night sounds. I saw bats swooping in the gloaming, heard the sound of foxes breaking from shelter. One shot across the path ahead and then stopped, superbly arrogant, his slim-nosed head following my scent as I thumped past in the quiet dusk.

This was easy—the downhill swoop, like flying through the twilight. And I didn't feel afraid, in spite of the darkness. Out here the trees weren't silent watchers behind the glass, but friendly presences, welcoming me into the wood, parting before me as I ran, swift and barely panting along the forest path.

It would be the uphill stretch that tested me, the run back along the rutted, muddy drive, and I knew I must make it to the drive before it got so dark that I could not see the potholes. And so I ran harder, pushing myself. I had no time to keep, no target to make. I didn't even know the distance. But I knew what my legs could do, and I kept my stride long and loose. I leaped over a fallen log, and for a minute I shut my eyes—crazy in this dim light—and I could almost imagine that I was flying, and would never meet the ground.

At last I could see the road, a pale gray snake in the deepening shadows. As I broke out from the woods I heard the soft hoot of an owl, and I obeyed Flo's instructions, turning right along the tarmac. I hadn't been running for long when I heard the sound of a car behind me, and stopped, pressing myself up against the verge. I had no wish to be run down by someone not expecting to find a runner out at this time.

The sound of the car came closer, brutally loud in the quiet night, and then it was upon me, the engine roaring like a chainsaw. My eyes were dazzled by the blinding headlights—and then it was gone, into the darkness, only the red of its rear lights showing like ruby eyes in the darkness, backing away.

Its passing had left me blinking and night-blind and even though I waited, hoping my eyes would readjust, the night seemed infinitely darker than it had a few moments before, and I was suddenly afraid of running into the ditch at the side of the road, or tripping on a branch. I felt in my pocket for Flo's head torch and wrestled it on. It felt awkward, tight enough for the buckle to dig in, but loose enough for me to worry about it falling off as I started running again. At least now I could see the patch of tarmac in front of me, the white markings at the side of the road glittering back at me in the torch beam.

A sudden break showed me that I was at the turning, and I slowed and rounded the corner.

Now I was grateful for the headlamp, and it was not a matter of running anymore, but a sort of slow, cautious jog, picking my way around muddy troughs and avoiding the potholes that might break an unwary ankle. Even so, my trainers were caked, and every step felt like I was dragging a brick—half a pound of clotted mud on the sole of each shoe. I'd have fun cleaning them when I got back.

I tried to remember how far it was—half a mile? I rather wished I'd gone back through the wood, dark or no dark. But far up ahead I could see the beacon of the house, its blank glass walls shining golden in the night.

The mud sucked at my feet, as if trying to keep me here in the dark, and I gritted my teeth and forced my tired legs to go a bit faster.

I was maybe halfway when there was a sound from below, back on the main road. A car, slowing down.

I didn't have a watch, and I'd left my phone back at the house, but surely it couldn't be six yet? I hadn't been running for an hour, nothing like it.

But there it was, the sound of an engine idling as the car made the turn, and then a gritting, growling roar as it began to plow up the hill, bouncing from pothole to pothole.

I flattened myself against the hedge as it got closer, and stood, shielding my eyes from the glare and hoping that the car wouldn't splash me with too much mud as it passed, but to my surprise it stopped, its exhaust a cloud of white against the moon, and I heard the whirr of an electric window and a blast of Beyoncé, quickly muffled as someone turned the volume down.

I took a step closer, my heart pounding again, as if I'd been running much faster than I had.

The headlamp had been angled to point at the ground, for walking rather than talking, and I couldn't work out how to adjust it back up. Instead, I pulled the apparatus from my head, holding it in my hand, and shone it into the pale face of the girl in the car.

But I didn't need to.

I knew who it was.

Clare.

"Lee?" she said, as if in disbelief. The light was full in her eyes, and she blinked and shielded them from the torch beam. "My God, is it really you? I didn't . . .

"What are you doing here?"

chapter 7

For a minute I didn't understand. Had there been some horrible mistake? Was it possible she *hadn't* invited me at all, and this was all Flo's stupid idea?

"It— I'm— Y-your hen," I stammered. "Didn't you—?"

"I know that, silly!" She laughed, a nervous gust of white breath in the cold air. "I meant, what are you doing out here? Are you training for an Arctic expedition or something?"

"Having a run," I said, trying to make it sound like the most normal thing in the world. "It's not that c-cold. Just a bit nippy." But I *was* cold now, standing still, and I ruined the last words by shivering convulsively.

"Get in, I'll give you a lift up to the cottage." She leaned across and opened the passenger door.

"I'm— My trainers, they're pretty gross—"

"Don't worry. It's a hired car. Get in already, before we both freeze!"

I squelched around to the passenger's side and got in, feeling the heat of the car strike through my cold, sweat-soaked thermals. The mud had penetrated my trainers—my toes were squishing inside the lining in a way that made me shudder.

Clare put the car back into gear and hushed "Single Ladies" with a click of the Mute button.

The silence was suddenly deafening.

"So . . ." She looked sideways at me. She was just as beautiful as ever. I'd been crazy to think ten years could have made a difference to Clare. Her beauty was bone-deep. Even in the dim light of the car, muffled up in an old hoodie and a giant snoodlike scarf, she looked startling. Her hair was piled on top of her head in an adorably messy knot that spilled down over her shoulders. Her nails were painted scarlet, but chipped—not trying too hard—no one could accuse Clare of that. Pitch perfect, more like.

"So," I echoed back. I had always felt like the poor relation in comparison to Clare. Ten years had changed nothing, I realized.

"Long time no see." She was shaking her head, her fingertips tapping on the wheel. "But God, I mean . . . it's good to see you, Lee, you know?"

I said nothing.

I wanted to tell her I was not that person anymore—I was Nora now, not Lee.

I wanted to tell her it wasn't her fault, the reason I hadn't kept in touch was nothing to do with her—that it was *me*. Only . . . that wasn't completely true.

Most of all, I wanted to ask her why I was here.

But I didn't. I didn't say anything. I just sat, staring up at the house as we wound closer.

"It's *really* good to see you," she said again. "So, you're a writer now—is that right?"

"Yes," I said. The word seemed strange and false in my mouth, as if I were lying, or telling stories about someone else, a distant relative perhaps. "Yes, I'm a writer. I write crime fiction."

"I heard. I saw a piece in the paper. I'm so—I'm really pleased for you. That's amazing, you know? You should be very proud."

I shrugged.

"It's just a job." The words came out stiff and bitter-sounding—I didn't mean them like that. I know I'm lucky. And I worked hard to get here. I should be proud. I *am* proud.

"What about you?" I managed.

"I'm in PR. I work for the Royal Theatre Company."

PR. That figured, and I smiled, a genuine smile, not a false one this time. Clare was always amazing at spinning a story, even at twelve. Even at *five*.

"I'm— I'm very happy," she said softly. "And listen, I'm sorry we lost touch—seeing you . . . we had some good times, didn't we?" She glanced at me in the ghostly green light from the dashboard. "Remember having our first fag together?" She gave a laugh. "First kiss . . . first joint . . . first time sneaking into an adult film . . ."

"First time getting chucked out," I retorted, and then wished I hadn't sounded so snide. Why? Why was I being so defensive?

But Clare only laughed.

"Ha, what a humiliation! We thought we were being so clever—getting Rick to buy the tickets and sneaking through to the loos. I didn't think they'd check at the screen door as well."

"Rick! I'd forgotten him. What's he up to these days?"

"God knows! Probably in prison. For underage sex, if there's any justice."

Rick had been Clare's boyfriend for a year when we were fourteen or fifteen, a greasy long-haired twenty-two-year-old with a motorbike and a gold tooth. I'd never liked him—even at fourteen I'd found it bizarre and disgusting that Clare would want to sleep with a bloke that age, despite the fact that he could get into clubs and buy alcohol.

"Ugh, he was such a creep," I said, before I thought better of it. I bit my tongue, but Clare only laughed.

"Totally! I can't believe I couldn't see it at the time. I thought I was so sophisticated having sex with an older guy! Now it seems like—

like one step away from pedophilia." She gave a snort and then an exclamation as the car bounced off a pothole. "Oops. Sorry."

There was silence for a while as she negotiated the last and most rutted part of the drive, and then we swung onto the graveled space at the front of the house, tucking in neatly between Nina's hire car and Flo's Land Rover.

Clare turned off the engine, and for a minute we just sat in the dark car, contemplating the house, with the players inside ranged out like actors on a stage, just as Tom had said. There was Flo, beavering away in the kitchen, bending over the oven. Melanie was hunched over the phone in the living room. Tom was sprawled across a sofa directly opposite the plate-glass window, flicking through a magazine. Nina was nowhere to be seen—out having a fag on the balcony, most likely.

Why am I here? I thought again, with a kind of agony this time. *Why did I come?*

Then Clare turned to me, her face lit by the golden light streaming from the house.

"Lee," she said, at the same time as I said, "Look—"

"What?" she asked. I shook my head.

"No, you go first."

"No, you, honestly. It wasn't important."

My heart was beating painfully in my throat, and suddenly I couldn't ask it anymore, the question on the tip of my tongue. Instead, I forced out, "I'm not Lee anymore. I'm Nora."

"What?"

"My name. I don't go by Lee anymore. I never liked it."

"Oh." She was silent, digesting this. "Okay. So it's Nora now, huh?"

"Yes."

"Well, I'll do my best to remember. It's going to be hard though—after, what, twenty-one years of knowing you as Lee."

But you never knew me, I thought involuntarily, and then frowned. Of course Clare had known me. She'd known me since I was five. That was exactly the problem—she knew me too well. She saw through the thin adult veneer to the scrawny, frightened child beneath.

"Why, Clare?" I said suddenly, and she looked up, her face blank and pale in the darkness.

"Why what?"

"Why am I here?"

"Oh God." She looked down at her hands. "I knew you'd ask that. I suppose you wouldn't believe me if I said, 'Auld lang syne' and all that?"

I shook my head.

"It's not that, is it? You had ten years to make contact if you wanted to. Why now?"

"Because—" She took a deep breath, and I was astonished to realize that she was nervous. It was hard to process. I'd never seen her anything less than totally self-possessed; even at age five, she'd had a stare that could make the most hardened teacher melt, or wilt—whichever she chose. It was, I suppose, why we'd been friends, in a strange way. She had what I craved: that all-encompassing self-possession. Even standing in her shadow I'd felt stronger. But not anymore.

"Because—" she said again, and I saw her chipped lacquered nails glint, red as blood, as her fingers twisted together and her nails caught the light from the house and reflected it back into the car. "Because I thought you deserved to know. Deserved to be told—face-to-face. I promised . . . I promised *myself* I'd do it to your face."

"What?" I leaned forward.

I wasn't frightened, only puzzled. I'd forgotten my stained, wet shoes, and the stench of sweat on my clothes. I'd forgotten everything apart from this: Clare's worried face, filled with an edgy vulnerability I'd never seen before.

"It's about the wedding," she said. She looked down at her hands. "It's about— It's about who I'm marrying."

"Who?" I said. And then—to make her laugh, to try to break the tension that was filling the car and infecting me—I said, "It's not Rick, is it? I always knew—"

"No," she broke in, meeting my eyes at last, and there was not a shred of laughter there, only a kind of steely determination, as if she were about to do something unpleasant but utterly necessary. "No. It's James."

chapter 8

For a minute I stared at her, willing myself to have misheard.

"What?"

"It— It's James. I'm marrying James."

I said nothing. I sat, staring out at the sentinel trees, hearing the blood in my ears hiss and pound.

Something was building inside me like a scream. But I said nothing. I pushed it back down.

James?

Clare and *James*?

"That's why I asked you." She was speaking fast now, as though she knew she didn't have much time, that I might get up and bolt from the car at any moment. "I didn't want— I thought I shouldn't invite you to the wedding. I thought it would be too hard. But I couldn't bear for you to hear it from somewhere else."

"But—then who the hell is William Pilgrim?" It burst out of me like an accusation. For a second Clare looked at me blankly. Then she realized, and her face changed, and at the same second I knew where I'd heard that name before, and realized how stupid I'd been. Billy Pilgrim. *Slaughterhouse-Five.* James's favorite book.

"It's his Facebook name," I said dully. "For privacy—so fans don't find his personal profile when they search. That's why he doesn't have a profile picture. Right?"

Clare nodded wretchedly.

"I never meant to mislead you," she said pleadingly. She reached her warm hand out towards my numb, mud-spattered one. "And James thought you should know before—"

"Wait a minute." I pulled my hand away abruptly. "You talked to *him* about this?"

She nodded and put her hands to her face.

"Lee, I'm so . . ." She stopped and took a deep breath, and I got the feeling she was marshaling herself, working out what to say next. When she spoke again, it was with a trace of defiance, a flicker of the Clare I remembered, who would have attacked, who would have died fighting rather than lie down under an accusation. "Look, I won't apologize. Neither of us have done anything wrong. But please, won't you give us your blessing?"

"If you haven't done anything wrong"—my voice was hard—"why do you need it?"

"Because you were my friend! My best friend!"

Were.

We both registered the past tense at the same time, and I saw my own reaction reflected in Clare's face.

I bit my lip, so hard that it hurt, crushing the soft skin between my teeth.

You have my blessing. Say it. Say it!

"I—"

There was a sound from the house and the door opened, and there was Flo, standing in the rectangle of light, shading her eyes as she looked out into the darkness. She was standing on the tips of her toes, almost toppling as she craned to see into the darkness, and there was an air of suppressed excitement about her, like a child before a birthday party who might tip over into hysteria at any moment.

"Hellooo?" she called, her voice shockingly loud in the still night air. "Clare? Is that you?"

Clare let out a trembling breath and opened the car door.

"Flopsie!" Her voice shook, but almost imperceptibly. I thought, not for the first time, what an amazing actress she was. It was not surprising she'd ended up in theater. The only surprise was that she wasn't onstage herself.

"Clare-Bear!" Flo shrieked, and catapulted down the steps onto the gravel. "Oh my God, it *is* you! I heard a noise and thought . . . but then no one came." She was stumbling hastily down the path in front of the house, her bunny slippers shushing in the grit. "What are you doing out here in the dark all by yourself, you silly moo?"

"I was talking to Lee. I mean, Nora." Clare waved a hand at my side of the car. "I ran into her on the way up the drive."

"Not literally, I hope! Oops!" There was a crunch as Flo tripped over something in the dark and fetched up on her knees in front of the car with a rush. She jumped up, brushing herself off. "I'm fine! I'm fine!"

"Calm down!" Clare laughed, and hugged Flo. She whispered something into her hair that I didn't hear, and Flo nodded. I pulled at the door handle and got stiffly out of the car. It had been a mistake not to walk those last few yards up to the house—going from running to sitting so abruptly, my muscles had seized up. Now it was an effort to straighten.

"You all right, Lee?" Clare said, turning back at the sound of my getting out. "You look like you're hobbling a bit."

"I'm fine." I tried to match her in keeping my voice light. James. *James*. "Want a hand with your bags?"

"Thanks, but I've not got much." She popped the boot and picked up a shoulder bag. "Come on then, Flops, show us my room."

- - -

Nina was nowhere to be seen when I climbed the last, painful step up to our room, holding my muddy trainers by the laces. I peeled off my spattered leggings and sweaty top, and crawled under the duvet in my bra and knickers. Then I lay, staring into the pool of light cast by the bedside lamp.

This had been a mistake. What had I been thinking of?

I'd spent ten years trying to forget James, trying to build a chrysalis of assurance and self-sufficiency around myself. And I'd thought I was succeeding. I had a good life. No, I had a *great* life. I had a job I loved, I had my own flat, I had some lovely friends, none of whom knew James or Clare or anyone else from my former life in Reading.

I was beholden to no one—emotionally, financially, or in any other way. And that made me feel fine. Absolutely fucking fine, thanks very much.

And now this.

The worst of it was, I couldn't blame Clare. She was right: she and James had done nothing wrong. They didn't owe me anything, either of them. James and I had broken up over a *decade* ago, for Christ's sake. No. The only person I could blame was myself. For not moving on. For not being *able* to move on.

I hated James for his hold over me. I hated that every time I met a man, I was comparing them in my head. The last time I slept with someone—two years ago—he had woken me in the night, his hand on my chest.

"You were having a dream," he'd said. "Who's James?" And when he saw my stricken face, he'd swung his legs out of bed and got up and got dressed and walked out of my life. And I never even bothered to phone him back.

I *hated* James and I hated myself.

And yes—I am fully aware that this makes me sound like the biggest loser in existence: the girl who meets a boy at age sixteen and obsesses over him for the next ten bloody *years*.

Believe me, no one is more aware of that than me. If I met myself in a bar and got talking, I would despise myself, too.

I could hear the others downstairs, talking and laughing, and caught the smell of pizza floating up the stairs.

I was going to have to go down there and talk and laugh, too.

Instead, I curled myself into a ball, my knees to my chest, my eyes tight shut, and I screamed a silent scream inside my head.

Then I straightened, feeling my tired muscles protest, got out of bed, and picked up the topmost towel off the pile Flo had stacked carefully on the foot of each bed.

The bathroom was on the landing, and I locked the door and let the towel drop to the floor. Over the bath was another of those uncurtained plate-glass windows, looking out over the forest in an incredibly unnerving way. It was angled so that, in practice, you wouldn't be able to see inside the room unless you were perched on top of a fifty-foot pine, but as I took off my bra and knickers I had to fight the urge to cross my hands over my breasts, covering my nakedness from the watchful darkness.

For a minute I considered getting straight into my change of clothes, but I was tired and mud-spattered, and I knew I'd feel better if I had a hot shower, so I climbed carefully into the walk-in enclosure and turned the lever, stretching gratefully as the huge showerhead coughed twice, and then flooded me with an enormous, forceful gush of hot water.

Standing like this, I could look out of the window, though it was too dark to see much. The bright bathroom light turned the glass into a sort of mirror, and aside from a pale ghostly moon, all I could see was my own body reflected in the fast-steaming glass as I soaped and shaved my legs. What kind of person was Flo's aunt anyway? This was a house for voyeurs. No, that was people who liked to watch. What was the opposite? Exhibitionists. People who liked to be seen.

Perhaps it was different in summer, when the light came flooding in until late into the evening. Perhaps then it was a house for looking out of, across the forest. But now, in the dark, it felt like the opposite. It felt like a glass display case, full of curiosities to be peered at. Or a cage in a zoo. A tiger's enclosure, with nowhere to hide. I thought of those caged animals pacing slowly backwards and forwards, day after day, week after week, going slowly crazy.

When I was finished, I climbed carefully out and peered at myself in the steam-misted mirror, swiping away the condensation with my hand.

The face that looked back startled me. It looked like someone ready for a fight. It was partly my short hair; after my shower and a rough dry with the towel, it looked aggressively spiky and defiant, like a boxer between rounds. My face was white and stark under the bright lights, my eyes dark and accusing and surrounded by shadows, like I'd taken a beating.

I sighed, and got out my wash bag. I don't wear much makeup, but I had lip gloss and mascara; the basics. No blusher, but I rubbed a bit of lip gloss into my cheekbones in an effort to brighten the pallor, then yanked on clean skinny jeans and a gray top.

From somewhere far below, music started up. Billy Idol, by the sounds of it. "White Wedding." Someone's idea of a joke?

"Le— I mean, Nora!" Flo's voice floated up the stairs, above the sound of Billy Idol telling us to start again. "Are you ready for something to eat?"

"Coming!" I shouted back, and with a sigh, I bundled my dirty underwear into my towel, picked up my wash bag, and opened the door.

chapter 9

While I had been in the shower, the hen night had started in earnest.

In the living room, Tom and Clare had plugged in someone's iPhone and were dancing around the living room to Billy Idol, while Melanie laughed at them from the sofa.

Over in the kitchen, which was hot as hell from the overworked oven, I could see someone shoveling industrial quantities of pizza onto boards and dumping tubs of hummus, guacamole, and cheese and chive dip into bowls. For a disorienting minute I thought it was Clare—the person was wearing the same gray jeans and silver vest that Clare had been wearing next door. Then she straightened up and wiped the hair off her forehead and I saw it was Flo. She was wearing exactly the same clothes as Clare.

Before I could pick that apart any further, my thoughts were interrupted by a strong smell of charring.

"Is something burning?" I asked.

"Oh my God! The pitas!" Flo shrieked. "Lee, can you rescue them before they set the alarm off?"

I ran across the rapidly smoke-filling kitchen and grabbed the pita breads from the toaster, before dumping them in the sink. Then I set about wrestling with the door at the far end of the kitchen. It was locked, and there was a trick to the handle, but finally I managed to fling it wide open. Freezing air gusted in, and I saw to my surprise that the puddles on the lawn were frosting over.

"I've looked in the wine rack, and I can't find any tequila." Nina's voice came from the doorway, and then, "Bloody hell, it's freezing! Shut the door, you mentalist!"

"The pitas were burning," I said mildly, but I swung the door shut. At least the temperature in the room was closer to normal now.

"It's not in the cellar?" Flo said, brushing sweaty hair out of her eyes. Her face was scarlet from the heat. "Blast. Where on earth could it be?"

"You tried the fridge?" Nina asked. Flo nodded.

"Freezer?" I asked. She clapped a hand to her forehead.

"Freezer! Of course—I remember now, thinking it'd be better if we wanted frozen margaritas. Ugh, I'm such an idiot."

Amen! Nina mouthed at me, as she bent and opened the freezer under the counter.

"Here it is." Her voice came slightly muffled by the whir of the freezer fan. She straightened up, a frosted bottle in her hand, and scooped up two limes from the fruit bowl. "Nora, grab a board and a knife. Oh, and the saltshaker. Flo, did you say there were shot glasses through there?"

"Yup, behind that mirrored door at the end of the living room. But do you think we should start with shots? Wouldn't it be more sensible to start with a cooler first—like mojitos maybe?"

"Screw sensible," Nina said, as she left the kitchen, and then, under her breath to me as we crossed the hall, "I need something as strong as possible to get me through this."

As we entered the living room, Clare and Tom turned, and Clare gave a whoop and danced over to take the bottle from Nina's hand and the knife from mine. She shimmied back to the coffee table, her top scattering motes of light around the dimly lit room as she banged them both down on the glass with a crack.

"Tequila slammers! I haven't done these since my twenty-first. I think it's taken this long for the hangover to wear off."

Nina let the limes bounce onto the table alongside the rest, and then turned to hunt in the cupboard for glasses while Clare knelt on the rug and started slicing.

"Hen first!" Melanie said, and Clare grinned. We all watched as she shook a pinch of salt into the hollow of her wrist, then picked up a chunk of lime. Nina filled a shot glass to the teetering brim, and pushed it into her hand.

Clare licked her wrist, gulped the shot, and then bit hard into the lime, her eyes squeezed shut.

Then she spat it out onto the rug and slammed the shot glass down on the tabletop, shuddering and laughing at the same time.

"Jesus! Oh my God, my eyes are watering. My mascara'll be half-way down my face if I have any more."

"Lady," Nina said sternly, "we are just getting started. Le— I mean, Nora, you're next."

"You know . . ." Tom said, as I knelt at the table. "If you want something a bit more upmarket, we could have tequila royales."

"Tequila royales?" I watched as Nina overfilled the tiny glass, liquor splashing down and puddling on the glass tabletop. "What's that? Champagne?"

"Possibly. But not the way I make them." Tom dug in his trouser pocket and held up a little bag of white powder. "Something a bit more interesting than salt?"

Christ. I glanced up at the clock. Not even eight o'clock. At this rate we'd all be climbing the walls by midnight.

"Coke?" Melanie said. She folded her arms as she looked coolly across at Tom, and there was a note of distaste in her voice. "Really? We're not students anymore. Some of us are parents. I don't think pumping and dumping's going to sort that one out."

"So don't do it," Tom said with a shrug, but there was an edge in his voice.

"Grub's up!" The awkward pause was broken by Flo, standing in the doorway, her arms trembling beneath the weight of a huge board covered with melting pizza. There was a bottle wedged under her arm. "Can someone clear the coffee table before I deposit this little lot all over my aunt's rug?"

"Tell you what," Clare said as she watched Nina and me make space on the table. She reached over and gave Tom a salty, citrusy kiss. "Let's save it for dessert."

"No problem," Tom said lightly. He pushed the packet back into his pocket. "I've no wish to force my rather expensive drugs on people who don't appreciate them."

Melanie gave a rather thin smile and took the bottle out from under Flo's arm as Flo slid the tray onto the table and straightened up. "Hm. Talking of champagne . . ."

"Well! It is a special occasion," Flo said. She beamed, seemingly oblivious of the undercurrent of tension flowing between Melanie and Tom. "Pop the cork, Mels, and I'll get the glasses."

As Melanie peeled off the foil, Flo opened the mirrored cupboard and began rooting around. She came up, slightly flushed and clutching a half-dozen flutes, just as there was a resounding *pop!!* and the cork flew through the air and bounced off the flat-screen TV.

"Whoops!" Melanie put a hand to her mouth. "Sorry, Flo."

"No worries," Flo said brightly, but she checked the TV screen surreptitiously as Melanie bent to pour out the champagne, rubbing it with her sleeve as she cast a slightly harassed look over her shoulder.

We each took a glass and I tried to smile. I don't actually like champagne—it gives me a roaring headache and acid indigestion, and I don't like fizzy drinks much, full stop—but no one had given us the opportunity to refuse.

Flo held up her glass and turned to look around the little circle, catching all of our eyes, and then stopping, her gaze on Clare.

"Here's to a *great* hen weekend," she said. "A *perfect* hen weekend, for the best friend a girl could ever have. To my rock. To my BFF. To my heroine and my inspiration: Clare!"

"And James," Clare said with a smile. "Otherwise, I can't drink. I'm not egotistical enough to toast myself."

"Oh," Flo said, after a slight check. "Well, I mean, I just thought— Shouldn't this weekend be just about you? I thought the whole point was to forget about the groom for a bit. But, of course, if you'd prefer. To Clare, and James."

"To Clare and James!" everyone chorused, and drank.

I drank, too, feeling the bubbles fizzing acidly in my throat, making it hard to swallow.

Clare and James. Clare and *James*. I still couldn't believe it—couldn't picture them together. Had he really changed so much in ten years?

I was still staring down into my glass when Nina nudged me in the ribs.

"Come on, are you trying to read your fortune in the dregs of the champagne? I don't think it'll work."

"Just thinking," I said with an attempt at a smile. Nina raised her eyebrows, and I thought for one stomach-churning moment that she was going to say something, one of her infamously blunt remarks that left you grazed and wincing.

But before she could speak, Flo clapped her hands and said, "Don't hold back, guys! Pizza time!"

Nina took a plate and helped herself to pizza. I did, too. The meat pizzas were covered in cheap pepperoni that was leaking a chemical-smelling red oil all over the board, but after my run I was hungry. I took a piece of pepperoni and a piece of spinach and mushroom, and then loaded up my plate with the charred pita and hummus.

"Guys, use napkins if you need to; I don't want to get oil on the rug," Flo said, hovering around as the others began to dig in. "Oh, and make sure you leave the veggie slices for Tom, please?"

"Flops." Clare put a hand on her shoulder. "I'm sure it's fine. There's no way Tom can eat all those slices. Plus there's more in the freezer if we run out."

"I know," Flo said. Her face was red and she pushed her hair impatiently back into its clip. There was pizza sauce on her silver top. "But it's a matter of principle. If people want the veggie option, they should order it. I've got no patience with people who hog the veggie meals just because they don't fancy the meat choice. It just means the veggie guests go without!"

"I'm sorry," I said. "Look, I took a piece of the mushroom. Do you want me to put it back?"

"Well, no," Flo said irritably. "It's probably got pepperoni all over it now."

For a second I thought about pointing out that there was already pepperoni oil over the whole lot, and that if she was that bothered maybe she should have put them on separate boards, but instead I bit my tongue.

"It's fine," Tom said. He'd stacked up his plate with three pieces of mushroom pizza and a big dollop of hummus. "This'll do me, honestly. If I eat any more, Gary'll have me doing pull-ups from here to Christmas."

"Who's Gary?" Flo said. She took a piece of pepperoni and sat on the sofa. "I thought your other half was called Bruce."

"Gary's my personal trainer." Tom looked down at his washboard stomach rather complacently. "He has an uphill job, poor love."

"You have a personal trainer?" Flo looked deeply impressed.

"Darling, anyone who's anyone has a personal trainer."

"I don't," Nina said flatly. She stuffed a slice of pizza into her mouth and spoke around it, her voice muffled. "I jus' go to the gym and work out. I don't need some tool yelling at me while I do it. Well"—she did a heroic swallow—"I do, that's what I've got my iPod for. But I like to be able to put the tool on shuffle if the refrain gets monotonous."

"Come on!" Tom was laughing. "I can't be the only one here, surely! Nora, what about you? You don't look like you suffer from writer's arse."

"Me?" I looked up from my pizza, startled at being suddenly in the headlight beam of everyone's attention. "No! I don't even have a gym membership, I just run. The only tools I have yelling at me are the kids in Victoria Park."

"Clare then?" Tom pleaded. "Melanie? Come on! Someone back me up here. It's a perfectly normal thing!"

"I have a trainer," Clare admitted. "But"—she held up her hand as Tom started to crow—"*only* because I needed to lose a few pounds to get into my wedding dress!"

"I never understand why people do that." Nina took another bite of pizza. There was pepperoni oil dribbling down her chin, and she caught it with her tongue before continuing. "Buy a dress two sizes too small, I mean. After all, presumably the dude proposed to you when you were a lard arse."

"'Scuse me!" Clare had started laughing, but there was something a bit brittle about her tone. "I was not a 'lard arse'! And it wasn't about James, although he has a trainer, too, I might add. It was about me wanting to look my best on the day."

"So only thin people look good?"

"That's not what I said!"

"Well, you said 'your best' equals you minus two dress sizes—"

"Minus a few pounds," Clare put in hotly. "*You* said two dress sizes. Anyway, you can talk! You're skinny as a rake!"

"By accident," Nina said loftily. "Not design. I'm not size-ist. Ask Jess."

"Oh, for crying out loud." Clare put her plate down on the table. "Look, I happen to think that *I personally* look better nearer a size ten than a size twelve. Okay? It's nothing to do with anyone else."

"Nina," Flo said warningly. But Nina was in full flow, nodding earnestly and playing up to Tom's snickered laughter behind his hand, and Melanie's half-hidden smirk.

"Yeah, I get it," she was saying. "It's nothing to do with ridiculous Western idealization of anorexic models and the constant portrayal of stick-thin waifs in the media. In fact—"

"Nina!" Flo said again, more angrily this time. She stood up, banging her plate down, and Nina looked up, startled, midsentence.

"I beg your pardon?"

"You heard me. I don't know what your problem is, but leave it, okay? This is Clare's night, and I will *not* have you picking a fight."

"Who's picking fights? I'm not the one throwing plates around," Nina said coolly. "What a shame, when you were so keen to take care of your aunt's things."

We all followed the direction of her gaze, and saw the crack across the plate Flo had smacked onto the coffee table.

For a second I had the image of a goaded bull, about to charge.

"Look," Flo said furiously, and the room went quite still, pizza slices suspended in midair, glasses half sipped, waiting for the explosion to happen.

"It's okay," Clare said, into the tense pause. She put her hand out, pulling Flo back to sit beside her, and she was laughing. "Honestly. It's just Nina's sense of humor. You'll get used to her. She's not having a go at me. Much."

"Yeah," Nina said. She nodded, completely straight-faced. "I'm sorry. I just think the cripplingly unrealistic body expectations of women are hilarious."

Flo looked at Nina for a long moment, and then back at Clare, her face uncertain. Then she gave a short laugh. It was not terribly convincing.

"Come on," Tom broke into the silence that followed. "This party is not *nearly* drunk and disorderly enough for my liking. Who's up for the next shot?" He looked around the group, and his eye fell on me. A wicked grin spread across his tanned face. "Nora. You're looking far too sober. You never did have that pre-dinner shot."

I groaned. But Nina was nodding vigorously and pushing a full shot glass at me, and Tom was holding out the lime wedge and saltshaker.

There was nothing for it. Best just to get it over with, like medicine.

Tom shook the salt into the crook of my wrist, and I licked it off, grabbed the shot from Nina and gulped it back, and then snatched the chunk of lime from Tom's hand. The juice exploded between my teeth, even as the tequila ran hot down the inside of my gullet. I waited for a moment, gasping and gritting my teeth against the taste, and then a familiar warmth began to spread through my capillaries, something loosening at the edge of my vision, a certain blunting of reality.

Perhaps this weekend would be a whole lot better, slightly drunk.

I realized they were all looking at me, waiting for something. The shot glass was still in my hand.

"Done!" I banged it down onto the table, and dropped the lime peel onto my empty plate. "Who's next?"

"Make it a royale?" Tom inquired, archly. He held up the white bag.

Clare nudged me in the ribs.

"Come on, for old times' sake, yeah? Remember our first line?"

I did, though I was pretty sure it hadn't been coke. Ground-up aspirin, more like, and I hadn't really wanted to do it even then. I'd just followed Clare, sheeplike, afraid of being left behind.

"We'll do it together," Clare told him. "Cut one for Nina, too; she partakes, don't you, Doctor?"

"You know doctors," Nina said with a dry smile. "Notorious self-medicators."

Tom knelt at the corner of the glass coffee table with his credit card and the bag of powder, and we all watched as he ceremoniously poured and chopped and separated the powder into four neat lines. Then he looked up and raised his eyebrows inquiringly.

"I'm assuming Mel 'pump 'n' dump' Cho will not be joining us, but what about you, Florence 'hostess with the mostess' Clay?"

I looked across at Flo. Her face was very pink, as if she'd drunk considerably more than the one glass of champagne I'd seen in her hand.

"Guys," she said stiffly. "I'm, I'm not very happy with this. I mean it's my aunt's house. What if—"

"Oh, Flops!" Clare gave her a kiss and put her hand over her mouth, stopping her protests. "Don't be ridiculous. Don't have any if you don't want to, but I really don't think your aunt's going to rock up here with her sniffer dogs and start taking names."

Flo shook her head, and pulled herself out of Clare's reach to start clearing plates. Melanie got up, too.

"I'll help you," she said pointedly.

"All the more for those who do!" Tom said with slightly aggressive cheerfulness. He rolled up a ten-pound note and snorted up his line, wiping his nose and rubbing the grains on his gums. "Clare?"

Clare knelt and did the same with a practiced swiftness that made me wonder how often she did this. She stood up, swayed slightly, and then laughed.

"Christ, I can't be high already. Must be the tequila! Nina?" She held out the tenner. Nina made a face.

"Thanks but no thanks! Palm that snot rag off on some unsuspecting shop assistant. I'll use my own, thanks." She ripped a strip off the cover of the *Vogue Living* that was lying on the hearth, and snorted up the third line. I winced, looking at the butchered cover and hoping Flo wouldn't notice when she came back from stacking the dishwasher with Melanie.

"Nora?"

I sighed. It was true that I'd done my first line with Clare. It had also been one of my last. Don't get me wrong, I smoked and drank and did various other drugs at college. But I never really enjoyed cocaine. It never did much for me.

Now I felt like an absurd caricature as I knelt awkwardly on the rug and let Nina vandalize *Vogue Living* a bit more. It felt like a scene from a bad horror movie—just before the slasher comes in and starts stabbing people. All we needed was a couple of kids making out in the pool house to be the first victims.

I snorted the line and stood up, feeling the blood rush away from my head and my nose and the back of my mouth grow numb and strange.

I was too old for this. It was never really me, even back at school. I'd gone along with Clare only because I was too weak-willed to say no. I remembered, as if through a haze, James holding forth about the hypocrisy of it all: "They make me laugh, doing sponsored fasts for Oxfam and protesting about Nestlé, and then funneling their pocket money off to Colombian drug barons. Tossers. Can't they see the irony? Give me a nice bit of homegrown weed, any day."

I sank back on the sofa and shut my eyes, feeling the tequila, champagne, and coke mixing in my veins. All night I had been trying to connect the boy I'd known with the Clare of today, and this only brought into sharp focus the strangeness of it all. Had he really changed that much? Did they sit in their London flat, snorting up, side by side, and did he think of what he'd said when he was sixteen and reflect on the irony of it, the irony that he was now one of those tossers he'd laughed at all those years ago?

The picture hurt, like an old half-healed wound griping unexpectedly.

"Lee?" I heard Clare's voice as though from far away, and opened my eyes, reluctantly. "Lee! Come on—focus, girl! You're not drunk already, are you?"

"No, I'm not." I sat up, rubbing my face. I had to get through this. There was no way out now, except forwards. "I'm not nearly drunk enough, in fact. Where's the tequila?"

chapter 10

"I have never . . ." Clare was sprawled across the sofa with her feet on Tom's lap and the firelight playing off her hair. She was holding a shot glass in one hand and a piece of lime in the other, balancing them as if weighing up her options. "I have never . . . joined the Mile High Club."

There was a silence around the circle and a burst of laughter from Flo. Then, very slowly, with a wry expression, Tom raised his shot glass.

"Cheers, darling!" He downed it in one, then sucked the lime, making a face.

"Oh, you and *Bruce*!" Clare said. Her voice hovered between a sneer and a laugh, but it was fairly good-natured. "You probably did it in first class!"

"Business, but point taken." He refilled and looked around the circle. "What, seriously? Am I drinking alone?"

"What?" Melanie looked up from her phone. "Sorry, I had half a bar of reception then, so I thought I'd try Bill, but it's gone. Was it truth or dare?"

"Neither, we've moved on," Tom said. His voice was slurred. He had certainly done a lot of weird shit in his time, and he was paying the price in this game. "We're playing I Have Never. And I *have* joined the Mile High Club."

"Oh, sorry." Melanie downed her shot absently and wiped her mouth. "There. Listen, Flo, could I use the landline again?"

"No, no, no, no!" Clare said, wagging her finger. "You don't get off as easily as that."

"Certainly not!" Flo said indignantly. "How and where, please, missus?"

"On honeymoon with Bill. It was a night flight. I gave him a blowie in the loos. Does that count? I've drunk now anyway."

"Well, technically *he's* joined the Mile High Club, not you, in that case," Tom said. He gave a slightly slow, leering wink. "But since you drank, we'll count it. Onwards! Right. My turn. I have never . . . fuck, what have I never done? Oh, I know, I've never tried water sports."

There was a burst of laughter, and no one drank, and Tom groaned.

"What, seriously?"

"Water sports?" Flo said uncertainly. Her glass was halfway in the air, but she looked around the circle, trying to work out what was funny. "What, like scuba diving and stuff? I've done sailing, does that count?"

"No, sweetie," Clare said, and she bent over and whispered in Flo's ear. As she did, Flo's expression changed to one of shock and then disgusted amusement.

"No way! How revolting!"

"Come on," Tom said pleadingly. "'Fess up for Uncle Tom; we're all girls here, there's nothing to be ashamed of." There was another silence, and Clare laughed.

"Sorry, that's what you get for coming away with squares like us. Come on, take it like a man."

Tom downed his shot, refilled, and then lay back on the sofa, his hand over his eyes.

"Bloody hell, I'm paying for a misspent youth now. The room's spinning."

"Your turn, Lee," Clare said from the sofa. Her face was flushed, and her golden hair straggled across her shoulders. "Spill."

My stomach turned.

This was the moment I'd been dreading. I'd spent the last round trying to grope my way past the fog of tequila and champagne and rum and think what to say, but every memory seemed to bring me back to James. I thought of all the things I'd never done, never said. I shut my eyes and the room seemed to lurch and shift.

It was one thing to play this game with a roomful of friends, who already knew pretty much everything there was to say, but not this uneasy mix of strangers and old acquaintances. I have never . . . oh God, what could I say?

I never found out why he did it.

I never forgave him.

I never got over him.

"Lee . . ." Clare said in a singsong voice. "Come on now, don't make me embarrass you in the next round."

There was a vile taste of tequila and coke at the back of my mouth. I couldn't afford to drink again. If I did, I'd be sick.

I never really knew him at all.

How could he be marrying Clare?

"I have never had a tattoo," I blurted out. I knew I was on safe ground with that, Tom had already admitted to having one.

"Crap . . ." he groaned, and downed his shot. Flo laughed.

"Come on! You don't get off that easily. Show and tell please."

Tom sighed and unbuttoned his shirt, revealing an expanse of tanned, toned chest. He slid the sleeve down one shoulder and turned to show us. It was an—I assume—ironic heart, pieced with an arrow and crossed with the flowing letters *Not So Dumb* in italic script.

"There." He began buttoning up his shirt. "Now come on, you others, I can't be the only one."

Nina said nothing, but simply pulled up the ankle of her jeans, showing a small bird of some kind on the tendon running up from her ankle.

"What is it?" Flo peered closer. "Blackbird?"

"It's a falcon," Nina said. She did not elaborate but simply pulled her jeans leg down and tossed back her shot. "How about you then?"

Flo shook her head.

"Too much of a scaredy-cat! Clare does, though!"

Clare grinned and heaved herself up off the sofa. She turned her back to us and pulled up her silver top. It shimmered like a fish skin. Twining up from the back of her jeans were two black Celtic designs, curving out towards her slim waist.

"Arse antlers!" Nina gave a snort.

"Youthful folly," Clare said, a touch ruefully. "Drunken trip to Brighton when I was twenty-two."

"They're going to look delightful when you're an old lady," Nina said. "At least they'll provide a homing path for the young man slated to wipe your arse in the nursing home."

"It'll give him something to look at, poor sod." Clare pulled down her top, laughing, and flung herself back on the sofa. She drained her shot. "Mels?" she called out.

But Melanie had dragged the phone out into the hall; only the trailing wire and the sound of her low, urgent voice gave away her location.

". . . and he took the bottle?" we heard from the hallway. "How many ounces?"

"Screw that," Nina said decisively. "Man overboard. Right. I have never . . . I have never . . . I have never . . ." She looked from me to Clare, and there was suddenly a very wicked expression on her face. My stomach flipped. Nina, drunk, is not always a nice person to be around. "I have never fucked James Cooper."

There was an uncertain laugh around the room. Clare shrugged and drank.

Then her cornflower-blue eyes, and Nina's coffee-brown ones, turned on me. There was an absolute silence, broken only by Florence and the Machine telling us that her boy built coffins.

"Fuck you, Nina." My hand was trembling as I tossed back the drink. Then I got up and walked out into the hallway, my cheeks burning, and suddenly feeling very, very drunk.

"You can always give him half a banana for breakfast," Melanie was saying. "But if you give him grapes, cut them in half first or use that mesh thing."

I pushed past her up the stairs; Flo's bemused "What? What happened?" followed me as I fled.

On the landing I burst into the bathroom and locked the door behind me. Then I knelt in front of the toilet retching and retching until there was nothing left to throw up.

Oh, Christ, I was drunk. Drunk enough to go downstairs and smack Nina for the shit-stirring bitch she was. Okay, she didn't know the full picture about James and me. But she knew enough to realize that she was putting me in a horrible position—and Clare.

For a minute I hated them all: Nina for goading me with her horrible needling questions, Flo and Tom for gawping as I drank. I hated Clare for forcing me to come. And most of all I hated James, for asking Clare to marry him, for starting this whole chain off. I even hated poor blameless oblivious Melanie, just for being here.

My stomach heaved again, but there was nothing left apart from a vile taste of tequila in my mouth as I stood and spat into the toilet bowl. Then I flushed, and went to the mirror to rinse out my mouth and splash water on my face. It was white, with a blotchy hectic flush on my cheekbones, and my mascara was smudged.

"Lee?" There was a knock at the door. I recognized Clare's voice and put my face in my hands.

"I n-need a minute." Ugh, I was stammering. I hadn't stammered since I left school. Somehow I had shed it, along with the sad, awkward personality of Lee, the moment I stepped out of Reading. Nora had never stammered. I was slipping back into Lee.

"Lee, I'm sorry—Nina shouldn't have—"

Oh fuck off, I thought. *Please. Just leave me alone.*

There was the sound of low voices outside the door, and I tried, with shaking fingers, to fix my mascara using toilet paper.

God, this was pathetic. It was like being back at school—bitch fights and sniping and everything. I had sworn never to go back. This had been a mistake. A dreadful, dreadful mistake.

"I'm sorry, Nora." It was Nina's voice, slurred with alcohol but tinged with real concern, at least it sounded so. "I didn't think . . . Please, come out."

"I need to go to bed," I said. There was a catch in my throat, hoarseness from throwing up.

"Le— Nora, *please,*" Clare begged. "Come on, I'm sorry. Nina's sorry."

I took a deep breath and slid back the lock.

They were standing outside, their expressions hangdog in the bright light from the bathroom.

"Please, Lee." Clare took my hand. "Come back down."

"It's fine," I said. "Honestly. But I really am tired, I was up at five to catch the train."

"All right . . ." Clare let go of my hand reluctantly. "As long as you're not going off in a snit."

I felt my teeth grit in spite of myself. *Be calm. Don't make this all about you.*

"No, I'm not g-going off in a 'snit,'" I said, trying to keep my voice light. "I'm just tired. Now, I'm going to brush my teeth. See you in the morning."

I elbowed past them to the bedroom to get my wash bag, and when I came back they were still there, Nina tapping her foot on the parquet.

"So you really mean it?" she said. "You're bailing out? Christ, Lee, it was just a joke. If anyone's got a right to be offended, it's Clare, and she's taking it okay. Have you lost your sense of humor since school?"

For a second I thought of all the replies I could make. It *wasn't* a joke. She knew full well what that question meant to me, and she'd deliberately brought James up in the one place and at the one time I couldn't dodge it, or smooth it over.

But what was the point? Like an idiot I'd taken the bait, exploded on cue. It was done.

"I'm not bailing out," I said wearily. "It's gone midnight. I've been up since five. Please, I really just want some sleep."

I realized, even as I said the words, that I was pleading, offering up excuses, trying to absolve myself of guilt for leaving the party. Somehow the realization stiffened my nerve. We weren't sixteen anymore. We didn't have to hang around like there was an invisible umbilical cord tethering us together. We'd gone our separate ways and all survived. My getting some sleep wasn't going to ruin Clare's hen forever, and I didn't have to justify the decision like a prisoner in the star chamber.

"I'm going to bed," I repeated.

There was a pause. Clare and Nina looked at each other, and then Clare said, "Okay."

For some irrational reason that single word annoyed me more than anything else—I knew she was only agreeing, but the word had a ring of "permission granted" that made my skin crawl. *I am not yours to boss around anymore.*

"Night," I said shortly, and pushed past them into the bathroom. Over the running water and the toothbrush's rasp I could hear them whispering outside, and I deliberately stayed in there, wiping off my mascara with unaccustomed care, until their voices disappeared, and I heard their footsteps on the parquet trailing away.

I let out a breath, releasing tension I hadn't even known I was holding, and felt the muscles in my neck and shoulder unclench.

Why? Why did they still have this power over me, Clare in particular? Why did I *let* them?

I sighed, shoved the toothbrush and toothpaste back into my wash bag, pushed open the door, and padded up the hallway to the bedroom. It was cool and quiet, quite different from the overheated, overpopulated living room. I could hear Jarvis Cocker in the background, his voice floating up the open hallway, but the sound muted to just a muffled bass line when I shut the bedroom door and flopped down on the bed. The relief was indescribable. If I shut my eyes, I could almost imagine myself back in my little flat in Hackney; only the sounds of traffic and honking horns outside were missing.

I wished myself back there, so powerfully that I could almost *feel* the worn softness of my flowered duvet cover beneath my palm, see the rattan blind that flapped softly at the window on summer nights.

But then there was a knock at the door, and when I opened my eyes, the blank blackness of the forest reflected back at me from the glass wall.

I sighed, gearing myself up to answer it, and then the knock came again.

"Lee?"

I got up and opened the door. It was Flo standing outside, her hands on her hips.

"Lee! I can't believe you're doing this to Clare!"

"What?" I felt immensely tired all of a sudden. "Doing what? Going to bed?"

"I've gone to loads of effort to make this a perfect weekend for Clare—I'll kill you if you ruin it on the very first night!"

"I'm not ruining anything, Flo. You're the one making this into a big deal, not me. I just want to go to bed. All right?"

"No, it's *not* all right. I won't have you sabotaging everything I've worked for!"

"I just want to go to bed," I repeated, like a mantra.

"Well, I think you're being a . . . a selfish *bitch*," Flo burst out. Her face was red, and she looked as if she was on the verge of tears. "Clare's—Clare's the best, okay? And she deserves . . . she deserves . . ." Her chin wobbled.

"Yeah, whatever," I said, and before I could think better of it, I shut the door in her face.

For a minute I heard her outside, breathing heavily, and I thought, If she sobs, I'm going to *have* to go out there and apologize. I can't sit here and listen to her breaking down outside my door.

But she didn't. By some huge effort, she got herself together and went downstairs, leaving me very close to crying myself.

I don't know when Nina came up, but it was late, very late. I wasn't asleep, but I was pretending to be, huddled under the duvet with my pillow over my head, as she padded heavily around the room, knocking over tubes of lotion and kicking her suitcase.

"Are you asleep?" she whispered as she slid into the twin bed next to mine.

I considered ignoring her, but then I sighed and turned over.

"No. Probably because you've knocked over every bottle in the place."

"Sorry." She huddled down under the sheets, and I saw the glint of her eye as she yawned and blinked tiredly. "Look, I'm sorry about earlier. I honestly didn't—"

"It's all right," I said wearily. "I'm sorry, too. I overreacted. I was just tired, and drunk." I'd already made up my mind to apologize to Flo in the morning. Whoever was at fault here, it certainly wasn't her.

"No, it was me," Nina said. She flung onto her back and put her hand over her eyes. "I was being my usual shit-stirring self. But, you know, it's been ten years. I think I could be forgiven for assuming . . ." She trailed off. But I knew what she meant. You could be forgiven for thinking a normal person would have got over whatever happened, moved on.

"I know," I said wearily. "D'you think I don't? It's pathetic."

"Nora, what happened? Clearly something did. You don't act like this over a normal breakup."

"Nothing happened. He dumped me. End of."

"That's not what I heard." She rolled onto her side again, and I felt her gaze on my face in the darkness. "I heard you dumped him."

"Well, you heard wrong. He dumped me. By text, if you must know."

I got rid of the phone, soon after. The cheerfully insouciant *cheep cheep* alert never stopped stinging.

"Okay . . . but still. Look, I never asked, but did he . . ."

She stopped. I could hear the cogs in her brain turning, trying to work out how to phrase something tricky.

I kept silent. Whatever it was she was thinking, I wasn't going to help her.

"Oh, fuck it, there's no way to say this without prying, but I have to say it. He didn't . . . he didn't hit you, did he?"

"What?"

I wasn't expecting that.

"Okay, clearly not, sorry." Nina turned onto her back. "I'm sorry. But honestly, Lee—"

"Nora."

"Sorry! Sorry, Clare's got me doing it. And you're right. It doesn't make any sense. But honestly, though, the way you reacted after you guys split up—you can't blame people for wondering—"

"People?"

"Look, we were sixteen—you leaving town and James falling apart was pretty dramatic. There was talk, all right?"

"Jesus wept." I stared up at the ceiling. There was utter silence, but for a strange soft patter outside, like rain, but softer. "Is that really what people thought?"

"Yup," Nina said laconically. "I'd say that was the most popular of the theories. That or he gave you an STD."

God. Poor James. In spite of what he'd done, he didn't deserve *that.*

"No," I said at last. "No, James Cooper did not beat me up. *Or* give me an STD. And you're very welcome to tell anyone that who 'wonders' about it in your hearing. Now good night, I'm going to sleep."

"What then? If it wasn't that? What happened?"

"Good night."

I turned on my side, listening to the silence, the sound of Nina's exasperated breathing, and the soft patter outside.

And then at last I slept.

chapter 11

Voices. In the corridor outside. They filter into my dream, through the morphine haze, and for a moment I think I'm back at the Glass House, and Clare and Flo are whispering outside my door, their shaking hands holding the gun.

We should have checked the house . . .

Then I open my eyes, and I remember where I am.

The hospital. The people outside my door are nurses, night orderlies . . . maybe even the police officer I saw earlier.

I lie there blinking, and trying to make my tired, drug-addled brain work. What time is it? The hospital lights are dimmed for night, but I have no sense of whether it's nine p.m. or four a.m.

I twist my head to look for my phone. Always when I wake, I check the time on my phone. It's the first thing I do. But the locker beside my bed is empty. My phone is not there.

There are no clothes hanging on the chair by the window, no pockets in the hospital gown I'm wearing. My phone is gone.

I lie there, looking around the small, dimly lit room. It's a private room—which seems odd—but maybe the main ward was full. Or perhaps that's just how they do things up here. There are no other patients to ask, and no clock on the wall. If the softly blinking green monitor by my head has a time display, I can't see it.

For a minute I think about calling out, asking the policewoman outside my door what the time is, where I am, what's happened to me.

But then I realize: she's talking to someone else; it was their low voices that woke me. I swallow, dry and sticky, and pull my head painfully off the pillow, ready to croak out an appeal. But before I can speak, one sentence filters through the thick glass of the door, and glues my dry tongue to the roof of my mouth.

"Oh Jesus," I hear, "so now we're looking at murder?"

chapter 12

I woke to a clear, bright silence, broken only by Nina's soft snoring in the bed next to mine.

But as I lay there, stretching my muscles and wishing I'd refilled my water glass, I began to disentangle the sounds of the forest: birdsong, a snap of twigs, and a soft *flump* that I didn't recognize, followed by a flurry of gentle sounds like sheets of paper falling to the floor.

I glanced at my phone—6:48—still no reception—and then grabbed a cardigan and padded to the window. When I drew back the curtain, I almost laughed—it had snowed in the night, not heavily, but enough to transform the landscape into a Victorian picture postcard. *That* was the strange pattering I'd heard the night before. If I'd got up and looked outside the window, I would have known.

The sky was a blaze of pinks and blues, the clouds peach-colored and lit from beneath, and the ground was a soft, speckled carpet of white, crisscrossed with bird prints and fallen pine needles.

The sight made my feet itch, and I knew immediately and piercingly that I *had* to go for a run.

My trainers on the radiator were crusted with mud from yesterday, but they were dry, and so were my leggings. I pulled on a thermal top and a hat, but I didn't think I'd need a coat. Even running on a frosty day, I give off enough heat to keep myself warm, provided the wind doesn't get up. The morning outside was still. Not a tree branch waved in the wind, and the only snowfalls were caused by gravity, not wind—tree branches bending beneath the weight of their load.

I could hear gentle snores from all the rooms as I padded quietly down the stairs in my socks, pulling on my trainers only when I got to the doormat, to save Flo's aunt's floors. The front door had an intimidating array of locks and bolts, so I tiptoed through to the kitchen door, which was the kind with just a handle and a key. The key turned smoothly, and I lifted the handle.

I winced as I pulled open the door, suddenly wondering if there was an alarm I should have deactivated—but no screaming siren rang out, and I slipped out into the frosty morning undetected and began my warm-up.

It was maybe forty minutes later when I jogged slowly back up the forest path, my cheeks glowing with the cold and the exertion, my breath a cloud of white against the piercing blue of the sky. I felt light and calm, the frustrations and tensions left somewhere back in the forest, but it was with a slightly sinking heart that I saw the combi boiler was emitting a cloud of steam like an express train. Someone was up, and using the hot water.

I'd been hoping to have a quiet hour to myself as the others slept, breakfast on my own terms, without awkward small talk. But as I came closer to the house, I saw that not only was someone up, but they'd been outside. There were footsteps leading from a side entrance to the garage, and back. How odd. All the cars were parked out in front of the house, in the open. What reason could anyone have for going into the garage?

But my sweaty top was starting to make me feel cold, now that I wasn't powering up the hill, and I wanted coffee. I turned and headed back to the house. Whoever was up would have an explanation.

"Hello?" I called quietly as I opened the door, not wanting to wake the others. "Only me."

Someone was sitting at the counter, bent over a mobile. She lifted up her head, and I saw it was Melanie.

"Hey!" She gave a smile, her deep peachy dimples coming and going in her cheek. "I didn't think anyone else was up. Have you been out for a run in that snow? You nutter!"

"It's gorgeous." I stamped the snow off my trainers on the outside mat and then pulled them off, holding them by the laces. "What's the time?"

"Seven thirty. I've been up for about twenty minutes. It's bloody ironic—my one chance to get a lie-in without Ben waking me up, and here I am, I can't sleep!"

"You've been conditioned," I said, and she sighed.

"Too bloody right. Want a tea?"

"I'd rather have coffee, if there's one going." Too late I remembered Flo's comment. "Oh, bugger, there's no coffee, is there?"

"Nope. I'm dying. I'm a coffee girl, too, at home. Always used to be tea at university, but Bill converted me. I've tried to drink enough tea to give me the equivalent caffeine, but I think my bladder can't physically take it."

Oh, well. Tea would be hot and wet, at least.

"I'd love a tea. D'you mind if I just hop in the shower first and change my clothes? I ran in these yesterday, too. I probably stink."

"No worries. I was making toast as well. I'll have it ready when you come down."

When I came downstairs ten minutes later, it was to the smell of toast and the sound of Melanie humming "The Wheels on the Bus."

"Hey," she said as I came into the kitchen, toweling my hair. "So there's marmite, marmalade, or strawberry jam."

"No raspberry?"

"Nope."

"Marmite then, please."

She spread it on and shoved the plate across at me, and then looked surreptitiously down at her phone on the countertop. I took a bite and asked, "Still no reception?"

"No." Her polite smile slipped. "It's really getting to me. He's only just six months, and he's been a bit unsettled since we started him on solids. I just— I know it's lame, but I hate being away from him."

"I can imagine," I said sympathetically, though I couldn't really. But I could relate to the longing for home, and that must be several times stronger with someone small and helpless waiting for your return. "What's he like?" I said, trying to cheer her up.

"Oh, he's lovely!" Her smile came back, a bit more convincing this time, and she picked up her phone and began flicking through gallery shots. "Look, here's a photo of him with his first tooth."

I saw a blurred shot of a moonfaced child with no discernible teeth at all, but she flipped past it looking for something else. We went past one that looked like an explosion in a Colman's mustard factory, and she grimaced.

"Oh God, sorry about that one."

"What was it?"

"Ben with a massive poo that went right up to his hair! I took a pic to show Bill at work."

"Bill and Ben?"

"I know." She gave a sheepish laugh. "We started calling him Ben in my tummy, as a joke, and somehow it stuck. I do feel a bit bad, but I figure, he's not going to be paired up with his dad very often in life. Oh, look at this one—his first swim!"

This one was clearer—a shocked little face in a bright blue pool, the mouth an outraged red "oh!" of furious indignity.

"He looks lovely," I said, trying not to sound wistful. God knows, I don't want a baby, but there's something about seeing someone else's happy family unit that feels excluding, even when it's not meant to be.

"He is," Melanie said, her face soft. "I feel very blessed." She touched the cross at her neck, almost unconsciously, and then sighed. "I just wish there were reception here. I honestly thought I was ready to leave him, but now . . . two nights is too much. I keep thinking, What if something goes wrong and Bill can't ring?"

"He's got the house phone number, though, hasn't he?" I took a bite of toast and marmite. Melanie nodded.

"Yes. In fact"—she looked at the time on her phone again—"I said I'd phone him this morning. He was nervous about ringing early in case he woke everyone up. D'you mind if I . . . ?"

"Not at all," I said, and she got up, drained her cup, and put it on the counter.

"Oh, by the way"—I suddenly remembered as she headed towards the door—"I meant to ask, did you go out to the garage?"

"No?" She looked surprised, her voice framing the word as a question, rather than an answer. "How come? Was it open?"

"I don't know; I didn't try the door. But there were footsteps going out there."

"How odd. Wasn't me."

"Bizarre." I took another bite and chewed thoughtfully. The footsteps were crisp, so they must have been made sometime *after* the snow had finished falling. "You don't think . . ." I said, then stopped.

"What?"

I hadn't thought through what I'd been about to say, and now, as I said the words, I felt an odd reluctance to voice them.

"Well . . . I assumed it was someone coming from the house to the garage and back. But it could have been the other way around."

"What . . . like someone snooping around? Were there footsteps coming up to the garage?"

"I didn't see any. But the garage is so close to the wood, and I don't think the tracks would show there—the snow's too patchy and broken up."

Plus, although I didn't say it, if there'd been any tracks on the forest path, my run had probably just effectively obliterated them.

"Never mind," I said, picking up the tea determinedly. "This is silly to be worrying about. It was probably just Flo going out to get something."

"Yeah, you're right," Melanie said.

She gave a shrug and left the room, and a minute later I heard the *ching* of the receiver as she picked up the handset. But instead of the sound of the dial clicking around, I heard another *ching, ching, ching* repetitively, and then a bang as the receiver was slammed down.

"For crying out loud, the phone line's down! Honestly, this is the last straw. What if something's happened to Ben?"

"Hang on." I put my plate in the dishwasher and followed her into the living room. "Let me try. Maybe it's his number."

"It's not his number." She handed me the receiver. "It's dead. Listen."

She was right. There was no dial tone, just an echoing empty line, and a faint sound of clicking.

"It must be the snow." I thought of the branches in the forest, weighted down by the burden of snow. "It must have brought down a tree branch and snapped the line. The engineers'll get it back up, I imagine, but—"

"But *when*?" Melanie said. Her face was pink and upset, and there were tears in her eyes. "I didn't want to make a big deal about this to Clare, but this was my first trip away, and to be honest, I'm having a pretty shitty time. I know I'm supposed to be all, like, 'Woo! Night out with the girls!' but I don't want to do this anymore—all this drinking and stupid pissing about. I don't give a fuck who slept with who. I just want to go home and cuddle Ben. You want to know the real reason I woke up early? Because my tits were rock hard with milk, and they were so painful they woke me up leaking all over the fucking bed." She was really crying now, her nose running. "I had to g-get up and pump into the sink. And now this is the l-last straw, I've got n-n-no idea if they're okay. I don't want to be here anymore."

I stared at her, biting my lip. Part of me wanted to hug her, the other part of me was recoiling from her tearstained, snot-dripping face.

"Hey," I said awkwardly. "Hey, look . . . if you're having a shit time—"

But I stopped. She wasn't listening. She was staring not at me, but out of the window at the snowbound forest, turning something over in her mind, breathing slowly as her sobs subsided.

"Melanie?" I ventured at last.

She turned to look at me, and wiped her face on her dressing-gown sleeve.

"I'm going to go," she said.

It was so sudden that I didn't know what to say.

"Flo will kill me, but I don't care. Clare won't mind. I don't think she gave a toss about having a hen in the first place; it was all Flo's weird obsession with being the world's best friend. Do you think I can get my car down the drive?"

"Yes," I said, "it's not that heavy, but look, what about Tom? You gave him a lift, didn't you?"

"Only from Newcastle." She wiped her face again. She looked calmer now her mind was made up. "I'm sure Clare or Nina or someone will take him back. It's not a big deal."

"I guess." I chewed the side of my nail, imagining Flo's reaction to all this. "Look, are you sure you don't want to give it a bit longer? They'll get the phone line up soon, I'm sure."

"No. I've made up my mind; I'm going now. I mean, I'll wait until Flo gets up, but I'm going up to pack now. Oh! What a relief." She was smiling suddenly, her face from cloud to sunshine in just a few moments, the dimples back in her cheeks. "Thanks for listening. I'm sorry I lost it a bit, but you've really straightened me out. I mean, you're right—if you're having a shit time, what's the point of being here? Clare wouldn't want me to hang around feeling miserable."

I watched her as she made her way slowly up the stairs, presumably to repack her stuff, and pondered her last words.

What *was* the point of being here? I realized, suddenly, that I hadn't wanted her to go. Not because I liked her, or would miss her. I didn't know her well enough for that—though she seemed perfectly nice. But because I'd had some fantasy of my own of escaping. And being one down would make it that much harder—there would be that small amount of extra pressure on the survivors to make up for Melanie's absence.

And without a car, and without the alibi of a small baby, what reason could I possibly come up with that wouldn't be construed as sour grapes over James, over the fact that the better woman had won and got my ex-boyfriend for herself?

I thought I had long since stopped giving a fuck what Clare Cavendish thought of me.

I realized, as I walked slowly back to the kitchen, that I was wrong.

chapter 13

This is how I met Clare. It was the first day at primary school, and I was sitting by myself at a desk trying not to cry. Everyone else had gone to the school nursery, but I hadn't, and I didn't know anyone. I was small and skinny with hard little braids that my mother knotted into the side of my scalp "to keep off the nits."

I could read, but I didn't want anyone to know. My mother had said that it would make me unpopular to look like little Miss Know-It-All and that the teachers would tell me how to do it properly, not my made-up way.

So I was sitting alone as the other children paired up into tables and chatted away, and then Clare walked in. I had never seen anyone so beautiful. Her hair was long and loose, in defiance of the school rules, and it shone in the sunlight like a Pantene commercial. She looked around the room, at the other children, one or two of whom were patting the chair beside themselves hopefully, and saying, "Clare! Clare, sit with me!"

And she chose me.

I don't know if you know what it's like being chosen by someone like Clare. It's as though a warm searchlight has picked you out and bathed you in its sunshine. You feel at once exposed, and flattered. Everyone looks at you, and you can see them wondering, Why *her*?

Clare sat beside me, and I felt myself transforming from a nobody into a someone. A someone people might actually want to talk to, be friends with.

She smiled, and I found myself smiling back.

"Hello," she said. "I'm Clare Cavendish, and my hair is so long I can sit on it. I'm going to be Mary in the school play."

"I'm—" I tried to answer. "I'm L-le . . ."

I'm Leonora, was what I was trying to say. But Clare only smiled.

"Hi, Lee."

"Clare Cavendish." It was the class teacher, banging the board eraser on the chalkboard to get our attention. "Why is your hair not tied back?"

"It gives me migraines." Clare turned her angelic, sunlit face towards the teacher. "My mum said I wasn't to. I've got a note from the doctor."

And that was Clare all over.

Was it really possible that she had a note from the doctor? Would any doctor in his right mind give a five-year-old a note allowing her to have loose hair?

But somehow it didn't matter. Clare Cavendish had said it, and so it became true. She did become Mary in the school play. And I became Lee. Mousy, stammering Lee. Her best friend.

I never forgot Clare's action that first day. She could have chosen anyone. She could have played the popularity card and sat with one of the girls with Barbie clips in their hair and Lelli Kelly shoes.

Instead, she chose the one girl who was sitting silent, by herself, and she transformed me.

As Clare's best friend I was always included in games, not condemned to sit, lonely but trying not to look it at the side of the playground, waiting for someone to ask me to play. I was invited to birthday parties, because Clare wanted me there, and when it became known that Clare had come to my house for a playdate and had spoken approvingly of my swing and doll's house, other girls began to accept my faltering invitations.

Five-year-olds can be incredibly cruel. They say things that no adult ever would—cutting comments about your looks, your family, the way you speak and smell, the clothes you wear. If someone spoke to you that way in an office, they'd get the sack for workplace bullying—but at school it's just the natural order of things. Every class has an unpopular scapegoat, the kid no one wants to sit with, the one blamed for everything and picked last in all the team games. And, perhaps just as inevitably, every class has a Queen Bee. If there was a Queen Bee in our class, then Clare was it, and without her friendship I might easily have become the scapegoat, sitting alone at that table forever. Part of me, the frightened five-year-old inside my adult shell, will be forever grateful for that.

Don't get me wrong, it wasn't always easy being Clare's friend. That searchlight beam of love and warmth could be withdrawn as quickly as it was bestowed. You might find yourself mocked and derided instead of defended.

There were plenty of days I came home crying because of something Clare had said, or something Clare had done. But she was funny, and generous, and her friendship was a lifeline I couldn't do without, and somehow I always ended up forgiving her.

My mother, on the other hand, did not approve of Clare, for reasons I could never quite work out. It made no sense, because in many ways Clare resembled the daughter my mother was always trying to make me be—charming, loquacious, popular, not too academic. When secondary school came around, my mother did not keep silent about her hopes that I would get into the local grammar and Clare would not. But she did. Clare was not a swot, no one could accuse her of that, but she was clever, and she could pull it out of the bag in exams.

Instead, my mum went to the teacher and asked that we be put into different classes. So in lessons I found a new friend, a companion just as unlikely: spiky, amusing Nina with her skinny brown legs and large, dark eyes. Nina was tall where I was short; she could run the 800 meters in two minutes thirty, and she was funny and not afraid of anyone.

Nina was dangerous to be around; her sharp tongue made no distinction between friend and foe, and you were as likely to be the butt of her wit as laughing at it. But I liked her. And in many ways, I felt safer with her than with Clare.

It made no difference, though. Outside lessons Clare sought me out. We spent lunchtimes together. We bunked off and went to spend our allowance at Woolworth's, on the CDs Clare liked and the sparkly nail polish we were forbidden to wear at school. We were caught only once, when we were fifteen. A heavy hand on the shoulder. Mr. Bannington from the Geography Department's furious face looming over our shoulder. Threats of suspension, of telling our parents, of detention for the rest of our natural lives . . .

Clare just looked up at him, her blue eyes limpid with honesty.

"I'm so sorry, Mr. Bannington," she said. "But it's Lee's granddad's birthday. You know, the one she lived with?" She paused and gave him a significant look, inviting him to remember, to join the dots. "Lee was upset and couldn't face lessons. I'm sorry if we did wrong."

For a minute I gaped. *Was* it Granddad's birthday? It was a year since he'd died. Had I really forgotten?

Then sense returned, and with it anger. No, no, of *course* it wasn't. His birthday was in May. We were only in March.

Mr. Bannington stood, chewing his mustache and frowning. Then he put his hand on my shoulder.

"Well, under the circumstances . . . I cannot condone this, girls; if there were a fire alarm, then lives could be put at risk looking for you. Do you understand? So please don't make a habit of it. But under the circumstances, we will say no more about it. This once."

"I'm sorry, Mr. Bannington." Clare's head drooped, chastened, deflated. "I was just trying to be a good friend. It's been hard for Lee, you know?"

And Mr. Bannington coughed a choked-up cough, gave one short sharp nod, and turned on his heel and left.

I was so angry I couldn't speak on the way back to school. How dare she. How *dare* she.

At the school gate she laid a hand on my shoulder.

"Lee, look, I hope you don't mind, I just couldn't think what else to say, you know? I was the one that persuaded you to bunk; I thought it was my responsibility to get us out of the mess."

My face was stiff. I tried to imagine what my mother would have said if I were suspended, and how Clare had got us both off the hook. I thought about May, and how I was going to have to go through the day—the real day—of my granddad's birthday without mentioning that fact, or referring to it ever again.

"Thanks," I said, in a hard, unnatural voice that did not stammer, that did not sound like me.

Clare only smiled, and I felt her sunshine warmth.

"You're welcome."

And I felt myself thaw, and smile back, almost in spite of myself. After all, Clare had only been trying to be a good friend.

"No."

"Flo—"

"You're not leaving."

Melanie stood for a moment in the middle of the kitchen, as if trying to think of something to say. At last she gave a snort of disbelieving laughter.

"And yet apparently . . . I am." She slung her bag on her shoulder and tried to push past Flo towards the door.

"No!" Flo shouted. There was an edge of hysteria to her voice. "I won't let you ruin it!"

"Flo, stop being such a basket case!" Melanie snapped back. "I know— I know this is important to you, but look at yourself! Clare doesn't give a flying fuck whether I'm here or not. You've got this picture in your head of how things should be, and you can't *force* people to go along with it. Get a grip!"

"You—" Flo stabbed with her finger at Melanie. "You— You are a bad friend. And a *bad person*."

"I'm not a bad friend." Melanie sounded very tired all of a sudden. "I'm just a parent. My life doesn't revolve around Clare bloody Cavendish. Now please, get out of my way."

She pushed past Flo's outstretched arms towards the hallway, and looked up.

"Clare! You're up."

"What's going on?"

Clare was coming down the stairs in a crumpled linen wrap. The sun was shining down from the window behind her head, illuminating her hair like a halo.

"I heard shouting. What's going on?" she repeated.

"I'm going." Melanie walked a few steps up, gave her a brisk kiss, and then hitched her bag farther up her shoulder. "I'm sorry—I shouldn't have come. I wasn't ready to leave Ben, and the situation with the phone is just making it worse."

"What situation with the phone?"

"The landline's down," Melanie said. "But it's not that. Not really. I'm just— I want to be back home. I shouldn't have come. You don't mind, do you?"

"Of course not." Clare yawned and brushed hair out of her eyes. "Don't be silly. If you're miserable, then go. I'll see you at the wedding anyway."

"Yeah." Melanie gave a nod. Then she leaned forwards, with a quick glance over her shoulder at Flo, and said in a low voice, "Look, Clare, help her to get a grip, yeah? It's not . . . it's not healthy. For anyone."

She walked briskly to the door, slammed it behind her, and the last we heard was the grate of her car tires as she bumped down the rutted driveway to the lane.

Flo began to cry, heavily and snottily. For a moment I stood, wondering what I should—could—do. Then Clare came down the stairs, took Flo's arm, and led her into the kitchen. I heard the bubble of the kettle beneath Flo's gulping, retching tears, and Clare's soothing voice.

"You saved my life," Flo gasped between sobs. "How am I supposed to forget that?"

"Honey," I heard Clare say. There was a kind of loving exasperation in her voice. "How many times . . ."

I retreated upstairs, backwards, keeping my steps light and silent, and then at the landing I turned and fled. I knew I was being a coward, but I couldn't help it.

The door to the bedroom I shared with Nina was closed, and I was just about to turn the handle and barge in when I heard Nina's voice from inside, filled with an uncharacteristic yearning softness.

". . . miss you, too. God, I wish I were home with you. Are you in bed?" Long pause. "You're breaking up. Yeah, the reception's awful,

I tried to phone you last night, but there was nothing. I've only got half a bar now." Another pause. "No, just some bloke called Tom. He's okay. Oh sweetheart, Jess, I love you . . ."

I coughed. I didn't want to burst in on the middle of her conversation. Nina doesn't let her guard down often and when she does, she doesn't like it to be seen. I know that from experience.

". . . wish I were snuggled up with you. I'm missing you so much. It's the back of beyond up here—nothing but trees and hills. I'm half tempted to leave, but I don't think Nora—"

I coughed again, louder, and rattled the handle, and she broke off and called, "Hello?"

I opened the door, and she grinned.

"Oh, Nora's just come in. We're sharing a room. What? It's breaking up again." Pause. "Ha—don't worry, definitely not! Yeah, I'll tell her. Okay, I'd better go. I can hardly hear you. I love you, too. Bye. Love you." She hung up and smiled up at me from the pile of pillows. "Jess says hi."

"Oh, glad you got through to her. Is she all right?" I love Jess. She is small and round and comfortable, with a smile that lights up a room and no snark about her at all—the exact opposite of Nina, in fact. They're the perfect couple.

"Yeah, she's fine. Missing me. Natch." Nina stretched until her joints popped, and then sighed. "God, I wish she was here. Or I wasn't. One of the two."

"Well, there's a vacancy. We're one down."

"What?"

"Melanie, she's gone. The landline's down and it was the last straw."

"Christ, you're kidding? It's like Agatha effing Christie and the *Ten Little Eskimos*."

"Indians."

"What?"

"*Ten Little Indians*. In the book."

"It was Eskimos."

"It bloody wasn't." I sat down on the bed. "It was the N word, actually, if you're going for the original, then Indians, then soldiers when they decided that offing ethnic minorities was maybe a bit strange. It was never Eskimos."

"Well, whatever." Nina dismissed the Eskimos with a wave of her hand. "Is there any coffee down there?"

"Nope. Just tea, remember?" I reached for a jumper, pulled it over my head, and smoothed my hair. "Clare doesn't drink coffee, so neither do we."

"Oh God, fucking Flo and the satellite of love. How's she taking Melanie's departure?"

"Hmm. Listen, and you might be able to . . ." I trailed off, and we both heard the unmistakable sound of heavy sobs coming up from the kitchen. Nina rolled her eyes.

"She is unhinged. I really mean that. She was weird when they were at university—have you noticed how she copies what Clare wears? She used to do that back then, too. But now . . ."

"I don't think she's unhinged." I shifted uncomfortably. "Clare's a powerful personality—if you're not very confident . . ."

I stopped, struggling to put into words the feeling that I'd always had—that my own personality was a space, a vacuum that someone like Clare could rush in to fill. It was something that I knew Nina would never understand—with all her faults, lack of personality was not one of them. She lay there, eyeing me speculatively from the pillow, and then shrugged.

"Clare's *perfect,* do you know what I mean?" I said at last. "It's easy to want that for yourself, and feel like imitation is the way to get it."

"Maybe." Nina sat up, pulling her skimpy vest top straight. "I still think Flo's a few cherries short of a trifle. But whatever. Look, I've been meaning to say—I really am sorry about last night. I had no idea it was such a sore spot for you. But seriously, why did you come if you still feel like that about it all?"

I sat, chewing my lip, thinking over what I had and hadn't told Nina. It's always my instinct to keep my cards close to my chest, I don't know why. I dislike giving people, even friends, the smallest hold over me—I've always been a private person, and that tendency has grown since I started to live alone and work alone. But I knew, too, that tendency could make me as crazy as Flo in my own way.

"I came because—" I took a breath, and then forced myself on. "Because I had no idea that Clare was marrying James."

"What?" Nina swung her legs out of bed and looked at me. I gave a tremulous shrug. Put like that, it did sound . . . kind of pathetic. "What, are you serious? So Clare, like, lured you here to spring that shit on you?"

"N-not exactly." Shit. *Stop* stammering. "She said she wanted to tell me to my face. That she felt she owed me that."

"Fuck that!" Nina pulled a shirt over her head, and for a moment her voice was muffled, then it cleared as her head popped out, her cheeks pink with indignation. "If she wanted to meet you face-to-face, the normal thing to do would be to invite you out for a drink! Not lure you into some godforsaken forest. What was she thinking?"

"I—I don't think she meant it like that." Christ, what was I doing defending her? "I think she just didn't think—"

"Ugh!" Nina stood up and began brushing her hair angrily, the strands crackling as she dragged the brush through them. "How does she get away with pulling this *crap*? And she comes out of it smelling like roses every time! Do you remember when she told everyone in year ten that I fancied Debbie Harry? And then claimed it was because she felt bad that I was having to 'live a lie' and everyone acted like she was doing me a fucking *favor*?"

"I . . ." I didn't know what to say. The Debbie Harry incident had been brutal. I still remembered Nina's shocked expression when she came into the classroom and Clare was humming "Hanging on the Telephone" with that particular smile on her face, and the whole class was sniggering.

"It's all about *her*. It's about how she looks and feels. Back then she wanted to look like the caring, liberal, accepting friend, and so out it comes, sod whether I'm ready to tell people, and now she wants to feel like she can swan off into the sunset with James and no guilt—so hey, presto. Force you into a position where you've got pretty much no choice at all over whether you forgive her."

I hadn't looked at it like that. But in a way, Nina was right.

"I'm not upset about what Clare's done," I said, although I knew in my heart that this was only partly true. "What's really been bothering me . . ."

"What?"

But suddenly, I couldn't say it. The feeling of nakedness was back, and I only shook my head and turned away, pulling on my socks.

What I had been about to say, before I lost my nerve, was this: How much did James know about it? Had he gone along with this plan?

"We can go," Nina said conversationally as she buttoned up her own jeans and stood up to stretch, all six feet one of her. "We could drive off into the sunset and leave Clare and Flo to the crazy together."

"And Tom."

"Oh, yeah, and Tom."

"We could, couldn't we?" It was an enticing picture, and I thought about it for a minute as Nina began brushing her hair.

But we couldn't. I knew that, really. Or rather *I* couldn't.

If I'd said no, before I even got here, that would have been one thing. But backing out now, halfway through the hen—there was only one interpretation. I could imagine them all speculating about it after I was gone: *Poor Nora, poor cow, she's so screwed up over James, she ruined Clare's hen because she couldn't be happy for her . . .*

And worst of all—*he* would know. I could see it now, the two of them in their perfect flat in London, curled up in bed together, Clare sighing with concern over me. *I'm worried, James—it's like she's never got over you.*

And he . . . and he . . .

I found my hands were clenched into fists, and Nina was looking at me curiously. I had to consciously relax them, and I gave a little, false-sounding laugh.

"If only—right? But we can't. It would be too much of a *fuck you* in the aftermath of Melanie leaving."

Nina looked at me, long and hard, and then shook her head.

"All right. I think you're kind of masochistic. But all right."

"We've only got one more night." I was convincing myself now. "I can take one more night."

"All right. One more night it is."

chapter 14

If only. If only I had gone then.

I wish I could sleep, but I can't, even with the soft *click* and *whir* of the morphine driver. Instead, I lie awake, listening to the voices in the corridor, the policeman and -woman discussing in low voices what has happened, and that one word reverberates inside my head. *Murder. Murder. Murder.*

Can it be true? Can it possibly be true?

Who is dead?

Clare? Flo? *Nina?*

My heart stops at that. Not Nina. Not beautiful, brash, vibrant Nina. Please . . .

I must remember. I must try to remember what happened next. I know that come daybreak they will come in here and ask me questions. They're waiting outside for me to wake up, waiting to talk to me.

I must have my version of events straight by then.

But what *did* happen next? The events of that day swirl and pound inside my head, mixing themselves up, tangling themselves together, the truth with the lies. I've only got a few hours left to try to sort it out.

Step by step then. What happened next?

My hand goes to my shoulder, to the spreading bruise.

chapter 15

When Nina and I got downstairs, Flo had stopped crying and had cleaned herself up, and she was eating toast and jam, evidently determined to pretend that nothing had happened.

"Any coffee?" Nina asked innocently, but I knew from her tone she was only needling.

Flo looked up miserably, and her lip wobbled again.

"I—I forgot, remember? But I promise I'll get some today when we go to the shooting range."

"What?"

That shut Nina up. We both stared at Flo, who gave a watery smile.

"Yeah, I wanted it to be a surprise. We're going clay-pigeon shooting."

I gave a short, shocked laugh. Nina didn't move.

"Seriously?"

"Of course. Why?"

"Because—it's just like . . . a hen night? Shooting?"

"I thought it would be fun. My cousin went on his stag."

"Yes, but . . ." Nina trailed off, and I could see the thoughts running through her head as clearly as if they were written on her forehead in ticker tape: Why can't we go to a bloody spa and then clubbing like normal people? But then again, she can't possibly make us wear pink feather boas at a shooting range, right? So it could be worse.

I wondered, too, if she was thinking of Colombia. Of the gunshot wounds she'd treated there not so long ago.

"Um . . . okay," she said at last.

"They're just like clay plates," Flo was saying earnestly. "So you don't need to worry if you're veggie or anti–blood sports."

"I'm not veggie."

"I know. But if you were."

"I'm not veggie." Nina rolled her eyes and made her way over to the bread bin, looking for more bread to toast.

"I thought we'd have a spot of brunch here—with some games maybe? I've done a quiz!"

Nina winced theatrically.

"And then we can head out after that. And come back here for drinks and curry."

"Curry?" We all turned to see Tom padding downstairs in his pajama bottoms and an open dressing gown, rubbing his eyes. His pajama bottoms were knotted very low, barely above his hip bones, and there was an impressive amount of buff muscle on display.

"Tim, hate to tell you, you forgot your shirt," Nina said. "I think you should put it on. You don't want to tempt poor Nora beyond what she can bear."

I threw a toast crust at her. She dodged, and it hit Flo.

"Oops. Sorry, Flo."

"Stop it, you two!" Flo scolded. Tom only yawned, but he belted up his dressing gown and winked at me.

"What's the plan for today then?" he asked as he took a piece of toast from the plate Flo shoved at him.

"Shooting," Nina said, deadpan. Tom's eyebrows nearly disappeared beneath his hair.

"I beg your pardon?"

"Shooting. Apparently, that's Flo's idea of a jolly."

Flo gave Nina a look, not quite sure if she was having the piss taken out of her or not.

"Clay-pigeon shooting *actually*," she said defiantly. "It's fun!"

"Okay." Tom chewed his toast and looked around the table. "Am I the last one up? Oh—no. Melanie's still asleep, I presume?"

"Melanie," Flo began indignantly, but at that moment Clare came in from the living room and answered, raising her voice firmly above Flo's.

"Melanie had to go," she said. "Family stuff. Don't worry, Tom, either Nina or I will give you a lift back to Newcastle. But the good news is, it means we can all fit in the same car now, so we don't have to worry about navigating—I'll drive, and Flo can direct, as she knows where it is."

"Great," Nina said. "Super. We can all sing 'Ten Green Bottles' and fight in the backseat. I can hardly wait."

"Okay, so I think it's time for the quiz," Flo said. She craned around in her seat to look at Nina, Tom, and me in the back. I was crushed in the middle and feeling carsick already, not helped by Tom's headily overpowering aftershave. Or maybe it was Clare's perfume. It was hard to tell in the confined space. I wanted to open a window, but it was snowing outside, and the heater was on full blast.

"It's Clare versus you guys," Flo continued. "Fingers on buzzers, please, for round one."

"Wait, wait," Nina shouted. "A quiz on what, and what's the prize?"

"A quiz on James, of course," Clare said from the front seat, amused. "Right, Flops?"

"Of course!" Flo said. She was laughing. I felt more and more like vomiting. "Prize . . . I don't know. Glory? Oh, no, I've got it. The losing team can wear these for the rest of the day!"

She dug around in her rucksack and brought out a handful of skimpy underwear, emblazoned with the slogan I ❤ JAMES COOPER on the bum.

I felt every muscle in my body go stiff with anger. Nina coughed, and glanced at me sympathetically.

"Um, Flo . . ." she said diffidently, but Flo plowed on.

"Don't worry! Over trousers, I mean—or on your head or something. Right, first question. This is for Team Backseat, with a bonus point to Clare for any that you fail to get that she guesses correctly. What is James's middle name?"

I shut my eyes against the carsickness and listened to Nina and Tom arguing it over.

"Pretty sure it begins with a *C*," Tom was saying. "So I'm thinking, Chris?"

Karl. With a *K*.

"It's not," Nina insisted. "It's something to do with Russia. His dad was a professor of Russian politics. Theodor. Or what's Stalin's first name?"

"Joseph. But I'm *sure* it's not Joseph. Besides, who'd name their kid after *Stalin*?"

"Okay, not Stalin then. Name another famous Russian."

I gritted my teeth. *Karl.*

"Dostoyevsky? Lenin? Marx?"

"Marx!" Nina shouted. "It's Karl. I'm sure of it."

In spite of my growing nausea, I had to crack a smile at her competitiveness. Nina was incapable of losing at anything—an argument, a board game—she often said it was the reason she didn't do any competitive sport, because she couldn't bear losing to *someone,* even if that someone was only Usain Bolt.

"Is that your final answer?" Flo asked seriously. My eyes were still closed, but I felt Nina nodding vigorously beside me.

"Karl. With a *K*."

"Correct! Question two. What is James's star sign?"

"He's old in the year," Nina said straight off. "I remember that. He's definitely September or October."

"No, I think it's August," Tom said. "I'm sure it's August."

They bickered amicably back and forth, swapping evidence, until Nina said, "Nora, what do you—Wait, are you okay? Your face is a bit green."

"I'm feeling a bit sick," I said shortly.

"Oh God." Nina recoiled almost physically, though there was a limit to how far she could get away from me in the narrow backseat. "Someone open a window. Tom. Tom, wind yours down, too." She nudged me in the ribs and said, "Open your eyes. Looking at the road helps—it's something to do with giving the brain the information that you're traveling."

Reluctantly, I opened my eyes. Flo was grinning in the front seat. Clare was driving along calmly, and I could see in the rearview mirror that she had an amused smile on her face. She caught my eye in the mirror for a fleeting moment, and the smile twitched. For a moment—just a moment—I wanted to slap her across her perfect, beautiful cheekbone.

"I'm *sure* it's August," Tom said again. "I remember going to the proms with him and Bruce one year."

"Oh, for crying out loud," I snapped. "It's September twentieth. I've no idea what sign that is."

"Virgo," Tom said instantly. He didn't seem to hold my shortness of temper against him. "Are you sure about the date, Nora?" I nodded. "Okay, Virgo. That's our answer."

"Two points to Team Backseat!" Flo said delightedly. "Clare, you *will* have some catching up to do. Next question: What is James's favorite food?"

I wanted to shut my eyes—but I didn't dare. This was torture.

I looked down at my lap, away from Clare, and I pushed my nails into my palm, trying to distract myself from the nausea, and the memories that were crowded in unbidden. I had a sharp, flashing picture of James, sprawled on his bed after school eating his way through a bowl of clementines. He loved those things. For a moment the scent was sharp in my nostrils—the sweet tang of the oil, the smell of his room, of tumbled sheets and him. I used to love clementines—love the smell of them on his fingers, finding the peel in his pocket. I never touch them now.

"Panang curry?" Tom said uncertainly, and Flo pulled a face.

"*Almost*—but I can only give you half a point for that. Panang with . . . ?"

"Tofu," Tom said promptly. Flo nodded.

"Three points! Two more questions to go before Clare's round. Question four: Which play was James's West End debut?"

"West End in what sense?" Tom asked. "I mean, are you counting the National as West End? Because personally I wouldn't."

There was some muttered discussion between Flo and Clare in the front seat, and Flo turned back around.

"Okay, let me rephrase that as *London* debut."

I Googled James. Once. Only once. Google was spattered with images of him—pictures of him in costume, onstage, publicity stills, shots of him smiling at charity functions and opening nights. The ones I couldn't bear were the ones in which he was looking directly at the camera, directly out of the screen, at me. When I scrolled down to one where he was naked onstage, in *Equus,* I had closed the browser with shaking hands, as if I'd stumbled on something violent or obscene.

Tom and Nina were conferring over the top of my head.

"We think it was as an understudy in *The History Boys*," Nina said at last. Flo sucked in her breath.

"Ooooh! Close. I'm sorry—that was his *second* role. Over to Clare?"

"Vincent in Brixton," Clare said. "One point to me."

"Never heard of it," Nina said. Tom leaned across me and punched her.

"It won the Laurence Olivier Award for Best New Play! *And* a Tony Award."

"Never heard of that, either. Who's Tony?"

"Jesus!" Tom threw up his hands. "I'm in a car with a bleeding philistine."

"Okay," Flo said loudly, talking over them. "Fifth and final question before we hand it over to Clare for her round. When and where did James propose to Clare?"

I shut my eyes again, listening to the chorus of protest from Tom and Nina.

"That's not fair!"

"They should at least be things that Clare has a *chance* of not knowing."

"He proposed on her birthday," Tom said, "I know that. Because they came to lunch with Bruce and me the next day, and Clare was flashing that ring. Where is it, Clare?"

"Oh, I . . ." I heard Clare fidget in the driver's seat and fumble the gearshift as we took a turn too fast. "I left it at home. To tell you the truth, I've not got used to wearing it yet, and I keep panicking I'm going to lose it."

"As for where . . ." I could hear the frown in Tom's voice. "I'm going to go for a pure punt and say, J. Sheekey?"

"Ooh, so close!" Flo sucked in her breath. "Birthday was right, but it was in the bar at the Southbank. Sorry, half a point there. So that's . . . three and a half points, and a point and a half to Clare."

"Some of those were fixes," Tom grumbled. "But we'll get our revenge."

"Right, round two, question one to Clare. What was James's first pet called?"

"Blimey." Clare sounded stumped. "I think it was a hamster, but I honestly don't know."

"Team Backseat?"

"No idea," Nina said. "Nora?"

She had the grace to sound awkward, as if she knew how painful this all was. I did know. But I was damned if I was telling them. I only shook my head.

"A guinea pig called Mindy. Null points. Question two. Who is James's ideal celebrity woman?"

Clare burst out laughing.

"Okay, for self-respect I'm going to say the person who looks most like me. Which is . . . God. Who do I look like? Christ. You always sound delusional whatever you say. Okay, he likes strong women, funny women. I'm going to say . . . Billie Piper."

"You don't look anything like Billie Piper!" Nina objected. "Well, except that you're both blond."

"Well, it's not Billie Piper," Flo said. "It's—" She consulted her piece of paper. "Jeez, I have no idea who this is: Jean, how do you say that? Morrow? Clare?"

"Never heard of her, either. Is she a stage actress, Tom?"

"Right here," Flo interjected, and we rounded the corner with a sickening swing.

"Jeanne Moreau," Tom said. "She's a French actress. She was in that Truffaut film. *Jules et Jim,* I think it was. But I didn't know she was James's favorite actress."

"Well, I'd hardly call her a celebrity," Clare grumbled as we lurched over a humpback bridge and picked up speed again. The sick feeling rose again. "Next question."

"What is James's favorite designer clothes label?"

Favorite designer clothes label? The James I'd known would have laughed at the very suggestion. I wondered if it was a trick question and Clare was about to say Oxfam.

Clare tapped her fingers on the wheel, thinking.

"I'm stuck between Alexander McQueen," she said at last, "and Comme des Garçons. But I'm going to go for . . . McQueen. Mainly because he actually wears McQueen."

Jesus wept.

"Correct!" Flo said. "Well, it actually says, 'If we're talking people I think are cool, then probably Vivienne Westwood, but if you mean designers I actually wear, then McQueen.' So I think that counts. Question four: Which body part"—she began to laugh—"did James accidentally slice off at age ten in a woodwork lesson?"

"He took a chunk off his knuckle," Clare said instantly. "The scar's still there."

I squeezed my eyes tighter shut. I remembered that scar so well, a white circle on the knuckle of his little finger, and a long silver line tracing up the outside of his wrist, pale against his tan. I remembered kissing my way along that line, up his forearm, to the soft crook of his elbow, and James lying there, stiff and shaking, trying not to laugh as my lips brushed the ticklish soft skin of his inner arm.

"Correct!" Flo said. "You're doing well. Leveled up. It's three and a half all around. So this final one is the decider. If Clare gets this, she wins, and you lot wear the pants. So drumroll, please. At what age did James lose his virginity?"

Nausea rose up in my throat and I opened my eyes.

"Stop the c-car."

"What?" Clare glanced at me in the rearview mirror. "Jesus, Lee, you're green."

"Stop the car." I put a hand over my mouth. "I'm going . . ." I couldn't say any more. I pressed my lips together, breathing through my nose as Clare bumped to a hasty halt, and then I scrambled out across Nina's lap and stood on the snowy verge, hands on knees, shivering with the strange aftermath of nausea.

"Are you okay?" I heard Flo's anxious voice behind me. "Want me to do anything?"

I couldn't speak. I just shook my head vehemently, wishing she'd go away. Wishing they'd *all* go away.

"Are you all right, Lee?" Clare's voice floated out of the window.

Nora, I thought, viciously. *You stupid bitch.* But I said nothing. Just waited for my shuddering breathing to go back to normal, and the sickness to subside.

"Are you okay, Nora?" It was Nina, beside me, her hand on my shoulder. I nodded, and then slowly straightened up, taking a long, shaky breath. The cold air stung the inside of my lungs, but it was a clear, cleansing cold, a relief after the hot stuffiness of the car.

"Yeah. Sorry. I just went a bit . . . I think it was sitting in the backseat."

"I think it was Flo's fucking nauseating quiz," Nina said. She didn't bother to lower her voice, and I winced on Flo's behalf and glanced behind me apologetically, but either she didn't hear, or she didn't care. She was chatting away to Clare unconcernedly. "Flo," Nina said, turning back to the car, "I think Nora should sit in the front, is that okay?"

"Oh yeah! Totally, totally fine. Totally. Nora, you poor thing! You should have said if you were feeling rubbish."

"I'm okay," I said stiffly, but I took the front seat that Flo had vacated and slid in beside Clare. She flashed me a sympathetic look, and when Flo said enthusiastically from the backseat, "Right! Back to the quiz!" Clare interjected.

"I think we'll just call it a draw, yeah, Flops? Maybe we've all had enough quiz for the moment."

"Oh." Flo's face fell, and I couldn't help but feel sorry for her. Whoever's fault this whole mess was, it wasn't hers. Her only crime was trying to be a good friend to Clare.

chapter 16

"Leonora." There is a hand shaking me, pulling me awake. "Leonora, I'm going to need you to wake up, duckie. Leonora."

I feel fingers pulling at my eyelids and a light—blindingly bright—shining in.

"Ow!" I blink and pull back, and a hand lets go of my chin.

"Sorry, ducks, are you awake now?"

The face is disconcertingly close, her eyes staring into mine. I blink again, and then nod.

"Yes. Yes, I'm awake."

I don't know when I dozed off. It felt like I was awake half the night, watching the silhouettes of the police through the glass, running through things in my head, trying to remember. The clay-pigeon shoot. That was the recoil bruise. I must remember to tell the police . . . if only I can keep things straight in my head.

But the closer things get to—to whatever happened, the hazier they get. What did happen? Why am I here?

I must have spoken the last words aloud, for the nurse gives a sympathetic smile.

"You had a bit of a car accident, my love."

"Am I okay?"

"Yes, nothing broken." She has a pleasant Northumberland burr. "But you've knocked your poor face something awful. You've got a couple of beautiful black eyes—but no fractures. But that's why I had to wake you. We have to do observations every few hours, just to make sure you've not had a funny turn in the night."

"I was asleep," I say stupidly, and then rub my face. It hurts as if I've headbutted a window.

"Careful now," the nurse says. "You've got a few cuts and bruises."

I rub my feet, feeling the grime and grit and blood. I feel disgusting. I need a pee.

"Can I have a shower?" I ask. My head feels bleary.

There is an en suite in the corner of the room, I can see. The nurse looks down at the chart at the foot of the bed and then says, "Let me ask the doctor. I'm not telling you no, but I'd like to just make sure."

She turns to go, and I catch sight of the silhouette outside the door, and it comes back to me: the conversation I heard last night. It has a nightmarish quality. Was it really true? Did I really hear what I thought I heard, or did I dream it?

"Wait," I say. "Wait, last night I heard the people outside . . ."

But she's gone already, the door flapping back behind her with a gust of food smells and sounds from the corridor. As she walks out, the policewoman outside catches at her arm, and I hear a burst of conversation, then see the nurse shaking her head emphatically.

"Not yet," I hear. ". . . permission from the doctor . . . have to wait."

"I don't think you appreciate"—the policewoman's voice is low, but her tones are clipped and clear as a newsreader's, and her words filter through the glass much more distinctly than the nurse's Northern burr—"that this is now a homicide investigation."

"Och, no!" The nurse is shocked. "The poor love didn't make it, then?"

"No."

So it's true. I didn't imagine it. It wasn't some product of too much morphine and my battered head.

It's true.

I struggle up against the pillows, my heart pounding in my throat, and on the monitor at my left I see the little green line echoing my panic, leaping with panicked jerks against the flat line.

Someone is definitely dead.

Someone is *dead.*

But who?

chapter 17

"Welcome to Tuckett's Wood," the man said in a slightly bored Australian accent. He was tanned and chiseled and reminded me of Tom Cruise, and from the way Flo was gazing at him, her green eyes wide and her mouth slightly open, I could tell that I wasn't the only one seeing the resemblance. "My name's Grigg, and I'll be your instructor here today."

He stopped, seeming to count heads, and then said, "Hang about, I've got six here on my booking. Someone gone AWOL?"

"Yes," Flo said tightly. "Someone certainly has. No prizes for guessing who *I'll* be imagining when I open fire."

"So we're five then today?" the instructor said easily, not seeming to notice Flo's tense annoyance. "Fair dinkum. Right, first off, I have to tell you about our safety precautions . . ."

He began a long speech about ear defenders, alcohol, the responsibilities of gun ownership, and so on.

Once we'd established that yes, we were all complete beginners, and no, none of us held a shotgun license, and yes, we were all over eighteen and sober, we signed a long waiver form and trooped through into the back half of the outward-bound center, where the instructor sized us up.

"All I can say is, thank God you're none of you wearing pink feather boas and all that malarkey. You wouldn't believe the trouble we have with hen parties. You"—he pointed at Flo—"Flo, was it? Your jacket's a bit thin. You probably want something a bit thicker against the recoil." He dug around in a chest behind him and fished out a padded Barbour. Flo made a face but put it on.

"Sorry, I have to ask," she said as she zipped it up. "Is your name really Grigg? Is that a nickname?"

"Nah, Grigg. Short for Grigory."

"Oh, *Greg*," Flo said, and laughed, a little too loudly. The man gave her a slightly odd look.

"Yeah, Grigg. That's what I said. Now the thing to remember," he continued, getting out a broken shotgun and laying it on a trestle table, "is that a gun is a wippon designed to kill. Never forget that. Treat it with respect, and it'll treat you with respect. Mess around with it, and like as not, you'll be the one that ends up messed up. And most important of all, never, never point a gun at anyone, loaded or unloaded. And if you get a misfire, don't go looking down the barrel to see what happened. All this sounds simple, but you'd be amazed how often people don't obey simple safety precautions.

"Right. Now we're gonna run through a few basics about loading, closing, and breaking the gun, and then we'll head out into the woods and try a few clays. Any questions, just shout. Now the first cartridges we'll be shooting with today . . ."

We all listened in silence as he talked through the technicalities, the silliness of the car journey quite gone. I was glad to have something to concentrate on, glad to stop thinking about Clare and James, and I got the impression that the others felt the same, or at least most of them. Nina and Clare had both changed the subject when Flo had tried to start discussing the honeymoon plans. Tom had said nothing, and had spent most of the remaining car journey tapping away on his BlackBerry, but I saw his quick glance up at Clare and me, and I knew that he was filing all this away.

If you write about this, I thought, I will fucking kill you, but I said nothing, just nodded as Greg said something about automatic traps.

At last the talk was done, and we all followed Greg and trooped out of the hut into the sparse pinewood, our guns broken and hooked over our arms.

"Hey, if you enjoy this, maybe you should put a shotgun on the wedding list!" Flo said to Clare, and gave her loud braying laugh. "Shotgun wedding in the most literal sense, huh?"

Clare laughed.

"I think James'd kill me if I started messing around with the gift list now. It took the best part of a day in John Lewis to get it whittled down to what we've got now. You wouldn't believe the arguments we had—just choosing a coffeemaker took about two hours. Is a Heston Blumenthal endorsement a plus or a minus? Do we need a milk frother? Should we get bean to cup, or one of those pod machines—"

"Oh, bean to cup, surely?" Tom interrupted. "George Clooney can say what he likes, but pods are so noughties. They're the Soda Stream de nos jours. Catchy, but fundamentally pointless and inconvenient."

"You sound exactly like James!" Clare said. "But then, bean to cup is all very well, but what do you do if the grinder goes? That was my argument. You're stuck with a useless machine. Whereas if you get a separate grinder . . ."

"True, true," Tom said, nodding. "So what did you decide?"

"Well, I'm a tea gal, as you know. James is the coffee fiend. So I gave him the casting vote, and he went for the Sage by Heston Blumenthal bean to cup." She stumbled over a log, recovered, and went on. "The salesperson convinced us because it's not fully integrated the way some of them are, in that you can still use it as a solo espresso machine if you want. I mean, yes, they're expensive, but hopefully it'll be worth the investment. The only downside is that it's bloody huge. I hate to think how much space it'll take up in the kitchen."

"Bruce looked at one of those last year. Hefty beast. And best part of six hundred quid, from what I remember?"

"About that," Clare agreed.

Nina caught my eye and went cross-eyed. I tried to keep my face expressionless, but my heart was with her. Six hundred pounds for a coffee machine? I like coffee, but six hundred pounds? And on a gift list, too. I knew she meant nothing by it, but there was something unintentionally offensive about Clare's casual assumption that people could spend that much on her. Or would want to.

Or maybe it was James's assumption.

The thought left a bad taste in my mouth.

"Right," Greg called as the trees thinned out into a large grassy clearing. There was a little breeze-block wall over the far side. "Everybody hold up here. Now the kind of cartridge that we'll be using today," Greg said, with the air of someone reciting a well-worn spiel, "is seven-five. This is a good midrange type of shot, suitable for pretty much all types of clay shooting, whether that's sport, skeet, or trap.

"This"—he held up a cartridge—"is a live seven-five round, with the shot itself packed into the tip"—he tapped the rounded end—"the wad in the center, and the gunpowder and primer at this metal end here. Now, before we get going, I'm gonna show you the effects of a cartridge full of seven-five on a human body."

"Don't be asking for volunteers next!" Flo hooted. Greg turned a deadpan face onto her.

"Very kind of you to step forward, young lady."

Flo gave a nervous laugh. She looked taken aback, but at the same time slightly thrilled.

"It should be the hen, really!" she protested, as Greg beckoned, but she went and stood beside him anyway, blushing and covering her face in pantomime fear.

"Right. So Flo here has kindly volunteered to help demonstrate the effects of a barrel full of shot at close quarters." He paused for a beat and then winked. "But don't worry, she's not gonna be on the business end. What I have here"—he held up a large sheet of paper with a black outline on it—"is a paper target, more usually used for handgun target practice."

He fished in his pocket, pulled out some tacks, and pinned the target sheet to a nearby tree. The bark was blistered and pockmarked with wounds, and it wasn't hard to guess what was about to happen next.

"Everybody stand back, please. Ear defenders on, Flo."

"I feel like a DJ!" Flo said, grinning as she pulled the neon headphones over her ears.

"Now, I'm loading the cartridge into the gun"—he slid it into place—"and shutting the barrel as we demonstrated back at the center. Flo, come up here, stand in front of me. Right, bring the gun up to your shoulder." He held it against her, steadying it in place. Flo gave a slightly hysterical titter.

"Our Greg's quite dishy, isn't he?" Tom whispered into my ear. "I wouldn't mind having him correct my stance. Flo certainly looks like she's not about to object."

"Hold it firm," Greg said. "Now, finger on the trigger." He held Flo's hand in place, steadying the stock and barrel against her. "And gently squeeeeze the trigger. No sharp movements . . ."

There was a deafening crack, Flo gave a little squeak and staggered back against Greg's chest, and the paper in front of us exploded into pieces.

"Jesus!" Tom said.

I'd seen target shooting on American films—nice neat little holes, close to the bull's-eye of the outlined figure. But this was something else. The shot had hit the paper full in the chest, and the whole middle section of the piece was virtually destroyed. As we watched, the legs fluttered free and drifted gently to the leafy ground.

"Quite." Greg took the gun off Flo and walked across to stand close to us. Flo's face, as she trotted beside him, was a mixture of alarm and excitement, her cheeks pink. I wasn't sure if it was the thrill of the explosion or whether, as Tom had suggested, she had enjoyed Greg's one-to-one attention.

"As you can see," Greg continued, "this single shot at close quarters has done quite a bit of damage. If that was a person, it's doubtful he'd make it as far as the reception center, let alone the local hospital. So the moral of this is, ladies and gentlemen, respect your weapon. Okay. Any questions?"

We all shook our heads, mutely. Only Flo was beaming. Nina looked distinctly grim. I remembered the gun wounds she'd treated with MSF, and wondered what she was thinking.

Greg nodded, once, as if satisfied, and we all followed silently after him to face the trap.

chapter 18

"That was so much fun!"

Flo collapsed backwards onto the sofa and kicked off her boots. Her socks were pink and fluffy. She shook the snow out of her hair—it had started again on the drive back.

"That was ace! Tom, you were a crack shot!"

Tom grinned and slumped back into an armchair.

"I used to do a lot of archery as a teen. I guess the skills are similar."

"Archery?" Nina eyed him disbelievingly. "As in, Robin Hood and his Merry Men? Did you have to wear tights?"

"As in, the stuff they do at the Olympics," Tom said. He was obviously well used to teasing, and it barely registered. "No tights involved. I used to do competitive fencing, too. It's very good for you. Very physical. I'm out of shape now."

He flexed one bicep and looked at it with what was supposed to be a rueful expression, but the undertone of slight self-satisfaction rather showed through.

Nina made a sympathetic face.

"God, yeah, it must be awful having pecs the size of a teen girl's boobs and a six-pack to match. I don't know how Bruce puts up with it."

"Stop it, you two!" Flo scolded. Clare watched them from the far sofa, and I found myself watching her, remembering how she loved to observe, how she used to throw a remark out, like a pebble into a pond, and then back quietly away to watch the ripples as people scrapped it out. It was not an endearing habit, but it was one I could not condemn. I understood it too well. I, too, am happier watching than being watched.

Clare turned her head and caught me watching her watch Tom and Nina squabbling, and she smiled, a small conspiratorial smile that said, *I see you.*

I looked away.

What had she hoped to accomplish by inviting me here? Nina saw it as an attempt to salve her conscience at my expense—the equivalent of an adulterous husband confessing to his wife.

I did not. I don't think Clare lost any sleepless nights over hooking up with James. And in any case she didn't deserve my approbation. She owed me nothing. James and I broke up long ago.

No. I thought that perhaps . . . perhaps she had merely wanted to watch. To see how I took it. Perhaps that was the same reason she outed Nina. Like a child who sees a teeming anthill and simply can't *not* poke it.

And then she steps back . . . and watches.

"How about you, Lee?" Flo said suddenly, and I looked away from Clare, jerked out of my thoughts.

"Sorry, what?"

"Did you enjoy that?"

"Ish." I rubbed my shoulder, where I could feel a bruise already forming. "My shoulder hurts though."

"You got a right whack from the recoil on that first shot, didn't you?"

The kick of the gun had surprised me, whacking back against my shoulder bone with a *whump* that knocked the breath out of me.

"You have to hold it firm in the first place," Tom said. "You were like this, look." He reached up and took down the shotgun over the mantelpiece and braced it against his shoulder, showing me the loose stance that had cost me a bruise.

The muzzle of the gun was pointing directly at me. I froze.

"Hey," Nina said sharply.

"Tom!" Clare struggled up straighter against the sofa cushions, looking from me to Tom and then back again. "Put that down!"

Tom just grinned. I knew he was joking—but in spite of myself, I felt every muscle in my body tense.

"God, I feel like Jason Bourne," he said. "I can literally feel the power going to my head as I speak. Hmm . . . let's interrogate a few people. How about this for starters: Nora, why in all the years I've known Clare has she never mentioned your name?"

I tried to speak, but my throat was suddenly so dry I could barely swallow.

"Tom!" Clare said more sharply. "Call me paranoid, but should you be waving that thing around after all Greg's wise words about guns fucking you up?"

"It's not loaded," Flo said, and yawned. "I already explained to the others, my aunt just uses it for scaring rabbits."

"Still," Clare said.

"Just kidding around," Tom said. He gave another wolfish grin, showing those unnaturally white teeth, and then lowered the muzzle and hooked the shotgun back on its rack.

I slumped back against the sofa, feeling the wave of adrenaline recede and my fingers uncurl from their rigid fists. My hands were shaking.

"Ha fucking ha," Clare said. She was frowning like someone totally failing to see any funny side at all. "Next time you want to wave that thing around, can you make sure it's not one of my friends on the sharp end?"

I shot her a grateful look, and she rolled her eyes at me as if to say *dick.*

"Sorry," Tom said mildly. "Like I said, just kidding, but I apologize if any offense was caused." He gave a mock bow in my direction.

"Right, 'scuse I," Flo said with another yawn. "I'd better make a start on supper."

"Want a hand?" Clare said, and Flo's face lit up. Her smile was extraordinary—it transformed her whole face.

"Really? I feel like you should be acting like the queen of the day."

"Nah, come on. I'll chop or something."

She heaved herself up off the sofa and they left the room, Clare's arm slung companionably around Flo's shoulders. Tom looked after them, as they left.

"Funny couple, aren't they?" he said.

"What do you mean?" I said.

"I can't quite fit the Clare I know together with Flo. They're so . . . different."

The remark shouldn't have made sense, given that they were so physically similar, and both dressed in an almost identical uniform of gray stonewash jeans and stripy top. But I knew what he meant.

Nina stretched. "They've got one really important interest in common though."

"What's that?"

"They both think Clare's the center of the fucking universe."

Tom snorted, and I tried not to laugh. Nina only looked sideways out of her glinting dark eyes, a little wry smile twitching at the corner of her mouth. Then she stretched, and shrugged, all in one fluid movement.

"Right. I might phone the old trouble and strife." She pulled out her mobile and then made a face. "No reception. How's yours, Lee?"

Nora. But there were only so many times I could correct people without seeming obsessively controlling.

"I don't know," I said, and felt in my pockets. "That's odd. It's not here. I'm sure I had it at the shooting range—I remember checking Twitter. Maybe I left it in the car. I don't think I'd have any reception either, though—I haven't had a bar since I got here. You got a bit of reception from our room earlier, didn't you?"

"Yeah." Nina had picked up the phone receiver and was jiggling the cradle. "This one's still out. Okay. I'm going upstairs to hang off the balcony and try to get a bar or two. Maybe I can send a text."

"What's so urgent?" Tom asked.

Nina shook her head. "Nothing. Just . . . you know. I miss her."

"Fair play."

We both watched as she disappeared upstairs, long legs eating up the stairs two at a time. Tom sighed and stretched out on the couch.

"Are you not phoning Bruce?" I asked. He shook his head.

"To tell the truth we had a bit of a . . . disagreement, let's call it. Before I left."

"Oh, right." I kept my voice neutral.

I never know what to say in these situations. I hate people prying into my business, so I assume others will feel the same way. But sometimes they want to spill, it seems, and then you look cold and odd, backing away from their confidences. I try to be completely nonjudgmental—not pushing for secrets, not repelling confessions. And in truth, although part of me really doesn't want to hear their petty jealousies and weird obsessions, there's another part of me that wants to egg them on. It's that part of me that stands there nodding, taking notes, filing it all away.

It's like opening up the back of the machine to see the crude workings grinding away inside. There's a disappointment in the banality of what makes people tick, but at the same time, there's a kind of fascination at seeing the inner coils and cogs.

The trouble is that the next day they almost invariably resent you for having seen them naked and unguarded. So I'm deliberately reserved and noncommittal, trying not to lead them on.

But somehow it doesn't seem to work. All too often I end up pinned to the wall at parties, listening to a long tale of how so-and-so fucked them over, and then he said this, and then she got off with him, and then his ex did that . . .

You'd think people would be wary of spilling to a writer. You'd think they'd *know* that we're essentially birds of carrion, picking over the corpses of dead affairs and forgotten arguments to recycle them in our work—zombie reincarnations of their former selves, stitched into a macabre new patchwork of our own devising.

Tom, if anyone, should have known that. But it didn't stop him. He was speaking now, his voice a bored drawl that didn't disguise the fact that he was clearly still angry with his husband.

"What you've got to understand is that Bruce gave James his first big chance; he directed him in *Black Ties, White Lies* back in . . . God, what, we must be talking seven, eight years ago? And maybe—I mean, I don't know—I never asked what went on, but Bruce wasn't exactly renowned for his professional chastity. We weren't together then, of course. But naturally Bruce feels that James owes him a certain amount, and maybe equally naturally James feels that he doesn't. I know that Bruce was pretty angry over the business with *Coriolanus* and the fact that Eamonn sided with James . . . And then when those rumors got around about him and Richard, well, there was only one place those could have come from. Bruce swore he never sent that text to Clive."

He carried on, a stream of names and places that meant nothing to me, and plays that had only the sketchiest impression in my own cultural landscape. The politics flowed over me, but the point was clear: Bruce was angry with James and had a past with him—of whatever kind. Bruce had not wanted Tom to come to this hen night. Tom had come.

"So anyway, fuck him," Tom said at last, dismissively. I wasn't sure if he was talking about Bruce or James. He walked across to the sideboard where a cluster of bottles stood: gin, vodka, the pathetic remnants of last night's tequila. "Want a drink? G and T?"

"No, thanks. Well, maybe just a tonic water."

Tom nodded, went out for ice and limes, and then came back with two glasses.

"Bottoms up," he said, his face set in lines that made him look a good ten years older. I took a sip and coughed. Tonic, there was. But also gin. I could have made a fuss, but Tom raised one eyebrow with such perfect comic timing that I could only laugh, and swallow.

"So tell me," he said, as he drained his own glass and went back for a refill, "what happened with you and James? What was last night about?"

I didn't answer at first. I took another long sip of my drink, swallowing it slowly, thinking about what to say. My instinct was to shrug it off with a laugh, but he would get it out of Clare or Nina later. Better to be honest.

"James is . . . was . . ." I swirled the drink in my glass, the ice cubes chinking as I tried to think how to phrase it. "My ex," I said at last. It was true—but so far from the whole truth that it felt almost like a lie. "We were together at school."

"At *school*?" Tom raised both eyebrows this time. "Good Lord. Dark ages. Childhood sweethearts?"

"Yes, I guess so."

"But you're friends now?"

What could I say? No—I haven't seen him since the day he texted me.

No—I've never forgiven him for what he said, what he did.

No.

"I . . . not exactly. We sort of lost touch."

There was a sudden silence, broken only by the sounds of Clare and Flo chatting next door, and the hiss of a shower upstairs. Nina must have given up on trying to phone Jess.

"So you met at school?" Tom asked.

"Sort of. We were in a play together . . ." I said slowly. It was strange to be talking about this. You don't bring it up much as an adult: how you got your heart broken for the first time. But Tom was the next best thing to an anonymous stranger. I was highly unlikely to meet him again after this weekend, and somehow telling him felt like a release. "*Cat on a Hot Tin Roof.* I was Maggie and James was Brick. Ironic, really."

"Why ironic?" Tom said, puzzled. But I couldn't answer. I was thinking of Maggie's words in the last act of the play, about making the lie true. But I knew that, of all people, Tom would know what that meant if I quoted the line, he would know what Maggie was referring to.

Instead, I swallowed and said, "Just . . . ironic."

"Come on," he said, and smiled, his tanned cheek crinkling. "You must have meant something."

I sighed. I wasn't going to tell him the truth. Or not the truth I'd been thinking of. A different truth then.

"Well, I was supposed to be the understudy. Clare was cast as Maggie—she was the lead in almost every play we ever did, right from primary school onwards."

"So what happened?"

"She got glandular fever. Missed a whole term of school. And I got pushed onstage." I was always the understudy. I had a good verbal memory, and I was conscientious. I felt Tom looking at me, puzzled about where the irony in that lay.

"Ironic that she should have been the one to get together with him, and now she is? Is that what you mean?"

"No, not exactly . . . It's more just ironic, given that I hate being looked at, being watched. And there I was in the main role. Maybe all writers prefer being behind the page to being onstage. What do you think?"

Tom didn't answer. He only turned to look out of the great glass window, out into the forest, and I knew he was thinking of his remark the night before: of the stage. The audience. The watchers in the night.

After a moment I followed his gaze. It looked different from last night: someone had switched on the external security lights, and you could see the blank white lawn stretched out, a perfect unbroken snowy carpet, and the sentinel trees, their trunks bare and prickly beneath the canopy. It should have made me feel better—that you could see the blank, unspoiled canvas, visual evidence that we were alone, that whoever had disturbed the snow before had not come back. But somehow it was not reassuring. It made it feel even more stagelike, like the floodlights that illuminate the stage, and cast the audience into a black morass beyond its golden pool, unseen watchers in the darkness.

For a moment I made myself shiver, imagining the myriad eyes of the night: foxes with their eyes glowing yellow in the lamplight, white-winged owls, frightened shrews. But the footsteps of this morning had not been animal. They had been very, very human.

"It's stopped snowing," Tom said unnecessarily. "I must admit, I'm quite glad. I didn't really fancy being snowed in here for days on end."

"Snowed in?" I said. "In November? Do you think that could really happen?"

"Oh, yes." Flo's voice came from behind us, making me jump. She was carrying a tray of crisps and nuts, and clamped her tongue rather sweetly between her teeth as she set it carefully down on the table. "Happens all the time in January. It's one of the reasons my aunt doesn't really live here in winter. The lane gets impassable if you get a big dump. But it never snows as heavily in November, and I don't think it'll happen today. There's no more forecast for tonight. And it looks pretty, doesn't it?"

She straightened up, rubbing her back, and we all stared out of the window at the black lowering trees and the white snow. It didn't look pretty. It looked stark and unforgiving. But I didn't say that. Instead, I asked the question that had been nagging at me.

"Flo, I meant to ask, the footprints going out to the garage this morning—was that you?"

"Footprints?" Flo looked puzzled. "What time?"

"Early. They were there when I got back from my run at about eightish. Maybe before, I didn't look going out."

"It wasn't me. Where did you say they were?"

"Between the garage and the side door of the house."

Flo frowned.

"No . . . it definitely wasn't me. How odd." She bit her lip for a moment and then said, "Look, if you don't mind, I might just lock up now—that way we won't forget later."

"What do you mean? You think it could have been someone else? Someone from outside?"

Flo's cheerful face looked suddenly uncomfortable.

"Well, my aunt had a lot of trouble when she built this place—there were a lot of planning objections; local people didn't like the fact that it was a second home for a start, and there were quite a lot of complaints about the style of the build and the site."

"Don't tell me," Tom drawled. "Native American ancient burial ground, right?"

Flo hit him with a paper towel and cracked a smile through her worry. "Nothing like that. The only thing buried around here are sheep, as far as I know. But this *is* a protected area—I'm not sure if it's actually *in* the national park, but it's near as makes no odds. It got through because it was extending an existing building—an old croft-type place. But people said it wasn't in the spirit of the original . . . anyway, to cut a long story short, it burnt down halfway through construction and I think it was pretty much accepted that it was arson, although nothing was ever proved."

"Jesus!" Tom looked horrified. He glanced out of the window, as though expecting to see flaming torches coming up the hill at any moment.

"I mean, it was fine!" Flo reassured us. "It was midbuild, so the place was empty, and actually it worked out really well for my aunt because the insurance was very good, so she ended up with a higher-spec build, overall. And according to the original plans, she had to keep a bit of the original croft in place, but that burnt to the ground, so it meant she didn't have to bother with that anymore. Overall I'd say they did her a favor. But you know. It kind of affected how she feels about the neighbors."

"*Are* there any neighbors?" Tom wanted to know.

"Oh yes. There's a little cluster of houses about a mile through the forest that way." She pointed. "And a farm down the valley."

"You know"—I was thinking aloud—"what really creeps me out isn't the footprints, or not as such. It's the fact that if it hadn't have been for the snow, we'd never have known."

We looked out—contemplating the unbroken white carpet across the path to the forest. My own steps from the run that morning had been filled in, and now you would never have known a human foot had passed. For a long moment we all stood in silence, thinking about that fact, thinking about all the times we could have been observed, completely unaware.

Flo walked to the window to try the latch. It was firmly locked.

"Good!" she said brightly. "I'm going to check the back door, and then I think we should stop all this gloomy talk and have another drink."

"Hear, hear," Tom said soberly. He picked up my empty glass, and this time, when he poured me a double, I didn't complain.

chapter 19

When I went up to change for dinner, I found Nina sitting on the bed, her head in her hands. She looked up as I came in, and her face was gray and pinched, her expression so different from her usual wry sarcasm that I did a double take.

"Are you all right?"

"Yeah." She pushed her dark glossy hair back from her face and stood up. "I'm just . . . ugh, I'm *so* fed up of being here. It feels like we're back in school and I'm remembering everything I hated about myself back then. It's like we've slipped back ten years, don't you think?"

"I don't know." I sat down on my own bed and pondered her words. Although I'd had very similar thoughts last night, in the light of day they felt unfair. The Clare I remembered from school wouldn't have put up with Flo for a second—or not unless she had some powerful motive. She would have nodded along with Flo's dumber remarks, stringing her along into saying something painfully weird, at which point she would have stood back, pointed, and laughed. I'd seen none of that cruelty this weekend. Instead, I'd been impressed by her tolerance. It was clear that Flo was a damaged person in some way—and I admired Clare's compassion in trying to help her. I didn't know if I could have put up with Flo for ten days, let alone ten years. Clare was obviously a bigger and better person than I'd given her credit for.

"I think Clare's changed a lot actually," I said. "She seems a lot more . . ." I stopped, searching for the right word. Maybe there wasn't one. "She just seems *kinder*, I guess."

"People don't change," Nina said bitterly. "They just get more punctilious about hiding their true selves."

I chewed my lip while I thought that over. Was it true? *I* had changed—at least, I told myself I had. I was far more confident, more self-sufficient. All through school I'd relied on my friends for self-esteem and support, wanting to be one of a pack, wanting to fit in. At last I had learned that wasn't possible, and I'd been happier—albeit more lonely—ever since.

But perhaps Nina was right. Perhaps it was simply that I'd learned to hide the awkward, desperate-to-fit-in child I had been. Perhaps the me I'd become was just a thin veneer, ready to be peeled painfully back.

"I don't know," Nina said. "I just . . . didn't you think lunch was painful?"

Lunch had been painful. It had been exclusively wedding talk. Where the reception was to be held. What Clare was wearing. What the bridesmaids were wearing. Whether smoked salmon was overdone as a starter, and why the vegetarian option always contained goat cheese. It had been made worse by the realization that I'd crossed an invisible line and gone past the point where I could have admitted I wasn't invited. I should have said something straightaway, fessed up, made a joke out of it on the first night. Now it had gone too far to look like anything other than deception, and I was trapped in a lie by omission.

"I'm not going to say 'bridezilla,'" Nina continued, "because actually here I think it's more like a bridesmaidzilla. But if I have to hear one more time about wedding favors, or leg waxes, or best-man speeches . . . can you imagine James in the middle of all this?"

I had been purposely avoiding thinking about James and the wedding, like a sore bit of skin you can't bear to have touched. But now, as I tried, I realized that I couldn't. The James I remembered—with his head shaved at the back and a scraped-up topknot, and his ripped school tie, the James who'd got drunk on his dad's whiskey and climbed on the school war memorial at midnight to shout Wilfred Owen poems to the night sky, the James who wrote Pink Floyd lyrics on the head teacher's car in lipstick on the last day of the summer term . . . That James, I couldn't imagine him in a dinner jacket, kissing Clare's mother and laughing dutifully at the best-man speech.

The whole thing had been painful to the point of nausea, made worse by covert sympathetic looks from Nina. If there's one thing I dislike more than being hurt, it's being seen to be hurt. I've always preferred to creep away and lick my wounds in private. But Nina was right. It wasn't a case of Bridezilla-itis. In fact, Clare had been uncharacteristically quiet all through lunch. The conversation had been driven by Flo, egged on by Tom. At one point Clare had even suggested they change the subject. It was not likely that she had lost her love of the limelight since leaving school. More likely, she was thinking of me.

"If I had more balls, I'd have said no," Nina said glumly. "To the wedding, I mean. But Jess would've killed me. She loves weddings. It's like some obsessive-compulsive disorder with her. She's already bought a new fascinator for this one. I ask you. A fucking fascinator."

"She'd have forgiven you," I said lightly. "Though you might have had to propose to make it up to her."

"It may yet come to that. Would you come?"

"Of course." I gave her a punch on the arm. "I'd even come to your hen. If you had one."

"Sod that," Nina said. "If—and I repeat—*if* I ever get married, I'm having a night out clubbing, and that's that. None of this prancing about in cottages in the arse end of beyond." She sighed and dragged herself upright. "Do you know what Flo's got sorted for us tonight?"

"What?"

"Only a fucking Ouija board. I'm telling you, if she's got one with 'sexy' answers on the board I'm pulling that gun down off the mantelpiece and shoving it up somewhere painful—blanks or no blanks."

"Okay, *this*," Flo said, spreading out sheets of paper on the coffee table, "should be fun."

"Magic Eight Ball says *don't count on it*," Nina muttered. Clare shot her a look, but either Flo hadn't heard, or chose to ignore, the dig. She carried on busily setting up the table, dotting candles among the half-empty wine bottles.

"Anyone got a lighter?"

Nina dug in the pocket of her denim miniskirt and produced a Zippo, and Flo lit the candles with an air of ceremonial reverence. As each candle on the table caught, a corresponding flame kindled in the reflected view in the window. Flo had turned off the outside security lights, and the forest was dark, apart from a little light from the moon, but the room was dimly lit enough that we could see the dark massing shapes of the trees, the pale snow, and the silhouette of the forest canopy against the slightly luminous sky.

Now, it looked as if little will-o'-the-wisps were dancing in the trees, fragile ghostly flames, twice reflected in the double glazing.

I walked to the window, huffing on the glass and cupping my hands to see out into the night. It was perfectly still. But I thought again of the footsteps leading out to the barn, and the broken phone line, and I couldn't stop myself from surreptitiously checking the latch of the French windows. It was fastened.

"Mel would have hated this," Clare said thoughtfully as I rejoined the table, and Flo lit the last candle. "I'm pretty sure she's even more Christian than she was at uni."

"I really can't see that communing with one imaginary friend is any different than communing with a bunch of them," Nina said spikily.

"Look, it's her faith, all right? There's no need to be offensive."

"I'm not being offensive. You cannot, by definition, offend someone who's not here. Offense has to be taken, not just given."

"If a tree falls in an empty forest, does it make a noise?" Tom said, with a dry smile. He lay back on the sofa and took a long gulp of wine. "Blimey, it's years since I've done this. My aunt was very into all this communing with the spirits. I used to go around to her house after school and she'd make me do the traditional Ouija board, you know, the one with the letters on it."

I knew what he meant—those were the kind of Ouija boards I'd seen on films. The one Flo was setting up was a bit different, more like a biro on wheels.

"It's easier this way," Flo said, her tongue between her teeth as she tried to fix the pen in the holder. "I've tried it before, and the problem with the pointer is that unless you're very quick, you can miss loads of letters. This way there's a permanent record."

"Did you get anything?" Clare asked. "When you tried it before, I mean?"

Flo nodded, seriously.

"Oh yes. I usually get some kind of message. My mum says I've got a natural resonance with the beyond."

"Uh-huh," Nina said. Her face was deadpan, but I could tell some kind of sarcastic remark was building up.

"What did it say?" I put in hastily, trying to head her off at the pass. "Last time, I mean."

"It was about my grandfather," Flo said. "He wanted to tell Granny that he was happy and that she should remarry if she wanted. Anyway, there, all set up. Are we ready?"

"As ready as I'll ever be," Clare said. She downed the rest of her wine and set aside her glass. "Right. What do we do?"

Flo motioned to us all to come closer.

"Right—put your hands on the planchette. Just gently—you're not trying to guide it, just be the conduit for any impulses you receive from the beyond."

Nina rolled her eyes but put her fingertips on the planchette, a heart-shaped piece of wood with a holder for a pen. Tom and I followed suit. Clare was the last.

"Ready?" Flo asked.

"Ready," Clare said.

Flo took a deep breath and shut her eyes. Her face in the candlelight was glowing, as if lit from within. I saw her eyes move beneath her lids, darting from side to side, seeking something she could not see.

"Is there a spirit there who wants to speak to us?" she intoned.

The planchette swirled uneasily in loops and spirals, not forming any shapes that made sense. No one was pushing it, that was for sure.

"Is there a spirit here tonight?" Flo repeated seriously. I saw Nina hide a smile. The planchette began to move in a more purposeful way.

Y.

"Oh wow!" Flo breathed. She looked up, her face alight. "Did you see that? It was like it was being pulled by a magnet. Did everyone feel that?"

I had felt something. It felt more like it was being pushed by someone else in the circle, but I said nothing.

"What is the name of the spirit?" Flo said eagerly.

The planchette began to move again.

te . . . qui . . . long pause . . . *te . . . qui . . .*

"Qui means *who* in French," Flo breathed. "Maybe we've got a French spirit guide?"

l . . .

Both Tom and Nina began to laugh as the last *a* trailed out from beneath the planchette. Even Clare gave a smothered snort, and the planchette veered off towards the edge of the paper and then clattered to the floor as we all began to giggle.

Flo looked at the page for a moment, frowning, not getting the joke. Then she saw it. She knelt back from the table, her arms crossed.

"Right." She looked from Clare, to Tom, and then to me. I tried to straighten my face. "Who did that? This is not a joke! I mean, yes, it's a bit of fun, but we're never going to find anything out if you keep playing around! Tom?"

"It wasn't me!" Tom threw up his hands. Nina was wearing her most innocent expression, and I strongly suspected it had been her.

"Well, whoever it was"—Flo's face was pink and annoyed—"I'm not impressed. I've gone to a lot of trouble and you're ruining—"

"Hey, hey, Flops." Clare put out a hand. "Chill, okay? It was just a joke. They won't do it again. Will you?" She looked sternly around the circle of faces. We all put on our most contrite expressions.

"All right," Flo said sulkily. "But last chance! If you mess around again, I'm putting this away, and we'll all play . . . we'll all play Trivial Pursuit!"

"What a threat," Tom said seriously, though the corner of his mouth was twitching. "I promise I for one will behave like an angel. Don't threaten me with the pink Camembert."

"Okay," Flo said. She drew a deep breath and waited as we all rested our fingers on the planchette again. It twitched, and I saw Nina's shoulders were still shaking with suppressed giggles, but she bit her lip and subsided with an effort as Clare stared at her.

"We are sorry for the levity of *some* of our circle," Flo said meaningfully. "Is there a spirit here who would like to speak to us?"

This time the planchette moved more slowly, more as if it were drifting of its own accord. But, unmistakably, it was forming another *Y,* and then it stopped.

"Are you a friend of someone here?" Flo breathed.

? said the planchette.

This time I didn't think anyone else was pushing—and I could see the others felt the same way. They had stopped laughing. Clare even looked slightly uneasy.

"Do you know, Flops, I'm not sure . . ." she said.

Tom patted her hand. "It's fine, darling. I used to do it all the time with one of my aunts when I was younger. It's not really spirits—just the subconscious of the group making words. Sometimes the results are quite illuminating."

"Who is here?" Flo had shut her eyes. Her fingers rested very lightly on the planchette. If anyone was controlling it, I was sure it wasn't her. The planchette moved again, forming letters in a looping, free-form hand. Tom read them aloud as they appeared.

"*M . . . A* maybe? Or was that *N*? . . . *X . . . W . . . E . . . L . . . L . . .* Okay, well, that's a word. Maxwell. Anyone know a Maxwell?"

We all shook our heads.

"Maybe it's the spirit of one of the former crofters," Nina said seriously. "Come to warn us against trampling on their sacred sheep bones."

"Maybe," Flo said. She opened her eyes. They were wide and green in the darkness. She looked very pale, her pink crossness of before quite gone. She closed them again and said in a hushed, reverent tone, "Is there anyone here you wish to speak to, Maxwell?"

Y.

"Do you have a message for one of the group?"

Y.

"Who of the group?"

f . . . fl . . . f . . .

"Me?" Flo's eyes flew open. She looked startled to the point of alarm. In fact, she looked like she was regretting this idea already. "Do you have a message for *me*?"

Y.

Flo gulped. I saw that her free hand—the one not resting on the planchette—was gripping the edge of the coffee table so hard her knuckles were white.

"Okay," she said bravely. But the planchette was already moving.

B . . . u . . . it traced slowly, and then in a sudden, skittering rush: *y coffee.*

There was a moment's silence, and then Nina broke it with a short, barking laugh.

"Fuck OFF!" Flo shouted. We all jumped, and I realized it was the first time I could remember her swearing. She jumped up and sent the planchette skittering across the table. Wineglasses and candles crashed to the floor, spattering wax on the carpet. "Who was that? This isn't a joke, guys! I am fed *up*. Nina? Tom?"

"It wasn't me!" Nina said, but she was laughing so hard there were tears coming from her eyes. Tom was trying harder to hide his mirth, but he was snickering, too, behind his hand.

"I'm sorry," he said, trying hopelessly to straighten his expression. "I'm sorry. It's n-not f-f—" But he couldn't complete the sentence.

Flo swung accusingly around at me. I was dabbing up wine from the rug.

"You're very quiet, Lee, sitting there pretending butter wouldn't melt!"

"What?" I looked up, genuinely surprised. "I beg your p-pardon?"

"You heard me! I'm fed up with you sitting there like a malignant little mouse, laughing behind my back."

"I'm not," I said uncomfortably, remembering the way I had succumbed to laughing at Nina's teasing when we first arrived. "I mean—I didn't mean—"

"You all think you're so perfect." Flo was breathing heavily, in great sobbing gasps. I thought she was about to burst into tears. "You all think you're so great, with your degrees and your jobs and your flats in London."

"Flo," Clare said. She put her hand on Flo's arm again, but Flo shook it off.

"Come on," Tom said soothingly. "Look, I don't know who did that, but I promise it's the last time anyone will mess around, right?" He looked at the group. "Right, everyone? We promise, okay? This time it's for real."

He was trying to help, but I felt my stomach twist uncomfortably. We should have packed up when Flo blew up the first time—pushing on like this was asking for trouble, with Flo in her furious, heightened state.

"Don't you th-think—" I said nervously.

"I th-think you should just shut up," Flo said furiously, imitating my stutter with an uncanny precision. I was so shocked I didn't say anything, just sat with my mouth open, staring at her. It was as if a Teletubby had spat in my face.

"Hey, come on, now," Clare said. "One more chance, okay, Flops? And I promise everyone will take it seriously this time. They'll have me to answer to if not."

Flo downed her glass of wine with a hand that shook. Then she sat heavily down at the table and put her hand on the planchette.

"Last chance," she said savagely. Everyone nodded, and, reluctantly, I put my fingers back on the board.

"Let's ask it a question this time," Tom said soothingly. "Help keep it on track. How about . . . Will Clare and James have a long and happy life?"

"No!" Clare said loudly. We all turned, shocked by the vehemence of her response. "No—look, I'm just— I don't want to start dragging James into this. Okay? It feels wrong. This is a bit of fun, but I don't want some pen telling me I'll be divorced before the age of thirty."

"All right," Tom said mildly, but I felt his surprise. "How about me then. What wedding anniversary will Bruce and I celebrate?"

We all rested our fingertips on the board, and, very slowly, I felt it begin to move.

This time it was quite different from before. Not the stuttering push and tug, but a long, languid flowing script that looped in spirals around the page.

"Pa . . . Pa . . ." Flo spelled out. "Papa? What does that mean? That's not a wedding anniversary."

"Paper, maybe?" Tom was frowning at the sheet. "That makes no sense, though. Paper's like . . . year two or something. We celebrated that last year. Maybe it means opal. That first *P* could be an *O*."

"Maybe it's telling us its name," Flo said breathlessly. Her rage of a moment before was gone, and she looked excited—almost hyper with it. She refilled and then drained her glass with three reckless gulps, and then set it unsteadily back on the floor, and I saw that her silvery-gray top, the twin of the one Clare was wearing, had a red wine stain down one sleeve. "They don't always perform to order, you know. Let's ask it. What is your name, Spirit?"

The pen started again, looping swiftly over the page in large, quickly formed letters that ate up the space, scribbling over the other writing from before.

Pa . . . I saw and then . . . *by* farther across the page. Then it slowed to a halt and Flo craned her head to read out the text.

"*Papa Begby.* Wow. Who on earth is that?"

She looked around the circle of shrugging shoulders and shaking heads.

"Nora?" Flo said suddenly. "Do you know who that is?"

"Christ, no!" I said, reflexively. To tell the truth, I was more than a little creeped out. The other stuff had been fairly obvious joking around. This felt distinctly odder. The others looked as unnerved as I felt. Clare was chewing the end of a piece of hair. Nina was looking elaborately unconcerned, but I could see her fingers playing with her lighter in her pocket, nervously twisting it around beneath the cloth. Tom looked frankly shocked, his face pale even in the dim light. Only Flo looked genuinely thrilled.

"Wow," she breathed. "A real spirit. Papa Begby. Maybe he's the guy who owned this croft? Papa Begby," she spoke respectfully into the space above our heads. "Papa Begby, do you have a message for us here tonight?"

The pen started moving again, more jerkily this time.

M . . . I read. For a moment my heart sank. Not more jokes about coffee.

M . . . m . . . m . . .

The script went faster and faster and then there was a sudden crunch and the planchette grated to a juddering halt. Clare lifted it up and put her hand to her mouth.

"Oh, Flops, I'm so sorry."

I looked down at the table. The biro had gone clean through the page, and into the polished wood beneath.

"Your aunt . . ."

"Oh, never mind," Flo said impatiently. She pushed the planchette away and lifted up the sheet. "What does it say?"

We all looked, reading over her shoulder as she turned the page slowly this way and that, reading the curving spiral of writing.

M m mmmmuurderrrrrrrrrrrer

"Oh my God." Tom put his hand to his mouth.

"That's not funny," Nina said. Her face was pale, and she took a step back from the group, scanning our faces. "Who wrote that?"

"Look," Tom said. "Hands up, I did the coffee one. But I didn't say that. I wouldn't!"

We all looked at each other, searching for guilt in each other's eyes.

"Maybe you're barking up the wrong tree," Flo said. Her flush was back, but this time, I thought, it had an edge of triumph rather than anger. "Maybe it was a real message. After all, I know some things about you, about you all."

"What do you mean?" Tom said. His voice was wary. "Clare, what's she on about?"

Clare said nothing, just shook her head. Her face was quite white, her lips bloodless beneath the gloss. I found I was breathing hard and fast, almost hyperventilating.

"Hey," Nina said suddenly. Her voice had an odd faraway quality. "Hey, Nora, are you okay?"

"I'm fine," I said, or tried to say. I wasn't sure if the words came out. The room seemed to be closing in, even as the great glass window opened out, like a mouthful of pointed piney teeth, waiting to swallow us all. I felt hands grabbing at my arms, pushing me down on the sofa, my head between my knees.

"You're all right." I heard Nina's firm voice, and suddenly it was easy to remember that she was a doctor, a professional medic and not just a friend I went drinking with every few months. "You're all right. Someone get a bag, a paper bag."

"Drama queen," I heard Flo say in an angry hiss, and she stomped out of the room.

"I'm fine," I said. I tried to sit up, pushing away Nina's hands. "I don't need a paper bag. I'm okay."

"You sure?" Nina looked into my face searchingly. I nodded, trying to look convincing.

"I'm absolutely fine. Sorry, I don't know why I came over so funny. Too much wine. But I'm all right, I promise."

"Too much drama," Tom said under his breath, but he said it soberly, and I knew he didn't mean me.

"I just— I think I'll go and get some fresh air. It's too hot in here."

It was hot, the stove was pumping out heat like a furnace. Nina nodded.

"I'll come with you."

"No," I said, more violently than I meant. And then, more calmly, "Honestly, I'd rather be by myself. I just want a breather. Okay?"

Outside, I stood with my back against the glass door of the kitchen. The sky above was deep blue velvet, and the moon was astonishingly white, ringed with a pale halo of frost. I felt the cold night air envelop me, the chill cooling my hot face and sweaty palms. I stood, listening to the pounding of my own heart, trying to slow its beats, trying to calm down.

It was absurd to be so ridiculously panicked. There was nothing to say the message was about me. Though, what was it Flo had said at the end?

I know some things about you . . .

What had she meant? Which one of us was she talking to?

If it was me, there was only one thing she could have been referring to. And Clare was the only person who knew what had happened. Had she told Flo?

I wasn't sure. I wanted to think not. I tried to remember all the secrets I'd confided in Clare over the years, secrets she'd kept faithfully.

But I remembered going back to school to sit my French comprehension exam, and one of the other girls in the queue putting a hand on my arm. *I'm so sorry,* she'd said, *you're so brave,* and there was genuine pity in her face, but also a kind of glee, the sort you see sometimes when teens are interviewed about the tragic death of a friend. The sadness is there, and it's real, but there's an underlying thrill at the drama of it all, the *realness* of it all.

I didn't know for sure what she meant—she might have been talking about James and me breaking up. But her reaction seemed extreme for that, and I began to wonder if Clare had told someone what had happened.

All through the exam I worried, and worried at the question. And by the time the two hours was up, I knew what I had to do. Because I knew that the doubt would send me insane.

I never went back.

Now, I shut my eyes, feeling the cold on my face, and the snow penetrating my thin socks, and listening to the soft sounds of the night, the crackle and rush of snow-laden branches breaking beneath their weight, the hoot of an owl, the strange haunting shriek of a fox.

I had never lived in the country. I'd grown up on the outskirts of Reading, and then moved to London as soon as I turned eighteen. I'd lived there ever since.

But I could imagine living here, in the silence and the solitude, seeing people only when I wanted to. I wouldn't live in a vast glass bell jar, though. I'd live somewhere small, inconspicuous, part of the landscape.

I thought of the crofter's cottage that had once stood here, before it had been burned to the ground. I imagined a long low building, its silhouette like an animal trying to go to ground, like a hare flattening its form into the grasses. I could have lived there, I thought.

When I opened my eyes, the light blazing from the house onto the snow hurt my retinas. It was so brash, so wasteful—like a golden lighthouse, beaming its presence into the darkness. Only . . . a lighthouse was to tell ships to keep away. This place felt more like a beacon, like a lantern drawing in the moths.

I shivered. I must stop being so superstitious. This was a beautiful house—we were lucky to be staying here, even for just a few days. But I didn't like it, I didn't trust Flo, and I couldn't wait to be away tomorrow morning. I wondered how early I could decently leave. Nina and I had seats on the five p.m. train, but my ticket was flexible.

"Are you okay?" The voice came from behind me, followed by a long exhalation of cigarette smoke, and I turned and saw Nina standing there, fag in one hand, the other arm wrapped around her ribs against the cold. "Sorry. I know you said you wanted to be alone. I just . . . I needed a fag. Needed to get away. Ugh, that Flo! She gives me the heebie-jeebies. What was all that weird stuff about knowing secrets about us?"

"I don't know," I said uncomfortably.

"It was probably just bullshit." Nina dragged on her fag. "But I must admit, I was sitting there ticking off all the stuff I've told Clare over the years, and it wasn't a very comfortable feeling, thinking about what she might have passed on to Flo. And Tom looked pretty shaken up, didn't he? Wonder what the skeleton in his closet is?"

"I don't know," I repeated. The cold was starting to strike through to my bones, and I shivered.

"I think Melanie had it right," Nina said at last. "Flo's not normal. And her weirdness about Clare—'not healthy' is an understatement. All that copying Clare's clothes—it's a bit *Single White Female,* isn't it? If you ask me, she's a couple of Xanax away from reenacting the shower scene in *Psycho*."

"Oh, for God's sake," I snapped. Flo was odd, but that was really not fair. "She's not psycho; she's just not very confident. I know what it's like, always feeling second best. Clare's not always the easiest person to be friends with."

"No. No, don't try to make excuses for her, Nora. The clothes and stuff—I mean, whatever. It's weird, but if Clare wants to put up with it, it's her call. But that little exhibition tonight was directed squarely at us, and I'm not having it. Look, I was thinking, tomorrow—I know we're booked on the five p.m., but—"

"But can we go early? I was thinking the exact same thing."

"I've had it up to here, to be honest. If I was sober, I'd go tonight, but I'm in no state to drive. What do you reckon—straight after breakfast?"

"Flo will flip," I said soberly. There were more activities planned for tomorrow—I wasn't sure what, but the instructions had been clear: leave at two p.m., not before.

"I know. I was actually thinking . . ." Nina took a long drag. "I was thinking we could just slip away. Is that cowardly?"

"Yes," I said definitely. "Very."

"Oh, all right." She sighed, exhaling a cloud of smoke, white in the moonlight. "Maybe I can invent some sort of hospital crisis. I'll think of an excuse tonight."

"How would you know?" I said. "Given there's no mobile reception and no phone?"

"Well, that's another fucking thing, isn't it? Supposing the crazed locals *do* come up the hill, banjos playing, pikes alight, what the hell are we supposed to do? Throw snowballs at them?"

"Don't be so melodramatic. There aren't any crazed locals. Flo's aunt probably torched the place herself as an insurance job and blamed it on the farmers."

"I hope you're right. I've seen *Deliverance*."

"I'm happy for you, but back to the problem at hand . . ."

"Oh, I'll just pretend a stray text got through overnight. Anyway, even if Flo doesn't believe me, what can she say?"

Plenty, was my guess, but unless she barricaded the door, I didn't think it would work to deflect Nina. There was a long silence, Nina blowing smoke rings with her cigarette into the still night air, me huffing out clouds of white breath.

"What happened back there?" Nina asked at last. "That little panic attack, I mean. Was it the message?"

"Sort of."

"But you didn't think it was about you, did you?" She looked at me sideways, curiously, and blew out a smoke ring. "I mean, what could you have possibly done to kill someone?"

I shrugged.

"No, not really. Anyway, it might not have been *murderer.* It could have been *murder.* There were so many repeats I'm not sure what the word actually was."

"What, like a warning, you mean?" Nina asked. "So, we're back to the crazed locals, are we?" I shrugged again. "I'm not going to lie." She puffed out another ring. "I thought maybe it was directed at me. I mean— I've never killed anyone purposely, but there're people who've died because of mistakes I made, for sure."

"What—you thought it was a genuine message?"

"Nah." She took another drag. "I don't believe in any of that kind of thing. I just meant, I thought someone was taking a stab in the dark, trying to wind me up. It was definitely Flo, no question. I think she was pissed off because we were messing around at the beginning and decided to punish us. I did that *tequila* message. She probably knew."

"Do you think?" I looked up at the clear sky. It was not black, but deep, navy blue, a color so pure it made my eyes hurt. Far up a satellite was traveling towards the moon. I tried to think back, to Flo's face as she read out the word, to her closed eyes and rapturous expression. "I don't know. I've been standing out here trying to think it out, but I'm not sure it was her. She looked genuinely shocked. And she was the only person who really believed in the whole thing—I don't think she'd have messed with the spirits by pushing it."

"So now *you* reckon it was real?" There was skepticism in Nina's voice.

I shook my head. "No, I didn't mean that. I think someone was pushing it. I'm just not sure it was her."

"So what . . . that leaves Tom and Clare?" Nina dropped her cigarette and ground it out in the snow with a hiss. "Really?"

"I know. That's partly what upset me. I think it was . . ." I stopped, trying to disentangle my unease at the whole thing. "It wasn't the message, it was the spite. Whatever you think—whoever you think did that, human or not, it was a horrible thing to say. Someone in that room wanted to fuck with our heads."

"And they did."

We both turned to look back at the house. Through the window I could see Clare moving around the living room, rounding up glasses and picking nuts out of the carpet. Tom was nowhere to be seen—I guessed he had gone up. Flo was loading the dishwasher in the kitchen with a nervous, savage energy, crashing the glasses in so hard I was surprised they didn't break.

I didn't want to go back in. For a second, in spite of the snow, in spite of the subzero temperatures that were already making me shiver, I was seriously tempted to borrow Nina's keys and sleep in the car.

"Come on," Nina said at last. "We can't stay out here all night. Let's go back in, say good night, and head straight up. Then first thing in the morning, we're out of here. Right?"

"All right."

I followed her back through the kitchen door, and closed it behind us.

"Lock it, please," Flo said shortly. She looked up from the dishwasher. Her face was bleary, her mascara halfway down her cheeks, her hair straggling down her face.

"Flo, leave it," Nina said. "Please. I promise we'll help in the morning."

"It's fine," Flo said tightly. "I don't need any help."

"All right!" Nina threw up her hands. "You said it. See you at breakfast." She turned and then muttered, *"Fucking martyr,"* as she left the room.

chapter 20

I didn't sleep well. Nina fell asleep almost instantly, and lay there, sprawled out like a tanned daddy longlegs, snoring away.

I lay awake, trying to go to sleep, but instead I was thinking about the evening and the strange little group Clare had gathered around her this weekend. I wanted to leave so badly it hurt—to be back at home, in my own bed, with my own things, in the blissful peace and quiet. Now I was counting down the hours, and listening to Nina's soft snores and behind that to the silence of the house and the forest.

Not quite silence, though. As I was drifting off, there came a quiet creak and then a bang, not a loud one, just as if a door was banging in the wind.

I was almost drowsing when it came again, a long, slow *ekkkkkkk,* and then a staccato *clack.*

The strange thing was, it sounded like it was inside the house.

I sat up, holding my breath, trying to hear the noise above Nina's snores.

Ekkkkkkkk . . . clack!

This time there was no doubt. The sound was certainly not coming from outside the window, but floating up the stairwell. I got up, grabbed my dressing gown, and tiptoed to the door.

When I opened it, I almost screamed: a ghostlike figure was standing on the landing, bending over the banister.

I didn't scream. But I must have made some kind of choked gasp because the figure turned and put her finger to her lips. It was Flo, dressed in a white nightgown with pink flowers, bleached pale in the moonlight.

"You heard it, too?" I whispered.

She nodded.

"Yes, I thought it might be a gate in the garden, but it's not, it's *inside* the house."

There was a creak behind us, and we both turned to see Clare coming out of the bedroom, rubbing her eyes.

"What is it?"

"Shh," Flo whispered. "There's something downstairs. Listen."

We all paused.

Eeeeekkkkk . . . clack!

"It's just a door in the wind," Clare said, yawning. Flo shook her head vehemently.

"It's inside the house. What wind could there be inside the house? Someone must have left a door open."

"Impossible," Clare said. "I checked them all."

Flo put her hands over her throat, looking suddenly frightened. "We've got to go down, haven't we?"

"Let's wake Tom," Clare said. "He looks tall and menacing."

She tiptoed into his room, and I heard her shaking him and whispering, "Tom! Tom! There's a noise in the house."

He came out, bleary-eyed and pale, and we all crept slowly down the stairs.

There was a door open; you could tell it as soon as we reached the ground floor. It was cold as ice, and a breeze was blowing through the hallway, coming from the kitchen. Flo turned completely pale.

"I'm getting the gun," she whispered, her voice so slight you could hardly hear.

"I thought you said," Clare mouthed, "that it was loaded with blanks?"

"It is," Flo whispered crossly. "But *he* won't know that, will he?"

She jerked her head at the living room door.

"You first, Tom."

"Me?" Tom said in a horrified whisper, but he rolled his eyes and edged his head, very quietly, around the living room door. Then he beckoned silently, and we all followed him, in a sort of relieved rush. The room was empty, moonlight flooding the pale carpet. Flo reached up above the mantelpiece and took down the gun. Her face was pale but determined.

"You're *sure* about the blanks?" Clare asked again.

"Completely sure. But if someone's there, it'll give them a pretty good scare."

"If you're holding the gun, I'm going behind you," Tom hissed. "Blanks or no blanks."

"All right."

Whatever I'd thought of Flo, I couldn't fault her courage. She stood for a moment in the hallway, and I could see her hands shaking. Then she took a deep, shuddering breath, and flung open the kitchen door so hard it crashed back against the tiled wall.

There was no one there. But the glass kitchen door was standing open in the moonlight, and a light dusting of snow blew across the tiled floor.

Clare was across the room in a moment, her bare feet soft on the cold tiles. "There's footsteps, look." She pointed out across the lawn: big shapeless prints, like those made by wellies or snow boots.

"Fuck." Tom's face was pale. "What happened?" He turned to me. "You were out of that door last. Didn't you lock it?"

"I— I'm sure I did." I tried to remember. Nina offering to help, Flo's angry crashing. I had a clear memory of my hand on the lock. "I did. I'm certain I locked it."

"Well, you can't have done it properly." Flo rounded on me. In the moonlit dark she looked like a statue, her face hard and unyielding as marble.

"I *did*." I was beginning to feel angry. "Anyway, I thought you said Clare checked?"

"I just rattled each door," Clare said. Her eyes were huge, with shadows like bruises in the sockets. "I didn't check every lock. If it didn't open, I assumed it was shut."

"I locked it," I said stubbornly. Flo made a small furious noise, almost like a growl. Then she tucked the shotgun under her arm and stalked upstairs.

"I locked it," I repeated, looking from Clare to Tom. "Don't you believe me?"

"Look," Clare said, "it's no one's fault." She walked across to the door and slammed it hard, twisting the key as she did. "It's damn well locked now, anyway. Let's get up to bed."

We trooped back up the stairs, feeling the spent adrenaline in our systems fading to sour jitters. Nina was at the top of the stairs as I rounded the landing, rubbing her eyes confusedly.

"What happened?" she asked as I drew level. "Why did I just see Flo stamp past holding that fucking shotgun?"

"We had a scare," Tom said shortly, coming up from behind me. "Someone"—he glanced at me—"left the kitchen door unlocked."

"It *wasn't* me," I said doggedly.

"Well, whatever. It was open. We heard it banging. There were footprints outside."

"Bloody hell." Nina was as wide awake as the rest of us now. She passed a hand over her face again, rubbing the sleep out of her eyes. "Had they gone? Was anything missing?"

"Nothing I noticed." Tom looked at Clare and me. "Anything you can think of? Telly was there. All the obvious stuff like that. Did anyone leave a wallet lying around? Mine's in my room."

"Mine, too," Clare said. She turned and glanced out at the drive. "And all the cars are still there."

"My bag's in my room, I think," I said. I put my head around the door to check. "Yup. It's there."

"Well . . . looks like it wasn't robbery they were after," Tom said uneasily. "If it wasn't for the footsteps, you could almost think it was just a faulty lock."

But there *were* the footsteps. There undeniably were.

"Think we should call the police?" he asked.

"We can't, can we?" Nina said acidly. "No landline and no bloody reception."

"You had a couple of bars yesterday," I reminded her, but she shook her head.

"Must have been a blip. I've had nothing since. Well, look on the bright side, there's no smell of petrol, so with luck, it's not the crazed locals with their jerry cans come back for a second bonfire."

There was a silence. Nobody laughed.

"We should go back to bed, try to get some sleep," Clare said at last. We all nodded.

"Want to pull your mattress in with us?" Nina said unexpectedly to Tom. "I wouldn't want to be by myself."

"Thanks," Tom said. "That— That's really nice. But I'll be fine. I'll lock my door, just in case anyone's after my virtue. Not that I've got much left."

- - -

"That was nice," I said to Nina after we had said good night to Tom and Clare and were huddled up in our own beds. "What you said to Tom, I mean."

"Nice, schmice. I felt sorry for the poor guy. Plus, he looks like he'd have a mean right hook if anyone did break in." She sighed, and then rolled over. "Want me to leave the light on?"

"No, it's okay. That door's locked now—that's the main thing."

"Fair enough." She clicked off the light, and I saw the glow of her phone. "Gone two o'clock. Bloody hell. And still not a single bar of reception. How about you? Got anything?"

I reached for my phone.

It wasn't there.

"Hang on, I need to put the light on. I can't find it."

I flicked the switch and looked around, beneath the bed, beneath the bedside table. Then inside my bag. No phone. No phone anywhere, in fact—just the unhooked charger lead trailing across the floor. I tried to remember when I'd last had it. In the car maybe? I remembered using it at lunchtime. But after that, I couldn't be sure. I'd got out of the habit of checking it here—with no reception, it seemed pointless. I *thought* I remembered taking it up here to charge it before supper—but maybe that was Friday. Most likely it had slipped out of my pocket in the car.

"It's not here," I said. "I think I must have left it in the car."

"Never mind," Nina said. She yawned. "Just remember to find it tomorrow before we leave, yeah?"

"All right. Night."

"Good night."

There was a rustle of duvet, as she huddled down. I closed my eyes. I tried to sleep.

- - -

What happened next . . .

Oh God. What happened next. I'm not sure I can . . .

I am still sitting there, trying to put my confused tumble of thoughts in order when the door swings wide and the nurse comes back in pushing a trolley.

"The doctor wants to have a wee look at your scans, but he says very likely you can have a bath after that. And I've got some breakfast for you here."

"Listen." I try to sit up against the sliding, shifting pillows. "Listen, the police outside the door . . . are they here for me?"

She looks uncomfortable, and her gaze slides off to the small square of glass as she sets out Rice Krispies in a little carton, a jug of milk, and a single clementine.

"They're investigating the accident," she says at last. "I'm sure they'll want tae speak to you, but the doctor has to sign you off. I've told them, they're not barging into a hospital ward at this hour. They'll have tae wait."

"I heard . . ." I swallow, hard, my throat hurting as if something is trying to escape—a sob or a scream. "I heard them say something about a d-death . . ."

"Och!" She looks annoyed, banging the locker drawer shut with unnecessary force. "They shouldna be worriting you, with your poor head."

"But it's true? Someone died?"

"I can't say about that. I cannae discuss other patients."

"Is it *true*?"

"I'll have tae ask you tae calm down." She spreads out her hands in a professionally soothing gesture that makes me want to scream. “It’s not good for your head to be getting upset like this.”

“Upset? One of my friends is probably dead, and you’re telling me I shouldn’t be upset? Who? For God’s sake, who? And why can’t I remember? Why can’t I remember what happened before the accident?”

“It’s quite common,” she says, her voice still in that strange soothing cadence, as if she’s speaking to a small child, or someone hard of understanding. “Following a head injury. It’s tae do with the way the brain transfers short-term to long-term memory. If something interrupts the process you can lose a bit of time.”

Oh God, I *must* remember. I must remember what happened because someone is dead, and the police are outside. They are going to come and ask me, and how can I know, how can I know what I’m saying, what I’m revealing, if I don’t know what happened?

I see myself—running, running through the forest with the blood on my hands and on my face and on my clothes . . .

“Please,” I say, and my voice is close to cracking, close to pleading, and I hate myself for being so weak and needy. “Please tell me, please help me, what’s happened? What’s happened to my friends? Why was I covered in such a lot of blood? My head wound wasn’t that bad. Where did all the blood come from?”

“I don’t know,” she says softly, and there’s real compassion in her voice this time. “I don’t know, pet. Let me get the doctor, and perhaps he can tell you more. In the meantime, I want you tae eat some breakfast; you’ve got to keep your strength up, and the doctor will want to see an appetite.”

And then she backs out of the door, with the trolley in front of her, and the door swings shut, and I am alone, with my plastic bowl of Rice Krispies, popping and clicking away as they soak into sugary mush.

I should get up. I should force my weak, woolly limbs to do their duty, and I should swing them out of bed and march into the corridor and demand answers from those police officers outside.

But I don't. I just sit there, and tears roll down my face and drip off my chin into the Rice Krispies, and the smell of the clementine is heady and overripe, reminding me of something I cannot remember, and cannot forget.

Please, I think, *please. Pull yourself together, you stupid bitch. Get up. Find out what happened. Find out who's dead.*

But I don't move. And not just because my head hurts, and my legs hurt, and my muscles feel like wet tissue.

I don't move because I am afraid. Because I don't want to hear the name the police are going to say.

And because I am afraid they are here for me.

chapter 21

The brain doesn't remember well. It tells stories. It fills in the gaps, and implants those fantasies as memories.

I have to try to get the facts . . .

But I don't know if I'm remembering what happened—or what I *want* to have happened. I am a writer. I'm a professional liar. It's hard to know when to stop, you know? You see a gap in the narrative, you want to fill it with a reason, a motive, a plausible explanation.

And the harder I push, the more the facts dissolve beneath my fingers . . .

I know that I woke with a jump. I don't know what time it was, but it was still dark. Beside me Nina was sitting up in bed, her dark eyes wide and glittering.

"Did you hear that?" she whispered.

I nodded. Footsteps on the landing. A door opening very softly.

My heart was beating in my throat as I pushed back the duvet and grabbed my dressing gown. I remembered the kitchen door swung wide, the footsteps in the snow.

We should have checked the rest of the house.

At the door I stood listening for a second, and then opened it with infinite caution. Clare and Flo were standing outside, their eyes wide, their faces bleached pale with fear. Flo was holding the gun.

"Did you hear something?" I whispered, as low as I could. Clare gave a single, sharp nod, and pointed to the stairs, her finger stabbing downwards. I listened, hard, trying to still my shaky breathing and thudding heart. There was a scratching sound, and then a clear definite *thunk,* as of a door being softly closed. There was someone down there.

"Tom?" I mouthed. But even as I did, his door opened a crack and his face peered out.

"Did you . . . that sound?" he whispered. Clare gave a grim nod.

This time it was no open door. No wind. This time we could all hear it: clear footsteps as someone made their way through the tiled kitchen, across the parquet floor of the hallway, and then the soft, definite creak of a foot on the first of the stairs.

Somehow we had drawn together into a little knot; I felt someone's hand scrabbling for mine. Flo was at the center, the gun raised, though its muzzle was shaking badly. I put my free hand out to steady it.

There was another creak on the stairs and an indrawn breath from all of us, then a figure rounded the newel post halfway up, silhouetted against the plate-glass window that overlooked the forest.

It was a man—a tall man. He was dressed in some kind of dark hoodie, and I couldn't see his face; he was looking down at his phone, the screen glowing ghost-white in the darkness.

"Fuck off and leave us alone!" Flo screamed, and the gun went off.

There was a deafening, catastrophically loud bang, and the sound of shattering glass, and the gun kicked like a horse. I remember that—I remember that people fell over.

I remember that I looked up to see—it didn't make sense—the huge plate-glass window at the landing, shattered—the glass spattered outwards onto the snow, clattering onto the wooden stairs.

I remember the man on the stairs gave one choking exclamation—more of shock than of pain, it sounded like, and then he fell all of a heap, thudding slowly down the stairs like a stuntman in a film.

I don't know who turned on the lights. But they flooded the tall hallway with a brightness that made me wince and cover my eyes—and I saw.

I saw the pale frosted stairs, splashed with blood, and the shattered window, and the long, slow smear of gore where the man's body had slithered slowly down to the ground floor.

"Oh my God," Flo whimpered. "The gun . . . the gun was loaded!"

When the nurse comes back, I am crying.

"What happened?" I manage. "Someone is dead—please tell me, please tell me who's dead."

"I can't tell you, love." She looks genuinely sorry. "I wish I could, but I can't. But I've brought Dr. Miller here to take a look at you."

"Good morning, Leonora," he says, coming across to the bed. His voice is soft, pitying. I want to punch him, and his fucking compassion. "I'm sorry we're a bit tearful today."

"Someone is dead," I say very clearly, trying to keep my breath even, keep myself from gulping and sobbing. "Someone is dead, and no one will tell me who. And the police are sitting outside. Why?"

"Let's not worry about that at the moment—"

"I *am* worried!" I shout. Heads in the corridor turn. The doctor puts out a soothing hand, patting my leg beneath the blanket in a way that makes me want to shrug and shudder. I am bruised. I am hurt. I am wearing a hospital gown that's open at the back, and I've lost my dignity along with everything else. Do not fucking touch me, you patronizing arsehole. I want to go *home.*

"Look," he says, "I understand that you're upset, and the police will hopefully have some answers for you, but I'd like to examine you, ensure that you're up to speaking to them, and I can only do that if you're calm. Do you understand, Leonora?"

I nod my head mutely, and then turn my face to the wall while he examines the dressing on my head, checks my pulse and blood pressure against the readings on the machine. I close my eyes, let the indignities fade away. I answer his questions.

My name is Leonora Shaw.

I'm twenty-six.

Today is . . . here I have to be helped, but the nurse prompts me. It's Sunday. I have not even been here twelve hours. In which case, it's November 16. I think this counts as disorientation rather than memory loss.

Elizabeth Windsor is on the throne.

No, I have no nausea. My vision is fine, thanks.

Yes, I am having trouble recovering some memories. There are some things that you shouldn't have to remember.

"Well, you seem to be doing remarkably well," Dr. Miller says at last. He hangs his stethoscope around his neck and puts his little torch back in his top pocket. "All the observations overnight are fine, and your scan is very reassuring. The memory trouble is concerning me a little bit—it's quite typical to lose the few minutes before a collision, but it sounds like you're having trouble a little bit further back than that, is that right?"

I nod, reluctantly, thinking of the patchy staccato blasts of images that invaded my head throughout the night. The trees. The blood. The swinging headlights.

"Well, you may find it starts coming back. Not all causes of memory trouble"—he avoids the word *amnesia,* I have noticed—"are down to physical trauma. Some are more . . . stress related."

For the first time in a little while I look up, meet his eyes directly. "What do you mean?"

"Well, this is not my speciality, you understand—I work with the physical head trauma. But sometimes, sometimes the brain suppresses events that we're not quite ready to deal with. I suppose it's a . . . coping mechanism, if you will."

"What kind of events?" My voice is hard. He smiles. His hand is back on my leg again. I resist the urge to flinch.

"You've had a difficult time, Leonora. Now, is there anyone we can call? Anyone you would like to be with you? Your mother has been informed, I understand, but she's in Australia, is that right?"

"That's right."

"Any other relations? Boyfriend? Partner?"

"No. Please." I swallow, but there is no sense in putting this off any longer. The agony of *not* knowing is becoming more painful. "Please, I'd like to see the police now."

"Hmm." He stands, looks at his chart. "I'm not convinced you're up to it, Leonora. We've already told them you're not fit to answer questions."

"I'd like to see the police."

They are the only people who will give me answers. I *have* to see them.

I stare at him, while he pretends to study the chart in front of him, making up his mind.

At last he lets out a breath, a long frustrated half sigh, and shoves the chart into the holder at the foot of the bed.

"Very well. They're only to have half an hour at the most, Nurse, and I don't want anything too stressful. If Miss Shaw starts to find the interview difficult . . ."

"Understood," the nurse says briskly.

Dr. Miller puts out his hand, and I shake it, trying not to look at the scratches and blood on my arm.

He turns to go.

"Oh— Wait, sorry," I blurt out, as he reaches the door. "Can I have a shower first?" I want to see the police, but I don't want to face them like this.

"A bath," Dr. Miller says, and gives a short nod. "You've got a dressing on your forehead which I'd prefer you not to disturb. If you keep your head above water, yes, you can have a bath."

And he turns to go.

It takes a long time to unhook everything from the machine; there are sensors, needles, and the huge incontinence pad between my legs, which makes me hot and cold with shame as I swing my legs to the floor, feeling its bulk. Did I wet myself in the night? There's no sharp smell of urine, but I can't be sure.

The nurse gives me her arm as I stand, and although I want to push her away, I find I'm pathetically grateful for it, and I lean on her harder than I want to admit as I hobble painfully to the bathroom.

Inside the light flickers on automatically, and the nurse starts to run a bath, then helps me with the tapes of my gown.

"I can do the rest myself," I say, cringing at the thought of undressing in front of even a professional stranger, but she shakes her head.

"I can't let you get into the tub without a hand, I'm sorry. If you slip . . ." She doesn't finish, but I know what she's saying: another bang on top of what's already happened to my head . . .

I nod, step out of the hideous adult nappy (the nurse whisks it away before I can worry about whether it's soiled or not), and then I let the gown fall to the floor, shivering in my nakedness even though the room is sweatingly hot.

I smell, I realize to my shame. I smell of fear and sweat and blood.

The nurse holds my hand as I step unsteadily into the bath, catching onto the grab rails as I lower myself into the scalding water.

"Too hot?" the nurse says quickly, as I let out a little gasp at the heat of the water, but I shake my head. It's not too hot. *Nothing* could be too hot. If I could sterilize myself with boiling water, I would.

At last I'm lying back in the water, shivering with the effort.

"Can I— I'd like to be alone, p-please," I say, awkwardly. The nurse sucks in her breath and I can see her about to refuse, and suddenly I can't bear it anymore—I can't bear their scrutiny, and their kindness, and their constant watch. "Please," I say, more roughly than I meant. "For God's sake, I won't drown in six inches of water."

"All right," she says, though there is reluctance in her tone. "But don't even think about trying to get out—you're to pull the cord, and I'll come in and help you."

"All right." I don't want to admit defeat, but I know in my heart that I would not be safe getting out of that bath myself.

The nurse goes, leaving the door just a crack ajar, and I close my eyes and sink into the steaming water, shutting out her watchful presence outside the door, shutting out the hospital smells and sounds and the buzz of the fluorescent light.

As I lie in the bath I run my hands down all the cuts and scrapes and bruises, feeling the small clots and scabs soften and dissolve beneath my palms, and I try to remember what set me running through the woods, with blood on my hands. I try to remember. But I'm not sure if I can bear the truth.

After the nurse has helped me out, I towel myself gently dry, looking at my familiar body with its unfamiliar tracing of cuts and stitches. There are slashes on my shins. They are deep, ragged scratches across the front of the bone, as if I'd run through brambles or barbed wire.

There are cuts on my feet and hands, from running barefoot over glass, from shielding my face from flying debris.

Finally, I walk across to the mirror and swipe away the steam, and I see myself for the first time since the accident.

I've never been the kind to turn people's heads—not like Clare, whose beauty is hard to ignore, or Nina, who's not conventionally beautiful but is spectacular in a lean, Amazonian kind of way.

But I was never a freak. Now, as I peer at myself in the steam-bleeding mirror, I realize that if I saw myself on the street, I would turn away, out of pity or horror.

The huge dressing at my hairline doesn't help—it looks as if my brains are being barely held in place—and nor do the smaller cuts and scratches dappled across my cheekbones and forehead, but they're not the worst. The worst is my eyes—two dark bronze-colored shiners that blossom out from the bridge of my nose, leaching in blackened circles beneath my lower lids, before they fade to yellow across my cheekbones. The right one is spectacular, the left one less so. I look like I've been punched in the face, repeatedly. But I am alive, and someone is not.

It is that thought that makes me pull on the hospital gown, lace up the ties, and shuffle out to face the world.

"Admiring your shiners?" The nurse gives a comfortable laugh. "Don't worry, they've done all the scans, you've no basilar fracture. You just got a bang to the face. Or two."

"B-basilar?"

"Type of skull fracture. It can be very nasty. But they've ruled it out, so don't fret. Black eyes aren't uncommon following a car crash, but they'll clear up in a few days."

"I'm ready," I say. "For the police."

"Are you sure you're up to it, then? You don't have to."

"I'm up to it," I say firmly.

- - -

I'm back in bed, sitting up with a cup of what the nurse claimed was coffee but—unless the head trauma has damaged my taste perception—is not, when there is a knock on the door.

I look up, sharply, my heart thudding. Outside, smiling through the wire-hatched glass pane in the door, there is a policewoman. She's in her forties, maybe, and she is incredibly striking, with the kind of sculpted looks you might see on a catwalk. It feels shockingly incongruous, but I don't know why. Why shouldn't police officers have the face of David Bowie's wife?

"C-come in," I say. *Don't stammer.* Fuck.

"Hello." She opens the door and comes into the room, still smiling. She has the slender, greyhound frame of a long-distance runner. "I'm Detective Constable Lamarr." Her voice is warm, and her vowels are plum-colored. "How are you feeling today?"

"Better, thank you." Better? Better than what? I'm in hospital, in a gown with no back and two black eyes. I'm not sure how much worse it could get.

Then I correct myself: I've been unhooked from the machine, and they've removed the nappy. Apparently, I can be trusted to pee by myself. This is, indeed, better.

"I've spoken to your doctors: they tell me you may be up to a few questions, but if it's too much, we can stop, just say. Is that all right?"

I nod, and she says, "Last night . . . can you tell me what you remember?"

"Nothing. I remember nothing." It comes out harder and terser than I meant. To my horror, I feel a lump in my throat and I swallow fiercely. I will not cry! I'm a grown woman, for fuck's sake, not some child who's scraped her knee in the playground, wailing for her daddy.

"Now, that's not true," she says, but not accusingly. Her voice is the gently encouraging tone of a teacher, or an older sibling. "Dr. Miller tells me that you're pretty clear about events leading up to the accident. Why don't you start at the beginning?"

"At the beginning? You don't want my childhood traumas and stuff, do you?"

"Maybe." She sits on the foot of the bed, in defiance of hospital regulations. "If they're relevant to what happened. I tell you what, why don't we start with some easy questions, just to warm up? What's your name, how about that?"

I manage a laugh, but not for the reasons she thinks. What *is* my name? I thought I knew who I was, who I had become. Now, after this weekend, I'm no longer sure.

"Leonora Shaw," I say. "But I go by Nora."

"Very well then, Nora. And you're how old?"

I know she must know all this already. Perhaps it's some sort of test, to see how bad my memory really is.

"Twenty-six."

"Now tell me, how did you end up here?"

"What, in the hospital?"

"In the hospital, here in Northumberland, generally, really."

"You haven't got a Northern accent," I say irrelevantly.

"I was born in Surrey," she says. She gives me a little complicit smile to acknowledge that this is not quite procedure, that she should be asking questions, not answering them. But this is a little token of something . . . I can't quite work out what. An exchange: a piece of her for a piece of me.

Except that makes me sound broken.

"So," she resumes, "how did you end up here, then?"

"It was . . ." I put my hand to my forehead. I want to rub it, but the dressing is in the way, and I'm afraid to dislodge it. The skin beneath is hot and itchy. "We were on a hen weekend, and she went to university here. Clare did, I mean. The hen. Listen, can I ask you something—am I a suspect?"

"A suspect?" Her beautiful, rich voice makes music of the word, turning the chilly, spiky noun into a sol-fa exercise. Then she shakes her head. "Not at this stage of the investigation. We're still gathering information, but we aren't ruling anything out."

Translation: not a suspect—yet.

"Now, tell me, what do you remember of last night?" She returns to the subject like a very beautiful, well-brought-up cat circling a mousehole. I want to go home.

The scab beneath the dressing tingles and tickles. I can't concentrate. Suddenly, out of the corner of my eye I see the uneaten clementine sitting on the locker, and I have to look away.

"I remember . . ." I blink, and, to my horror, I feel my eyes fill with tears. "I remember . . ." I swallow fiercely, and I dig my nails into my torn and bloody palms, letting the pain drive out the memory of him lying on the honey-colored parquet, bleeding into my arms. "Please, please tell me—who . . ." I stop. I can't say it. I can't.

I try again.

"Is . . ."

The word chokes in my throat. I shut my eyes, count to ten, dig my nails into the cuts on my palm until my whole arm is shaky with pain.

I hear an exhalation from D.C. Lamarr, and when I open my eyes, she looks, for the first time, worried.

"We would like to get your side of the story before we muddy the waters," she says at last, but her face is troubled, and I know, I know what it is she is not allowed to say.

"It's all right," I manage. Something is coming apart inside me, breaking up. "You don't need to tell me. Oh G-god—"

And then I cannot speak. The tears come and come and come. It's what I feared.

It's what I knew.

"Nora—" I hear from Lamarr, and I shake my head. My eyes are shut tight, but I feel the tears running down my nose and stinging the cuts on my face. She gives a small, wordless sound of sympathy, and then she stands.

"I'll give you a moment," she says. And I hear the door of the room creak open, and then flap shut, swinging on its double hinges. I am alone. And I cry, and cry, and cry until there are no tears left.

chapter 22

I ran down the stairs as quickly as I could, trying not to cut my feet on the glass, holding on to the banister so as not to slip in the wetness of the man's blood, and there he was, curled in a small pathetic heap at the bottom of the stairs.

He was alive.

I could hear his soft whimpers as he struggled to breathe.

"Nina!" I bellowed. "Nina, get down here! He's alive! Someone dial nine nine nine!"

"There's no fucking signal," Nina shouted back as she scrambled down the stairs.

"Leo," the man whispered, and my heart froze. And then he raised his face from his painful hunch, and I knew. I knew. I knew.

I remember that moment with complete, heart-stopping clarity.

"James?" It was Nina who spoke first, not me. She slipped rather than walked down the last few stairs, landing in a heap beside us on the floor, and her voice cracked as she gently felt for his pulse. "James? What the fuck are you doing here? Oh my God." She was almost crying, but her hands were doing their automatic work, checking where the blood was coming from, checking his pulse.

"James, talk to me," she said. "Nora, keep him talking. Keep him awake."

"James . . ." I didn't know what to say. We hadn't spoken for ten years and now—and now . . . "James, oh my God, James . . . why, how?"

"Te . . ." he said, and he coughed, blood flecking his lips. "Leo?"

It sounded like a question, but I didn't know what he meant. Tell? Tell Leo? I only shook my head. There was so much blood.

Nina had his hoodie unzipped, and she had found scissors from somewhere and was ripping up his T-shirt. I almost shut my eyes at the sight of his body, that skin that I had kissed and touched, every inch, spattered with blood and gunshot wounds.

"Oh fuck," Nina moaned. "We need an ambulance."

"Did . . ." James was trying to speak, in spite of the blood bubbling at his lips. "Did she . . . tell you?"

About the wedding?

"He's got a punctured lung. He's probably bleeding internally. Press on this." Nina guided my hand to a pad of torn-up T-shirt pressed against James's thigh, from where blood was pumping frighteningly fast.

"What can we do?" I was trying not to cry.

"For the moment? Try to stop him bleeding out. If that artery keeps going like that, he's dead no matter what. Press harder, it's still bleeding. I'll try a tourniquet, but—"

"Oh my God." It was Flo. She looked like a ghost, standing there, her hands over her face. "Oh my God. I'm— I'm so sorry— I can't, I can't deal with b-blood . . ."

She gave a little gasping sigh, and collapsed, and I heard Nina swear under her breath, long and low.

"Tom!" she bellowed. "Get Flo away from here! She's fainted. Get her to her room." She pushed the hair back from her face. There was blood on her cheekbone and on her brow.

"Clare . . ." James said. He licked his lips. His eyes were fixed on mine, like there was something he was trying to tell me. I squeezed his hand, trying to hold it together.

"She's coming." Where the hell was she? "Clare!" I shouted. No answer.

"No . . ." James managed. "Clare . . . text . . . did she say?" His voice was so faint it was hard to work out what he was trying to say.

"What?"

He had closed his eyes. His hand in mine was relaxing.

"He's dying," I said to Nina, hearing the hysteria rising in my own voice. "Nina, do something."

"What the fuck do you think I am doing? Playing tea parties? Get me a towel. No, wait—don't let go of that pad on his thigh. I'll get it. Where the *fuck* is Clare?"

She got up and ran for the kitchen, and I heard her banging through drawers.

James lay very still.

"James?" I said, suddenly panicked. "James, stay with me!"

He opened his eyes painfully, and lay looking up at me, his eyes bright and dark in the soft light from the hall. His T-shirt was split open like a peeled fruit, and his bloodstained chest and belly were bare to the cold air. I wanted to touch him, to kiss him, to tell him everything was okay. But I could not. Because it was a lie.

I gritted my teeth and pressed harder on the pad on his thigh, willing the blood to stop pooling and pooling.

"I'm . . . sorry . . ." he said, very faint, so faint that I thought I had misheard.

"What?" I put my head closer, trying to hear.

"I'm sorry . . ." His hand squeezed mine, and then, to my astonishment, he reached up, his arm trembling with the effort, and touched my cheek. His breath rattled in his throat, and a thin trickle of blood came from the corner of his mouth.

I squeezed my eyes shut, trying not to cry.

"Don't be silly," I managed. "It was a long time ago. It's all over now."

"Clare . . ."

Oh fuck, where is she?

A tear dripped off my nose onto his chest, and he reached up again, and tried to wipe it away, but his arm was too weak and he let it fall back.

"Don't . . . cry . . ."

"Oh, James." It was all I could manage, a gulping exhortation that tried to say everything I couldn't. *James, don't die, please don't die.*

"Leo . . ." he said softly, and he closed his eyes. Only James ever called me that. Only him. Always him.

I am still crying when the knock on the door comes, and I struggle up against the pillows, before remembering the electric button that raises the head of the bed automatically.

The bed grinds me into a sitting position, and I take a deep shuddering breath and swipe at my eyes.

"Come in."

The door opens, and it is Lamarr. I know my eyes must be red and wet, and my throat croaky, but I can't find it in myself to care.

"Tell me the truth," I say, before she can say anything else—before she's sat down, even. "Please. I'll tell you everything I can remember, but I have to know. Is he dead?"

"I'm sorry," she says, and I know. I try to speak, but I can't. I sit, shaking my head and trying to make the words come, but they don't.

Lamarr sits in silence, while I struggle for control, and then at last, when my breathing eases, she holds out the paper tray she's carrying.

"Coffee?" she asks gently.

I shouldn't care. James is dead. What does coffee matter?

I nod, half reluctantly, and when she hands it to me, I take a long sip. It's hot, and strong. It is as unlike the watery hospital gravy as chalk from Gorgonzola, and I feel it running into every cell of my body and waking me up. It is impossible to believe that I can be alive and James can be dead.

When I put the cup down, my face feels stiff and my head aches.

"Thank you," I manage, my voice rough. Lamarr leans across the gap between us and squeezes my hand.

"It was the least I could do. I'm sorry. I didn't want you to find out like that, but I was asked—" She stops and rephrases. "It was thought advisable not to tell you more than you knew already. We wanted to get your version. Uninfluenced."

I don't say anything. I just bow my head. I have written about this kind of thing, this kind of interview, all my adult life, and I never imagined for one moment I would be here.

"I know this will be painful," she says at last, as the silence stretches, "but please, can you think back to last night? What do you remember?"

"I remember up to the—the shooting," I say. "I remember running down the stairs, and seeing him . . . seeing him, lying there . . ." I grit my teeth and pause for a moment, the breath hissing between my teeth. I will not cry again. Instead, I gulp at the coffee, not caring that it scalds as I swallow. "You must know about the shooting?" I say at last. "Did they tell you, the others? Nina and Clare and everyone?"

"We have several different accounts," she says, a hint of evasiveness in her voice. "But we need to get all the perspectives."

"We were scared," I say, trying to think back. It seems like a hundred years ago, swathed in a fog of adrenaline as we all crept around the house, half hysterical with a mixture of drunken excitement and genuine fear. "There was a message on the Ouija board, about a murderer." The irony, as I say it, is almost unbearable. "We didn't believe it—most of us, anyway—but I suppose it made us edgy. And there were footprints, in the snow outside. And when we woke up, the first time, I mean, the kitchen door had come open."

"How?"

"I don't know. Someone had locked it—or said they had. Flo, I think. Or was it Clare? Someone had checked, anyway. But it blew open, and it just made us all more crazed and frightened. And so when we heard the footsteps . . ."

"Whose idea was it to get the gun?"

"I don't know. Flo had it from earlier, I think. From when the door blew open. But it wasn't supposed to be loaded. It was supposed to have blanks."

"And you were holding it, is that right?"

"Me?" I look up at her with genuine shock. "No! It was Flo, I think. It was definitely her."

"But your fingerprints are on the barrel."

They have fingerprinted the gun? I stare at her. Then I realize she's waiting for an answer.

"On the b-barrel, yes." *Fuck.* Do not stammer. "But not the—the other bit. The handle bit. The stock, I mean. Look, she was waving it around like a crazy thing. I was trying to keep it away from us."

"Why, if you thought it wasn't loaded?"

The question takes me aback. Suddenly, in spite of the sun, the room feels cold. I want to ask again if I'm a suspect, but she has said I'm not, and won't it look strange to keep asking?

"B-because I don't like having a gun pointed at me, no matter what it's loaded with. All right?"

"All right," she says mildly, and makes a note on her pad. She flips over a sheet and then turns back.

"Let's go back a bit. James—how did you know him?"

I shut my eyes. I bite the inside of my cheek to keep from crying.

There are so many options open to me: We went to school together. We were friends. He is Clare's fiancé. *Was,* I correct myself silently. It is impossible to believe he is gone. And I realize, suddenly, the selfishness of my grief. I have been thinking about James. But Clare—Clare has lost everything. Yesterday she was to be a bride. Today she is . . . what? There's not even a word for what she is. Not a widow—just bereft.

"He . . . we used to be together," I say at last. It's better to be honest, surely? Or at least as honest as I can be.

"When did you break up?"

"A long time ago. We were . . . oh . . . sixteen or seventeen."

The "oh" is a little dishonest. It makes it sound like a guesstimate. In fact, I know to the day when we broke up. I was sixteen and two months. James was just a few months away from his seventeenth birthday.

"Amicably?"

"Not at the time, no."

"But you've made up since? I mean, you were on Clare's hen weekend . . ." She trails off, inviting me to jump in with platitudes about how time heals everything, how betrayals at sixteen are the stuff you laugh about at twenty-six.

Only I don't. What should I say? The truth?

Something cold is stealing around my heart, a chill in spite of the hospital heat and the warmth of the setting sun.

I don't like these questions.

James's death was an accident: a gun that should never have been loaded, going off by mistake. So why is this policewoman here, asking about long-dead breakups?

"What relevance does this have to James's death?" I say abruptly. Too abruptly. Her head comes up from her notepad, her plum-colored lips forming a silent "oh" of surprise. Damn. Damn damn *damn*.

"We're just trying to form a complete picture," she says mildly.

I feel cold all up and down my spine.

James was shot by a gun that was supposed to be unloaded. So who loaded it?

I feel the blood drain from my cheeks.

I very, very much want to ask the question I asked before: Am I a suspect?

But I can't. I can't ask, because to ask would be suspicious. And suddenly, I very much want not to be suspicious.

"It was a long time ago," I say, trying to recover. "It hurt a lot at the time, but you get over things, don't you?"

No, you don't. Not things like that. Or at least, I don't.

But she doesn't hear the lie in my voice. Instead, she smoothly changes tack.

"What happened after James was shot?" she asks. "Can you remember what you all did next?"

I shut my eyes.

"Try to walk me through it," she says. Her voice is soft, encouraging, almost hypnotic. "You were with him in the hallway . . ."

I was with him in the hallway. There was blood on my hands, on my nightclothes. His blood. Masses of it.

His eyes had drifted closed, and after a few minutes I put my face down to his, trying to hear if he was still breathing. He was. I could feel his halting breath on my cheek.

How different he was from when we had been together—there were lines around his eyes, a five o'clock shadow on his jaw, and his face had become leaner and more defined. But he was still James. I knew the contours of his brow, the ridge of his nose, the hollow beneath his lip where the sweat beaded on summer nights.

He was still my James. Except he was not. Where in God's name was Clare?

I heard footsteps behind me, but it was Nina, holding a length of white cloth that looked like a sheet. She knelt and began binding James's leg very tight.

"I think our best hope is to stabilize you until we get you to hospital," she said, very loud and clear, talking to James, but to me as well, I knew. "James, can you hear me?"

He didn't respond. His face had gone a strange waxen color. Nina shook her head and then said to me, "Clare had better drive. You direct. I'll go in the back with James and try to keep him going until we get there. Tom had better stay with Flo. I think she's in shock."

"Where's Clare?"

"She was trying to get a signal up the far end of the garden—apparently, you can sometimes get one there."

"But there's nothing," a voice came from over my shoulder. It was Clare. Her face was the color of skimmed milk, but she was dressed. "Can he talk?"

"He was saying a few words," I said. My throat was cracked and hoarse with tears. "But I—I think he's unconscious now."

"Oh fuck." Her face went even whiter, even her lips bloodless pale, and there were tears in her eyes. "I should have come down sooner. I just thought—"

"Don't be silly," Nina cut her off. "It was the right thing to do—getting an ambulance was the most important thing, if we could only have got a fucking signal. Right, I think that tourniquet is as good as I can make it—I'm not going to try to do anything else now, let's get him out of here."

"I'll drive," Clare said instantly. Nina nodded.

"I'll come in the back with James." She looked out of the window. "Clare, you go and bring the car as close to the front door as you can get it." Clare nodded and left to get her car keys. Nina carried on, talking to me this time, "We'll need something to lift him on. It'll hurt him too much if we just pick him up."

"What sort of thing?"

"Something flat ideally, like a stretcher." We both gazed around, but there was nothing obvious.

"We could take a door down." Tom's voice came from behind us, making us both jump. He gazed down at James, now fully unconscious on the floor in a spreading pool of his own blood. There was a kind of horror in his expression. "Flo's out cold in the bedroom. Is he going to be okay?"

"Honestly?" Nina said. She glanced at James, and I saw her face was weary and, for the first time since she had taken over, showing traces of fear. "Honestly, I don't know. It's possible he'll make it. Door's a good idea. Can you find a screwdriver? I think there was a box of stuff under the stairs."

Tom gave a short nod and disappeared. Nina put her face in her hands.

"Fuck," she said, into her cupped, muffling palms. "Fuck, fuck, fuck."

"Are you all right?"

"No. Yes." She looked up. "I'm fine. Just— Oh my God. What a fucking stupid wasteful way to die. Who the hell fires a gun when they don't know what it's loaded with?"

I thought of Tom, waving it around yesterday as a joke, and I felt suddenly sick.

"Poor Flo," I said.

"Did she pull the trigger?" Nina asked.

"I— I assume so. I don't know. She was holding it."

"I thought you were."

"Me?" I felt my jaw drop with surprise and horror. "God, no. But it could have been anyone who jolted her—we were all standing so close."

There was a growl from outside, and I heard Clare's tires crunching through the snowy gravel outside the front door. At the same time there was a thud from the living room and Tom appeared, dragging a heavy oak door with the handles still attached.

"It weighs a ton," he said, "but we've only got to get it as far as the car."

"Okay." Nina took charge again. Her authority was effortless. It always amazed me how, in these moments of crisis, she transformed so completely from the sarcastic joker I'd known all my life, into a fearsomely competent doctor. "Tom, you take his shoulders. I'll take his feet. Nora, you support his hips as we lift and shift them onto the door; try not to disturb that dressing on his thigh, and be careful not to catch anything on the door handle. Ready? On my count of lift; three, two, one, lift."

We all heaved, there was a kind of groaning, involuntary whimper from James that brought a fresh spatter of blood to his lips, and then he was onto the makeshift stretcher. I ran to open the huge steel front door—thanking God for the first time for the scale of this house, the internal door would fit through easily—and then back to help Nina with the foot end of the door. It was immensely heavy, but we wrestled it down the hallway and out into the freezing night, where Clare was waiting, the engine ticking over, the exhaust a white cloud in the cold air.

"Is he okay?" she asked over her shoulder, reaching to unlatch the rear door. "Is he still breathing?"

"He's still breathing," Nina said, "but it'll be touch and go. Okay, let's get him off this door."

Somehow, in a horrible trembling blood-spattered rush, we got him into the backseat, where he lay, slumped, and breathing in a shallow rasping way that frightened me. His leg was hanging out of the car, and, grotesquely, I saw that the seeping blood was steaming in the chilly air. The sight stopped me in my tracks, and I was just standing there, too shocked to think what to do next as Tom folded the leg gently into the footwell and then shut the door.

"There's not going to be enough room for both of us," Nina said. For a minute I didn't know what she was talking about, and then I realized: James was taking up all the backseat by himself. There was no way Nina could fit in the back as she'd suggested.

"I'll stay," I said. "You should go with them."

Nina didn't try to argue.

"Nora?" Lamarr's voice is gentle but insistent. "Nora? Are you awake? Can you tell me what you remember?"

I open my eyes.

"We got James out to the car. We didn't have anything to carry him, so Tom took down a door. Clare was driving. Nina was supposed to go in the backseat with James, and I was going to direct."

"Supposed to?"

"It— There was a misunderstanding. I'm not sure what happened. We got James into the car, and we realized there wasn't going to be room for all of us. I told Nina she should go with him—she's a doctor—and I'd stay. She agreed, and we ran back into the house to get her phone and blankets for the car. But something happened . . ."

"Go on."

I shut my eyes, trying to remember. The events are starting to blur together. I remember Clare gunning the engine, and Tom calling something over his shoulder.

"Why not?" Clare shouted back. And then, impatiently, "Oh, never mind, I'll call when I get there."

And then there was the grinding sound of tires on gravel, and I saw the red of her taillights as she bumped off down the rutted track to the road.

"What the fucking fuck?" Nina shouted from upstairs. She skittered down the stairs and bellowed, "Clare! What are you doing?"

But Clare was gone.

"There was a misunderstanding," I say to Lamarr. "Tom said that he told Clare we were just coming, but Clare must have thought he said, *They're not coming.* She started off without Nina."

"And what next?"

What next? But that's what I'm not sure of.

I remember Clare's coat was hanging over the porch rail. She must have intended to take it and forgotten. I remember, I picked it up.

I remember . . .

I remember . . .

I remember Nina crying.

I remember standing in the kitchen, with my hands beneath the tap, watching James's blood run down the drain.

And then . . . I don't know if it's the shock, or what happened after, but things begin to fragment. And the harder I push, the more I'm not sure if I'm remembering what happened, or what I *think* happened.

I remember picking up Clare's coat. Or was it Clare's? I have a sudden picture of Flo at the clay-pigeon shooting, wearing the same black leather jacket. Was it Clare's? Or was it Flo's?

I remember picking up the jacket.

I remember the jacket.

What is it about the jacket I can't remember?

And then I'm running, running through the woods, desperate to stop them.

Something started me running. Something had me shoving my feet into my cold trainers with panicked desperation, and tumbling headlong down the narrow forest track, the torch swinging wildly in my hand.

But what?

I look down. My fingers are cupped as though I'm trying to hold on to something small and hard. The truth, perhaps.

"I can't remember," I say to Lamarr. "This is when it starts to get really fuzzy. I can remember running through the trees . . ."

I stop, trying to piece it all together. I gaze up at the harsh strip light, and then back down at my hands, as if they can give me an inspiration. But my hands are empty.

"We've got a statement from Tom," Lamarr says at last. "He says that you were holding something, looking down at it in your palm, and then you just took off, without even putting your coat on. What made you set off?"

"I don't *know*." There is rank desperation in my voice. "I wish I did. I can't remember."

"Please try, it's very important."

"I know it's important!" It comes out as a shout, shockingly loud in the small room. My fingers are clenched on the thin hospital blanket. "D-do you think I don't know that? This is my friend, m-my—"

I can't speak. I can't come up with a word for what James is to me . . . *was* to me. My knees are drawn up to my chest, and I am panting, and I want to hit my head on my knees and keep on hitting until the memories bleed out, but I can't, I can't remember.

"Nora—" Lamarr says, and I'm not sure if her voice is trying to soothe or warn me. Perhaps both.

"I want to remember." My teeth are gritted. "M-more than you can believe."

"I believe you," Lamarr says. There is something sad in her voice. I feel her hand on my shoulder, and then there's a bang at the door and the nurse comes in, pushing a trolley.

"What's going on here?" She looks from me to Lamarr, taking in my tearstained face and unconcealed distress, and her pleasant round face puckers in disapproval. "You, missie, I'll not have you upsetting my patients like this!" She stabs a finger at Lamarr. "She's not twenty-four hours after nearly killing herself in a car crash. Out!"

"She didn't . . ." I try. "It wasn't . . ."

But it's only part true. Lamarr *has* upset me, and in spite of my protest I'm glad to see her go, glad to curl on my side under the sheets as the nurse dishes up cottage pie and limp green beans, muttering under her breath about the high-handedness of the police, and who do they think they are, barging in here without so much as a by-your-leave, upsetting her patients, setting them back days if not weeks . . .

A school-dinner smell fills the room as she plops and ladles and sets the tray down beside me with a bang.

"Eat up now, pet," she says, with something close to tenderness. "You're just skin and bone. Rice Krispies are all very well, but they're no food to get well on. You need meat and veg for that."

I'm not hungry, but I nod.

When she's gone, though, I don't eat. I just lie on my side, holding my aching ribs, and try to make sense of it.

I should have asked how Clare was, where she was.

And Nina, where is Nina? Is she okay? Why hasn't she come and seen me? I should have asked all this, but I missed my chance.

I lie, staring at the side of the locker, and I think about James and about all we meant to each other, and everything I've done and lost. Because what I realized, as I held his hand and he bled all over the floor, was that my anger, which I had thought was black and insuperable and would never fade, was already going, bleeding out over the floor along with James's life.

It has defined me for so long, my bitterness about what happened. And now it's gone—the bitterness is gone, but so is James, the only other person who knew.

There is a lightness about that knowledge, but also a terrible weight.

I lie there, and I think back to the first time—not the first time I met him, for that must have been when we were twelve or thirteen, younger perhaps. But the first time that I noticed him. It was summer term in year ten, and James was playing Bugsy Malone in the school play. Clare was—of course—Blousie Brown. It was a toss-up between that and Tallulah, but Blousie gets her man at the end and Clare never did like playing the loser.

I'd seen James before, in lessons, horsing about, flicking paper planes and drawing on his arm. But onstage . . . onstage he somehow lit the room. I had just turned fifteen, James was a few months off sixteen—one of the oldest in our year—and that year he had shaved a savage undercut into his hair, and twisted the remaining black curls on top into a little knot at the back of his skull. It looked punky and rebellious, but for Bugsy he had smoothed it down with hair oil, and somehow, even at rehearsals in his school uniform, that simple thing made him look completely and utterly like a 1930s gangster. He walked like one. He stood like one, an invisible cigar clenched in the corner of his mouth so convincingly that I could smell the smoke—though there was nothing there. He spoke with a laconic twang. I wanted to fuck him, and I knew that every other girl in the room—and some of the boys—felt the same way.

I knew what Clare thought, for she'd told me, hanging over the row of chairs behind me, whispering into my ear, her pink Blousie lipstick tickling my hair.

"I'm going to *have* James Cooper," she told me. "I've made up my mind."

I said nothing. Clare usually got what she wanted.

Nothing happened over the summer holidays, and I began to wonder if Clare had forgotten her promise. But then we went back to school, and I realized, from a thousand tiny things—the way she flicked her hair, the number of buttons undone on her school shirt—that Clare had forgotten nothing. She was just biding her time.

The autumn-term play was *Cat on a Hot Tin Roof*, and when James got cast as Brick, Clare got the part of Maggie. She gloated to me about the extra rehearsal time it would necessitate, alone in the drama studio after hours, but not even Clare could charm her way out of glandular fever. She was signed off for the rest of the term, and her part was given to the understudy. Me.

And so, instead of Clare, *I* played Maggie, hot, sultry Maggie. I kissed James every night for a week, fought with him, draped myself across him with a sensuality I didn't know I even possessed until he called it out of me. I didn't stammer. I wasn't even Lee anymore. I've never acted like that, before or since. But James *was* Brick, drunken, angry, confused Brick, and so I became Maggie.

We had a cast party on the last night, Cokes and sandwiches in what we called the greenroom, but was in fact an empty classroom just up the corridor from the auditorium. And then, later, Jack and Cokes in the parking lot, and in the kitchen of Lois Finch's house.

And James took my hand, and together we climbed the stairs to Lois's brother's bedroom and we lay on Toby Finch's creaking single bed and did things that still make me shiver when I think about them, even here, in the hospital room, ten years on.

That was when James Cooper lost his virginity. Sixteen years old, on a winter's night, on a Spider-Man duvet cover, with model airplanes turning and wheeling over our heads as we kissed and bit and gasped.

And then we were together—that was simply how it was, with no more discussion than that.

My God, I loved him.

And now he is gone. It seems impossible.

I think of Lamarr's soft, plum-colored voice saying, *"And James—how did you know him?"*

What should I have said, if I were telling the truth?

I knew him so that if I touched his face in the dark, I would know it was him.

I knew him so that I could tell you every scar and mark on his body, the appendix slit to the right of his belly, the stitches from where he fell off his bike, the way his hair parted in three separate crowns, each swirling into the other.

I knew him by heart.

And he is gone.

I have not spoken to him for ten years, but I thought of him every single day.

He is gone—and, just when I need it most, so is the rage I have nursed all this time, even while I told myself that I no longer cared, that it was a part of my past shut away and gone and done.

He is gone.

Perhaps if I say it often enough, I will start to believe it.

chapter 23

I sleep the sleep of the dead that night—in spite of the noise and the beep of machines down the corridor and the intrusive lights. The nurses have stopped coming in to check on me every two hours, and I sleep . . . and sleep . . . and sleep.

When I wake, it's with a sense of disorientation: Where am I? What day is it? I look for my phone automatically.

It's not there. There's a plastic water jug instead.

And then the weight of the present comes crashing down on the back of my skull.

It is Monday.

I am in a hospital.

James is dead.

"Wakey, wakey," says a new nurse, coming briskly in and running a professional eye over my charts. "Breakfast will be coming around in a few minutes."

I'm still in the hospital gown, and as she goes to leave, I find myself calling out, "Wait!"

She turns, one eyebrow raised, plainly midrounds and in no mood to stop.

"I'm s-sorry," I stammer. "I was just wondering, c-could I, can I get any clothes? I'd like my own clothes. And my phone, if possible."

"We ask relatives to bring them in," she says briskly. "We're not a courier service." And then she's gone, the door flapping shut behind her.

She doesn't know, then. About me. About what has happened. And it occurs to me, the house is probably a crime scene. There's no way Nina and Clare and everyone can still be there, tiptoeing around James's congealing blood. They must have gone home—or been shipped off to a B and B. I'll have to ask Lamarr when she comes in. *If* she comes in.

For the first time I realize how very dependent on the police I am. They are my only line to the outside world.

It's around eleven a.m. when there is a knock on the door. I am lying on my side listening to Radio 4. It's the *Woman's Hour* drama, and if I shut my eyes hard enough, and press the headphones to my ears, I can almost imagine myself back home, a cup of coffee—proper coffee—at my side, the traffic roaring softly outside my window.

When the knock comes, it takes me a minute to adjust to Lamarr's face in the wire-hatched pane. I pull off the headphones and struggle up against the pillows.

"Come in."

She holds up a paper cup as she enters.

"Coffee?"

"Oh, *thank* you." I try not to sound desperate, try not to snatch the cup from her hands, but it's amazing how much these small things mean in the goldfish-bowl world of the hospital. I can tell by the feel of the cup that it's too hot to drink, and I nurse it while I think how to phrase what I want to say, and while Lamarr chats about the unseasonably beautiful winter weather, and how the roads are clearing up from the weekend's snow. At last she grinds to a pause, and I take my chance.

"Sergeant . . ."

"Constable."

"I'm sorry." I'm annoyed with myself for the mistake and trying not to get flustered. "Listen, I was wondering, how is Clare?"

"Clare?" She leans forward. "Have you remembered something?"

"What?"

"Have you started to remember what happened after you left the house?"

"What?" We stare at each other for a moment, and then she shakes her head ruefully.

"I'm sorry. I thought from what you said . . ."

"What do you mean? Has something happened to Clare?"

"Tell me what you remember," she says, but for a minute I say nothing, trying to read her beautiful, closed face. Her eyes meet mine, but I can't tell anything. There is something she's not telling me.

"I remember . . ." I speak slowly. "I remember running through the woods . . . and I remember a car's headlights and glass . . . and then after the accident, I remember stumbling along, I'd lost a shoe, and there were chunks of glass on the road." It's coming back to me as I speak, the lowering tunnel of bare branches, pale in the car headlights, and my limping run as I tried to flag down someone—anyone—someone to help. There was a van, swinging along the road, headlights raking the dark. I stood, waving frantically, the tears streaming down my face, and I thought he wouldn't stop. I thought for a moment he'd run me down. But he didn't—he skidded to a halt, his face pale as he wound down the window. *What the fuck?* he said, and then, *Have you been . . . ?* The rest of the sentence hovered unspoken.

"But that's it. Between that, it's so jumbled . . . it's like the images get more and more shaken up, and then there's just a blank spot. Listen, has something happened to Clare? She's not . . ."

Oh my God.

Oh my God. It cannot be.

I feel my fingers close on the bedsheet, my bitten nails digging in so hard that my fingers hurt.

Is she dead?

"She's okay," Lamarr says slowly, carefully. "But she was in the accident, the same accident as you."

"Is she all right? Can I see her?"

"No, I'm sorry. We've not been able to interview her yet. We need to get her version before . . ."

She trails off. I know what she is saying. She wants my truth, and Clare's truth—separate, so they can compare our stories.

Yet again I have that cold writhing feeling in the pit of my stomach. Am I a suspect? How can I find out without looking like one?

"She's still not really up to being interviewed," Lamarr says at last.

"Does she know about James?"

"I don't believe so, no." There is compassion in Lamarr's face. "She's not been well enough to be told, yet."

I don't know why, but it is *that* that rattles me more than anything else she has said so far today. I can't bear the idea that Clare is lying somewhere in this very hospital and doesn't know that James is gone.

Is she wondering why he hasn't come? Or is she too ill even for that?

"Is she going to be okay?" My voice cracks and breaks on the last word, and I take a long, aching gulp of coffee to try to hide my distress.

"The doctors say yes, but we're waiting for her family to come, and then they'll take a view about whether she's stable enough to be told. I'm sorry . . . I wish I could tell you more, but it's not really my place to be discussing her medical details."

"Yeah, I know," I say dully. There are tears trapped at the back of my throat, making my head ache and my eyes swim as I blink angrily, trying to clear them. "What about Nina," I manage at last. "Can I see her?"

"We're still taking statements from everyone else at the house. But as soon as that's concluded, I imagine she'll be allowed to visit."

"Today?"

"Hopefully today, yes. But it would be very, *very* helpful if you could remember what happened after you left the house. We want to get your version, not anyone else's, and we're worried that speaking to other people might . . . confuse things."

I cannot tell what she means by this. Is she worried that I am waiting, pretending memory loss so I can get my story straight with someone else's? Or is it simply that she's concerned that in the vacuum of my own memories, I might implant someone else's account unconsciously?

I know how easy that is to do—for years I "remembered" a childhood holiday during which I rode on a donkey. There was a photo of me doing it on the mantelpiece, I was about three or four, and I was silhouetted against the setting sun, just a dark blur with a halo of sunlit hair. But I could remember the salt wind in my face, and the glint of the sun off the waves, and the feel of the scratchy blanket between my thighs. It was only when I was fifteen that my mum mentioned it wasn't me at all, but my cousin Rachel. I was never even there.

So what are they saying? Cough up the memories, and we'll let you speak to your friend?

"I'm trying to remember," I say bitterly. "Believe me, I want to remember what happened even more than you want me to. You don't have to hold Nina out like a carrot."

"That's not it," Lamarr says. "We just want to get your account—I promise this isn't some kind of penalty."

"If I can't see Nina, can I at least get some of my own clothes? And my phone?" I must be getting better if I have started to worry about my phone. The thought of all those e-mails and messages building up . . . and no way of answering them. It's Monday now. A working day. My editor will have been in touch about the new draft. And my mum—has she been trying to call? "I really need my phone," I say. "I could promise not to contact anyone from the house if you're worried about that."

"Ah," she says, and there is something in her face, a kind of reserve. "Well, actually, that's one of the things we'd like to ask you. We'd like to take a look at your phone, if you don't mind."

"I don't mind. But can I have it back afterwards?"

"Yes, but we can't locate it."

That checks me. If they don't have it, where is it?

"Did you take it with you when you left the house?" Lamarr is saying.

I try to think back. I am sure I didn't. In fact, I can't remember having my phone for most of the day.

"I think it was in Clare's car," I say at last. "I think I left it there when we went clay-pigeon shooting."

Lamarr shakes her head.

"The car has been completely stripped. It's definitely not there. And we've made quite a thorough search of the house."

"Maybe the clay-pigeon range?"

"We'll try there"—she makes a note on her pad—"but we've been calling it and no one's picking up. I imagine if it had been left there, someone might have heard it ringing."

"It's ringing?" I'm surprised the battery is still working. I can't remember when I last charged it. "What, you mean you've been calling my number? How did you know what it was?"

"We got it off Dr. da Souza," she says briefly. It takes me a second to click that she means Nina.

"And it's definitely ringing?" I say slowly. "Not just going through to voice mail?"

"I . . ." She pauses, and I can see her trying to remember. "I'll have to check, but yes, I'm fairly sure it was ringing."

"Well, if it's ringing, it can't be at the house. There's no reception."

Lamarr frowns for a moment, a line between her slender, perfect brows. Then she shakes her head.

"Well, we've put the tech guys on it now, so no doubt they'll get us an approximate location. We'll let you know as soon as it's picked up."

"Thanks," I say. But I don't add the question that's buzzing in my head: Why do they want my phone?

Here is how I know I'm getting better.

The nurses are no longer coming in to check on me every two hours.

I'm bloody hungry—I looked at the lunch that came in a couple of hours ago and thought, That's it? It's like when you get those toy-sized meals on airplanes and you think, Who eats a tablespoon of mash and a sausage the size of my little finger? That's not a meal. That's a canapé in a pretentiously upmarket bar.

I am bored. Christ, I'm bored. Now I'm no longer sleeping as much, I have nothing to do. No phone. No laptop. I could be writing, but without access to my laptop and my current manuscript there's nothing I can do. I'm even getting angry with the radio. At home, where it's just a background to my routine, I love the constant repetition, the reassuring cycle of the day, the fact that *Start the Week* follows *Today,* and *Woman's Hour* follows *Start the Week,* as surely as Monday gives way to Tuesday and Wednesday. Here, it is starting to drive me a little mad. How many times can I hear the endless loop of news headlines before I go crazy?

But most of all, I'm frightened.

There's a kind of focusing effect that happens when you're very ill. I saw it with my granddad, when he was slipping away. You stop caring about the big stuff. Your world shrinks down to very small concerns: the way your dressing gown cord presses uncomfortably against your ribs, the pain in your spine, the feel of a hand in yours.

It's that narrowing that enables you to cope, I suppose. The wider world stops mattering. And as you grow more and more ill, your world shrinks further, until the only thing that matters is just to keep on breathing.

But I am going the other way. When I was brought in, all I cared about was not dying. Then yesterday I just wanted to be left alone to sleep and lick my wounds.

Now, today, I am starting to worry.

I am not an official suspect; I know enough from writing crime books to know that Lamarr would have had to interview me under caution if that was the case, offer me a solicitor, read me my rights.

But they are groping around, searching for *something.* They don't think James's death was an accident.

I remember the words floating through the thick glass last night, *Oh Jesus, so now we're looking at murder?*

At the time they seemed shocking but fantastical—all part of the drugged-up dream state I was caught in. Now they seem all too real.

chapter 24

When the knock comes again, I nearly don't answer. I'm lying with my eyes shut listening to Radio 4 on the headphones provided, trying to block out the noise and bustle of the ward next door, to imagine myself back at home.

The nurses don't knock—at least they do, but with a perfunctory tap and then they come in anyway. Only Lamarr knocks and waits for an answer. And I cannot face Lamarr, with her kind, calm, curiously dogged questions. I don't remember. I don't remember, all right? I'm not hiding anything, I just Don't. Fucking. Remember.

I screw my eyes shut, listening over the sound of *The Archers* to see if she's going away, and then I hear the door shush cautiously open, as if someone is putting their head around.

"Lee?" I hear, very quietly. "I mean, sorry, Nora?"

I sit bolt upright. It's Nina.

"Nina!" I rip off the headphones and try to swing my legs out of bed, but whether it's my head, or just low blood pressure, the room goes suddenly hollow and distant, and I am overcome with a wave of vertigo.

"Hey." Her voice is distant, through the hissing in my ears. "Hey, take it easy. They've only just sewn your brains back in, by all accounts."

"I'm all right," I say, though I'm not sure if I'm trying to reassure myself, or her. "I'm all right. I'm okay."

And then I *am* okay. The wave of faintness has passed, and I can hug Nina, breathing in her particular scent: Jean Paul Gaultier, and cigarettes.

"Oh Jesus, I'm so glad to see you."

"I'm glad to see you." She pulls back, looking at me with critical, worried eyes. "I have to say, when they told us you'd been in a car accident, I . . . well. Seeing one school friend bleed out was enough."

I flinch, and she drops her eyes.

"Shit, sorry. I— It's not that I—"

"I know." It's not that Nina doesn't feel stuff. She just deals with it differently than most people. Sarcasm is her defense against life.

"Let's just say, I'm glad you're here." She takes my hand and kisses the back of it, and I'm astonished and kind of touched to see her face is crumpled and soft. "Although, not looking your best, I have to say." She gives a shaky laugh. "Sheesh, I need a fag. Think they'd notice if I had one out the window?"

"Nina, what the hell happened?" I ask, still holding on to her hand. "The police are here—they're asking all these questions. James is *dead*, did you know?"

"Yes, I knew," Nina says quietly. "They came to the house early on Sunday. They didn't tell us straightaway, but . . . well, let's just say, you don't expend that kind of manpower on a nonfatal shooting. It was pretty obvious after they started printing us and taking gunshot-residue tests."

"What happened? How could that gun possibly be loaded?"

"As I see it," her voice is grimly steady, "there're two possibilities. One"—she holds up her forefinger—"Flo's aunt did not, in fact, keep that gun loaded with blanks. But from their line of questioning, I don't think they think that's likely."

"And two?"

"Someone loaded it."

It's only what I've been thinking. But it's still a shock, hearing it out loud in the small hermit cell of the hospital room. We both sit there in silence, contemplating this for a long while, thinking about Tom larking around with it the night before, thinking about all the hows and whys and what-ifs.

"How's Jess taking it all?" I ask at last, more to change the subject than anything else. Nina makes a wry face.

"As you can imagine, she was her usual measured self. Only forty-five minutes of hysteria down the phone. First she was furious they were keeping me up here to make a statement, and then she wanted to come up, but I told her not to."

"Why not?"

Nina gives me a look that's simultaneously sympathetic and disbelieving.

"Dude, are you kidding me? For whatever fucked-up reason, they think James was murdered. Would you want your nearest and dearest mixed up in that? No. Jess is not part of this, thank Christ, and it's staying that way. I want her far, far away."

"Fair point." I scoot back onto the bed and sit, hugging my knees. Nina takes the chair and picks up my chart, flicking through it with bald-faced curiosity.

"Do you mind?" I say. "I'm not sure I want you knowing details of my last bowel movement and all that."

"Sorry, professional nosiness. How's the head now? Sounds like you had quite a whack."

"Yeah, it felt like it. I'm okay, though. Just . . . I've been having memory trouble." I rub where the dressing sits, as if I can rub the jumbled images back into a semblance of order. "It's just the bit after I left the house."

"Hmm. Post-traumatic amnesia. It's usually only a matter of a few moments, though. Yours sounds like . . . I don't know. How long do you think?"

"It's kind of difficult to be sure since, oh, did I mention, I can't remember," I say. I can hear my voice going snappish, and my own peevishness annoys me, but Nina ignores it.

"It can't be long, though, right?"

"Look, I know you mean well"—I massage my temples—"but can we not talk about this? I spent all morning with a police officer trying to remember, and honestly, I've had enough. It's not coming. I worry if I try and force it, I'll just end up making something up and convincing myself it's the truth."

"Okay." She's quiet for a moment and then says, "Look, I told them about you and James. I said you used to go out. I thought you should know. I didn't know what you would have said, but . . ."

"It's fine. I don't want anyone to lie. I told Lamarr we were together. She's the police officer assigned—"

"I know," Nina breaks in. "She's been speaking to us, too. Does she know how you broke up?"

"What do you mean?"

"You know, the big secret. The STD. Or whatever you want to call it."

"For the last time, no one gave me an STD."

"So you keep saying. Did you tell her?"

"No, I didn't say anything. Did you?"

"No. I had nothing to tell. I just said you were together. And then you broke up."

"Well, quite. There's nothing to tell." I press my lips together.

"Really? Hmm, let's see." She begins to tick the points off on her fingers. "Breaking up, leaving school, dropping contact with half your friends, not speaking to him for ten years. Nothing to tell?"

"There's nothing to tell," I repeat doggedly, staring at my fingers, laced together over my knee. The cuts are starting to darken and scab over. Soon they'll be healed.

"Because the fact is," Nina continues, "James is dead, and they're looking for a motive."

At that I look up. I look her right in the eye. She meets my gaze without flinching.

"What are you saying?"

"I'm saying, I'm worried about you."

"You're implying I killed James!"

"Fuck off!" At that she stands and begins to pace around the room. "I am *not*. I'm saying— I'm trying—"

"You know n-nothing about it," I say. *Fuck*. Stop stammering! But it is true. Nina *does* know nothing about it. No one knows about that part of my life—not even my mum. The only person who knows anything is Clare, and even she doesn't know the full story. And Clare . . .

Clare is in hospital.

Clare is . . . what? Too ill to be interviewed? In a coma, even? But she will wake up.

"Have you seen Clare?" I say, my voice very low. Nina shakes her head.

"No. I think she's pretty bad. Whatever happened in that crash . . ." She shakes her head again, this time in frustration rather than denial. "You know the worst thing? James would probably have lived. He was very badly hurt, but I reckon there was at least a fifty percent chance he'd have survived."

"What do you mean?"

"It was the crash that killed him. Or else the delay caused by the crash—which comes to the same thing."

Suddenly, Lamarr's insistence on those missing minutes crystallizes.

What happened in the house was only the first half of the story.

The real killing came later, on the road.

I *have* to remember what happened.

I should never have come. I knew that. I knew it from the moment the e-mail pinged into my in-box.

You should never go back.

And yet. I think of James, lying on the floor, his dark eyes looking up into mine as his blood pooled around us both. I think of his hand, slippery with blood, gripping mine as if he were drowning and only I could save him. I think of his voice saying, *Leo . . .*

If I had known then what I know now, would I have deleted the e-mail?

Nina's hand reaches out for mine, and I feel her warm, dry grip, and her strong fingers tracing the lattice of scratches and cuts.

"It'll be okay," she says. But her voice is husky, and we both know she is lying—lying because whatever happens with me and Lamarr and the rest of the investigation, this has gone far beyond the point where things could ever be okay again. Whatever happens, whether Clare recovers or not, whether they suspect me or not, James is dead.

"H-how's Flo?" I say at last. Nina chews her lip, as if considering what to say, and then lets out a gust of breath.

"Not . . . great. To tell the truth, I think she's having a breakdown."

"Does she know about Clare?"

"Yes. She wanted to see her, but we were told no visitors."

"Has anyone seen her? Clare, I mean."

"Her parents, I think."

"And . . ." I swallow. I won't stammer. I won't. "And James's parents? Have they been?"

"I think so, yes. I believe they came yesterday and"—she looks down at my hands, runs her finger gently across the longest scratch—"and saw his body. They've gone home, as far as I know. We didn't see them."

I get a sudden piercing memory of James's mum as she was ten years ago, her long curly hair caught up in a clip, her bangles chiming as she gesticulated and laughed to someone on the other end of the phone, her scarves fluttering in the breeze from an open window. I remember her putting the phone to her shoulder as James introduced me: *This is Leo. She'll be coming around a lot. Get used to her face.*

And James's mum laughing and saying, *I know what that means. Let me show you where the fridge is, Leo. No one cooks in this house, so if you want something to eat: forage.*

It was so different from my house. No one was ever still. The door was always open, and they always had friends around, or students staying, and everyone was always arguing—laughing—kissing—drinking. There were no mealtimes. No curfews. James and I lay on his bed in the flooding sunlight, and no one came and knocked on the door and told us to stop whatever we were doing.

I remember James's dad, with his full beard and his accordion. He lectured on Marxist theory at the local uni and was always on the brink of resigning or being fired. He used to run me home after dark, in his battered car, swearing at the temperamental choke and regaling me with his awful puns.

James was their only child.

The thought of them both stricken down by grief—it's almost unbearable.

"Look." Nina gives my hand a final squeeze. "I'd better go. I only put an hour on the car parking ticket, and it's nearly gone."

"Thanks. Thanks for coming." I give her an awkward hug. "Listen, you didn't happen to grab any of my clothes when you left the house, did you?"

Nina shakes her head.

"No, I'm really sorry. They were really strict about what we could take. I've only got one change for myself. I could buy you some sweats, if you want?"

"Thanks, that'd be great. I can pay you back."

Nina makes a kind of derisory snort, and does a batting-away motion with her hand.

"Psssh, shut up already. You're a small, right? Any preferences?"

"No, anything's fine. Just . . . nothing too bright. You know me."

"Okay. Tell you what, I'll leave you this in the meantime." She peels off her cardigan, a navy-blue knitted thing with small buttons in the shape of dark blue flowers. I'm shaking my head, but she drapes it around my shoulders. "There you go. At least you can open the window without freezing."

"Thanks," I say, huddling it around myself. I can't believe how good it feels to be wearing something that's not hospital issue. Like I've got my personality back. Nina shrugs, kisses me—briskly this time—and then heads for the door.

"Stay sane, Shaw. We can't have two people going off the tracks, on top of everything else."

"Flo? Is she really bad then?"

Nina just shrugs, but her face is sad. Then she turns to go. I watch her stalking off down the corridor, and something suddenly occurs to me. The police guard outside my door is gone.

chapter 25

It's maybe half an hour later when there comes another, brisker knock at the door, and a nurse bustles in. For a minute I think it's supper, and my stomach growls and turns, but then I realize there's no smell of industrial catering floating through the door.

"We've got a young man here to see you," she says without preamble. "Name of Matt Ridout. Says he'd like to come and visit you if you're up to it."

I blink. I've never heard of him.

"Is he a policeman?"

"I don't know, pet. He's not in uniform."

For a minute I think about sending her back out there to find out more, but she's tapping her foot, plainly impatient and busy, and I realize it would be easier just to see him and get it over with.

"Send him in," I say at last.

"He can only have half an hour," she warns. "Visiting hours end at four."

"That's okay." Good. That will provide an excuse to get rid of him if he proves awkward.

I sit up, gathering Nina's cardie around myself and raking my hair off my face. I look like a car crash—literally—so I don't really know why I'm bothering, but it feels important to my self-respect that I at least make a token effort.

A few—a very few—minutes later, I hear steps in the corridor, and there's a knock on the door, a hesitant, diffident knock quite different from Nina's brisk tap and the nurse's perfunctory pretense.

"Come in," I say, and a man walks into the room.

He's about my age—maybe a few years older—and dressed in jeans and a faded T-shirt. His jacket is slung over his arm, and he looks hot and uncomfortable in the hospital's tropical atmosphere. He's got a scrubby Hoxton-style beard, and his hair is cropped close to his skull, not a buzz cut, but something like a Roman soldier, short curls, flat against his head.

But the thing that I really notice is that he's been crying.

For a minute I can't think of anything to say, and neither can he. He stands in the doorway, his hands in his pockets, and he looks shocked to see me.

"You're not from the police," I say at last, stupidly. He rubs a hand through his hair.

"I—my name is Matt. I'm—at least—" He stops, and his lip curls into a grimace, and I know he's fighting back some very strong emotion. He takes a deep breath, and begins again. "I was—James's best man."

I say nothing. We only sit, staring at each other, me clutching Nina's cardigan to my throat as if it's a suit of armor, he rigid and tense in the doorway. And then, unbidden, a single tear runs down the side of his nose, and he swipes at it furiously with his sleeve, and I say, simultaneously, "Come in. Come and sit down. Do you want a drink?"

"Got whiskey?" he says, and gives a short, shaky laugh. I try to laugh, too, but it doesn't sound like a laugh to me, more like a choke.

"I wish. Hospital tea or coffee from the vending machine, or water." I point to the plastic jug. "On the whole I'd recommend the water."

"I'm okay," he says. He comes and sits in the plastic chair next to my bed. But he's hardly sat down when he pushes himself to standing again. "Fuck, I'm so sorry. I shouldn't have come."

"No." I grab his wrist, and then look down at my hand, holding his arm, astonished at myself. What the hell am I doing? I let go at once, as though his skin burns. "I—I'm sorry. But I just meant . . ."

I trail off. What did I mean? I have no idea. Only that I don't want him to go. He is a link to James.

"Please stay," I manage at last. He stays, standing, looking down at me, and then gives a short, curt nod and sits.

"I'm sorry," he says again. "I wasn't expecting . . . you look . . ."

I know what he means. I look like I've been beaten within an inch of my life and then patched up again. Badly.

"It's not as bad as it looks," I say, and I surprise myself by managing a smile. "It's mainly just scratches and bruising."

"It's your face," he says, "your eyes. I see a fair bit of domestic violence in my line of work, but those shiners . . ."

"I know. I only saw them myself this morning. They're kind of spectacular, aren't they? They don't hurt, though."

We sit in silence for a second, and then he says, "Actually, you know what, second thoughts, I might get a coffee. Want one?"

"No, thanks." I'm still coasting on the remnants of the coffee Lamarr brought. I'm not yet desperate enough for the vending machine stuff.

Matt gets stiffly to his feet and walks out of the room, and I can see the tension in his shoulders as his back disappears down the corridor. I almost wonder if he's going to come back, but he does.

"Shall we start again?" he says as he sits down. "Sorry, I feel like I kind of cocked that one up. You must be Leo, right?"

I almost flinch. It's such a shock hearing it—James's name for me—from his lips.

"Yes, that's right. So James . . . he told you about me?"

"A bit, yeah. I know you were . . . I dunno. What would you call it? Childhood sweethearts?"

For some reason the words bring a rush of tears to the back of my throat, and I feel my lip wobble as I try to answer. Instead, I just nod, silently.

"Fuck." He puts his head in his hands. "I'm sorry— I just— I can't believe it. I was only speaking to him a couple of days ago. I knew there was stuff . . . things going wrong . . . but this . . ."

Things going wrong?

I want to ask more, to probe, but I can't quite get the words out, and Matt's still speaking.

"I'm really sorry to barge in like this. If I'd known how ill you were, I wouldn't have—the nurse didn't say. I just asked if I could see you, and she said she'd find out. But I heard, from James's mum, that you were with him when he—" He stops, gulps, and forces himself on. "When he died. And I know how much you meant to him, and I wanted—"

He stops again, and this time he can't carry on. He bends over his cup, and I know he's crying and trying to hide it.

"I'm sorry," he says at last, his voice croaky, and then he coughs to clear his throat. "I only found out last night. It's been— I can't get used to it. I kept thinking there'd been some mistake, but seeing you like this . . . it's kind of made it real."

"How . . . how did you know James?"

"We were at Cambridge together. We were both into theater—acting, you know, plays and stuff." He rubs his face on his sleeve, and then looks up, smiling determinedly. "Goes without saying, I was shit, but luckily I realized that in time. Didn't help that I was acting next to James. Nothing like seeing the real thing for showing up the fake."

"And you kept in touch?"

"Yeah. I used to go and see him in his plays, every now and then. Everyone else in our year became bankers and civil servants and stuff. Felt like he was the only one who made it. I'm kind of proud of him for that, you know? He never sold out."

I nod, slowly. Yes, that was the James I knew. The man he's describing is painfully familiar. The James I knew. *My* James. Completely unlike the unreal, materialistic person I've been hearing described all weekend. I thought James had changed. But perhaps he hadn't. Or not completely.

"So, what happened?" Matt said at last. "At—at the house? They said a shotgun went off, but it just seems . . . why was he even there?"

"I don't know." I shut my eyes, and my hand goes to the hot, sweaty dressing over my forehead. "I never asked. When we heard him walking around, we thought he was a burglar." I don't go into the rest of it—the door swinging wide, our stupid hysteria. It seems like something out of a horror movie, clichéd, ridiculous. "I suppose it was a prank, the groom turning up to surprise his future bride in bed."

"No." Matt's shaking his head. "I really don't think— He wouldn't have gone up there uninvited."

"Why not?"

"Well, first of all, you just don't, do you? You don't crash your girlfriend's hen. It's kind of . . . crass. It's her last chance at being single; you'd have to be kind of a wanker to take that away from her."

I guess. But I don't say anything. I'm waiting for the second reason. Matt takes a breath.

"And second . . . well . . . they weren't getting along that great."

"What?" I know, as soon as I've said it, that my voice was too loud, too emphatic, too shocked. Matt looks up, startled.

"Look, I don't want to overstate it, but—yeah. Did Clare not say?"

"No . . . at least . . . I don't think so." I think back, trying to remember what we talked about. But I know Clare. She would never admit to any kind of problem. The facade always had to be perfect, the mask never slipped. "What kind of problems?"

"I don't know." He looks uncomfortable. "I don't— We never really talked about it. I'm guessing it was just the usual pre-wedding jitters, right? I've seen enough mates down the aisle to know how it goes—perfectly normal girlfriend turns into Bridezilla, everyone gets tense, families chip in, friends get involved, small stuff is suddenly blown up into major feuds, and everyone takes sides."

"So why was he there?" I say at last.

"I don't know. I can only guess . . . someone asked him to come."

"Someone *asked* him? But—but—"

But who?

Clare? No. No way. She of all people knew what it would mean if James turned up at the cottage—there was no way she wanted him and me shut up together in the same place for two hours, let alone twenty-four. It would have resulted in my storming out, or an unholy row, and she knew it. That was why she hadn't invited me to the wedding. One of the others might have done it—out of ignorance, or malice. But there was no way Clare would purposely ruin her own hen weekend. Why would she?

Flo? Could she have done it as some kind of joke? She knew nothing about my past with James. She could have done it as a jolly jape to crown off her "perfect" weekend. And, after all, Melanie had gone. There was a spare double room. And then, too, that might explain her abrupt breakdown: not just guilt over waving a loaded gun around, but guilt over having set up the whole prank gone wrong in the first place. But then—surely she would have known it was probably James coming up the stairs. Why would she have fired the gun—even supposing it was unloaded? I had seen her face as that shadowy figure rounded the corner of the stairs. She had looked genuinely frightened. Either she's insane, or the most fantastic actress of all time.

Could it have been Tom? Had there been something about that row with Bruce, something that would have made him want to set James up for a fall? Or Nina, with her weird twisted sense of humor, playing a practical joke? But *why*? Why would either of them do such a thing?

I shake my head. This is sending me crazy. No one in that house invited James. No one. There's no way the shooting would have played out that way if they had.

"You're wrong," I say into the silence. "You must be. He must have just decided to come. If he and Clare had argued—he might have wanted to patch it up, don't you think? He was always . . ."

"A bit of an idiot?" Matt says. He gives a shaky laugh. "I guess maybe you're right. He's not known for his forethought. I mean—" He stops, and I see his fist on his knee is clenched. "I mean . . . he was." He stops. There is another silence, both of us thinking of the James who lives in our heads, in our thoughts. "I remember," he says at last, "I remember one time at uni . . . he climbed the college walls and put Santa hats on all the gargoyles. Idiot. He could have been killed."

As the last word drops from his lips I see him realize what he's said, and flinch, and before I can stop myself I put out a hand.

"I'd better go," he says. "I'm— I hope you're better soon."

"I'll be fine," I say. And then, forcing myself on, because I know if I don't say it, I'll regret it, "Will you— Can you come back?"

"I'm going back to London in the morning," he says. "But it'd be nice to keep in touch."

There's a pen on the chart, and he pulls it off and scribbles his number on the only bit of writable surface around—the side of his coffee cup.

"You were right," he says, as he puts the cup carefully on my bedside table. "Water would have been preferable. Bye, Leo."

"Bye."

The door swings slowly shut behind him, and through the narrow glass hatch I watch his silhouette disappearing down the corridor. And it's strange for a person who lives alone, for someone who's been craving solitude since coming here, but suddenly I feel very lonely . . . and it's a very foreign, peculiar feeling.

chapter 26

I'm eating supper when the knock comes again. It's not visiting hours—the sign on the wall tells patients and their families that these are two to four p.m. and seven to nine p.m.

So I'm surprised when I look up and it's Nina sliding around the door with a carrier bag. She puts her fingers to her lips.

"Shh. I only got in by pulling the old *Don't you know who I am?*"

"Did you tell them you were Salma Hayek's cousin again?"

"Puhlease! She's not even Brazilian."

"Or a doctor."

"Quite. Anyway, I said I'd be quick, so here you go." She throws down a bag on the bed. "I'm afraid they're not exactly haute couture. In fact, you were lucky they're not pastel velour. But I did the best I could."

"They're great," I say thankfully, riffling through the anonymous gray sweats. "Honestly. The only thing I care about is that they're not open at the back and logoed with 'Hospital Property.' Truly, I really, really appreciate it, Nina."

"I even got you some shoes—only flip-flops, but I know how grim the hospital showers can be, and I thought at least then if they kick you out at short notice, you'll have something to walk in. You're a six, right?"

"Five actually—but don't worry, six is brilliant. Here." I pull off her cardigan and hold it out. "Take this."

"Nah, don't worry. Keep it until your own stuff turns up. Do you need money?"

I shake my head, but she pulls out two tenners anyway and tosses them onto the locker.

"Can't hurt. At least then if you get sick of hospital food you can grab a panini. Okay. I'd better go."

But she doesn't. She just stands there, looking down at her short, square nails. I can tell she wants to say something and—with uncharacteristic nervousness—is holding back.

"Bye, then," I say at last, hoping to jolt her into speaking, but she just says, "Bye," and turns for the door.

Then, with her hand on the push panel, she stops and turns back.

"Look, what I said, earlier . . . I didn't mean . . ."

"What you said?"

"About James. About the motive. Look, I didn't really think you'd ever— Fuck." She thumps her fist gently on the wall. "This isn't coming out right. Look, I still think it was an accident, and that's what I told Lamarr. I never thought this had anything to do with you. But I was just worried, okay? *For* you. Not about you."

I let out a breath I didn't know I was holding and swing my legs out of bed. I walk uncertainly over to her and give her a hug.

"It's okay. I knew what you meant. I'm worried, too—for all of us."

She smooths my hair, and then I drop my arms and she looks at me.

"They don't think it was an accident, though, do they? Why on earth not?"

"Someone loaded that gun," I say. "That's the bottom line."

"But even so—that could have been anyone. Flo's aunt could have done it by mistake and been too scared to admit it to the police. The police keep banging on about the clay-pigeon shoot—was the ammunition properly secured, could anyone have got unsupervised access to a live round. They obviously think the cartridge came from there, or that's what they're trying to prove. But if one of us wanted to kill James, why the fuck would we lure him out to the back of beyond to do it?"

"I don't know," I say. My legs feel tired and wobbly from the effort of standing even just for that short conversation, and I let go of Nina's arm and walk shakily to the bed. All this talk—of guns and bullets—it's giving me a strange, queasy feeling. "I really don't know."

"I just think—" Nina starts, and then she stops.

"What?"

"I just think . . . oh, screw it. Look, whatever unmentionably awful thing happened with you and James, I just think you should tell them. I know"—she holds up a hand—"I know it's none of my business and I can fuck right off with my unsolicited advice, but I just think, whatever it is, it's probably not as bad as you think, and it'll just look a whole lot better if you tell them *now*."

I shut my eyes tiredly, and rub at the bloody bastard itching dressing on my forehead. Then I sigh and open them again. Nina is standing there, hands on hips, looking an odd mix of belligerent concern.

"I'll think about it," I say. "Okay? I will. I promise."

"Okay," Nina says. Her lower lip is stuck out like a child's, and I know if she still had it she would be clicking the ring she used to have there against her teeth. I remember the sound of it during exams. Thank God she took it out when she qualified. Apparently, patients didn't like seeing a surgeon with holes in her face. "I'll get going. Take care, Shaw. And if they kick you out at short notice, call me, okay?"

"I will."

I lie there after she's gone, thinking about her words, and thinking about how she's probably right. My head is hot and itching and words like *bullet* and *spatter* and *cartridge* are clattering around inside, and after a while I can't bear it any longer. I get up, walk slowly across to the bathroom with my old-woman gait, and click on the light.

The reflection that greets me inside is, if anything, worse than yesterday. My face feels better—much better—but the bruises are blazing from purple through to yellow and brown and green—all the shades a painter might use to paint the Northumberland landscape, I think with a twisted smile.

But it's not the bruises I'm looking at. It's the dressing.

I begin to pick at the corner of the tape, and then, oh the relief, off it peels with a kind of delicious tearing pain as the tape takes off the small hairs at my temples and hairline, and the dressing itself plucks at the wound.

I'd expected stitches—but there aren't any. Instead, there's a long, ugly cut, held together by small strips of tape and what looks like . . . can it really be Super Glue?

They've shaved a very small semicircle of hair at the edge of my scalp, where the cut snaked beneath the hairline, and it has started to grow. I touch it with my fingers. It feels spikily soft, like a baby's hairbrush.

The relief. The relief of the cold air on my forehead and the itch and pull of the dressing gone . . . I throw the bloodied pad into the bin, and walk slowly back to the bed, still thinking of Nina. And Lamarr. And James.

What happened between James and me has nothing to do with any of this. But perhaps Nina is right. Perhaps I should come clean. Maybe it would even be a relief, after all these years of silence.

No one knew. No one knew the truth except me, and James.

And I spent so long nursing my anger at him. And now it's gone. *He's* gone.

Perhaps I will tell Lamarr, when she comes in the morning. I'll tell her the truth—not just the truth, for everything I've said so far has been the truth. But the whole truth.

And the truth is this.

James dumped me. And yes, he dumped me by text.

But what I've held on to all these years is the reason *why.* He left because I was pregnant.

I don't know when it happened—which time, out of all those dozens, maybe hundreds, of times, made a baby. We were careful—at least we thought we were.

I only know that one day I realized I hadn't had a period for a long time, too long. And I did a test.

We were in James's attic bedroom when I told him, sitting on the bed, and he went quite white, staring at me with wide black eyes that had something of panic in them.

"Can't—" he started. Then, "Don't you think you could have . . ."

"Made a mistake?" I finished. I shook my head. I even managed a bitter little laugh. "Believe me, no. I took that test like eight times."

"What about the morning-after pill?" he said. I tried to take his hand, but he stood up and began pacing back and forth in the small room.

"It's much too late for that. But yes, we need—" There was a lump in my throat. I realized I was trying not to cry. "We need to d-decide—"

"We? This is your decision."

"I wanted to talk to you, too. I know what I want to do, but this is your b—"

Baby, too, was what I'd been going to say. But I never got to finish. He let out a gasp like he'd been smacked, and turned his face away.

I stood up and moved towards the door.

"Leo," he said, in a strangled voice. "Wait."

"Look"—my foot was already on the stairs, my bag over my shoulder—"I know, I sprang this on you. When you're ready to talk . . . call me, okay?"

But he never did.

Clare rang me when I got home, and she was angry.

"Where the hell *were* you? You stood me up! I waited half an hour in the Odeon foyer, and you weren't answering your calls!"

"I'm sorry," I said. "I had— I had stuff—" I couldn't finish.

"What? What's happened?" she asked, but I couldn't answer. "I'm coming over."

He never called. Instead, he texted, later that night. I'd spent the afternoon with Clare, agonizing over what to do, whether to tell my mum, whether James would be charged—we'd first done it when I was fifteen, although I was sixteen now and had been for a couple of months.

The text came through about eight p.m.

Lee. I'm sorry but this is your problem, not mine. Deal with it. And don't call me again. J.

And so I dealt with it. I never did tell my mum. Clare—actually, Clare was kind of amazing. Yes, she could be snappy, and snide, and even manipulative, but in a crisis she was like a lion. Looking back at that time, I remember why we were friends all those years. And it makes me realize again how selfish I was afterwards.

She took me to the clinic on the bus. It was early, early enough just to take the pills, and it was all over surprisingly soon.

It wasn't the abortion. I don't blame James for that—it was what I wanted myself; I didn't want a child at sixteen, and whatever happened, it was my fault as much as his.

And whatever people might think, it wasn't this that fucked me up. I don't feel a crucifying guilt over the loss of a cluster of cells. I refuse to feel guilty.

It wasn't any of that.

It was . . . I don't know. I don't know how to put it. It was pride, I think. A kind of disbelief at my own stupidity. The thought that I'd loved him so much, and had been so mistaken. How could I? How could I have been so incredibly, unbelievably wrong?

And if I went back to that school, I would have to live with that knowledge—the memory of us both together in everyone's eyes. The telling of a hundred people, *No, we're not together. Yes, he dumped me. No, I'm fine.*

I wasn't fine. I was a fool—a fucking stupid little fool. How could I have been so mistaken? I'd always thought myself a good judge of character, and I had thought James was brave, and loving, and that he loved me. None of that was true. He was weak, and cowardly, and he couldn't even look me in the eye to end it between us.

I would never trust my own judgment again.

We were on study leave when it happened, revising for our exams.

I went into school to take the exams, and then I never went back. Not to collect my results. Not for the autumn social. Not to see any of the teachers who'd coached and cheered me through my exams.

Instead, I changed to a sixth-form college two train rides away, one where I was sure no one could possibly know me. My day was insanely long—I left the house at five thirty in the morning and got home at six every night.

And then my mother moved house anyway, to be with Phil. I should have been angry, because she sold my grandfather's house where I grew up, where we'd all lived together for so many years, where all our memories were. And part of me was. But part of me was relieved—the last tie with Reading and with James was cut. I would never have to see him again.

No one knew what happened, apart from Clare, and even she didn't know about the text. I told her the next day that I'd decided I couldn't keep the baby and was breaking up with James.

She hugged me and cried and said, "You're so brave."

But I wasn't. I was a coward, too. I never faced James, I never asked him *why*. How could he do that? Was it fear? Cowardice?

I heard afterwards that he was sleeping his way systematically around Reading, girls and boys.

It confirmed what I already knew. The James Cooper I thought I knew never existed. He was a figment of my imagination. A false memory, implanted by my own hopes.

But now . . . now as I look back across ten years, I don't know. It's not that I absolve James for the thoughtless cruelty of that text, but I see myself: furious, righteous, and so hard on both of us. Perhaps I absolve myself. For the mistake I made in loving James. I realize how young we were—hardly more than children with the careless cruelty of childhood and the rigid black-and-white morality, too.

There is no gray when you're young. There's only goodies and baddies, right and wrong. The rules are very clear—a playground morality of ethical lines drawn out like a netball pitch, with clear fouls and penalties.

James was wrong.

I had trusted him.

Therefore, I was wrong, too.

But now . . . now I see a frightened child, confronted with an immense moral decision he was not equipped to make. I see my words as he must have seen them—an attempt to shift this irrevocable choice onto his shoulders, a responsibility he was not prepared for, and did not want.

And I see myself—just as frightened, just as ill prepared.

And I feel so very sorry for us both.

When Lamarr comes in the morning, I will tell her. I'll tell her the whole truth. Unpicked like this, in the dying light of the evening, it's not as bad as I feared. It's not a motive for murder, just an old, tired grief. Nina was right.

Then, at last, I sleep.

But when Lamarr comes in the morning, there's a new kind of grimness in her face. There's a colleague hovering behind her, and she's holding something in her hand.

"Nora," she says without preamble, "can you identify this for me?"

"Yes," I say in surprise, "it's my phone. Where did you find it?"

But Lamarr doesn't answer. Instead, she sits, clicks on her tape recorder, and says, in a grave, formal voice, the words I've been dreading.

"Leonora Shaw, we would like to question you as a suspect in the death of James Cooper. You do not have to say anything, but it may harm your defense if you do not mention when questioned something which you later rely on in court. Anything you do say may be given in evidence. You have a right to ask for a solicitor. Do you understand?"

chapter 27

If you're innocent, you have nothing to fear. Right?

Then why am I so frightened?

My previous statements weren't taped, and I hadn't been cautioned. They wouldn't stand up as evidence in court, so the first few minutes are spent going over stuff I already told Lamarr, reestablishing the facts for the purposes of the tape. I don't want a solicitor. I know it's stupid, but I can't get over the feeling that Lamarr is on my side—that I can trust her. If I can only convince her of my innocence, everything will be okay. What could a solicitor possibly do?

Lamarr finishes on the stuff we have already established and then starts on new ground.

"Can you take a look at this phone, please." She holds it out in a sealed plastic bag. "And let me know whether you recognize it?"

"Yes, it's my phone." I resist the urge to chew my nails. The last few days have ground them down to battered stubs.

"You're sure about that?"

"Yes, I recognize the scratch on the casing."

"And your phone number is . . ." She flips through her pad and then reads it out. I nod.

"Yes, that's c-correct."

"I'm interested in the last few calls and texts you made. Can you run me through what you can remember?"

I wasn't expecting this. I can't see what relevance it can possibly have to James's death. Maybe they're trying to corroborate our movements or something? I know they can triangulate locations from mobile phone signals.

I'm struggling to remember.

"Not many. There wasn't really any reception at the cottage. I checked my voice mail at the shooting range . . . and Twitter. Oh, and I returned a call from a bike shop in London; they're servicing my bike. I think that's it."

"No texts?"

"I . . . I don't think so." I'm trying to remember. "No, I'm pretty sure not. I think the last one I sent was to Nina, telling her I was waiting on the train. That was Friday."

She changes tack smoothly.

"I'd like to ask you a bit more about your relationship with James Cooper."

I nod, trying to keep my expression even, helpful. But I've been expecting this. Maybe Clare has woken up. My stomach does a little uneasy shift.

"You met back at school, is that right?"

"Yes. We were about fifteen, sixteen. We dated, briefly, and then we broke up."

"How briefly?"

"Four or five months?"

That's not quite true. We were together for six months. But I've already said "briefly," and six months doesn't sound that brief. I don't want to look like I'm contradicting myself already. Luckily, Lamarr doesn't quiz me about the dates.

"Did you keep in contact after that?" she says.

"No."

She waits for me to elaborate. I wait. Lamarr folds her hands in her lap and looks at me. I don't know what she's getting at, but if there's one thing I'm good at, it's keeping quiet. The pause hangs, heavy in the air. I can hear the tiny percussive tick of her expensive watch, and I wonder briefly where she gets her money from: that skirt wasn't bought on a police officer's salary; neither were the chunky gold earrings. They look real.

Still, it's none of my business. Just something to speculate on as the time ticks past.

But Lamarr can wait, too. She has a kind of feline patience, that quality of unblinking composure as she waits for the mouse to panic and make a bolt for it. In the end, it's her companion who cracks. D.C. Roberts, a big hulk of a man with a fleshy face that seems set in a permanent frown.

"You're telling us you've had no contact with him for ten years," Roberts says brusquely, "and yet he invited you to his wedding?"

Fuck. But there's no point in lying about this. It would take them two minutes to check with Clare's mother or whoever handled the guest list.

"No. Clare invited me to the hen, but I'm not coming to the wedding."

"That's a bit odd, isn't it?" Lamarr comes back in. She's smiling, as if this is girl talk over a cappuccino. Her cheeks are round and rosy, with high cheekbones that make her look like Nefertiti, and her mouth as she smiles is wide and warm and generous.

"Not really," I lie. "I'm James's ex. I imagine Clare thought it would be awkward—for me as much as her."

"So why invite you to the hen, to celebrate her wedding? Wouldn't that be awkward, too?"

"I don't know. You'd have to ask Clare."

"So you've had no contact with James Cooper at all since you broke up?"

"No. No contact."

"Texts? E-mails?"

"No. None."

I'm suddenly not sure where this is going. Are they trying to establish that I hated James? That I couldn't bear to have him near me? My stomach does another uneasy shift, and a little voice in my head whispers, *It's not too late to ask for a lawyer . . .*

"Look," I find myself saying, stress making my voice rise half a tone, "it's hardly unusual not to keep in touch with your exes."

But Lamarr doesn't answer. She switches track again, bewilderingly.

"Can you run me through your movements at the cottage? Were there any times you left the property?"

"Well, we went clay-pigeon shooting," I say uncertainly. "But you know about that."

"I mean by yourself. You went for a run, isn't that right?"

A run? I feel completely out of my depth all of a sudden. I hate not knowing what they're getting at.

"Yes," I say. I pick up a pillow and hug it to my chest. And then, feeling that I should look cooperative, I say, "Twice. Once when we arrived, on Friday, and once on Saturday."

"Can you give me the approximate times?"

I try to think back.

"I think the Friday one was about four thirty maybe? Perhaps a bit later. I remember it was fairly dark. I met Clare on the drive on the way back, about six o'clock. And the Saturday one . . . it was early. Before eight, I think. I can't pin it down much better than that. Definitely not earlier than six a.m.—it was light. Melanie was up—she might remember."

"Okay." Lamarr is writing down the times, not trusting to the tape. "And you didn't use your phone on the runs?"

"No." What the hell is this about? My fingers dig into the soft kapok of the pillow.

"What about Saturday night, did you go out then?"

"No." Then I remember something. "Did they tell you about the footprints?"

"Footprints?" She looks up from her pad, her face puzzled. "What footprints?"

"There were footprints, in the snow. When I came back from my run that first morning. They were leading from the garage to the back door."

"Hm. I'll look into it. Thanks." She makes a note. Then she changes tack again. "Have you remembered anything further about the period after you left the house on Saturday night? When you chased after the car?"

I shake my head.

"I'm sorry. I remember tearing down through the wood . . . I get flashes of cars and broken glass and stuff . . . but no. Nothing really concrete."

"I see." She shuts her notebook and stands up. "Thank you, Nora. Any further questions, Roberts?"

Her companion shakes his head, and then Lamarr gives the time and location for the tape and clicks off the recording and leaves.

I am a suspect.

I sit there trying to process it after they've gone.

Is it because they've found my phone? But what could my phone possibly have to do with James's murder?

And then I realize something, something I should have known before.

I was *always* a suspect.

The only reason they weren't interviewing me under caution before was because the interview was worthless as evidence anyway. With my memory problems, any lawyer could have shot a hole a mile wide in my statement. They wanted intelligence—the information I could provide. And they wanted it quick, enough to risk talking to me when I was in no state to be relied on.

But now the doctors have confirmed I'm lucid, and I'm well enough to be interviewed properly. Now they are starting to build a case. Now . . . now I'm a suspect.

I haven't been arrested. That's one thing to hold on to.

I haven't been charged.

Yet.

If only I could remember those missing few minutes in the wood. What happened? What did I do?

The desperation to remember rises inside me, sticking in my throat like a sob, and I clench my fingers on the soft pillow and bury my face in its clean whiteness, and I *ache* to remember. Without those missing few minutes, how can I hope to convince Lamarr that what I'm saying is true?

I close my eyes, and I try to think myself back there, to the quiet clearing in the forest, to the great glowing blocks of the house, shining out through the dark close-clustered trees. I smell again the scent of fallen pine needles; I feel the cold bite of the snow on my fingers and inside my nose. I remember the sounds of the forest, the soft patter of snow sliding from overladen branches, the hoot of an owl, the sound of an engine disappearing into the darkness.

And I see myself tumbling down that long straight track into the trees, feel the springy softness of the needles beneath my feet.

But I cannot remember what comes next. When I try, it's like I'm trying to snatch at a scene reflected in a pond. Images come, but when I reach for them, they break into a thousand ripples and I find that I'm holding only water.

Something happened in that darkness: to me, Clare, and James. Or some*one*. But who? What?

"Well, Leonora, I'm very pleased with you." Dr. Miller puts away his pen. "I'm a little bit concerned about the time you're still missing, but from what you're saying, those memories are starting to come back, and I don't see any reason to keep you here for much longer. You'll need further checkups, but they can all be arranged by your GP."

Before I can process what he's saying, he's carrying on.

"Do you have anyone at home who can give you a hand?"

What?

"N-no," I manage. "I live alone."

"Well, could you stay with a friend for a few days? Or have a friend come around to yours? You've done amazingly well, but I'm slightly reluctant to let you go home to an empty house."

"I live in London," I say irrelevantly. What can I tell him? I don't have anyone I could foist myself on for a week, and I can't see myself trekking out to Australia to my mother's waiting arms.

"I see. Is there anyone who can give you a lift back?"

I try to think. Nina, maybe. I could ask her to help me get home. But . . . but surely they can't be throwing me out so soon? Suddenly, I'm not sure I'm ready to leave.

"I don't understand," I say to the nurse, after the doctor has picked up his notes and gone out. "No one ever discussed this."

"Don't worry," she says comfortingly. "We won't throw you out with nowhere to go. But we do need the bed and you're no longer at risk, so . . ."

So I am no longer wanted here.

It's strange what a punch to the gut this news is. I realize that in the few short days I've been here, I've become institutionalized, in a way. For all this place feels like a cage, now the door is open, I don't want to leave. I've come to rely on the doctors and nurses and the routine of this place to protect me—from the police, from the reality of what happened.

What will I do, if I'm thrown out? Will Lamarr let me go home?

"You should speak to the police," I find myself saying. I feel strangely detached. "I don't know if they'll want me to leave Northumberland."

"Och, yes, I'd forgotten you were the poor lass who was in the accident. Don't worry, we'll make sure they know."

"D.C. Lamarr," I say. "She's the one who's been coming here." I don't want her to speak to Roberts, with his thick neck and his frown.

"I'll let her know. And don't worry. It won't be today anyway."

After she's gone I try to process what just happened.

I'm going to be thrown out. Maybe as early as tomorrow.

And then what?

Either I will be allowed to go back to London or . . . or I won't. And if I'm not, that means arrest. I try to remember what I know about my rights. If I'm arrested, I can be questioned for . . . what is it? Thirty-six hours? I think they can get a warrant to extend it, but I can't completely remember. Fuck. I'm a crime writer. How can I not know this stuff?

I must phone Nina. But I don't have my phone. I have a bed phone—but you need a bank card to buy call credit, and my wallet and all my belongings are with the police. I could probably call from the nurses' station—I'm sure they'd lend me a phone if it was for something necessary, like getting a lift out of here. But I don't know her number. All my contacts are in my mobile.

I try to recall any numbers I know by heart. I used to know Nina's parents' number—but they've moved. I know my own home number, but that won't help. There's no one there. I used to know our home number by heart, but that was the old house, where I grew up. I don't know Mum's number in Australia. I wish I had someone like Jess—someone I could turn to in any situation and say, without shame, I need you. But I don't. I always thought that being self-sufficient was a strength, but now I realize it's a kind of weakness, too. What the hell can I do? I guess I could ask the nurses to Google my editor—but the thought of facing her like this makes me go cold with shame.

Strangely, the one number I can recall perfectly is James's parents' number. I must have dialed it a hundred times. He was always losing his mobile. And they still live there, I know they do. But I can't call them. Not like this.

When I get back to London I must phone them. I must ask about the funeral. I must . . . I must . . .

I shut my eyes. I will not cry, not again. I can cry when I'm out of here, but for the moment I have to be practical.

I cannot think about James, or his mother and father.

And then my gaze alights on the paper cup beside my bed. Matt's number. I rip the cup carefully and fold the scribbled mobile number into my pocket. I can't phone him. He'll be on his way back to London. But it's an odd comfort to think that I have, at least, one person I could call, in a dire emergency.

Two days ago I had no idea he existed. And now, he's my one link to the outside world.

It will be okay, though. Nina will come back, or Lamarr will. I'll be able to get a message out to them.

I just have to wait.

I am still sitting, staring into space and biting my battered nails, when a nurse puts her head around the door.

"Call for you, duckie. I'll put them through on the bed phone."

She gestures to the white plastic phone suspended on an arm beside my bed and then slips out.

Who can it be? Who knows I'm here? Could it be my mum? I look at the clock. No—it would be the middle of the night in Australia.

Then, like a cold hand on the back of the neck, a thought comes to me. James's parents. They must know I'm here.

The phone starts to ring. For a moment I lose all courage, and I almost don't answer it.

But then I grit my teeth and force myself to pick up the receiver.

"Hello?"

There's a pause, and then a voice says, "Nora? Is that you?"

It's Nina. Relief floods through me, and for an irrational second I wonder about telepathy.

"Nina!" It's so good to hear her voice, to know I'm not stranded here. "Thank God you called. They might be chucking me out—and I realized I don't have your number or anything. Is that why you're calling?"

"No," she says shortly. "Listen, I'm not going to beat around the bush. Flo's tried to commit suicide."

chapter 28

For a minute I can't speak.

"Nora?" Nina says after a moment. "Nora, are you still there? Shit, has this thing cut me off?"

"Yes," I say dazedly. "Yes, yes, I'm here. I'm just— Jesus."

"I didn't want to tell you like this, but I didn't want you to hear it from one of the nurses or the police or something. She's being taken to your hospital."

"Oh my God. Is she—is she going to be okay?"

"I think so, yes. I found her, in the bathroom at the B and B where we're staying. She's been pretty off the wall, but I didn't realize . . . I . . ." She sounds shaken, and I realize for the first time the strain that she has probably been under. While Clare and I are in hospital, avoiding the brunt of the interrogations, Nina, Flo, and Tom have presumably been questioned around the clock. "It was pure luck I came back earlier than I said I would. I should've noticed. It's been horrible, but I never thought—"

"It's not your fault."

"I'm a bloody doctor, Nora." Her voice at the other end of the phone is anguished. "Okay, it's a while since I've done anything in mental health, but we're supposed to remember our basic training. *Shit.* I should have seen this coming."

"But she'll be okay?"

"I don't know. She took a bunch of sleeping pills, combined with some Valium and a hell of a lot of paracetamol, washed down with whiskey. It's the paracetamol that's worrying me—it's pretty nasty stuff—you can wake up feeling just fine in hospital and then your liver packs up just when you've decided suicide really isn't going to fit in with your spring calendar."

"Oh my God. Poor Flo. Did she say— Did she give a reason?"

"She just left a note saying she couldn't cope any longer."

"Do you think—" I stop. I can't think how to ask this.

"What? That she's got a guilty conscience?" I almost hear Nina's shrug down the phone. "I don't know. But whatever you think happened, she was holding the gun. I don't think Lamarr and Roberts went particularly easy on her."

"How did she get the pills?"

"She got prescribed the diazepam and the sleeping pills. She— We've all been under a lot of stress, Nora. She saw a man get shot. That's PTSD kind of stuff."

I shut my eyes. I've been safe here, wrapped in my cocoon of ignorance, while Flo has been falling apart.

"She was so obsessed," I say slowly. "Do you remember, the way she kept going on about giving Clare the *perfect* hen."

"I know," Nina says. "Believe me, we heard a lot about that the last couple of days. She's not done much except for cry and blame herself for what happened."

"But what did happen, Nina?" I realize suddenly that I'm gripping the white plastic receiver so hard that my fingers hurt. "Lamarr thinks it's murder. I know she does. They're asking weird questions about my phone. They've given me a formal caution. I'm a suspect."

"We're *all* suspects," Nina says wearily. "We were in a house when a man got shot and died. It's not just you. Fuck, I wish this were over. I'm missing Jess so much I can barely think. Why the fuck did we agree to this, Nora?"

She sounds tired. Tired not just of this, but of everything. And I can see her, suddenly, her and Tom alone in their B and B rooms, waiting to be questioned, waiting for answers, waiting for news on Flo and Clare and everything else.

They've taken her phone, too. They've asked her not to leave. She's just as trapped as me. Trapped by what happened in that house.

"Look, I've got to go," Nina says at last. "This is a crappy pay-as-you-go mobile, and I don't think there's much credit on it. But I'll phone back and leave the number at the desk, yeah? Tell them to call me if you get kicked out."

"Okay," I say at last. There's a catch in my throat, and I cough, trying to hide it. "Take care of yourself, you hear me? And don't beat yourself up over Flo. She'll be okay."

"I really don't know if she will," Nina says. Her voice is bleak. "I saw a few paracetamol overdoses when I was a med student, and I know how it goes. But thanks for trying. And Nora—" She stops.

"Yes?" I say.

"I— Oh fuck, look, it's pointless me saying this. Forget it."

"What?"

"I was just going to say—try to remember what happened after you left the house, yeah? There's a lot riding on this. No pressure," she says with a slightly shaky laugh.

"Yeah, I know," I say. "Bye, Nina."

"Bye."

She hangs up, and I rub my face. "No pressure," Nina said. I assume it was her idea of a joke. She knows as well as I do the pressure that we're under. All of us.

I must remember. I must remember.

I shut my eyes and try to remember.

"Nora." A hand on my shoulder, shaking me awake. "Nora."

I blink and try to sit up, try to process where I am and what's going on.

It's Lamarr. I've been asleep.

"What time is it?" I say blearily.

"It's nearly noon," she says. Her voice is crisp. There's no hint of a smile now. In fact, she looks very grave. D.C. Roberts is behind her, his glower fixed and unmoving. He looks like he was born with a pencil and a sour expression. It's impossible to imagine him cuddling a baby or kissing a lover.

"We'd like to ask you some more questions," Lamarr says. "Do you want a minute?"

"No, no, I'm okay," I say. I shake my head, trying to wake myself. Lamarr watches. "Go ahead," I say.

Lamarr nods, clicks on the tape recorder, and repeats the caution. Then she gets out a piece of paper.

"Nora, I'd like you to read this. It's a transcript of e-mails and text messages taken from your and James's phones over the last few days."

She hands the paper to me, and I sit up straighter and rub the sleep from my eyes, trying to focus on the closely typed sheets of paper. They're a list of texts, each annotated with the number they were sent from and a date, time, and some other information I can't interpret—GPS location maybe?

The first one is marked with my number, and a time of Friday at 4:52 p.m.

LEONORA SHAW: James, it's me, Leo. Leo Shaw.

JAMES COOPER: Leo?? Christ is that really you?

LEONORA SHAW: Yes, it's me. I really need to see you. I'm at Clare's hen weekend. Please can you come up? It's urgent.

JAMES COOPER: What, seriously?

JAMES COOPER: Has C told you?

LEONORA SHAW: Yes. Please come up. I can't say what this is about over the phone but I really need to speak to you.

JAMES COOPER: You really need me to come? Can't it wait until you're back in London?

LEONORA SHAW: No. It's really urgent. Please. I've not asked you for anything but you owe me this. Tomorrow? Sunday's too late.

There is a long pause. The next reply from James is date-stamped Friday, 11:44 p.m.

JAMES COOPER: I've got a matinee & an evening tomorrow I won't be finished at the theater till 10/11. I cd drive up but it'll take me 5+ hours. I'll be there in the middle of the night. You really want me to do this?

The reply is date-stamped Saturday at 7:21 a.m.

LEONORA SHAW: Yes

There's another pause. James's reply comes through at 2:32 p.m.

JAMES COOPER: ok.

LEONORA SHAW: THANK YOU. Leave your car in the lane. When you get to the house go round the back. I'll leave the kitchen door unlocked. My room is at the top of the stairs, second door on the right. I'll explain everything when you get here.

There is another long pause. James's reply is marked 5:54 p.m., and it almost breaks my heart.

JAMES COOPER: Ok. I'm so sorry Leo—for everything. Jx

And then, at 11:18 p.m.:

JAMES COOPER: I'm on my way.

And then that's it.

When I look up at Lamarr, I know that my eyes are swimming, and my voice is cracked and mute.

"The interviewee has finished reading the transcript," she says quietly, for the benefit of the tape. And then, "Well, Nora? Any explanation? Did you think we wouldn't find these? Deleting them was pretty pointless, you know; we recovered them off the server."

"I—I—" I try. I take a deep breath, force myself to speak. "I d-didn't send these."

"Really." It's not a question, just a flat, slightly tired acknowledgment.

"Really. You have to believe me." I know, even as I begin to gabble, that it's hopeless. "Someone else could have sent them. Someone could have cloned my SIM card."

"Believe me, we're used to that, Nora. These were sent from your phone, and the date stamps on your replies correspond to your runs in the forest, and the trip to the clay-pigeon range."

"But I didn't take my phone on my runs!"

"The GPS evidence is pretty conclusive. We know that you went out of the house and up the hill until you got a signal."

"I didn't send them," I repeat, hopelessly. I want to crawl back into bed and pull the covers over my head. Lamarr is looking down at me from her full height, no cozy sitting on the bed now. Her face is set, like carved ebony. There's compassion in her face but also a kind of rigor that I never noticed until now. Her face has the sort of unsparing detachment I imagine an angel might show—not an angel of mercy, but an angel of judgment. One come not to comfort, but to mete out justice.

"We've also got the report back on the analysis of the car, Nora. We know what happened."

"What happened?" I am trying not to panic, but I know my voice has got shaky and shrill. They know. They know something that I don't. "*What* happened?"

"Clare picked you up. And when she was safely on the road and traveling at speed, you grabbed the wheel. Do you remember? You grabbed the wheel and forced the car off the road."

"No."

"Your fingerprints are all over the wheel. The scratches on your hands, the broken nails—you were fighting Clare. She has defensive wounds on her hands and arms. Your skin was under her nails."

"No."

But even as I say it, I get a flash, like a nightmare breaking into day: Clare's terrified face, green-lit by the dashboard glow, my hands grappling with hers.

"No!" I say, but there is a sob in my voice. What have I done?

"What did Clare tell you, Nora? Did she tell you that she was marrying James?"

I can't speak. I just shake my head, but it's not a denial, I cannot deal with this, I cannot take these questions.

"The interviewee is shaking her head," Roberts puts in gruffly.

"Flo told us what happened," Lamarr says relentlessly. "Clare asked her to keep it under wraps. She was planning to tell you this weekend, wasn't she?"

Oh God.

"You've never had another relationship since you broke up with him, isn't that right?"

No. No. No.

"You were obsessed with him. Clare put off telling you because she was worried about your reaction. She was right to be worried, wasn't she?"

Please let me wake from this nightmare.

"And so you lured him up to the cottage, and then you shot him."

No. Oh Jesus. I must speak. I must say something to make Lamarr shut up, to make these smooth plum-colored vicious accusations go away.

"It's true, isn't it, Nora?" she says, and her voice is soft, and gentle, and finally, at last, she sits on the end of my bed and puts out her hand. "Isn't it?"

I look up. My eyes are swimming, but through it I see Lamarr's face, her sympathetic eyes, her heavy earrings, impossibly heavy for such a slender neck to support. I hear the click and whir of the tape recorder.

I find my voice.

"I want to see a solicitor."

chapter 29

I try to think back to the time stamp of the first text, the one I supposedly sent to James, the one sent from my phone—4:52 p.m. I was out on my run. My phone was unprotected, up in my room. So who else had access to it?

Clare hadn't arrived yet—I know that for sure since I met her in the drive coming up to the cottage, but it could have been any of the others.

But why? Why would they want to destroy me like this—destroy James, destroy *Clare*?

I try to think through the possibilities.

Melanie seems the least likely. Yes, she was there while I was out on my run; in fact, she was one of the few people who was up and about at the time of the second run. But I can't believe that she could possibly care about James or me enough to do this. Why risk everything to incriminate someone she'd never even met? And besides, she was gone by the time James arrived, by the time . . . by the time . . . I shut my eyes, trying to shut out the pictures of James lying shattered and bloody on the wooden floor. *She could still have swapped the cartridge,* a tiny voice whispers in the back of my mind. *She could have done that anytime. And maybe that would explain why she left in such a hurry . . . ?* It's true. She could have swapped the cartridge. But surely she couldn't have predicted the rest—the open door, the gun, the struggle . . .

Tom then. He had the means—he was there in the house when my phone was, he was there at the shooting. And—it suddenly strikes me—he was the one who sent Clare driving off into the forest alone. What did make her suddenly leave like that? We have only his word about what he said to her, and now, in the light of what's happened, the fact that she misheard him so radically seems a little convenient. Would she really just go haring off into the night like that, without double-checking? Nina was the doctor, after all. She was James's best chance of survival.

What if he *told* her to go? He could have said anything—that Nina wasn't coming, that she'd said to get going and wait for her at the hospital. As for motive . . . I think back to the drunken conversation we had about his husband and James. If only I'd paid attention. If only I'd listened! But I was bored—bored by the litany of names I didn't recognize, and the bitchy theater politics. Is it possible that there's something there—some grudge between Bruce and James? Or maybe—maybe quite the opposite.

It seems unlikely, though. And even if he *did* send Clare off into the night, what would it achieve? He couldn't have predicted what would happen.

Most important, though, he could not have known about my past with James. Unless—unless someone told him.

Clare could have told him. I can't get away from that. But the thing is this: this murder has been set up in such a way that it didn't just destroy James; it is destroying me and Clare, too. It doesn't just feel like collateral damage; there is something incredibly malicious and *personal* about the way I have been deliberately dragged in, reminding us both of long-forgotten sores. Who would do that? *Why* would anyone do that?

I try to look at this like the plot of one of my books. If I were writing this, I could imagine a reason for Tom to hurt James. And

I could probably manufacture a motive for him to hurt Clare in the process. But me? Why go to all these lengths to bring in someone he doesn't even know? The only person who could possibly want to do that would be someone who knows all three of us. Someone who was there at the time it all blew up. Someone like . . .

Nina.

But my mind shies away from that, flinching from the idea. Nina can be odd—sharp and sarcastic and often thoughtless. But there's no way she'd do something like that. Surely? I think of her face, set in stern lines like grief, as she remembered the gunshot wounds she'd treated in Colombia. She lives to help people. Surely she'd never do this?

But something is whispering in my ear, a little voice, reminding me of how callous Nina can be. I remember her saying once, very drunk, "Surgeons don't care about *people,* not in a touchy-feely way. They're like mechanics: they just want to cut them up, see how they work, dismantle them. Your average surgeon's like a little boy who takes apart his dad's watch to see how it works and then can't get it back together. The more skilled you get, the better you get at reassembling the parts. But we always leave a scar."

And I think, too, about her occasional shocking flashes of contempt for Clare. I think about her savagery that night when she talked about how Clare wanted to push and prod and get off on other people's reactions, her bitterness about the way Clare outed her all those years ago. Is there something there, some reason she's never forgiven Clare?

And finally, I think about her actions on the first night we arrived. The I Have Never game. I remember the deliberate malice of her drawling, *I have never fucked James Cooper.*

Suddenly, in the overheated little sauna of a room, I feel cold. Because *that* is the kind of cruel personal spite that lies behind this whole crazy situation. It wasn't just curiosity about James and me. It wasn't thoughtlessness. It was deliberate cruelty—to me and to Clare.

Who is pushing and prodding and getting off on people's reactions now?

But I shove that thought away. I will not think about Nina like this. I will not. This will send me mad if I let it.

Flo. Flo is the name I keep coming back to. Flo was there from the beginning. Flo invited the guests. Flo held the gun. Flo was the one who claimed it was loaded with blanks.

Flo—with her strange obsession with Clare. With her strange unstable intensity. She could have found out about James and me at any point—she's Clare's best friend, after all, has been since university. What more likely than that Clare would have confided in her about James and me?

Is that why she's taken an overdose? Has she realized what she's done?

I am looking up, looking into space as I think all this out, and then suddenly my eyes focus on something, on a movement outside the door.

And I realize what it is.

The guard is back—the police guard at my door. Only this time I have absolutely zero doubt: they are not there to protect me. They are there to keep me in. I'm not going home when they discharge me, I'm going to a police station. I will be arrested, and questioned, and most likely charged if they think they can make this stick.

Coldly, dispassionately, I try to examine the last person at the hen night: the case against myself.

I was there. I could have made those texts to James. I could have swapped the live round for the blanks. I had my hand on the gun when Flo fired. What could be more easy than nudging the barrel to ensure it was pointing at James as he came up the stairs?

And, more important, I was there at the second half of James's murder. I was in the car when it drove off the road.

What the hell happened in that car? Why can't I remember?

I think back to what Dr. Miller said: *Sometimes the brain suppresses events that we're not quite ready to deal with. I suppose it's a . . . coping mechanism, if you will.*

What is it that my brain cannot cope with? Is it the truth?

I realize I'm shivering as if I'm cold, even though the heat of the hospital is as stifling as ever, and I pull Nina's cardigan from the foot of the bed and huddle it around myself, breathing in her scent of fags and perfume, trying to steady myself.

It's not the thought of being arrested and charged that has shocked me so much—I still don't believe that will really happen. Surely, *surely* if I just explain everything, they will believe me?

What has really knocked me off balance is this: someone hates me enough to do this. But who?

I don't let myself think about the final possibility. It's one too horrible for me to allow it into my mind, except in tiny niggling whispers when I'm thinking about other things.

But as I huddle down beneath the thin hospital blanket, Nina's cardigan around my shoulders, one of those whispers comes: *What if it's true?*

The day goes slowly, as if I'm moving through air made of treacle. It feels like the nightmares I sometimes have where my limbs are too heavy to move. Something is pursuing me, and I have to get away, but I'm stuck in mud, my legs are numb and slow, and all I can do is wade painfully through the dream, with the unspecified horror behind me getting closer and closer.

My little room feels more and more like a prison cell, with the narrow hatch of reinforced glass, and the guard outside the door.

If they release me, I know now what will happen. The texts are enough evidence to hold me, along with the fact that I denied having sent them. Maybe even enough evidence to charge me.

I remember, a long time ago, when I wrote my first book, speaking to a policeman about interviewing techniques. *You listen,* he said. *You listen for the lie.*

Lamarr and Roberts have found their lie: I told them I did not send those texts. And yet, there they are.

I try to eat, but the food is tasteless, and I leave most of it on the tray. I try to do a crossword, but the words fall away from me; they are just type on a page, and my mind's eye is being invaded by other pictures.

Me, in the dock at court, in a prison cell.

Flo, on life support, somewhere in this very hospital.

Clare, flat on a bed, her eyes moving slowly beneath her closed lids.

James, in a pool of spreading blood.

Suddenly, my nostrils are filled with a flashback to the smell of it—the butcher's shop smell of his blood on my hands and on my pajamas and leaching into the floor . . .

I throw off the covers and stand up. I walk to the bathroom to splash my face with water, trying to wash away the stench of blood and the invading memories. But the memories that I want don't come. Is it possible . . . is it possible I *did* send those texts, and I have just buried it along with whatever happened in the car?

Who can I trust, if I can't even trust myself?

I put my face in my hands, and when I stand, I look at myself in the mirror, beneath the unforgiving fluorescent light. The bruises around my eyes are still there, but fading. I look jaundiced, hollow-eyed. There are dark patches in the hollows at the bridge of my nose, and beneath my lower lids, but I no longer look like a freak. If I had concealer, I could cover the shadows up. But I don't. I never thought to ask Nina for that.

I look thin, and old. My face is crumpled where I have been lying on the hard hospital sheets.

I think of the me I am inside. In my head I have been sixteen for nearly ten years. In my head my hair is still long. I find myself going to sweep it back in moments of stress, but it's not there.

In my head James is still alive. I cannot believe that he isn't.

Would they let me see his body?

I shiver, rake my wet hand through my crumpled hair, and rub my palms on the gray jogging bottoms.

Then I turn and leave the bathroom.

As I come out of the en suite, it strikes me that something is different. For a moment I can't work out what it is: my book is still there on the bed. My flip-flops are beneath. My water jug is half full on the locker, and the file of notes is still stuck crookedly into the holder at the foot of the bed.

Then I see.

The guard is not there.

I walk to the door, peering out through the wire-hatched pane. The chair is there. A cup of tea is there, steaming gently. But no guard.

A little prickle of adrenaline runs through me, making the hairs on my neck shiver. My body knows what I am about to do, even before my mind has processed it. My fingers are reaching for the flip-flops, easing them on. My hands are buttoning the buttons of Nina's cardigan. Lastly, I reach for the two ten-pound notes, still lying, folded, on the corner of the locker.

My heart is thumping as I press gently on the panel of the door, expecting at any moment to hear a shout of *Stop!* or just a nurse saying, "Are you all right, dear?"

But no one says anything.

No one does anything.

I walk out of the room and down the corridor, past the other bays, with my feet in my flip-flops going *plip, plip, plip* against the linoleum floor.

Past the nursing station—there is no one there. A nurse is inside the little office doing paperwork, but her back is to the glass.

Plip plip plip. Through the double doors and out into the main corridor, where the air smells less of Lysol and more of industrial cooking from the kitchens down the corridor. I walk a little faster. There is a sign saying WAY OUT, pointing around a corner.

As I turn it, my heart almost stops. There is the police officer, standing just outside the men's toilets, muttering into his radio. For a moment I falter. I nearly turn tail and run back to my room before he can discover I'm gone.

But I don't. I recover myself, and I walk on past, *plip, plip, plip,* with my heart going *bang, bang, bang* in time with my steps, and he doesn't give me a second glance.

"Roger," he says as I pass him. "Copy that."

And then I round the corner, and he's gone.

I keep walking—not too fast, not too slow. Surely someone will stop me? Surely you can't just walk out of a hospital like this?

There's a sign saying EXIT, pointing along the corridor between cubicles of beds. I'm almost there.

And then, as I'm almost at the last door before the lift lobby, I see something, *someone,* through the narrow pane of glass.

It's Lamarr.

My breath catches in my throat, and, almost without thinking, I duck backwards into a closed cubicle, praying that the occupant is asleep.

The curtains are already drawn, but I edge them stealthily around myself, my heart banging in my throat, and stand, waiting, listening. There's the noise of the main ward doors opening and closing, and then I hear her heels going *click, clack, click, clack* down the linoleum floor. At the nurses' station, almost opposite the cubicle where I'm hiding, the steps pause, and I stand, hands trembling, waiting for the curtain to be ripped back, waiting for the discovery.

But then she says something polite to the matron on duty, and I hear the heels go *click, clack, click, clack* down the corridor towards the toilets and my room.

Oh thank God, thank God, thank God.

My legs are weak and shaking with relief, and for a minute I don't think I can stand. But I have to. I have to get out of here before she gets to my room and realizes I'm gone. I suddenly wish I'd thought to put pillows in the bed or draw the little curtain across the window.

I take two or three deep breaths, trying to calm myself, and then I turn, ready to apologize to the occupant of the cubicle behind me.

But when I see who is in the bed, my heart almost stops.

It's Clare.

Clare—lying with her eyes closed, her golden hair spread out across the pillow.

She is very pale, and her face is even more badly cut up than mine. There's a monitor clipped onto her finger, and more wires leading under the blankets.

Oh my God. Oh Clare.

For a moment—and I know it's crazy, but I can't stop myself—my hand strays towards her face, and I brush a strand of hair away from her lips. Her eyes flicker beneath her lids, and I hold my breath, but then she relaxes back into whatever state she's in—sleep? coma?—and I let out a gasping sigh.

"Clare," I whisper, very soft, so that no one will hear, but perhaps it will filter through into her dreams. "Clare, it's me, Nora. I swear, I'm going to find out the truth. I'm going to find out what happened. I promise."

She says nothing. Her eyes shift under her lids, and I remember Flo at the séance, blindly searching for something none of us could see.

I think my heart might break.

But I can't stop. They could be looking for me right now.

Carefully, stealthily, I peer out of the closed cubicle curtains. The corridor is empty—the nurses' station is unmanned, they are all dealing with patients, and the matron has disappeared.

I slip out, closing Clare's curtains behind me, and then I almost run for the doors at the end of the ward, and stumble out into the lift lobby.

I press the buttons, not once, but five, ten, fifteen times, pressing again and again, as if it will make the lifts come faster.

Then there's a sudden grating noise and a *ping,* and the farthest lift doors open. I half walk, half run inside, my heart thudding. A porter is pushing a woman in a wheelchair and hissing Lady Gaga through his teeth. Please, please let me make it.

The lift bumps to a halt, and I stand back to let the porter and the woman in the chair out first, and then follow the signs to the main entrance. A bored-looking woman is sitting at the desk flicking through a copy of *Hello.*

As I draw level with her, her phone starts to ring, and I cannot stop myself walking a little faster.

Don't pick it up. Don't pick it up.

She picks it up.

"Hello, reception desk."

I am walking too fast, I know I am, but I can't stop myself. I must look like a patient. How can she not notice I'm wearing flip-flops, for Christ's sake? Normal people, visitors, don't wear flip-flops in November. Not with gray jogging bottoms and a blue knitted cardigan.

She is going to stop me—I know it. She's going to say something, ask me if I'm okay. The two ten-pound notes clutched in my fist are damp with sweat.

"Really?" the receptionist says sharply as I draw level. She winds the phone cord around one finger. "Yes, yes, all right. I'll keep an eye out."

My heart is in my mouth. She knows. I can't bear it.

But she doesn't look up. She's nodding. Maybe it's not me they're talking about.

I'm almost at the door. There's a sign telling people to use the alcohol rub on entry and exit. Should I stop? Will someone notice more if I stop, or more if I don't?

I don't stop.

At the desk the woman is still talking and shaking her head.

I am in the revolving door. For a moment I have a brief flashing fantasy that it will stop midcycle, that I will be trapped in a triangle of air, with maybe just a sliver of a gap to the outside, enough to reach an arm out, but not escape.

But of course it doesn't happen. The door continues its smooth revolution.

The cold air hits me like a blessing.

I am free.

I am out of the hospital.

I have escaped.

chapter 30

The air is cold in my face, and I feel completely lost. This place is totally strange to me—and I realize suddenly and piercingly that I was brought here unconscious and have no idea how I got here or how to get away.

I'm shivering after the heat of the hospital, and there are flecks of snow on the breeze. I look up, as if searching for a miracle, and one comes, in the form of a sign saying TAXIS and an arrow.

I walk slowly, shiveringly, around the corner of the building, and there, at the sign saying TAXI QUEUE STARTS HERE, is a single cab, light on. A man is inside, at least I think he is; it's hard to see through the fog on the windows.

I limp closer—the flip-flops are starting to chafe the inner side of my foot—and knock on the window. It rolls down a crack, and a cheerful brown face grins at me.

"What can I do you for, love?" he asks. He is a Sikh, his turban a smart black, with a pin in the center with his taxi company's logo on. His accent is a disconcerting mix of Punjabi and Newcastle that momentarily makes me want to laugh. Thank God I don't.

"I—I need to get to . . ." I suddenly realize I have no idea where to go. Back to London?

No.

"I need to get to the Glass House," I say. "It's a cottage, a house, just outside Stanebridge. Do you know the village?"

He nods and puts down his paper.

"Aye, I know it. Hop in, love."

But I don't. In spite of the cold, and the fact that I'm shivering hard now, I hesitate, my hand on the door handle.

"How much will it be, please? I've only got twenty quid."

"It's twenty-five normally," he says, "but for you, I'll say twenty."

Thank God. I manage a smile, though my face feels like it's frozen, and might crack with the effort.

"Th-thank you," I say, not stammering now, but my teeth chattering with cold.

"Get in, love." He opens the door behind him. "Or you'll freeze. Hop in, now."

I get in.

The car is like a cocoon of warmth that folds around me. It smells of worn plastic and pine air freshener and old cigarettes, the smell of every taxi everywhere, and I want to curl into the soft warmth of its seats and go to sleep and never wake up.

My fingers as I buckle my belt are trembling, and I realize how tired I am, how weak my muscles are after my hospital stay.

"Sorry," I say, as he glances back to make sure I'm buckled up. "Sorry. I'm nearly there."

"No worries, love. No hurry."

And then the seat belt shuts with a reassuring click, and I sit back, feeling my body ache with tiredness.

The driver starts the engine. I close my eyes. I am away.

"Eh, love. Wake up, miss."

I open my eyes, confused and bleary. Where am I? Not at home. Not in the hospital.

It takes a minute before I realize that I'm in the backseat of the taxi, in my hospital clothes, and the car has stopped.

"We're here," he says. "But I can't get up to the house. The road's blocked."

I blink, and wipe the condensation off the window. He's right. A roadblock has been put across the lane, two aluminum crowd-control barriers lashed together with police tape.

"It's all right." I rub the sleep out of the corners of my eyes and feel in my pocket for the money. "Here you go, twenty, was that right?"

He takes the money, but says, "Are you sure you'll be all right, love? Looks like the house is shut up."

"I'll be fine."

Will I? I have to be. There must be a way in. I imagine the police will have secured the property, but I can't believe they will have turned it into Fort Knox, not out here. There's no one to come and disturb the scene.

The taxi driver's face is unhappy as I get out of the car, and he watches me, the engine idling, as I edge around the barrier. I don't want him to. I can't bear him to see me stumbling up the rutted track in my pathetic flip-flops. Instead, I stand with my hands on the barrier, trying not to shiver, and wave at him determinedly.

He winds down the window, his breath gusting white into the cold air.

"Are you sure you're all right? I can stay if you like, tek you back to Stanebridge if there's nobody about. I won't charge. It's on me way back anyway."

"No, thanks," I say. I grit my teeth, trying not to let them chatter. "I'm fine. Thanks. Good-bye, now."

He nods, still unhappy, and then revs the engine, and I watch as his car disappears into the falling dusk, the red taillights illuminating the falling snow.

Jesus, this drive is long. I had forgotten how long. I remember the run, when I met Clare halfway up, my legs tired and aching and my skin cold.

That was nothing to this. What has happened to my muscles in hospital?

I'm not even halfway up, and my legs are trembling with those muscle shakes that come after you've pushed yourself too hard and too fast. My feet in the hard plastic flip-flops are bleeding, but they're so numb I can't feel any pain. I only know what has happened from the smears of red that mingle with the flecks of snow.

The mud, at least, has frozen, so I'm not fighting against the cloying lumps sticking to my feet. But when I stumble into a particularly deep rut, there's a crack, and my foot goes through the thin crust of ice into the freezing pool of muddy water beneath.

I gasp and make a kind of squeaking whimper as I pull my foot painfully out through the sharp ice. It is a thin pathetic sound, like a mouse being caught by an owl.

I am so cold. I am so very, very cold.

Have I been very stupid?

But I have to carry on. I'm halfway. There's no sense in going back—even if I could flag down someone on the road, where would I go? Back to the hospital and the waiting cuffs of Lamarr? I've run away, absconded. I have to see this through. There is no way back.

I force my feet, one in front of the other, my arms wrapped around myself for warmth, thanking God and Nina for the blue cardigan, which is the only thing keeping me from hypothermia. The wind blows again, a low moaning howl through the trees, and I hear the snow shake and patter to the ground.

One more step.

And one more after that.

I cannot tell how close I am—with the house empty, there's no glowing lights to guide me. I have no sense of how long I've been walking in this bitter cold. Only that I have to keep going—because if I don't, I will die.

One more step.

There are pictures in my head as I get closer. Flo, her face twisted with fear, the gun across her chest. Nina's horrified expression, her bloodstained hands as she tried to stanch the flow.

James. James lying in a pool of his own blood, dying.

I know now what he was trying to say, when he said *te . . . Leo?*

It wasn't "tell." It was "text." He was asking me why I'd brought him here. And why I'd let him die like this.

He came for me. He came because I asked him.

Did I ask him?

I'm no longer sure. Oh my God, I'm cold.

It's hard to keep things straight in my head.

I remember the texts Lamarr showed me on that printed paper, and I'm no longer sure if I'm remembering them from when she showed me, or before that.

Did I ask James to come?

I didn't know that Clare was marrying James until she told me in the car. I didn't know. So why would I have texted him?

I must cling to that—I must cling to what I'm sure of.

It *must* have been Flo. She was the only person who could have controlled all this—who chose the guests, who picked the cottage, who knew about the gun.

She was in the house when the texts were sent.

She knew I'd gone for a run.

I think again of her strange intensity, of her huge, explosive, terrifying love for Clare. Is it possible that she thought she might lose Clare to James? That she couldn't bear for him to come between them? And what better person to pin the blame on than me, James's ex-girlfriend, Clare's former best friend.

And then . . . then she realized what she had done. That she'd destroyed her friend as well as her rival. That she had ruined Clare's life.

And she couldn't take it anymore.

Oh my God, I'm so cold. And so tired. There's a fallen tree by the side of the lane. I could sit on it, just for a minute, just to stop the shaking in my legs.

Step by laborious step I make my way to it, then sink down onto its rough moss-covered side. I huddle my body down to my knees, breathing into my legs, desperately trying to conserve some warmth.

I shut my eyes.

I wish I could sleep.

No.

The voice comes from somewhere outside me. I know it's not real, and yet I hear it in my head.

No.

I want to sleep.

No.

If I sleep, I will die. I know that. But I don't care anymore. I am so tired.

No.

I want to sleep.

But something won't let me. Something inside me won't let me rest.

It's not a desire to live—I don't care about that anymore. James is dead. Clare is hurt. Flo is dying. There is only one thing left—and that is the truth.

I will not die. I will not die because someone has to do this—has to get to the truth of what happened.

I get up. My knees are shaking so much that I can hardly stand, but I do, steadying myself with a hand on the fallen tree.

I take a step.

And another.

I will keep going.

I will keep going.

chapter 31

I don't know how long it takes me. The hours seem to drift together, blurring into the snow that is speckling the frozen mud. I am tired—so tired that I can't think, and my eyes water as I walk into the wind that has begun to blow.

My face is quite numb, and my eyes are wet and blurred when, at last, I look up, and there it is: the Glass House.

It's no longer the great golden beacon I saw that first night—instead, it's dark and silent, blending into the trees, almost invisible. A half moon has risen, and it reflects off the bedroom window at the front, the bedroom that Tom slept in. There's a frost halo around it, and I know the night is only going to get colder.

The darkness is not the only difference. There's police tape across the door, and the broken window at the top of the stairs has been boarded over with a kind of metal grille, the sort you see on vacant houses in rough areas.

I walk the last few painful yards across the gravel and stand, shivering and staring at the blank glass wall in front of me. Now I'm here, I'm not sure I can do this, go inside, revisit where James died. But I have to. Not just because of James, not just because it's the only way I will ever find out the truth about what happened. But because if I don't get inside, into shelter, I will die of exposure.

The front door is locked, and there are no windows I can force.

For a moment I pick up a rock, and consider the huge glass wall of the living room. I can see inside, to the cold, dead wood burner and the flat blackness of the TV screen. I imagine heaving the rock at the giant pane—but I don't. It's not just the huge noise and destruction, but I don't think it would break—the pane is double, maybe even triple glazed. It took a shotgun blast to break the one in the hall; I'm pretty sure my puny rock would just bounce off this one.

I drop the rock and make my way slowly, painfully around to the back of the house. My feet are totally numb, and I stumble more than once, seeing the blood coming up between my toes as I do. I push away the thought of how I will get away from here—I can't walk, that's for sure. But I have a horrible feeling it will be in a police car. Or worse.

The back of the house looks equally unpromising. I try the long sliding French door to the rear of the living room, prizing my nails around the flat glass panel and trying to pull it sideways, hoping, desperately, that the catch is not locked. But it stays firm, and all I manage to do is bruise my fingers. I look up at the sheer side of the house. Could I climb up to the balcony where Nina smoked?

For a minute I consider it—there's a zinc drainpipe. But then reality bites. I'm kidding myself. There's no way I could climb that slippery glass wall, even with climbing shoes and a harness, let alone in flip-flops and with numb fingers. I was always the first person to fail the climbing ropes at school, hanging there pathetically, my skinny arms stretched above my head, before I dropped like a stone into a crumpled heap on the rubber mat, while other girls swarmed to the top and smacked the wooden bar overhead with the flat of their palm.

There's no rubber mat here. And the zinc pipe is slipperier and more treacherous than a knotted gym rope. If I fell, it'd be all over—I'd be lucky to get away with a broken ankle.

No. The balcony is not going to work.

At last, almost without hope, I try the back door.

And it swings open.

I feel something prickle across the back of my neck: shock, disbelief, a kind of fierce elation. I can't believe it. I can't believe the police didn't lock it. Can it really be this easy, after everything else has been so hard?

There's police tape across the opening, but I duck under it and half walk, half crawl inside. I straighten up, almost expecting sirens to go off, or a policeman to stand up from a seat in the corner. But the house is dark and quiet, the only movement a few flakes of snow scudding across the slate floor.

I put my hand out to swing the door shut, but it doesn't close properly. It hits the frame, but bounces back open. I grab it, to try again, and as I do I notice something. There's a piece of tape across the tongue of the latch, preventing it from shutting completely.

Suddenly, I understand why the door kept swinging open that night—why, even after we locked it, it was never secure. The lock is the kind that just immobilizes the door handle, stops it from turning the latch. But if the latch itself is pushed back, the handle is useless. It feels stiff when you rattle it, but there's nothing holding the door shut but its own inertia.

For a second I think about ripping the tape off—but then I realize how stupid that would be. This—finally—is proof. In front of me, hidden innocently within the doorframe, is cast-iron proof that someone set James up to die, and whoever placed the tape was that person. Carefully, without disturbing it, I push the door shut and then I drag a chair across the kitchen to rest against the inside of the glass.

Then, for the first time, I look around.

The kitchen looks strangely undisturbed. I don't know what I was expecting: fingerprint dust, perhaps, that strange silver sheen on every surface. But as soon as I think about this, I realize how pointless it would be. None of us ever denied being in the house. Our prints would be all over the place, and what would they prove?

I want, more than anything, to crawl upstairs to one of the beds, and sleep. But I can't. I may not have much time. By now they've probably discovered my room is empty. They'll know I can't have gone far under my own steam—not without money, shoes, and a coat. It won't take them long to find the taxi driver. And when they do . . .

I walk through the kitchen, my footsteps loud in the echoing silence, take a deep breath, and then open the door to the hallway.

They've cleaned up, to some extent anyway. Much of the blood has gone, along with most of the glass, although I can feel the occasional tiny sliver crunch under my plastic soles. In its place there are markings on the floor, on the walls, bits of tape with notations I can't read in the darkness. I don't dare switch on a light. There are no curtains to draw, and my presence would be visible from right across the valley.

But there are specks left here and there, dark rust splashes of something that used to be James—and now is not.

It's the strangest thing—he is gone, and his heart's blood is still here. I kneel on the soft wooden parquet, pitted with chunks of glass ground in by our shoes, and marked by the soaking blood, and I touch my fingers to the stained grooves of the wood, and I think, This was James. A couple of days ago, this was inside him, keeping him alive, making his skin flush and his heart beat. And now it's gone—it's lying here, wasted, and yet it's all that's left of him. Somewhere his body is being postmortemed. And then he'll be buried, or cremated. But a part of him will be here, in this house.

I get up, forcing my cold, tired legs to work. Then I go to the living room and grab one of the throws off the sofa. There are dirty wineglasses still on the table, from our last night. Fag butts are stubbed out in the dregs of wine, Nina's roll-ups bloated into soggy white worms. But the planchette has been packed away, and the paper has gone. I cannot suppress a shiver at the thought of the police reading those deranged scrawlings. What did it mean, that long, looping *murderrrrrer*? Did someone write it deliberately? Or did it simply float up from the group subconscious, like a sea monster surfacing from someone's innermost fears, and then sinking back down?

The throw smells of stale cigarette smoke, but I hug it around my shoulders as I glance up at the empty pegs above the fireplace, and away. I can't really bear to think of what I'm about to do. But I must do it. It's my only chance to get to what really happened.

I start at the top of the stairs, standing where we all stood, that night, in a little huddle. Flo was to my right, and I remember putting out my hand to the gun. Clare and Nina were on the other side, Tom behind us.

The scene, with the quiet and the darkness, and my own thudding heart, is so close to that night that for a moment I feel almost faint, and I have to stand and breathe through my nose, and remember that it is done, James is not coming up those stairs. We killed him—between us, with our drunken hysterical fear. We all held that gun.

I have to force myself to retrace what happened next, James's body tumbling down the stairs, Nina and I stumbling after. This time I walk down slowly, holding the banister. There is still glass on the stairs, from the broken window, and I don't trust my flip-flops in the darkness, not with the skidding shards underfoot.

Here was where Nina tried to resuscitate James.

Here was where I knelt in his blood, and he tried to speak.

I feel tears, wet on my face, but I scrub them away. There is no time for grief. The hours are ticking down until dawn, until they come and get me.

What happened next?

The living room door is still off its hinges from where Tom took it down—and we struggled with it out through the front door to where Clare was waiting in the car.

The front door is not deadlocked, and I open the lock from the inside without difficulty. When I do, the force of the wind nearly bangs the steel door into my face, and the snow rushes inside like a living thing, trying to get in, trying to force what little warmth is left in the house back out.

I screw up my eyes, and, holding the throw hard around my shoulders, I step out into the white blizzard and stand on the porch, where I stood that night waiting for Nina. I remember Tom calling out something to Clare, and Clare gunning the engine.

And then I remember noticing that her coat was lying over the porch rail.

I put out my hand, pretend to pick it up.

I'm shivering, but I'm trying as hard as I can to remember back to that night, to the shape of something small and round in the pocket.

I hold out my hand—my eyes watering with the hard pellets of driving snow.

And suddenly, I can remember. I can remember what I was holding in my hand.

And I know why it set me to running.

It was a shell. A shotgun shell. It was the missing blank.

Standing here, in my own footsteps, the thoughts shoot across my brain just as they did that night, and I can remember them: it's like watching the snow melt and seeing the familiar landscape emerge from beneath.

It could have been there from the clay-pigeon shoot earlier. But I know enough now, from our shoot, to tell the difference between a live round and a blank. Live shotgun rounds are solid in your hand, packed with pellets that make them feel heavier than their compact shape suggests. What I held that night was light as plastic with no shot at all. It was a blank. *The* blank. The blank that was supposed to have been in the shotgun.

Clare had been the one to substitute the live round for the blank.

And now she'd just driven off into the night with James dying in the back of the car.

Why? *Why?*

It made no sense then, and it still makes no sense to me now, but then I had no time to consider. I had only one option: to catch them up and confront Clare.

Now, I have time. I turn slowly and walk back into the house, and I shut and lock the door behind me. Then I go into the living room and sit, my head in my hands, trying to figure it out.

I cannot leave here until dawn—unless, that is . . . I get up, stiff with cold, and pick up the phone receiver.

No, it's still dead, the line simply hissing and crackling quietly. I am stuck then, stuck until daylight, unless I want to stagger back down that icy rutted lane in the darkness once more, and I'm not sure I'd even make it.

I go back to the sofa and huddle deeper into the throw, trying vainly to get some warmth back into my limbs. My God, I'm so tired—but I cannot sleep. I must figure this out.

Clare substituted the live round.

Therefore, Clare killed James.

But it makes no sense. Clare has no motive—and she is the only person who could not have faked those texts.

I have to *think.*

The question I keep coming back to is *why*: Why would Clare kill James virtually on the eve of their own wedding?

And then suddenly, with a coldness that's totally different from the chill in the air, I remember Matt's words in the hospital. James and Clare were having problems.

I shake it off almost immediately. This is ridiculous. Yes, Clare's life has to be perfect. Yes, she has incredibly high standards, but for God's sake, she's been dumped before. She held a massive grudge, I know that, because I sat by while she signed Rick's e-mail up to every porn site and Viagra newsletter she could find. But she sure as hell didn't kill the bloke.

But there is one big difference.

When Rick dumped Clare, Flo wasn't in the picture.

I think of Flo's words, as she sobbed outside the bathroom on the first night: "She's my rock, and I'd do *anything* for her. Anything."

Anything?

I remember her reaction to my going to bed—the way she'd exploded, accusing me of sabotage. "I'll kill you if you ruin it," she'd promised. I hadn't taken her seriously. But maybe I should have.

And that was just a hen. What would she do to the man who was planning to leave her best friend at the altar?

And who better to take the fall than the bad ex-friend who'd stolen Clare's rightful property and then walked away for ten long years?

But now it has all spiraled out of control.

And then I remember the matching clothes Flo was wearing on that last night—and suddenly I realize: What if it wasn't Clare's coat on the rail, but Flo's, and Clare simply picked it up by mistake?

Flo. Flo was the one who picked up the gun.

Flo was the one who told us it wasn't loaded.

Flo was the person who set this whole thing up, persuaded me to come, arranged the whole thing.

And Flo *could* have sent those texts.

I feel like a web is closing round me, like the more I fight the more I will be tangled in it.

James is dead.

Clare is dying.

Flo is dying.

And somewhere, Nina is in her B and B at the breaking point, and she and Tom are facing questions they cannot answer, suspicions they cannot shake.

Please let me wake from this.

I curl up on the sofa on my side, and draw my knees into my chest, the throw tucked around myself. I have to think—I have to decide what to do, but in this confused, exhausted state, I find myself going around in circles.

I have a choice: wait here for the police, try to explain my presence, explain about the blank and Flo's jacket, and hope they believe me.

Or I can leave at the crack of dawn, and hope they don't realize I was here.

But where do I go? To London? To Nina? How will I get away?

The police will find me, of course, but it will look better than finding me here.

Almost against my will, I can feel my eyes closing, and my limbs, quivery with tiredness, slowly relaxing, the muscles twitching with exhaustion every few minutes as they loosen into sleep. I cannot think. I will try to work it out tomorrow.

A great yawn comes up from somewhere deep inside, and I realize I have stopped shivering. I let the flip-flops fall off my feet, and feel a thin line of tears tracing down my cheek, from the yawn, but I am too tired to wipe them away.

Oh God, I need to sleep.

I will think about this . . . tomorrow . . .

- - -

It's night. It's the night of the shooting. And I'm crouched in the blazing hallway, bathed in the golden streaming light and in James's blood.

The blood is in my nostrils, on my hands, beneath my nails.

He's looking up at me, his eyes wide and dark, and shining wet.

"The text . . ." he says. His voice is hoarse. *"Leo . . ."*

I reach out to touch his face—and then suddenly he's gone, the blood is gone, and the light is gone.

I wake, it's dark, and my heart is racing in my chest.

For a minute I just lie there, feeling my heart thumping like a drum, trying to work out what has woken me. I can't hear anything.

But then I turn my head and I notice two things at the same time.

The first is that, outside the huge plate-glass window facing the front of the house, I can see a dark shape that wasn't there before. And I'm pretty certain it's a car.

The second is that I can hear a sound from the kitchen. It is a slow, juddering, scraping noise.

It's the sound of a chair being pushed across the slate tiles as someone opens the door.

chapter 32

There is someone in the house.

I sit bolt upright, the throw falling from my shoulders, my heart thumping so high in my throat I feel sick.

For a minute I think about calling out, challenging the intruder. Then I realize I'm insane.

Whoever is here, for whatever reason they've come, it's not a good one. It's not the police. They wouldn't come like this in the dead of night, creeping in through the back door. No, there're only two possibilities: some random burglar has gotten lucky and discovered the open back door. Or the murderer is here.

I would *love* for it to be a burglar. Which says something about how fucked up my life has become—that a random stranger breaking in here in the middle of the night would be the best possible explanation. But I know in my heart of hearts it's not. The murderer is here. For me.

Very, very carefully, I get up, holding the throw around myself like a shield, as if the soft red wool can protect me.

My one comfort is that the intruder won't want to put the lights on any more than I do. Maybe in the dark I can evade him, hide, escape.

Fuck. Where do I go?

The windows in here open onto the garden, but I'm sure they're locked—I tried them from the outside, and I remember Flo locking them that last night. She had a key. I have no idea where it is.

I can hear someone in the kitchen, walking softly across the tiles.

Two very strong impulses fight within me. The first is to run—run out the door, up the stairs, lock myself in the bathroom—to do whatever I can to get away.

The second is to stand, and fight.

I am a runner. This is what I do—I run. But sometimes you can't run anymore.

I stand, my fists clenched by my sides, my blood a roaring in my ears, my breath a tearing in my throat. Flight or fight. Flight or fight. Flight or—

Shoes crunch on the glass in the hallway. And then they stop.

I know the murderer is there, listening—listening for me. I hold my breath.

Someone is standing in the frame, and I cannot see who it is—in the dimness all I can see is a shape, black against the reflecting steel of the front door.

It could be anyone—the shape is huddled in a coat, and the face is hidden by the shadows. But then the figure moves, and I see the glint of blond hair.

"Hello, Flo," I say, my throat so tight I can barely speak.

And then she laughs.

She laughs and laughs and laughs, and for a long moment I have no idea why.

She moves, still smiling, into the strip of moonlight, her feet again crunching on glass.

And I understand.

Because it's not Flo.

It's Clare.

She's holding herself up against the wall, and I realize that she's as frail as me. Maybe she wasn't as ill as she pretended when I saw her in the hospital, but she's ill, all right. She holds herself like someone twice her age, like she's been beaten bloody and has only half healed.

"Why did you come back," she manages at last. "Why couldn't you just leave it?"

"Clare?" I croak. It doesn't make sense. Nothing makes sense.

She feels her way slowly to the sofa and then sinks down with a groan. In the thin, cloud-muted moonlight she looks awful—worse than me. Her face is cut, and there's a huge swollen bruise on one side of her forehead, black in the pale light.

"Clare—why?"

I can't make sense of this.

She says nothing. Nina's rolling tobacco is on the table, along with Rizlas, and she reaches for them, painfully, with a little gasp of relief as she sinks back into the cushions, and begins slowly, painstakingly, to roll up. She is wearing gloves, but in spite of that her hands are shaking, and she spills the tobacco twice before she lights up.

"I haven't smoked in years." She puts the end to her lips and takes a long drag. "God, I've missed it."

"Why?" I say again. "Why are you here?"

I still can't make my brain accept what's happening. Clare is here—therefore, she must be the killer. But why, *how*? There was no way she could have sent that first text—she was the one person in the cottage who could not have done it.

I should be running. I should be cowering behind the sofa, armed with a bread knife. But I can't make myself understand this. It's Clare, my brain keeps insisting. She's your friend. When she holds out the cigarette to me, I take it, half in a dream, and suck in the smoke, holding it deep until the trembling in my limbs stills and I feel my head get light.

I go to hand it back, and Clare shrugs.

"Keep it. I can roll another. God, it's cold. Want a tea?"

"Thanks," I say, still in this strange, dreamlike state. Clare is the killer. But she can't be. I can't seem to think what to do—and so I take refuge in these strange, automatic social responses.

She gets painfully to her feet and hobbles out into the kitchen, and in a few minutes I hear the click of the kettle and the bubbling hum as it begins to boil.

What should I do?

The roll-up has burnt out, and I set it gently onto the coffee table. There's no ashtray, but I no longer care.

I shut my eyes, rub my hands over my face, and as I do I get a flash, like a projection against the inside of my lids: James, the blood bright as paint under the lights.

The smell from my dream is still sharp in my nostrils, his hoarse voice is inside my head.

There's a small sound from the doorway, and I see Clare, shuffling painfully across the room with two mugs in her hand. She sets them down and I take one, and she lowers herself to the sofa and pulls a packet of pills from her pocket, and breaks two capsules into the tea, her fingers a little clumsy in their woolen gloves.

"Painkillers?" I ask, more for something to say.

She nods. "Yes. You're supposed to swallow the capsules whole, but I can't swallow pills." She takes a swig and shudders. "Oh God, that's disgusting. I'm not sure if it's the pills or if the milk's gone off."

I take a gulp of my own. It tastes vile—tea always tastes vile, but this is even viler than normal. It tastes sour and bitter below the sugar Clare has added—but at least it's hot.

We sip in silence for a moment, and then I can't keep quiet any longer.

"What are you doing here, Clare? How did you get here?"

"I drove Flo's car. She lent it to my folks, and they left the keys in my locker for Flo to collect. Only . . . she never did."

No. She never did. Because . . .

Clare looks up. Her eyes over the top of her cup are dilated in the dimness, and they shine. She is so beautiful—even like this, huddled in an old coat, with her face cut and bruised and no makeup on.

"As for what I'm doing here, I could ask the same about you. What are *you* doing here?"

"I came back to try to remember," I say.

"And did you?" Her voice is light, as though we're talking about what happened in an old episode of *Friends.*

"Yes." I meet her eyes in the darkness. The mug is hot between my numb hands. "I remembered about the shell."

"What shell?" Her face is blank, but there's something in her eyes . . .

"The shell in your jacket. I found it, in the pocket of your coat."

She is shaking her head, and suddenly, I find I am angry, very, very angry.

"Don't fuck with me, Clare! It was your coat. I know it was. Why would you come back here if not?"

"Maybe . . ." She looks down at the mug and then up at me. "Maybe, to protect you from yourself?"

"What the hell does that mean?"

"You don't remember what happened, do you?"

"How do you know that?"

"The nurses. They talk. Especially when you're asleep—or might be."

"So? So what?"

"You don't remember what happened in the forest, do you? In the car?"

"What the hell are you on about?"

"You grabbed the wheel," she says softly. "You told me that you couldn't live without James, that you'd been fucked up over him for ten years. You told me that you dreamed about him—that you'd never got over what happened, what he said to you in that text. You drove us off the road, Lee."

For a second it washes over me like a wave. I feel my cheeks tingle with the shock, as if she's slapped me—and then it recedes, and I'm left gasping.

Because it's the truth. As she says it, I get a sharp, agonizing flash—hands on the wheel, Clare fighting me like a demon, my nails in her skin.

"Are you sure you're remembering this right?" she says, her voice very gentle. "I saw you, Lee. You had your hand on the barrel of the gun. *You* nudged it towards James."

For a minute I can't say anything. I'm sitting here, gasping, my hands gripping the tea mug like it's a weapon. Then I am shaking my head.

"No. No, no, no! Why are you here, in that case? Why aren't you denouncing me to the police?"

"How do you know," she says quietly, "that I haven't already done that?"

Oh my God. I feel weak with horror. I take a long gulp of tea, my teeth chattering at the edge of the mug, and I try to think, try to gather the strands of all this together.

This is *not* true. Clare is screwing with my head. No sane person would be sitting here drinking tea with a woman who murdered her fiancé and tried to drive her car off the road.

"The shell," I say doggedly. "The shell was in your coat."

"I have no idea what you're talking about," she says, and there's a catch in her voice. "Please, Lee, I love you. I'm scared for you. Whatever you've done . . ."

I can't think. My head hurts, I feel so strange, and there's a vile taste in my mouth. I take another gulp of tea to try to swill it away, but the taste only intensifies.

I shut my eyes and the picture of James swims in front of my closed lids, dying in my arms. Is this the picture that I'm going to see when I close my eyes for the rest of my life?

"Text . . ." he gasps, *"text, Leo,"* and there is blood in his lungs.

And then suddenly, amid the swimming haze of memories and tangled suspicion—something catches.

I know what James was saying. What he was trying to say.

I put down the mug.

I know what happened. And I know why James had to die.

chapter 33

Oh my God, I've been so stupid. I can't believe how stupid—for ten years, I never even noticed. I sit there, stock-still, running through all the what ifs—how different everything could have been if I'd only realized what was sitting in front of my face, all those years ago.

"Lee?" Clare says. She is looking at me, her face the picture of concern. "Lee, are you okay? You look . . . you don't look well."

"Nora. My name is Nora," I say hoarsely.

For ten years. For ten years that fucking text has been engraved on my heart, and I never even noticed.

"Lee," I say to Clare. She takes a gulp of tea and stares at me over the mug, her beautiful, narrow brows drawn into a puzzled frown. "Lee," I repeat. "I'm sorry but this is your problem, not mine. Deal with it. And don't call me again. J."

"What?"

"Lee."

"What the hell are you on about?"

"Lee. He never called me Lee. James never called me Lee."

For a minute she stares at me in utter incomprehension—and I am reminded, all over again, what an amazing actress she was. *Is.* It shouldn't have been James on the stage. It should have been Clare. She is amazing.

And then she sets down her tea and gives a rueful grimace.

"Jesus. It was a long time ago, Lee."

It's not an admission—not quite. But I know her well enough to know that it might as well be. She's not protesting anymore.

"Ten years. I'm slow," I say bitterly. Bitter, not just because my mistake ruined my own life, but because if I'd been a little quicker on the uptake, James might still be alive. "Why did you do it, Clare?"

She reaches out her hand to me; I flinch away, and she says, "Look, I'm not saying what I did was right—I was young, and it was stupid. But Lee, I did it for the best. You'd have been screwing up both your lives. I went around to see him that afternoon—the guy was shitting himself; he wasn't ready to be a dad. You weren't ready to be a mum. But I knew between the two of you, neither of you would have the guts to make the decision."

"No," I say. My voice is shaking.

"You wanted it to happen, both of you."

"No." It comes out like a sob.

"You can deny it all you want," she says softly. "But you were the one who walked away, and he let you. All it would have taken was one text, one message, one call—the truth would have come out. But between you, you couldn't even manage that. The fact is, he wanted out—he was just too much of a coward to make a break for it himself. I did it for the best."

"You're lying," I say at last. My voice is hoarse and choked. "You don't care—you never cared. You just wanted James—and I was in the way."

I remember—I remember that day in the school hall, the hot sun streaming in through the tall glass windows, and Clare saying laconically, "I'm going to *have* James Cooper."

But instead, he became mine.

"He found out, didn't he?" I stare at her pale face, her draggled hair silver white in the moonlight. "About the text. How?"

She sighs.

And then at last she speaks what sounds like the truth.

"I told him."

"What?"

"I told him. We were having a discussion—about honesty, and marriage. He said that before we got married he wanted to get something off his chest. He asked, Could he tell me something—and would I forgive him? And I said, Yes, anything, absolutely anything. I said that I loved him, that he could tell me anything. And he told me that at that party where we met up again, his friend had been interested in me—we'd spent all night flirting, I remember. I gave this friend my number at the end of the night—and James said that he found the piece of paper in his friend's pocket, and kept it himself—he told his friend that I wasn't interested, and instead, *he* texted me, said that he got my number off Julian, and did I want to go out for a drink."

She sighs and stares out of the window.

"He said it had been eating at him all these years," she carries on. "That our relationship had started with a lie, that it was his friend who should have ended up with me. But he said that Julian was a womanizer, and he'd done it partly for selfish reasons, but partly for me. He couldn't bear for Julian to string me along, screw me, and then dump me. He was expecting me to be angry—but as he talked, all I could think was that he'd lied and cheated to get me, bent his own scruples. You know what James is like . . . *was* like."

I nod. The movement makes my head swim, but I know what she means. James was a strange contradictory mix—an anarchist with his own rigid moral code.

"It was strange." Clare is speaking slowly now. I think she's almost forgotten about me. "He thought his confession would make me love him less. But it didn't—it only made me love him more. I realized what he'd done was for *me,* for love of *me.* And I realized that the same was true of me. That I had lied out of love for him. And I thought . . . if I can forgive him . . ."

I can see it. I can see her strange twisted logic. And her one-upmanship: you have done this for me; I have done worse for you. I love you even *more.*

But she fatally misunderstood James.

I sit, trying to imagine his face as she confessed what she'd done. Did she try to justify it to him, as she did to me? He wasn't ready to be a dad—she was absolutely right. But that wouldn't have swayed James. He would have seen only the cruelty of the deception.

"What did you say to him?" I say at last. I am light-headed with tiredness, and my body feels strange and disconnected, my muscles like wool. Clare looks just as bad—her wrists seem thin enough to snap.

"What do you mean?"

"You must have told him something else. Otherwise, he would have rung me. What did you say?"

"Oh." She rubs her temple, hooks back a lock of hair that has fallen over her face. "I can't remember. I said something about . . . you'd told me to tell him you needed time alone—that you thought he'd screwed up your life and you didn't want to see him. He shouldn't ring you—you'd contact him when you were ready."

But of course I never did. I went back to school only to take my exams, and ignored him steadfastly. Then I moved away completely.

Part of me wants to smack him for being so stupid, for being taken in so easily. Why didn't he overcome his scruples and just *call* me? But I know the answer. It's the same reason I never called him. Pride. Shame. Cowardice. And something else—something more like shell shock, that made it easier just to keep on going, not look back. Something momentous had happened in our lives—something we were totally unequipped to deal with. And we were both dazed from the fallout, trying not to think too much, feel too much. Easier just to shut down.

"What did he say?" I manage at last. My throat is sore and croaky, and I take another gulp of tea. It tastes even worse cold, but perhaps the sugar and caffeine will help keep me awake until morning, until the police come. I am so tired—so very, very tired. "Afterwards, I mean. When he found out."

Clare sighs.

"He wanted to call off the wedding. And I begged and pleaded—I said he was being like Angel in *Tess of the D'Urbervilles*—you know, when Angel confesses to adultery but then can't bear it when Tess says she had Alex's baby."

We studied the book at GCSE. I can still remember James's impassioned condemnation of Angel to the class. *He's being a fucking hypocrite!* he shouted, and got sent out for swearing in front of a teacher.

"He said he needed time to think, but that the only way he could ever even try to forgive me was if I told you the truth. So I told him I'd invited you to my hen party so that I could tell you then." She laughs then, unsteadily, like someone suddenly seeing the point of a joke. "It's just occurred to me how ironic it is: I always thought hen dos were completely lame, and James spent ages trying to persuade me to have one—and in the end he was the one who persuaded me, just not for the reason he thought. If he hadn't kept going on about it, I'd probably never even have thought of all this."

I understand now. I understand completely.

Clare—Clare could never be in the wrong. Someone else always had to take the fall. Someone else had to take the blame.

Did James ever really know her? Or did he just love some illusion of Clare, an act that she presented to him? Because I know, from twenty years of knowing Clare, that his plan was never going to work. Hell would freeze over before Clare would admit to something like that. Not just because she would be in the wrong to me—but because she would be in the wrong to *everyone,* forever. I could not be expected to keep quiet about what happened—it would have all come out: ten years of lying and deception and, most humiliating of all, the fact that Clare Cavendish had had to resort to this to get her man.

She must have known, too, that James's decision was on a knife's edge. I don't know what he said to Matt, but it was clear that if he was prepared to talk about his distress to other people, it must go very deep indeed. And he'd made no promises to Clare—only said that he *might* be able to forgive her if she confessed.

I didn't think, knowing James, that he would have succeeded.

No. Clare had everything to lose by being honest, and nothing to gain.

She had two options: tell the truth and expose herself; or refuse to go along with James's plan and lose her fiancé—and then the truth would have had to come out anyway. Either way, she would be destroyed, and the image she had built up so carefully over so many years—the image of a good friend, a loving girlfriend, and a caring, honorable person—would be shattered.

I know how hard it is to walk away from your past and start again—and Clare's life is happy and glittering and successful. She must have looked at all she'd done and built and won, and balanced that against a lie.

She could come out of this destroyed—or she could kill James and walk away a tragic and inspiringly brave widow, ready to start again.

James *had* to die—his execution was regretful but necessary.

But mine—mine is a punishment. It was not enough that James die. Someone must carry the can for his death—it cannot possibly be Clare's fault, even as an accident.

No, someone must be to blame, just as someone *always* has to be to blame. And this time, that someone is me.

Why me? I almost say. But I don't. Because I know.

I stole her man. Ten years ago I came between Clare Cavendish and her rightful property, stealing him out from under her nose while she was too ill to fight for what was hers, and now I have done it again, rising up from the past like a hand from the grave, to come between her and James one last time.

I will not leave this cottage now, I know that.

Clare cannot afford to let me leave.

My heart is beating very, very hard in my chest, so hard that I feel strange and light-headed, as if I might fall. I stand up unsteadily, holding my cup, and I stagger and drop it. Clare reaches for it, trying to grab it before it spills, but her gloved fingers fumble on the china, and the cup slips from between her fingers and skitters across the coffee table.

And as the dregs spill out across the glass top I see . . . I see the white residue at the bottom of the cup. Not sugar—that had all dissolved. But something else. Something that made the tea taste even worse than usual.

I understand now. I understand my light-headedness. I understand why Clare has said so much, has allowed me to get this far. And I understand, oh God, I understand the gloves.

She looks down at the cup, and then up at me.

"Oops," she says. And then she smiles.

chapter 34

For a moment I do nothing. I just stand there—staring stupidly at the cup, feeling the lethargy in my arms and legs, and the swirling confusion in my head that prevented me from noticing the effects of the drug before. What are they? Painkillers? Sleeping pills?

I stand there, swaying, trying to get myself together. Trying to balance.

And then I stumble towards the door.

I am not quick. I am slow—nightmarishly slow.

But as Clare leaps towards me, her battered limbs don't quite obey. Her foot catches in the rug, and she comes crashing down, her hip smacking into the wickedly sharp edge of the coffee table. She gives a scream that sets the echoes in the hallway ringing and makes my already-spinning head feel even stranger—and I stagger into the hallway.

I am struggling with the lock of the front door—the lock that seemed so simple and straightforward just a couple of hours ago. My fingers are slipping—the lock won't turn—and then I have done it, and I am out, snapping through the flimsy police tape, into the blessedly cold fresh air.

My limbs feel like rubber, and my head is sick and dizzy.

But this is what I do. I run. I can do this.

I take a step. And then another. And another and another and another. And then the forest swallows me up.

It is incredibly, indescribably dark. But I cannot stop.

The air is cold in my face and the shapes of the trees are black against black. They rear out of the chilly dark, and I dodge and weave, ducking under branches, my hands held out to protect my face.

Bracken and brambles catch at my shins, ripping at the skin, but my legs are numb and cold, and I hardly feel the slashes, only the tearing thorns holding me back.

It is my nightmare. Only this time it's not James I'm trying to save—it's myself.

Behind me I hear the slam of a car door and an engine revving. Full-beam headlights glimmer through the tree trunks, sweeping around in a great curve, as the car does a slow U-turn and then begins to bump down the rutted drive.

The drive goes around in a long curve, so as not to climb the hill too steeply. The woodland footpath is direct. If I run fast, I can do this. I can get to the road before Clare. And then what?

But I cannot think about that. My breath sobs between my gritted teeth, and I force my shaking muscles to work harder, faster.

I just want to live.

I'm gaining speed. The path is steeper here, and my muscles aren't forcing me on now, but trying to check my headlong rush. I leap a fallen branch and a badger's set, a dark hole in the pale scattered snow—and then, with a suddenness that punches the breath out of me, I smack into a tree.

I fall onto my hands and knees in the snow, my head ringing in agony. My nose is streaming blood—I can see it dripping into the snow as I pant, and pant, and when I touch Nina's cardigan, the front is dark and soaked with gore. I shake my head, trying to clear the shards and sparks shooting across my vision, and the blood spatters across the clearing.

I can't stop. My only chance is to get to the road before Clare can cut me off. I steady myself, one hand on the tree trunk, trying to overcome the sick dizziness, and then I begin to run again.

As I run, pictures shoot through my head, sudden flashes, like a landscape illuminated by lightning.

Clare, in her wellies—slipping quietly out of the house in the early morning to send those texts from my phone, from the point in the forest where reception kicked in, leaving her footsteps in the snow for me to find.

Clare—waiting until Nina was safely gone, and then driving off into the dark—to what? To park quietly in a lay-by, and wait for James to bleed to death?

Clare—her face white in the moonlight, and stiff with shock, as I burst out of the forest in front of the car, screaming at her to stop, let me in.

She stamped reflexively on the brakes, I scrambled into the passenger's side. As I slammed the door, she glanced at James and me, both without seat belts, and then, without trying to explain, gunned the engine and stamped on the accelerator.

For a second I didn't understand. She was steering *towards* the tree that loomed out of the darkness.

And then I realized.

I grabbed for the steering wheel, my nails in her skin, wrestling for control of the car—and there it goes blank.

Oh God, I have to get to the road before she does. If she parks across the foot of the track and cuts me off, I'm lost.

Everything hurts. Jesus—everything hurts *so* much. But the pills that Clare gave me have one silver lining. They've taken the edge off enough to allow me to keep going, combined with my own fear and adrenaline.

I want to live. I never knew how much until now.

Oh Christ, I want to live.

And then—suddenly—almost without realizing it—I'm at the road. The forest path spews me out onto the tarmac so fast that I stumble, trying to slow down enough to stop myself shooting into the path of a car. I stand there, hands on my knees, gasping and panting, and trying to work out which way to go.

Where is Clare?

I can hear a noise, I realize, the growl of an engine as it shoots over potholes and around bends. It's not far off. She's almost at the foot of the track. And I can't do it—I can't run anymore. I've pushed my body beyond what it can do.

I have to run, or I will die.

And I can't. I can't. I can barely stand—let alone put one foot in front of the other.

Run, I scream inside my own head. *Run, you fucking waste of space. Do you want to die?*

Clare's car is at the road. I see the blaze of her headlights just around the bend, lighting up the night.

And then there's a horrendous, screaming squeal of tires, and a bang like nothing I've ever heard. There's shrieking rubber, and the screech of metal, car on car: a sound that seems to echo forever in the forest tunnel, shrill in my ears. I stand, my eyes wide with horror, staring towards the sound of the collision.

And then silence—just the hiss of a radiator venting into the night air.

I cannot run anymore. But I manage to walk—my legs shaking. I have lost my flip-flops and the tarmac must be cold as ice—but I can't feel anything.

In the stillness I hear the sound of sobbing gasps, and the crackle of a radio. Then, with a suddenness that makes me jump and almost stumble, the trees are illuminated by a ghostly blue, flickering like flames.

One more step. One more. I force myself on, around the bend—towards whatever has happened.

But before I get there I hear a voice, a shaking female voice. She's speaking into something—a phone? But as I get closer I see it's a police radio.

It's Lamarr. She is standing by the open door of her police car. There is blood running down her face, black in the flashing blue lights of the emergency siren. She's speaking into the radio.

"Ground control, urgent message." Her voice is shaking; there's a sob in it. "Request immediate assistance and an ambulance, to the B4146 just outside Stanebridge, over." She's standing there listening to the crackling reply. "Roger," she says at last, and then, "No, I'm not hurt. But the other driver—look, just send the ambulance. And a fire crew, with—with cutting equipment, over."

She sets the radio carefully down and then goes back to the other car.

"Lamarr," I say croakily, but she doesn't hear. My limbs are so heavy—I don't think I can go another step. I brace myself up against a tree by the side of the road. "Lamarr . . ." I manage, one more time, my voice a shaking thread against the hissing of the engine and the crackle of the radio. "Lamarr."

She turns, and looks, and then at last I let my knees give way, and I kneel on the cold, snow-wet tarmac, and I don't have to run anymore.

"Nora!" I hear through the fog. "Nora! Christ, are you hurt? Are you hurt, Nora?"

But I can't find the words to reply. Lamarr is running towards me, and I feel her strong hands beneath my armpits as I collapse onto the road; and she's holding me, lowering me slowly to the ground.

It's over. It's all over.

chapter 35

"Nora." The voice is gentle but insistent, tangling in my confused restless sleep like a hook, dragging me back to reality. I know the voice. Who is it? Not Nina. It's too low for Nina. "Nora," the voice says again.

I open my eyes.

It's Lamarr. She is sitting on the chair at the edge of my bed, her dark eyes wide and bright, her shiny hair smoothed back from her sculpted forehead.

"How are you feeling?"

I struggle up against the covers and notice that she's wearing a neck brace—incongruous against her silk tunic.

"I came by yesterday," she says, "but they shooed me away."

"Are you in the hospital, too?" I croak. She passes me water, and I gulp it gratefully. She shakes her head, her heavy gold earrings swaying gently.

"No. Walking wounded—I got sent home from casualty yesterday morning. Good thing, really, my kids hate me being away overnight. The littlest one is only four."

She has children? This information feels like a peace offering. Something in our relationship has changed.

"Am I . . . " I manage, and then swallow and start again. "Is it over?"

"You're okay," Lamarr says, "if that's what you mean. And as for the case, we're not looking for anyone other than Clare in connection with James's death."

"How's Flo?"

I'm not sure if I imagine it, but it feels like a shadow flits across Lamarr's face. I can't put my finger on what changes, her expression is as smooth and calm as before, but there's suddenly a presence in the little room, a dread.

"She's . . . holding on," Lamarr says at last.

"Can I see her?"

Lamarr shakes her head.

"She's . . . she's with her family. The doctors aren't permitting any visitors right now."

"Have you seen her?"

"Yesterday, yes."

"So she's worse today?"

"I didn't say that," Lamarr says, but her eyes are troubled. I know what she is not saying. I know what she's skirting around. I remember Nina's words about paracetamol overdoses, and I know that the destructive ripples from Clare's actions have not yet stopped, even now.

Of everything Clare did, I think that was the cruelest. What she did to James, what she tried to do to me, at least she had a reason. But Flo—Flo's only crime was loving Clare.

I don't know when she began to realize the truth—when she started to put two and two together about the text Clare asked her to send from my phone when I arrived at the cottage. It was innocent enough: *James, it's me, Leo. Leo Shaw.* I don't know what Clare told her—something silly, I expect. A hen-night prank.

The first inklings were probably when Nina spilled the beans about my past with James, and she began to wonder why Clare, of all people, would want to stir things up again. Then when Lamarr started asking questions about phones . . . and texts . . . she must have realized that something was wrong.

I don't suppose she guessed the truth—or not at first. She tried to see Clare in the hospital, but they wouldn't let her. Clare was too ill, and the police weren't keen on the witnesses at the B and B visiting the hospital anyway. Nina said she'd had to fight like a tiger to see me, and then only after they'd gone over her statement a hundred times. And Clare at that stage was still feigning confusion and semiconsciousness, waiting to see what transpired with Lamarr and me, I suppose, before "waking up."

No. Flo stayed at the B and B, fretting, and wondering, and unable to ask Clare about what to say. She lied. She tripped herself up in her lies. She wondered what she'd done, what she'd set in motion. She started to doubt Clare's motives. She got desperate.

"Do you know?" I say, swallowing hard, trying to push away the thoughts of Flo lying somewhere up the corridor, struggling for life. "Do you know what happened? Did Clare tell you?"

"Clare's too ill to answer questions," Lamarr says grimly. "At least that's what her lawyer says. But we've got enough to piece the case together. Between what you told us, the tox report on the drugs Clare gave you, and, most important, Flo's statement, we've got enough. She never did phone the ambulance, you know."

"What do you mean?"

"From the cottage. When James died. There was no record of her ever trying nine nine nine. That should have tipped us off, but we were too busy looking elsewhere." She sighs. "We'll need to take a formal statement, of course, when you're well enough. But we can worry about that another day."

"I thought it was Flo," I say at last. "When I found Clare's jacket, with the shell in it. I thought it was Flo's jacket. I thought she'd changed the shells. I just couldn't work out why Clare would do such a thing; she finally had what she wanted—the perfect life, the perfect fiancé. Why would she throw that all away? It was only when I thought about the text, *really* thought about it, I realized: James never called me Lee. She didn't make that mistake twice. But I should have realized."

"She did it before, you know," Lamarr says. Her beautiful, rich, plum-colored voice is like a soft warm blanket around the coldness of her words. "Or a variant. It took us a while to dig it up, but there was a professor at her university. He was sacked for sending inappropriate e-mails to undergraduates, implying that they would get better grades if they slept with him and that there might be penalties if they told anyone. He denied it throughout, but there was no doubt that the students did receive the e-mails, and when his machine was raided, they were there in the Deleted folder, all of them, although he'd made a clumsy attempt to destroy them.

"It seems pretty clear now that Clare was involved, although at the time no one ever suspected her. She wasn't one of the students he was e-mailing. But a few weeks before, he had raised concerns with her that one of her papers was plagiarized, threatened to take it further. Of course in the ensuing furor the accusation was forgotten—but one of his colleagues remembered his discussing it. She said she'd always wondered . . ."

I shut my eyes, feeling a single tear trace down the line of my nose. I don't know why I'm crying. It's not relief. I don't think it's even grief for James anymore. Maybe it's just fury and frustration at the waste of it all, anger at myself for not realizing sooner, for being *so* stupid.

And yet, what then? If I had noticed? Would it have been me lying with my guts splattered across the white wood and the frosted glass?

"I'll leave you," Lamarr says softly, and she gets up, the plastic leather of the chair creaking. "I'll come back tomorrow, with a colleague. We'll take your formal statement, if you're up to it."

I don't speak, I only nod, with my eyes still tightly shut.

After she's gone there is silence, broken only by a soap theme tune next door, filtering through the wall.

I sit and listen to it, and to the breaths I draw in and out of my nose.

And then, into the middle of the calm, there's a knock at the door.

I open my eyes at once, assuming it's Lamarr come back, but it's not. There's a man outside. For a second my heart flip-flops, and then I see it's Tom.

"Knock knock," he says, putting his head around the door.

"Come in," I say. My voice is croaky.

He shuffles inside. His expression is diffident, unsure of his welcome. He looks pale, and far from the groomed *urbanisto* I'd met just a few days before. His checked shirt is crumpled and has some kind of visible stain on it. But I can tell from his expression that I must look even worse myself. The black eyes are fading to yellow and brown, but they're still shocking if you haven't seen them.

"Hi, Tom," I say. I pull my hospital gown up where it's slipped down my shoulder, and he smiles, the stiff, frozen smile of someone whose social graces have temporarily deserted them.

"Look, I have to get this off my chest," he blurts at last. "I thought it was you. I mean, there was all that stuff about your past with James, and then when the police started on about your phone and the texts, I just assumed . . ." He trails off. "I'm— I'm very sorry."

"It's okay," I say. I gesture to the chair beside the bed. "Look, sit down. Don't worry about it. The police thought it was me, too, and they weren't even there."

"I'm so sorry," he repeats, with a crack in his voice, as he sits awkwardly, hugging his knees. "I just— I never thought . . ." He stops, and then sighs. "Do you know, Bruce never liked her. He loved James. I mean, really loved him, even though they had their ups and downs. But he never had much time for Clare. When I rang him last night and told him everything that's happened, he said, 'I'm shocked, but I'm not surprised. She never stopped acting, that girl.' "

We sit in silence for a while as I ponder Bruce's words, the judgment of a man I've never met on one of my oldest friends. And I realize he's right. Clare never stopped acting. Even as a small child she was acting a part, the part of a good friend, the part of the perfect student, the ideal daughter, the glamorous girlfriend. And I realize, suddenly, that perhaps that's why I found it so hard to reconcile the Clare I knew with these other people. Because she was, quite literally, a different person to each of us. What will happen to her? I wonder. Will a jury convict anyone so charming, so kind, so very, very beautiful?

"I wonder . . ." I say aloud, and then stop.

"What?" Tom asks.

"I keep thinking, What if I hadn't said yes? To the hen night, I mean. I so nearly didn't come."

"I don't know," Tom says slowly. "Nina and I were talking about the same thing last night. The way I see it, you weren't the point of all this. The point was James. You were just the icing on the cake."

"So you mean . . ." I'm silent, working it out, and he nods.

"I think if you hadn't been there, it would have been one of us instead."

"It would have been Flo," I say sadly. "She sent the text, after all."

Tom nods.

"It wouldn't have been hard for Clare to twist the truth a bit," he says. "Start saying she was afraid of Flo, that Flo was jealous of James, acting irrationally. The worst thing is, we'd probably have backed her up."

"Have you seen her?" I ask.

"I tried," he says. "They aren't letting anyone in. I think . . . I'm not sure . . ."

He trails off. We both know what he's not saying.

"I'm going back to London tonight," he says at last. "But it would be great to keep in touch." He fishes in his wallet and pulls out a thick, glossy card, embossed with *Tom Deauxma* and his mobile and e-mail.

"I'm sorry," I say, "I don't have a card, but if you've got a pen . . ."

He holds out his phone, and I type my e-mail address into the "to" field, and watch while he sends me a blank e-mail.

"There," he says at last, standing up. "Well, I'd better get on the road. Take care of yourself, Shaw."

"I will."

"How are you getting back to London?"

"I don't know."

"I do," says a voice from the door. I turn and there is Nina, lounging in the doorframe, an unlit cigarette between her lips. She speaks around it, like a dime-store detective. "She's coming with me."

chapter 36

Home. Such a small word, and yet, when I close the door of my tiny flat behind myself and lock the door, I feel a spreading flood of relief that seems too huge to be encompassed by those four letters.

I am home. I am *home*.

Jess drove us back. She came all the way up from London to pick up Nina and me, and take us home. When they got to my road, they offered to come in, help me carry my case up the three flights of stairs, but I said no.

"I'm looking forward to being alone," I said, and it was true. And I knew that they were looking forward to being alone, too—alone together. I'd seen the quiet affectionate gestures on the long drive, Nina's hand resting in Jess's lap, Jess rubbing Nina's knee as she changed gear. But I didn't feel excluded—it wasn't that.

I just never knew how much I loved my own space until now.

Flo died on the evening of the day I saw Tom—the third day after she'd taken the overdose. Nina was right about that. And right, too, that she'd changed her mind by the end. I never saw her, but Nina visited her, and listened while she cried, and talked, and planned for the future and what she'd do when she left hospital. Her parents were with her when she died. I don't know if it was peaceful—Nina wouldn't tell me, which makes me think not.

I sigh and let my case fall to the floor. I am tired, and parched, and stiff from the long drive.

I open up the coffeemaker, pour in the water, and fold the filter paper just so. Then I open up my glass coffee jar and sniff the grounds. They're a week old—but still fresh enough to make the inside of my nose sing.

The sound the machine makes as it percolates is the sound of home, and the scent of the steaming grounds is the smell of home, and then at last I curl my battered body on the bed, my still-packed case on the rug, and I take a long, slow sip. The winter sun is filtering through the rattan blinds, and the traffic below makes a soft roar, too far away to disturb, more like the sound of the sea on a shore.

I think of the Glass House, far away, in the stillness of the forest, with the birds swooping past and the woodland animals padding quietly through the garden. I think of its blank glass walls, reflecting the dark shapes of the trees, and the moonlight filtering through.

Flo's aunt is selling, apparently. Flo's parents told Nina. Too much blood spilled, too many memories. And she said she was planning to burn the planchette, when the police released it.

That's the one part I don't understand. The séance.

Everything else was necessary. Everything else was part of the plan. But the Ouija board, and that creepy, creepy message?

I can still see it now, looping and scrolling across the page.

M m mmmmuurderrrrrrrrrrrer

Lamarr thought it was deliberate—all part of the plan to unnerve everyone, get them sufficiently on edge so that when the back door swung open, we'd be more inclined to panic, and react to a suggestion to get out the gun.

But I'm not so sure. I think again about what Tom said, about the messages that float up from the subconscious . . . was it Clare's unwilling hand, spelling out what she was so desperately trying to suppress?

I shut my eyes, trying to shut it out, the memory of that night. But there *is* no way of shutting it out completely. Flo is gone, but the rest of us—Tom, Nina, and me—we'll have to live with what happened, with what Clare did, with what we *all* did, for the rest of our lives.

My case is on the floor, and I open it up and pull out my laptop. The police still have my phone, but at least I can check my e-mails. It's more than a week since I left London, and as I fire it up and click Send and Receive, a message flickers up: "Downloading 1 of 187 e-mails."

I sit and watch as they drop, one by one, into my in-box.

There's an e-mail from my editor. And another. Two from my agent. One from my mum, headed "R U OK?"

Then, last of all comes the e-mail from my Web site address. Hot Thai Babes. One weird tip to melt belly fat! You have three comments waiting for approval.

And in among the spam . . .

From: Matt Ridout. Subject: Coffee

I feel in my pocket for the curling piece of cardboard, torn off a paper cup. It's nearly unreadable now, his number. The ink is blurring into nothing, and there's a crease across the middle two digits, but I think I can make out that they're both sevens, or possibly both ones.

I was going to let fate decide. If I got my phone back from the police before the number disappeared . . .

And now this.

I remember the way he buried his face in his hands as he cried over James.

I remember his smile.

I remember the expression in his eyes as he said good-bye.

I'm not sure I can do this. I'm not sure I can let go of everything that happened, start again. For a minute my finger hovers irrationally over the Delete button.

And then I click.

acknowledgments

A huge thank-you to Alison Callahan, Nina Cordes, and everyone at Scout Press for taking such care of *In a Dark, Dark Wood.* And much gratitude also to everyone at Harvill in the UK, particularly my editor, Alison Hennessey, who first said the words "hen party" to me and set everything else in motion.

Thanks always to my first readers, Meg, Eleanor, Kate, and Alice, for being brutal and supportive in the necessary proportions and asking all the right questions.

Many thanks to the writers and friends who took time out from their own problems to ponder mine; online and off, please know that you make life better and more amusing every day.

For technical help, I owe a great debt to Sam, Jon, Richard, and Lorna, who all helped with details of policing, medical protocol, and firearms. Needless to say, any errors are mine (and I apologize for the dramatic license I have taken with some of their advice).

Enormous thanks to Eve and Jack at the Eve White literary agency, for all their care and support.

And finally to my dear family, particularly Ian and the children—thank you for letting me tap away in the spare room when you would so often have rather been doing other things. I love you all.

Scout Press proudly presents
an excerpt from Ruth Ware's novel

The Death of Mrs. Westaway

Available now from Scout Press

Turn the page for a preview of *The Death of Mrs. Westaway*. . . .

One for sorrow
Two for joy
Three for a girl
Four for a boy
Five for silver
Six for gold
Seven for a secret
Never to be told

29th November, 1994

The magpies are back. It's strange to think how much I used to hate them, when I first came to the house. I remember coming up the drive in the taxi from the station, seeing them lined up along the garden wall like that, preening their feathers.

Today there was one perched on the frost-rimed branch of yew right outside my window, and I remembered what my mother used to say when I was little and whispered "Hello, Mr. Magpie" under my breath, to turn away the bad luck.

I counted them as I dressed, shivering next to the window. One on the yew tree. A second on the weathervane of the folly. A third on the wall of the kitchen garden. Three for a girl.

It seemed like an omen, and for a moment I shivered. Wishing, wondering, waiting . . .

But no, there were more on the frozen lawn. Four, five . . . six . . . and one hopping across the flags of the terrace, pecking at the ice on the covers over the table and chairs.

Seven. Seven for a secret, never to be told. Well, the secret part may be right, but the rest is wide of the mark. I'll have to tell, soon enough. There'll be no choice.

I had almost finished dressing when there was a rustle in the leaves of the rhododendrons in the shrubbery. For a minute I could not see the cause, but then the branches parted, and a fox slunk quietly across the leaf-strewn lawn, its red-gold fur startlingly bright against the frost-muted winter colours.

At my parents' house they were quite common, but it's rare to see one in daylight around here, let alone one bold enough to cross the huge exposed stretch of lawns in front of the house. I've seen slaughtered rabbits, and split bags of rubbish left from their scavenging, but they are almost never this bold. This one must have been very brave, or very desperate, to stalk in full sight in front of the house. Looking more closely, I thought perhaps it was the latter, for he was young, and terribly thin.

At first the magpies didn't notice, but then the one on the terrace, more observant than the others, registered the shape of the predator easing its way towards them, and it flew up from the icy flags like a rocket, chak-chakking its alarm, the warning loud and clear in the morning quiet. The fox had no hope after that. The other birds took to the sky, one by one, until at last only one was left, sitting on the yew, safely out of the fox's reach, and like a stream of molten gold, it slunk back over the grass, low to the ground, leaving the solitary magpie on the branch, crowing out its triumph.

One. One for sorrow. But that's impossible. I will never feel sad again, in spite of everything, in spite of the storm that I know is coming. As I sit here in the drawing room, writing this, I can feel it—my secret—burning me up from the inside with a joy so fierce that I think it must sometimes be visible through my skin.

I'll change that rhyme. One for joy. One for love. One for the future.

CHAPTER 1

The girl leaned, rather than walked, into the wind, clutching the damp package of fish and chips grimly under one arm even as the gale plucked at the paper, trying to unravel the parcel and send the contents skittering away down the seafront for the seagulls to claim.

As she crossed the road her hand closed over the crumpled note in her pocket, and she glanced over her shoulder, checking the long dark stretch of pavement behind her for a shadowy figure, but there was no one there. No one she could see, anyway.

It was rare for the seafront to be completely deserted. The bars and clubs were open long into the night, spilling drunk locals and tourists onto the pebbled beach right through until dawn. But tonight, even the most hardened partygoers had decided against venturing out, and now, at 9:55 p.m. on a wet Tuesday, Hal had the promenade to herself, the flashing lights of the pier the only sign of life, apart from the gulls wheeling and crying over the dark restless waters of the channel.

Hal's short black hair blew in her eyes, her glasses were misted, and her lips were chapped with salt from the sea wind. But she hitched the parcel tighter under her arm and turned off the seafront into one of the narrow residential streets of tall white houses, where the wind dropped with a suddenness that made her stagger and almost trip. The rain didn't let up. In fact, away from the wind it seemed to drizzle more steadily, if anything, as she turned again into Marine View Villas.

The name was a lie. There were no villas, only a slightly shabby little row of terraced houses, their paint peeling from constant exposure to the salty air. And there was no view—not of the sea or anywhere else. Maybe there had been once, when the houses were built. But since then taller, grander buildings had gone up, closer to the sea, and any view the windows of Marine View Villas might once have had was reduced to brick walls and slate roofs, even from Hal's attic flat. Now the only benefit to living up three flights of narrow, rickety stairs was not having to listen to neighbors stomping about above your head.

Tonight, though, the neighbors seemed to be out—and had been for some time, judging by the way the door stuck on the clump of junk mail in the hall. Hal had to shove hard, until it gave and she stumbled into the chilly darkness, groping for the automatic timer switch that governed the lights. Nothing happened. Either a fuse had blown, or the bulb had burned out.

She scooped up the junk mail, doing her best in the dim light filtering in from the street to pick out the letters for the other tenants, and then began the climb up to her own attic flat.

There were no windows on the stairwell, and once she was past the first flight, it was almost pitch-black. But Hal knew the steps by heart, from the broken board on the landing to the loose piece of carpet that had come untacked on the last flight, and she plodded wearily upwards, thinking about supper and bed. She wasn't even sure if she was hungry anymore, but the fish and chips had cost £5.50, and judging by the number of bills she was carrying, that was £5.50 she couldn't afford to waste.

On the top landing she ducked her head to avoid the drip from the skylight, opened the door, and then at last, she was home.

The flat was small, just a bedroom opening off a kind of wide hallway that did duty as both kitchen and living room, and everything else. It was also shabby, with peeling paint and worn carpet, and wooden windows that groaned and rattled when the wind came off the sea. But it had been Hal's home for all of her twenty-one years, and no matter how cold and tired she was, her heart never failed to lift, just a little bit, when she walked through the door.

In the doorway, she paused to wipe the salt spray off her glasses, polishing them on the ragged knee of her jeans, before dropping the paper of fish and chips on the coffee table.

It was very cold, and she shivered as she knelt in front of the gas fire, clicking the knob until it flared, and the warmth began to come back into her raw red hands. Then she unrolled the damp, rain-spattered paper packet, inhaling as the sharp smell of salt and vinegar filled the little room.

Spearing a limp, warm chip with the wooden fork, she began to sort through the mail, sifting out takeout fliers for recycling and putting the bills into a pile. The chips were salty and sharp and the battered fish still hot, but Hal found a slightly sick feeling was growing in the pit of her stomach as the stack of bills grew higher. It wasn't so much the size of the pile but the number marked *FINAL DEMAND* that worried her, and she pushed the fish aside, feeling suddenly nauseated.

She *had* to pay the rent—that was nonnegotiable. And the electricity was high on the list too. Without a fridge or lights, the little flat was barely habitable. The gas . . . well it was November. Life without heating would be uncomfortable, but she'd survive.

But the one that really made her stomach turn over was different from the official bills. It was a cheap envelope, obviously hand-delivered, and all it said on the front, in ballpoint letters, was "Harriet Westerway, top flat."

There was no sender's address, but Hal didn't need one. She had a horrible feeling that she knew who it was from.

Hal swallowed a chip that seemed to be stuck in her throat, and she pushed the envelope to the bottom of the pile of bills, giving way to the overwhelming impulse to bury her head in the sand. She wished passionately that she could hand the whole problem over to someone older and wiser and stronger to deal with.

But there was no one. Not anymore. And besides, there was a tough, stubborn core of courage in Hal. Small, skinny, pale, and young she might be—but she was not the child people routinely assumed. She had not been that child for more than three years.

It was that core that made her pick the envelope back up and, biting her lip, tear through the flap.

Inside there was just one sheet of paper, with only a couple of sentences typed on it.

Sorry to have missed you. We would like to discuss you're financal situation. We will call again.

Hal's stomach flipped and she felt in her pocket for the piece of paper that had turned up at her work this afternoon. They were identical, save for the crumples and a splash of tea that she had spilled over the first one when she opened it.

The message on them was not news to Hal. She had been ignoring calls and texts to that effect for months.

It was the message *behind* the notes that made her hands shake as she placed them carefully on the coffee table, side by side.

Hal was used to reading between the lines, deciphering the importance of what people *didn't* say, as much as what they did.

It was her job, in a way. But the unspoken words here required no decoding at all.

They said, *We know where you work.*

We know where you live.

And we will come back.

THE REST OF THE MAIL was just junk and Hal dumped it into the recycling before sitting wearily on the sofa. For a moment she let her head rest in her hands—trying not to think about her precarious bank balance, hearing her mother's voice in her ear as if she were standing behind her, lecturing her about her A-level revision. *Hal, I know you're stressed, but you've got to eat something! You're too skinny!*

I know, she answered, inside her head. It was always that way when she was worried or anxious—her appetite was the first thing to go. But she couldn't afford to get ill. If she couldn't work, she wouldn't get paid. And more to the point, she could not afford to waste a meal, even one that was damp around the edges, and getting cold.

Ignoring the ache in her throat, she forced herself to pick up another chip. But it was only halfway to her mouth when something in the recycling bin caught her eye. Something that should not have been there. A letter in a stiff white envelope, addressed by hand, and stuffed into the bin along with the takeout menus.

Hal put the chip in her mouth, licked the salt off her fingers, and then leaned across to the bin to pick it out of the mess of old papers and soup tins.

Miss Harriet Westaway, it said. *Flat 3c, Marine View Villas, Brighton.* The address was only slightly stained with the grease from Hal's fingers and the mess from the bin.

She must have shoved it in there by mistake with the empty envelopes. Well, at least this one couldn't be a bill. It looked more like a wedding invitation—though that seemed unlikely. Hal couldn't think of anyone who would be getting married.

She shoved her thumb in the gap at the side of the envelope and ripped it open.

The piece of paper she pulled out wasn't an invitation. It was a letter, written on heavy, expensive paper, with the name of a solicitor's firm at the top. For a minute Hal's stomach seemed to fall away, as a landscape of terrifying possibilities opened up before her. Was someone suing her for something she'd said in a reading? Or—oh God—the tenancy on the flat. Mr. Khan, the landlord, was in his seventies and had sold all of the other flats in the house, one by one. He had held on to Hal's mainly out of pity for her and affection for her mother, she was fairly sure, but that stay of execution could not last forever. One day he would need the money for a care home, or his diabetes would get the better of him and his children would have to sell. It didn't matter that the walls were peeling with damp, and the electrics shorted if you ran a hair dryer at the same time as the toaster. It was home—the only home she'd ever known. And if he kicked her out, the chances of finding another place at this rate were not just slim, they were nil.

Or was it . . . but no. There was no way *he* would have gone to a solicitor.

Her fingers were trembling as she unfolded the page, but when her eyes flicked to the contact details beneath the signature, she realized, with a surge of relief, that it wasn't a Brighton firm. The address was in Penzance, in Cornwall.

Nothing to do with the flat—thank God. And vanishingly unlikely to be a disgruntled client, so far from home. In fact, she didn't know anyone in Penzance at all.

Swallowing another chip, she spread the letter out on the coffee table, pushed her glasses up her nose, and began to read.

Dear Miss Westaway,

I am writing at the instruction of my client, your grandmother, Hester Mary Westaway of Trepassen House, St Piran.

Mrs Westaway passed away on 22nd November, at her home. I appreciate that this news may well come as a shock to you; please accept my sincere condolences on your loss.

As Mrs Westaway's solicitor and executor, it is my duty to contact beneficiaries under her will. Because of the substantial size of the estate, probate will need to be applied for and the estate assessed for inheritance tax liabilities, and the process of disbursement cannot begin until this has taken place. However if, in the meantime, you could provide me with copies of two documents confirming your identity and address (a list of acceptable forms of ID is attached), that will enable me to begin the necessary paperwork.

In accordance with the wishes of your late grandmother, I am also instructed to inform beneficiaries of the details of her funeral. This is being held at 4 p.m. on 1st December at St Piran's Church, St Piran. As local accommodation is very limited, family members are invited to stay at Trepassen House, where a wake will also be held.

Please write to your late grandmother's housekeeper Mrs Ada Warren if you would like to avail yourself of the offer of accommodation, and she will ensure a room is opened up for you.

Please accept once again my condolences, and the assurance of my very best attentions in this matter.

Yours truly,
Robert Treswick
Treswick, Nantes and Dean
Penzance

A chip fell from Hal's fingers onto her lap, but she did not stir. She only sat, reading and rereading the short letter, and then turning to the accepted-forms-of-identification document, as if that would elucidate matters.

Substantial estate . . . beneficiaries of the will . . . Hal's stomach rumbled, and she picked up the chip and ate it almost absently, trying to make sense of the words in front of her.

Because it *didn't* make sense. Not one bit. Hal's grandparents had been dead for more than twenty years.

CHAPTER 2

Hal wasn't sure how long she sat there, puzzling over the letter, her eyes flicking between the folded white sheet and the search page of her phone. But when she looked up, the clock on the microwave said five to midnight, and she stretched, realizing with a pang of anxiety that the gas fire had been burning the whole time. She stood and turned it off, listening to the cooling click of the elements, mentally adding on another fifty pence to the gas bill already lying there, and as she did, her gaze fell on the photograph on the mantelpiece.

It had been there almost as long as Hal could remember—ten years at least—but now she picked it up, looking at it afresh. It showed a girl, maybe nine or ten years of age, and a woman, standing on Brighton beach. They were laughing, with their eyes screwed up against a gusting wind that blew their long dark hair into identical comic upsweeps. The woman had her arm around the girl, and there was a look of such freedom, such trust between them that Hal felt her heart clench with a pain that she had almost grown used to over the last three years, but which never seemed to fade.

The girl was Hal—and yet she wasn't. She wasn't the girl who stood in front of the fire now, her hair cropped short as a boy's, her ears pierced, the tattoos on her back just peeping out from the neck of her threadbare T-shirt.

The girl in the photograph had no need to mark her skin with remembrances because everything she wanted to remember was right beside her. She didn't dress in black, because she had nothing to mourn. She didn't keep her head down and her collar up when she walked home, because she had nothing to hide from. She was warm, and well-fed, and most of all she was loved.

The fish and chips had grown cold, and Hal bundled them up in the paper and pushed them into the bin in the corner of the room. Her mouth was dry with salt, and her throat ached with grief, and the thought of a hot mug of tea before bed was suddenly comforting. She would make the tea, and fill a hot-water bottle with the rest of the kettle, something to take the chill off the sheets, help her to sleep.

As the kettle began to hum, Hal rummaged in the cupboard above it for the box of tea bags. But almost as if it were what she had really been looking for, her hand found something else. Not the lightweight cardboard box, but a glass bottle, half-full. She didn't need to get it out to know what it was, but she took it down anyway, weighing it in her hand, feeling the liquid slosh greasily inside. Vodka.

She only rarely drank these days—she didn't really like the person she became with a glass in her hand—but then her eye caught on the two notes lying across the coffee table, and with a quick movement she twisted off the cap and poured a generous measure into the cup she had been intending for the tea.

The kettle bubbled as she lifted the cup to her lips, smelling the acrid, slightly petrolly smell, watching the meniscus tremble in the dim light coming in from the streetlamp. For a moment the imagined taste was sharp in her mouth—the fiery burn, followed by that little addictive buzz. But then something inside her stomach seemed to turn, and she poured it down the sink, swilled out the cup, and made the tea instead.

As she carried it through to the bedroom, she realized with a kind of weariness that she had forgotten the hot-water bottle. But it didn't matter. She was too tired to care, and the tea was hot and good. Hal curled up in bed, fully clothed, sipping the tea and staring at the bright screen of her phone.

On the screen was Google images, and it showed a hand-tinted postcard, from perhaps 1930, featuring a country house. It had a long frontage of cream-colored stone with Georgian-style windows, covered in ivy. Chimneys poked up from a slate-tiled roof, a dozen or more, all in different styles. To the rear was more of the house, which seemed to be redbrick and built in a different style. A lawn spread out in front of the building, falling away, and a scrawled inscription across the picture read, *We had a very good tea at Trepassen House before driving on to Penzance.*

That was Trepassen House. *That* was Trepassen House. Not a modest little bungalow, or a Victorian terrace with a pretentious name. But a bona fide country seat.

A share, however small, of a place like that could do more than pay off her bills. It could give her back the security she had lost when her mother died. Even a few hundred pounds would give her more breathing room than she could remember for months.

The clock at the top of the screen showed half past midnight, and Hal knew she should sleep, but she did not close down her phone.

Instead she sat there in bed, with the steam from the tea misting her glasses, searching, scrolling, and feeling a strange mix of emotions spreading through her, warming her more than the tea.

Excitement? Yes.

Trepidation too, a good deal of it.

But most of all something she hadn't dared to feel in many years. Hope.

CHAPTER 3

Hal woke late the next morning. The sun was already up, slanting through the bedroom curtains, and she lay still, feeling the mingled excitement and dread in the pit of her stomach, and trying to remember the source.

Recollection came like a twin punch to the gut.

The dread was the pile of bills on the coffee table—and, worse than bills, those two typed notes, hand-delivered. . . .

But the excitement . . .

She had spent all last night trying to talk herself out of it. Just because it was where Hester Westaway had lived, there was no guarantee that she had actually owned that huge rambling place on the postcard. People just didn't have houses that size these days. The fact that she'd died there didn't mean she owned it. In all likelihood, it was a retirement home now.

But the housekeeper, whispered a voice in the back of her head. *And that line about opening up a room for you. They wouldn't say that about a retirement home, would they?*

"It doesn't matter," Hal said aloud, startling herself with the sound of her own voice in the silent flat.

She stood, smoothing down her rumpled clothes, and picked up her glasses. Settling them on her nose, she gave herself a stern look in the mirror.

It didn't matter whether Hester Westaway owned a room, or a wing, or a cottage in the grounds, or the whole damn place. There had clearly been some sort of mistake. She was not Hal's grandmother. The money belonged to someone else, and that was all there was to it.

Tomorrow she would write back and tell Mr. Treswick that.

But today . . . Hal looked at her watch, and shook her head. Today she had barely time for a shower. It was 11:20 and she was very nearly late for work.

SHE WAS IN THE SHOWER, the hot water drumming on her skull, driving out all other thoughts, when the voice whispered again, beneath the roar of the water.

But what if it's true? They wrote to you, didn't they? They have your name and address.

It wasn't true, though, that was the long and the short of it. Hal's only grandparents had died years ago, long before she was born. And her grandmother hadn't been called Hester, she had been called . . . Marion?

Maybe Marion was a middle name. People do that, right? They use one name for everyday, and have a different one on their papers. What if—

Shut up, Hal said inwardly. Just shut up. You know it's not true. You're persuading yourself because you want it to be true.

Still, the voice niggled away in the back of her head, and at last, more in an effort to convince herself than anything else, Hal turned off the shower, wrapped a towel around her shoulders, and made her way back into the bedroom. Beneath the bed was a heavy wooden box, and she dragged it out, wincing at the screech of castors on the wooden floor, and hoping that the downstairs neighbors weren't treating themselves to a lie-in.

Inside was a rat's nest of important papers—insurance documents, the rental contract on the flat, bills, her passport. . . . Hal sifted through the layers, feeling like an archaeologist of her own history. Past the insurance schedule, past the bill for the time a pipe had burst in the attic, and then down to a stratum that was nothing but pain—her mother's death certificate, the copy of her will, the police report, her faded driver's license, never used again. Beneath them all was a veil, folded into a neat square—fine black gauze, edged with droplets of jet.

There was a lump in Hal's throat as she put it aside, hurrying past the bitter memories to the older stuff underneath—papers her mother had chosen to keep, more neatly filed than Hal's haphazard shoving. There was an envelope with her own exam certificates, a program for a school play she had been in, a photograph of herself looking sheepish with a long-gone boyfriend.

And then at last a plastic folder marked *Important—birth certs* in her mother's neat hand, and inside, two red-and-cream certificates, handwritten, and topped with the extravagantly ornate crown emblem. *Certified copy of an entry,* read the top of the page. First Hal's: *Harriet Margarida Westaway, born 15th May 1995. Mother: Margarida Westaway, occupation: student.*

The space for "father" was left blank, a line drawn firmly through the box, as though to stop anyone from adding their own theories.

And then, beneath it, another certificate, older and more creased—*Margarida Westaway*. Her mother. Hal's eyes skipped to the "parents" column—*Father: William Howard Rainer Westaway, occupation: accountant* and beneath that *Mother: Marion Elizabeth Westaway, maiden name: Brown*. No occupation was given for her grandmother.

Well, that was that then.

She didn't realize how much she had been hoping against hope until the sense of deflation set in, tentative thoughts of debt repayment and security collapsing like a pricked balloon.

Substantial estate . . . whispered the voice in her ear, seductively. *Beneficiaries of the will . . . family members . . .*

There's always your father, whispered the voice again, as she dressed. *You have another grandmother, you know.* Hal shook her head bitterly at that. If your subconscious could betray you, Hal's just had.

For years she had fantasized about her father, spinning increasingly elaborate tales to the girls at school to cover her own ignorance and her anger at her mother for telling her so little. He was a pilot who had gone down in a crash in the sea. He was an undercover policeman who had been forced to return to his real life by his superiors. He was a celebrity, whose name couldn't be revealed, or they would be hounded by the tabloids, and her father's life would be ruined.

At last, when the rumors had reached the ears of the teachers, someone had had a quiet word and Hal's mother had taken her aside and gently told her the truth.

Hal's father had been a one-night stand—a student her mother had met in a nightclub in Brighton and had slept with for the first and last time on the night they met. He had a Spanish accent, and that was all Hal's mother knew.

"You didn't even find out his *name*?" Hal had asked incredulously, and her mother had bitten her lip and shaken her head. Her cheeks were scarlet, and she looked more uncomfortable than Hal could ever remember.

She was very sorry, she said. She hadn't wanted Hal to find out this way, but Hal *had* to stop spinning these . . . Her mother had stopped there, too kind to say the word she had been thinking; but even at seven, Hal was good at reading people, and perceptive enough to understand what it was her mother hadn't said.

These lies.

The truth was, her father was no one special. Who he was, where he lived now, she had no idea, and would probably never know. He had likely gone back to Spain or Mexico or wherever he had come from in the first place. But one thing she did know for sure—he was most certainly not a Westaway.

Wherever the mistake had come from, it wasn't there. But a mistake it was. Somewhere, wires had been crossed. Maybe there was some other Harriet Westaway in another city, rightfully entitled to this money. Or maybe it was like one of those heir-hunter programs, where someone had died without legitimate heirs, and the money would go to waste if the executors didn't track down some relative, however distant, to scoop the pot.

Whatever the truth was, the money wasn't hers, and she couldn't claim it. And the voice inside her head had no answer to that.

Hurrying now, Hal shoved the papers back underneath the bed and dressed. Her hairbrush seemed to have gone missing, but she combed her hair as well as she could with her fingers, and checked herself in the mirror by the front door. Her face looked even paler and more pinched than usual, the forlorn wet spikes of black hair making her look like an extra from *Oliver Twist*. Makeup would have helped, but it wasn't really Hal's style.

But as she pulled on her coat, still damp from the night before, the voice piped up with one last remark. *You could claim this money, you know. Not many people could, but if anyone can pull this off, it's you.*

Shut up, Hal said inwardly, gritting her teeth. Shut. Up.

But she didn't say it because she didn't believe it.

She said it because it was true.

In a Dark, Dark Wood

Ruth Ware

Introduction

Mystery novelist Leonora, known to some as Nora and others as Lee, lives a solitary but comfortable life in London. Her days hinge on routine: coffee, run, shower, write, repeat—until she is unexpectedly invited to a weekend away by an old childhood friend she hasn't seen and spoken to in a decade. Nora (Lee?) surprises even herself and reluctantly decides to make the trip to an eerie glass house, deep in the woods and far from the city.

As the weekend progresses, old rivalries and new relationships bubble to the surface and the getaway takes a dangerous turn, leaving Nora (Lee?) battered and bruised in a hospital bed. As she struggles to reconstruct the sequence of events that brought her to the hospital, secrets emerge about her past and present that force her to question everything she knows about herself—and everyone she's ever loved.

Topics and Questions for Discussion

1. Nora is a mystery writer who thrives on routine. As a novelist, she is in control of each book's narrative; in her personal life, she takes utmost care to control her environment, her health, and her social life. Why is it so important for Nora to be in control? How is she stripped of that control throughout the novel? How does Nora respond as her mental state and her freedom become increasingly uncontrollable?

2. What techniques does the author use to increase the tension and suspense throughout the novel? Discuss specific moments that were unnerving for you as a reader, and how the author kept you on edge. How did the author use humor to lighten the mood periodically?

3. The protagonist goes by Nora, Lee, Leo, or Leonora, depending on to whom she is speaking. Even her novels are published under a different name: L. N. Shaw. What do Nora's various past and present identities say about her personality and her motivations? Why is she so adamant that everyone at the hen party call her "Nora"? Why does Lee stutter, but Nora does not?

4. *In a Dark, Dark Wood* shifts between past and present. How did this shifting structure impact your reading of the novel and your perspective on the various characters? What is gained by switching back and forth between time periods?

5. How does the author foreshadow the harrowing events of Saturday night? Did you see the twists coming, or were you surprised by the novel's outcome?

6. Why is running so important to Nora's well-being and her mental state? Why does Nora always feel a need to escape, and what are her fears when she is not able to run?

7. How does the glass house become a character in the book? How does the author convey its remoteness, and how does the house itself take on an increasingly sinister quality over the course of the weekend? How does Flo's story about the house's construction and her aunt's struggle with the villagers impact your perception of the house?

8. Describe Nora's relationship with James. Is it reasonable to think that her feelings toward him would be what they are after a decade?

9. Why is Flo so extremely loyal to Clare? Is she simply a weak person looking to latch on to someone more confident and secure, or is there something else at play in their relationship? How are Nora and Flo's relationships with Clare similar? Why does Clare act the way she does, especially toward Nora and Flo? What does Clare stand to gain by identifying herself with and buoying up people who are so different from her?

10. Did you find Nora to be a reliable narrator? Identify key moments where you trusted her, and key moments where you doubted her. What techniques does the author use to make Nora seem both reliable and unreliable at various points in the novel?

11. Many of the characters are actors, and there is a great deal of talk about various plays and shows—Tom met Clare while working in the theater, and Nora and James first met when Clare fell ill

and Nora, the understudy, took on Clare's leading role. The glass house is referred to numerous times as a stage with an audience of trees beyond its windows. Why is all this talk of actors and performances so significant in the novel? Which characters perform the most, and why? Which performances did you see through, and which did you believe?

12. What do you think happens to the characters after the novel is over? How do you think the events of the weekend will impact each of them in their lives and relationships going forward?

Enhance Your Book Club

1. Plan a book club meeting that's also a hen night! Keep things light and festive (unlike the hen party in the book) with fun cocktails and games like "Never Have I Ever."

2. If you're not too superstitious (and if the scene in the book didn't scare you for good), break out your Ouija board and ask some questions about the members of your book club.

3. Bring a copy of your favorite scary story and read it aloud to the group (bonus points if you read it in the dark!).

A Conversation with Ruth Ware

***In a Dark, Dark Wood* is your debut novel. How does it feel to have received so much attention months prior to publication?**

Well, amazing, obviously! But also a little weird, in the best kind of way. Seeing my book on a billboard in New York was a bucket list–type thing, but also a deeply surreal moment. I had to keep reminding myself that, oh, yes, *I wrote that book.* I am mainly just delighted that people seem to find the idea of a murder on a hen night as intriguing as I did when I first sat down to write. The only downside has been that it has been *very* hard to concentrate on what to do next—the characters from *In a Dark, Dark Wood* are still running around inside my head, just when I need to be thinking about new people!

Have you always been interested in writing psychological suspense?

I've always written, but this is the first manuscript I came up with that could be described as a crime thriller, which is kind of strange, really, since I've written in every conceivable other genre, including some absolutely terrible fantasy sci-fi that I wrote as a teenager, and which I am very glad never saw the light of day! But looking back, I think with everything I wrote, even creative writing exercises back at school, I was always looking at suspense and life-or-death moments, so I guess the seeds were there.

What books or films influenced you while writing this novel?

I absolutely adore classic crime and read a huge amount as a teen—Agatha Christie, Dorothy L. Sayers, Sherlock Holmes, Josephine Tey, and many more. I didn't totally realize it when I was writing, but I think they definitely influenced the structure of the book. Several readers have pointed out how Christie-ish the setup is, with a finite cast of people in a remote house they can't escape from. I suppose I did know that at some level, hence the reference Nina makes to *And Then There Were None,* but I'm not sure I thought other people would see the links so strongly.

I also read and watched a fair bit of horror—Christopher Pike and Wes Craven–type stuff. I think there are definite influences there, too; the glass house is pretty much lifted from all those films like *Scream* and *A Nightmare on Elm Street* where the camera is in the eyes of the killer, circling the house and peering through the windows. I always watched those films shrieking internally, "Why don't they shut the bloody curtains!" I suppose the glass house was me taking that feeling to its logical conclusion—a house where you actually *can't* shut the curtains, and you're constantly exposed to the eyes of the forest.

Are there any real-life events that inspired the book? Hopefully you haven't been to a hen weekend that was similar to the one in the book!

Ha—no, thank goodness! It's not remotely autobiographical, except insofar as the way some of the characters act and react are inspired by my own memories of being a child and a teen. I am certainly not brooding over ten-year-old wrongs, but I do have vivid memories of my first day at school and feeling like a fish out of water in a way similar to Nora, and the brutal playground dynamics where you can be in favor one day and a pariah the next. And I still occasionally wake up in the night wincing at stuff I said, or did, or should have done while I was at high school. In my case it's all minor stuff, but I think the wounds you sustain at that age cut very deep and leave scars in a way that experiences later in life don't have the power to do.

Which character do you identify with most, and why?

I think I identify with all of them, to some degree—I can't write a character without inhabiting them and understanding their motives and actions, even the less sympathetic ones. Nina is the person I'd most like to have a drink with—I think she would be brilliant fun, and she's probably the most representative of my impatient, snappy side. Flo is probably the character I feel most sympathy towards—she's least like me, but she is the only person who's acting out of entirely good motives. She doesn't always do the right thing, but she's entirely altruistic. Everyone else is covering his or her own back or being selfish to some degree. Tragically, in terms of my day-to-day life, I think I am probably closest to Melanie at the moment! I've certainly been the person in the bar looking stealthily at my watch while everyone else is drinking, because I need to get back and feed the baby.

There seems to be a recent trend in fiction toward novels that feature violent and sociopathic females. Why do you think we are so drawn to stories that show a darker version of femininity?

You could see it as wish fulfillment, I guess. We spend so much of our lives swallowing our true feelings and being polite, and doing stuff we don't particularly want to do for fear of being seen as unfriendly or unpleasant, or just downright bitchy. I guess this is Nora at the start of the novel—she absolutely does *not* want to go on the hen weekend, yet she allows herself to be guilt-tripped into it by Flo, appealing to her role as a friend and making her feel ungrateful. Maybe we enjoy reading about women who've gone beyond giving a damn?

Partly, though, I think it's just that we still take notice and are surprised when a woman is cast in that role. It's kind of the reverse of the Joss Whedon quip about Buffy: "So, why do you write these strong female characters?" "Because you're still asking me that question." We've had decades and decades of men doing horrible things in novels and films. Why is it still noteworthy when a woman is cast in the role of the psychopath?

How did you decide to have Nora's memory loss be so central to the novel? Did you do any research about memory loss and traumatic brain injury?

I love unreliable narrators, but I felt like I'd read a lot of novels where the narrator is deliberately *choosing* to withhold information, or selecting the story he or she presents. I was interested in doing something where the narrator was kind of unreliable in spite of herself, where she wanted to tell the truth but didn't know what that truth was. Plus, I guess, what more frightening situation is there than to know a crime has been committed, but not be sure of your own role in it?

I did a lot of research into brain injury, although most of it didn't end up in the novel—mainly I just wanted to be sure that the scenario I had constructed was plausible, that someone could respond like that to a traumatic head injury, and how the doctors would proceed in terms of diagnosis and scans. Luckily, I have several medics among my family and friends, so they were able to help me find the information I needed. Ultimately, though, I think Nora's amnesia is mainly a coping mechanism.

What is your writing process like? Did you have the entire book plotted from the start or did it change and take shape as you went along?

I knew the basic shape—the jumping off point, what motivated the characters, roughly where they would end up. But I didn't know the exact detail of what would happen along the way. I tend to plot fairly loosely (the book I'm working on at the moment has an outline you could fit comfortably on a postcard, although there are more details in my head).

When I'm trying to describe the process to friends, I tend to liken it to a car journey to a place you've never been—you know where you're starting off, and you know roughly where you want to end up, even if in some cases all you have is a point on a map. You might also know a few details about the places you'll take in along the way, but the exact journey and the things you'll see are a surprise. You might be surprised by something traumatic out of the blue—a car accident, a crow bursting out of a thicket and smashing into your windshield. Or you might make a diversion to check out a particularly promising side route. Ultimately, though, you have to get your characters where they are going and not get lost along the way.

Do you ever scare yourself when you're writing? There was one night where I put the book down and then stayed awake for an hour listening for strange noises in my apartment! Do you find it difficult to take your mind out of such a dark place when you're done writing for the day?

Not at all—it's very cathartic in that respect! I rarely scare myself, I think because I'm in the driving seat and I know what's going to happen. It's a bit like tickling yourself—without that element of suspense of when and where the jolt is going to come, it's just not that scary. I do find myself sharing the moods of my characters, though. If I'm writing a furiously angry scene I have to consciously snap out of it when I shut down the computer, or I find myself growling at my family. I felt completely exhausted writing the sections where Nora is ploughing through the mud and snow up to the house, and had to keep breaking off for coffee and biscuits.

I am always surprised when people tell me they found *In a Dark, Dark Wood* scary, though. I'm a pretty cowardly reader and can't deal with much in the way of violence or sadism, which is why I deliberately didn't write about that. To me, the book is tense, but not terrifying.

What do you think happens to the characters after the end of the book?

I am not sure! I prefer to let readers make up their own minds. In my own head, I think Nora ends up with Matt, though I'm not sure if it would work out long-term.

What are you working on next?

Another thriller. This one is about a woman who witnesses a murder on a cruise (or thinks she does), but when she calls security, the victim was never there. I guess having ticked "what if you might have committed a murder but you can't remember?" off my list, my next phobia is "what if you thought you witnessed a murder but no one believed you?" If I run out of middle-of-the-night fears, then I'll really be stuck.